The Forgotten Letters
of Esther Durrant

The Forgotten Letters of Esther Durrant

Kayte Nunn

HARPER LARGE PRINT

An Imprint of HarperCollins*Publishers*

Originally published as *The Forgotten Letters of Esther Durrant* in Australia in 2019 by Hachette Australia.

HarperCollins books may be purchased for educational, business, or sales promotional use. For information, please e-mail the Special Markets Department at SPsales@harpercollins.com.

FIRST HARPER LARGE PRINT EDITION

ISBN: 978-0-06-297930-8

Library of Congress Cataloging-in-Publication Data is available upon request.

20 21 22 23 24 LSC 10 9 8 7 6 5 4 3 2 1

For my great-grandmother Phoebe Sly.
I wish that your story had ended differently.

Like the touch of rain she was
On a man's flesh and hair and eyes
When the joy of walking thus
Has taken him by surprise.

—"Like the Touch of Rain,"
EDWARD THOMAS

The Forgotten Letters
of Esther Durrant

Chapter One
London and Little Embers, Autumn 1951

It wasn't their usual destination for a holiday and the timing was hardly ideal. John and Esther Durrant generally took a week in Eastbourne or Brighton in the final week of August, so the far southwest tip of England was an odd choice, even more so considering it was early November. John, however, had been adamant. "It'll do you good," he said to his wife, in a tone of false jollity, when he suggested—no, *insisted* on—the trip. "Put some color back in your cheeks. Sea air." Never mind that a bitter cold gripped the nation with the kind of weather that you wouldn't put the cat out in and Esther couldn't have felt less like a week away even had she spent the previous year down a coal mine. She also didn't understand why they were leaving Teddy behind with the nanny, but she couldn't begin to summon the necessary enthusiasm for an argument.

Before catching the train south, they dined at a restaurant near Paddington station. Esther wasn't hungry, but she allowed John to decide for her nonetheless. After a brief perusal of the menu and dispatching their order to the black-clad, white-aproned waitress, he unfurled his *Telegraph* and spent the time before the arrival of their food absorbed in its pages. Winston Churchill and the Conservative Party had been returned to power she saw, noticing the headline on the front page. John was pleased, although privately she believed Mr. Churchill terribly old and probably not up to the job. They didn't discuss politics anymore, for they saw the world quite differently, she had come to realize.

Esther managed a little of the soup that arrived in due course, and half a bread roll, while John cleared his dish and several glasses of claret. Then Dover sole and tiny turned vegetables, all of which he ate with gusto while she pushed the peas and batons of carrot around on her plate, pretending to eat. Her husband made no comment.

Esther declined dessert but John, it appeared, had appetite enough for both of them and polished off a slice of steamed pudding made with precious rationed sugar and a generous dollop of custard. He glanced at his watch. "Shall we make our way to the train, my dear?" he asked, wiping the bristles of his mustache on a starched napkin. She couldn't help but be reminded of an otter who'd just had a fish supper: sleek, replete, and satisfied with himself. He was wearing the dark suit—his favorite—and the tie she'd given him several birthdays ago, when she had been expecting Teddy and the future felt as if it were the merest outline, a sketch, waiting for them to paint it in bold and vivid colors. Something to look forward to, not to fear.

She nodded and he rose and reached for her hand, helping her to her feet. It was a short walk from the restaurant to the station, but Esther was glad of her thick coat and gloves. She'd not ventured from the house in weeks—the November weather had been simply ghastly—and she shivered as she felt the wind slice through her outer garments and numb the tip of her nose and lips.

They entered the cavernous terminal and Esther was almost overwhelmed by the bustle and noise, the hissing of the giant steam engines and the raucous cries of porters as they effortlessly maneuvered unwieldy barrows top-heavy with luggage. It was as if they were part of the opening scene of a play, the moments before the main characters take the stage. She might once have enjoyed the spectacle, found the purposeful activity invigorating, but today she gripped John's arm as he steered her toward Platform One. "We'll be there in a jiffy," he said, reassuring her.

Everywhere she looked, lapels were splashed with poppies, blood-red against dark suits. A brief frown creased the pale skin of her forehead as it took her a moment to place them. Then she remembered: it would soon be Armistice Day. The terror, uncertainty, and deprivations of the recent war were a scarlet tattoo on every Englishman and woman's breast.

Eventually, the train was located, tickets checked, and they were ushered to their carriage by a porter. She took careful steps along a narrow corridor and they found their cabin: two slim berths made up with crisp cotton sheets and wool blankets the color of smoke.

She breathed a quiet sigh of relief that they would not be expected to lie together. In recent months John had taken to sleeping in his dressing room and she was still not ready for him to return to the marital bed. "I confess I am rather tired," she said, pulling off her gloves. "I might settle in." She opened a small cupboard, put her hat on the shelf inside, and hung her coat on a hook that was conveniently placed underneath.

"I shall take a nightcap in the Lounge Car. That is if you don't mind, darling," John replied.

He had taken the hint. So much between them went

unsaid these days. Esther turned around and inclined her head. "Not at all, you go. I shall be perfectly fine here."

"Very well." He left in a hurry, likely in pursuit of a dram or two of single malt.

She sat heavily on the bed, suddenly too exhausted to do more than kick off her shoes and lie back upon the blankets. She stared up at the roof of the cabin as it curved above her, feeling like a sardine in a tin. It wasn't unpleasant: if anything, she was cocooned from the activity going on outside and wouldn't be bothered by it.

Before long, a whistle sounded and, with a series of sudden jerks, the train began to move away from the station, shuddering as it gathered speed. After a few minutes it settled into a swaying rhythm and Esther's eyelids grew heavy. She fought to stay awake. Summoning the little determination she still possessed, she rallied and found her night things. It would not do to fall asleep still fully clothed, only to be roused by her husband on his return from the lounge.

John had asked their daily woman, Mary, to pack for them both, telling Esther that she needn't lift a finger. Normally she wouldn't have countenanced anyone else going through her things, but it had been easier not to object, to let them take over, as she had with so much recently. She had, however, added her own essentials to the cardigans, skirts, and stockings, and tucked away among her underwear was a small enameled box that resembled a miniature jewelry case. She found it, flipped the catch, and the little red pills inside gleamed at her like gemstones, beckoning. As she fished one out, she noticed her ragged nails and reddened cuticles. A different version of herself would have minded, but she barely gave them a second thought, intent as she was on the contents of the box. Without hesitating, she placed the pill on her tongue, swallowing it dry.

She put the box in her handbag, drew the window shades, and changed quickly, removing her tweed skirt and blouse and placing them in the cupboard with her hat and coat before pulling a fine lawn nightgown over her head. After a brief wash at the tiny corner basin, she dried her face on the towel provided and ran a brush through her hair before tucking herself between the starched sheets like a piece of paper in an envelope. She was lost to sleep hours before John returned.

On their arrival in Penzance the next morning he escorted her from the train, handling her once more as if she were his mother's best bone china. She didn't object, for she knew he meant well. His concern for her would have been touching had she been able to focus her mind on it—or anything else for that matter—for more than a few minutes, but it was as if there were a thick pane of glass, rather like the ones in the train windows, separating her from him, the world and everything in it.

In Penzance harbor, John engaged a small fishing dinghy—"hang the expense" he had said when Esther looked at him with a question in her eyes. "There is a ferry—the *Scillonian*—but there was a nasty accident last month, she hit the rocks in heavy fog by all accounts, and anyway it doesn't call at the island we want to reach. I looked into the possibility of a flight—there's an outfit that flies Dragon Rapides from Land's End, which could have been awfully thrilling, but they only operate in fine weather."

Esther had no idea what a "Dragon Rapide" might be, but thought that a boat was probably the safer option. As he spoke, she glanced upward. The sky was low and leaden, the gray of a pigeon's breast, and the air damp with the kind of light mist that softened the edges of things but didn't soak you, at least not to begin with. She huddled further into her coat, hands deep in her pockets. What on earth were they doing here? The boat looked as though it would scarcely survive a strong breeze. The hull was patched and its paintwork faded; translucent scales flecked its wooden rails and it reeked of fish.

"Shall we embark?" His face was hopeful.

Esther did as she was bid and climbed aboard, doing her best to avoid stepping on the purple-red slime that stained the decking. It was definitely the guts of some sea creature or other.

They huddled on a bench in the dinghy's small cabin as the captain got them under way. Beneath a pewter sky and afloat on an even darker sea, she was reminded of Charon, the ferryman of Hades, transporting newly dead souls across the Acheron and the Styx. The air was undoubtedly fresh here though. Sharply scented. Briny. Far more pleasant than the filmy London fog, which coated your hair, your skin, even your teeth with a fine layer of dirt. It roused her a little from her somnambulant state and she glanced about the cabin, seeing a dirty yellow sou'-wester, a length of oily rope acting as a paperweight on a creased and frayed shipping chart.

"Look!" John called out as they puttered out of Penzance's sheltering quay. "St. Michael's Mount. Centuries ago the English saw off the Spanish Armada from its battlements. At low tide you can walk across the causeway. Shame we didn't have time for it."

"Perhaps on our return?" she offered, her voice almost drowned out by the roar of the engine and the sound of the water slapping against the hull of the boat.

John didn't reply, looking out to sea instead. Had he even heard her?

"Oh look! Kittiwakes."

Esther raised her eyes toward the horizon; there were several gray and white gulls wheeling above them, their shrieks rending the air. To the left, a trio of torpedo-shaped birds whipped past. "And puffins!" he cried. The new sights and sounds had invigorated him, while she was already feeling queasy as the dinghy pitched and rolled. She registered their fat cheeks and bright orange bills and was reminded briefly of a portly professor friend of her father's. She tried but failed to match John's enthusiasm, pasting what felt like a smile on her face and swallowing hard to prevent herself from retching.

The captain cheerfully pointed out the site of several shipwrecks but Esther did her best not to pay too much heed to his story of a naval disaster in the early eighteenth century, where more than fifteen hundred sailors lost their lives. "One of the worst wrecks in the whole British Isles," he said with a kind of proud awe. As he spoke, a lighthouse, tall and glowing white against the gray sky, came into view. It hadn't done its job then. But then perhaps it had been built afterward, to prevent such a tragedy happening again.

They motored on as the rain thickened and soon a curtain of fog erased the horizon completely. Esther's stomach churned and bile rose in her throat. Even John's high spirits seemed dampened and they sat, saying nothing, as Esther fumbled in her pocket for a handkerchief and pressed it to her mouth, hoping that she was not going to empty the contents of her stomach onto the decking. She tried not to think about them mingling with the fish guts and saltwater that sloshed just beyond the cabin. She gritted her teeth against the spasms of nausea while her insides roiled and twisted as if she had swallowed a serpent.

The boat pitched and heaved in the rising swell as the waves frothed whitecaps beside them. "It's getting a bit lumpy," said the captain with a grin. "Thick as a bog out there too." John hadn't mentioned the name of the particular godforsaken speck of land that they were headed for and Esther didn't have the energy to ask. She tried to think of something else, anything but this purgatory of a voyage, but there were darker shapes in the yawning wasteland of her mind, so she forced herself instead to stare at the varnished walls of the cabin, counting to five hundred and then back again to take her mind off her predicament. She was only vaguely aware now of John next to her and the captain, mere inches away at the helm. Outside, the sea appeared to be at boiling point, white and angry, as if all hell had been let loose, and she gripped a nearby handhold until her fingers lost all feeling. She no longer had any confidence that they would reach their destination. She had ceased caring about anything very much months ago, so it hardly mattered either way.

Eventually, however, an island hove into view, and then another, gray smudges on the choppy seascape. Almost as soon as they had appeared they disappeared again into the mist, leaving nothing but the gray chop of the water. The captain's expression changed from sunny to serious as he concentrated on steering them clear of hidden shoals and shelves. "They'd hole a boat if you don't pay attention. Splinter it like balsa," he said, not lifting his eyes from the horizon.

All at once the wind and rain eased a fraction, the fog lifted, and they puttered alongside a small wooden jetty that stuck out from a sickle curve of bleached-sand beach. Like an arrow lodged in the side of a corpse, Esther imagined.

The bloated carcass of a seabird, larger than a gull, but smaller than an albatross, snagged her attention. Death had followed her to the beach. Her thoughts were so dark these days; she couldn't seem to chase them away. There was, however, some slight relief at having arrived, that the particular nightmare of the journey might soon be ended. For now that would have to be enough. "Small mercies," she whispered. She tried to be grateful for that.

The captain made the boat fast, then helped them and their luggage ashore, even as the boat bobbed dangerously up and down next to the jetty, its hull grinding, wood on wood, leaving behind flecks of paint. An ill-judged transfer and they would end up in the water. Esther stepped carefully onto the slippery boards, willing her shaky legs to hold her up.

Once they were both safely on land, the captain slung several large brown-paper-wrapped parcels after them. "Pop them under the shelter and when you get there, let the doc know that these are for him—he can send someone down for them before they get too wet. The house is up thataway. A bit of a walk, mind, and none too pleasant in this weather. There's not many that care to come this far."

The pelting rain had begun to fall again, blown sideways at them by the wind, and Esther silently agreed with him; she couldn't see the point of this wearisome journey, but John hefted their suitcases, looking at her with anticipation. "Think you can manage it, darling?"

Some small part of her didn't want to disappoint

him and she nodded faintly, still no clearer as to exactly where they were.

The walk wasn't long, but the wind buffeted them this way and that and Esther was obliged to hold on to her hat, a small-brimmed, dull felt affair that did little to keep off the rain. She faltered as she almost tripped on an object on the path and stopped to see what it was.

The doll lay on its back. Naked. China limbs splayed at unnatural angles. Eyes open, staring vacantly at the sky. A tangled mat of dirty yellow hair strewn with leaves and feathers. Esther stepped over it, feeling as she did, a tingling in her breasts and a spreading warmth at odds with the blustery, chilled air. It was a moment before she realized what it was, bewildered that her body still had the ability to nurture, in spite of everything.

John strode ahead, his steps unfaltering. He didn't appear to have noticed the abandoned toy, or if he had, had paid it no heed. Angling her chin down, Esther drew her coat in closer, its astrakhan collar soft against her cheeks, her grip tight on the handbag at her elbow.

As if sensing she'd stopped, John turned to look back at her. "Not far now." His expression coaxed her forward.

She gave him a curt nod and continued on, leaving the doll where it lay. The path ahead wound steeply upward and was pockmarked with shallow pools the color of dishwater. Esther had to watch her step to avoid them. Her shoes were new, barely worn in, not that she cared particularly about getting them wet. The avoidance of the puddles was an automatic action, a force of long habit, like so many were for her now.

A few steps farther on she glanced up, seeing the grasses on either side of them rippling and swaying, pummeled by the unrelenting gusts blowing off the ocean. Westward, cliffs like fresh scars marked where the land ended, rising abruptly as if forced upward from the earth's bowels. Huge boulders lay scattered at their base, a giant's playthings. It was a wholly foreign landscape for someone used to red brick, stone, pavement, and wrought iron.

"Nearly there, darling." John's tone was meant to encourage her, but it sounded a false note. Ersatz, her mother would have called it. And she would have been right.

Chapter Two
Aitutaki, South Pacific, February 2018

Rachel eased herself from the arms of her lover, sliding from beneath the thin sheet, being careful not to wake him. It was not yet dawn, but a waxing moon cast a glow through the uncurtained window. She located her shift, tossed on the tiled floor the night before, and shimmied it over her shoulders, down onto her torso, smoothing it over her thighs. She twisted her long hair into a knot and worked a kink out of her back, twisting and rolling the stiffness from her shoulders. Picking up her sandals, she tiptoed toward the door.

As she laid her hand on the latch, she allowed herself a single backward glance. He was beautiful: Adonis-like, with skin the color of scorched caramel, dark lustrous hair that she loved to curl around her fingers, and full, curving, skillful lips. Young, as always.

Closing the door gently so as not to wake him, she stood outside the straw-roofed bungalow and gazed across to the lagoon. The moon glistened on the water, and a faint light was visible on the horizon. On a clear night here, the sky was a sea of stars, with the Milky Way a wide belt arcing across the heavens. She would miss these skies more than the man she had just left behind. She checked her watch. Only three hours until her flight.

"Rachel!" The Adonis stood in the doorway. He had woken and found her missing. Damn. She'd lingered too long, taking in the beauty before dawn one last time.

She turned, meeting his gaze. "You knew I was leaving."

"Yes, but like this? No chance to say good-bye?"

"I thought it would be easier."

"On you perhaps." He looked sulky, his lower lip jutting out.

She tried, but couldn't feel sorry for him. He was young and gorgeous and would soon find someone else. Eager female research assistants would be falling over themselves to take her place. "You'll be fine," she said.

The sultry climate of the islands, where a permanent sheen of perspiration covered the skin, together with their remoteness, meant that relationships sprang up as quickly as the plants that flourished here. Generally their roots were as shallow, too.

"Come here?" It was more a question than a statement.

Rachel steeled herself against the pleading tone even as her footsteps led her back to him. Taller and broader than her, he easily enveloped her in his arms. "I'll miss you," he murmured into her hair.

"You too." Her voice was brusque, hiding anything softer.

"Somehow I doubt that," he laughed. "You have the blood of a lizard." He released her and placed his palm below her collarbone. "There is a stone where a heart should be."

They weren't entirely unfair comments and she didn't have time to argue with him.

"Stay in touch, eh?"

She gave a noncommittal shrug.

He kissed her forehead and hugged her once more before releasing her. "Au revoir, Rachel. Travel well."

She almost raced along the path to her bungalow in her haste to get away.

An hour later, she burst through the doors of the tiny airport and dumped her backpack at the check-in counter. "*Kia orana,* LeiLei," she greeted the woman waiting to take her ticket.

"*Kia orana,* Rachel." She gave her a smile that split her face. The island—atoll to be precise—was small enough that Rachel had gotten to know most of its permanent inhabitants in the time she'd spent there. LeiLei, who did double duty checking in passengers on Air Pacific and mixing fresh coconut piña coladas at Crusher Bar—both with equal enthusiasm—was a favorite.

LeiLei examined her ticket. "Flying home?"

"Something like that." The real answer was a complicated one. Growing up in a military family, Rachel had been to six different schools by the time she was twelve, moving from place to place, leaving friends behind and being forced to make new ones almost every year. She still remembered the name of her best friend when she was five. Erin. Could still recall the curly hair that never stayed in its pigtails and the swarm of freckles across her face. The two of them had been inseparable from their first day in Mrs. Norman's kindergarten class, sitting next to each other, spending every recess and lunchtime together. Rachel had cried as though her heart would break when her parents told her they were moving away. The next time it happened, she made a deliberate decision not to give her heart to people or places again. It was undoubtedly part of the reason she was still a rolling stone.

Home had, for a few years in her teens, been Pittwater, at the northern tip of Sydney. Accessible only by boat. She'd loved those years living with the rhythm of the tides, never more than footsteps away from saltwater, so it came as no surprise that after graduation she sought research postings on islands or waterways.

It was on Pittwater that she learned to drive a small aluminum boat powered by an outboard motor that passed for transportation in that corner of the world. At fifteen, she was part of the tinny tribe, ferrying herself and her younger brother to and from the high school on the mainland and racing their friends across the sheltered waters, something they'd been expressly forbidden to do. She learned to pilot the tiny boat through pouring rain and bustling gales, as well as on days where barely a breath of wind rippled the water's glassy surface and none of them hurried to lessons.

She'd learned where to find the plumpest oysters and when to harvest them; where the shoals were shallowest and likely to ground the tinny. To appreciate the beauty of the pearly light of dawn during the solitary joy of a morning kayak, her paddle pleating the water into ripples that stretched out in her wake. It had been hard to leave and go to university in the city.

When her dad had retired, he and her mother had returned to Pittwater, to a house built into the side of a hill and surrounded by gum trees and overrun with lantana.

She planned to squeeze in a week or so with them on her way through Australia, but hadn't phoned. Wanted to surprise them. Her mouth watered at the thought of her mum's scones, warm and spread thick with home-made jam. They'd be disappointed she wouldn't stay longer, but she couldn't help that.

Rachel shed lives as easily as a snake its skin, starting afresh somewhere new every couple of years, never stopping to look back. The new posting, to a group of islands off the coast of southern England, was an interesting one—to her anyway. She would be studying the unattractively named *Venus verrucosa*, or warty venus clam. Another bivalve, if rather smaller than her beloved pa'ua. Clams, it seemed, had become her thing.

She was to survey the islands, estimating the *verrucosa* population to determine changes and their correlation to ambient and sea temperatures. She would be entirely on her own, not part of a group as she had been previously, and it was this, as much as the actual project, that most appealed to her.

The irony that she studied sessile sea creatures, ones that barely moved once they fixed themselves to the ocean floor, when she drifted through the world like weed on the current, was not lost on her. Unlike the clams that cemented themselves to the seabed with sticky byssal threads, she never became attached, to anything, anywhere, or anyone.

"Safe travels," said LeiLei, coming around the counter to engulf her in a plump, sweetly scented hug and handing back her passport. "Come and see us again soon."

She smiled at her friend, turned, and didn't look back.

Chapter Three
London, Spring 2018

Rachel arrived in London at the same time as a vicious cold snap. Its effect on her was made worse by the fact that she'd come straight from a sultry southern hemisphere autumn. Before flying north, she had spent a couple of weeks in Pittwater catching up with her parents and siblings. Her parents both looked older than the last time she'd seen them more than three years earlier, although they still appeared to be spry.

Her father, long retired from the navy now, spent most of his days vigorously attacking the weeds that threatened to engulf their home, attempting to marshal them into the same kind of order that he had once imposed on the sailors under his command. Her mother busied herself with an endless round of yoga, twilight sailing, and baking for what seemed like the entire community. They both lived as if in perpetual motion and Rachel sometimes wished she had half their energy.

She spent most of her time there on the verandah overlooking the water, reading or watching the bright lorikeets flash by. She and her dad kayaked in the early morning stillness, holding their breath as the rising sun chased away wisps of fog that hung over the water.

Her younger brother was on the other side of the country, but one Sunday, her older brother and sister drove up from their homes in the city, bringing with them Rachel's nieces and nephews, several of whom were now well into their teens but still loved to hear her stories of turtles and stingrays, whale sharks and giant clams, particularly the pa'ua. She showed them photographs of *Tridacna gigas* and *Tridacna derasa*. "They were introduced from Australia actually," she explained, flicking through the pictures on her phone. "And no two are the same. A bit like fingerprints." They delighted in the vibrant purple and turquoise, jade and scarlet, tiger-striped and cheetah-spotted markings of their mantles. "They can live for more than a century and weigh up to two hundred and fifty kilos," she added as they jostled to get a better view.

"No way!" Jasper, her nephew exclaimed. He was still young enough to be impressed by such things.

Later, as they sat outdoors, toasting the last rays of the sun with glasses of cold white wine and slapping away the mozzies, Rachel let herself imagine what her life might be like if she too lived in Sydney. She wasn't sure if it was a frightening or appealing prospect. She loved her family, but even they could get too much for her sometimes.

"It'd be nice if you could make it for Christmas one year Noes," her brother said. Noes—short for "nosey parker"—had been his childhood nickname for her: she had liked to spy on him, torn between wanting to join in games with him and his friends and standing on the sidelines, an observer. "The kids will be gone before we know it and I know it would make Mum happy."

"What would make me happy?" her mother asked, stepping out onto the verandah.

"Coming back here more often," said Rachel. "Especially for Christmas."

"I can't deny that," said her mum, placing a reassuring hand on Rachel's shoulder. "But you have to live your life as you choose. If nothing else, I'm proud we gave you all the gift of independence."

"Some of us took it more literally than others." Her brother was only half-kidding.

"One year. I promise," said Rachel, meaning it. She didn't think either of them believed her.

Now, on a freezing gray day and completely under-dressed (she was wearing her lucky T-shirt with *don't sweat the detials* printed on the front), Rachel caught the tube to South Kensington, arriving exactly on time for her appointment with Dr. Charles Wentworth. He was the supervisor of the project she was about to un-dertake and worked in the Life Sciences department at the Natural History Museum.

They'd spoken via a pixelated Skype call, the con-nection sporadically dropping out, while she was in Aitutaki, and he'd followed up by email with confirma-tion of the job and this appointment.

She found the research offices and presented herself to the receptionist. The room was warm and she felt herself begin to defrost, curling and uncurling her fin-gers as the feeling returned to them.

"Ah, hello there, you must be Miss Parker." She looked up to see the man in front of her holding out a hand in greeting. "Dr. Wentworth. But call me Charles."

"Rachel," she said, getting to her feet and taking his hand. He had a firm grip and cool, dry skin and she decided she liked the look of him. Heavy tortoiseshell glasses balanced precariously on the end of his nose, his shoulders had the slightly hunched look of someone who spent too many hours looking through a micro-

scope and his tie appeared to have some of his breakfast clinging to it. Egg yolk, if she wasn't mistaken. His
smile was warm and genuine and she found herself returning it easily.

He led her into his office and proceeded to outline
the previous study and what it had entailed, handing
over several thick manila folders of information. "They
pertain to the original work and also outline what we
expect you will address in your research, but basically
you'll be looking at this one particular clam and deter-
mining any indicators of ecosystem change."

"Yes," said Rachel. "*Venus verrucosa.*"

"Indeed. I gather from our previous conversation
that you are something of a fan of such bivalves, though
I confess, this hardly compares to the spectacular species you have been studying on Aitutaki."

As he said this, a dreamy look came over him. It
often did, Rachel had noticed, when people mentioned
the tropical islands of the South Pacific, Tahiti, Bora
Bora, the Cooks . . . Gauguin had a lot to answer for.

She inclined her head. "Nevertheless, this is equally
as important."

"Oh absolutely. It'll form part of a nationwide
study on the effects of climate change on our marine
life, and the rate at which the increasing acidification
of our waters affects their growth patterns." His eyes

shone behind his glasses. "The Scilly Isles are a favorite of mine. If I didn't have to put my children through school, I'd be down there like a shot."

"I've heard they're stunning," she said politely, noticing that his attention had been diverted elsewhere as he riffled through the paperwork on his desk.

"Ah, yes, here it is." He held a sheet aloft and peered at it. "There's just a slight hiccup with the funding, but not to worry, I'm certain it will all sort itself out. Paperwork, details . . . that's all."

Rachel felt a faint stirring of alarm. She'd quit her previous job for this.

"Haven't quite got it signed off, but it'll all be tickety-boo in a week or so," he added.

Tickety-boo. She hoped that meant what she thought it did.

"No need for you to be concerned, dear girl . . ."

Rachel ground her teeth. She was a thirty-five-year-old woman, not someone's "dear girl." She held herself in check. Charles Wentworth *was* her supervisor and she was depending on him for this job.

"Should I delay my journey?" she asked, hoping his answer would be a negative one. She had no desire to cool her heels in London any longer than necessary. Big cities were anathema to her: they were dirty, crowded, and exhausting. They sapped her spirit and she found herself becoming irritable and anxious the more time she spent in them. London, with its kamikaze cyclists threatening to wipe her out every time she tried to cross the road, and the press of people on buses and the tube in rush hour, made her especially claustrophobic.

"Oh, I don't think that will be necessary," he said breezily. "It's a mere formality. I must say," he added, sifting through some more papers, "your references are excellent."

Rachel had gotten on well with her previous supervisor, and although he had been sad to see her leave, he'd promised to sing her praises. She smiled and sent a mental note of thanks to him.

"Now, why don't we talk about what you will be expected to produce. Since you will be unsupervised down there, I—and the higher-ups—will need a weekly report emailed to us outlining your activities and progress."

Rachel nodded. "Of course. That won't be a problem at all."

"As I mentioned when we last spoke, there's a cottage: two-up two-down." He caught her puzzled look. "Two rooms upstairs, and two downstairs," he explained.

"It sounds more salubrious than my last accommodation," she reassured him, thinking of the one-room thatched-roof bungalow that she had shared with an ever-changing insect population.

"Jolly good then. I think that about covers it. Did you have any questions?"

She shook her head.

"Well, then good luck and I expect you'll be in touch if anything does come up. Nice T-shirt by the way."

Rachel smiled again. After her meeting, her next pressing task was to kit herself out with a new wardrobe suitable for the northern hemisphere winter.

He stood up and Rachel did the same, shaking hands once more before stowing the folders in her daypack and retracing her path to the entrance. She needed to find an outdoor gear store for waterproofs, hiking boots, and thermal layers. A cold wind bit through the thin cotton of her top and she wrapped her arms around herself and shivered as she hurried in the direction of the nearest tube station.

Chapter Four
Little Embers, Autumn 1951

"Ah, here it is," said John. Esther followed his gaze. The path had come to an abrupt end in front of a low wall, over which she could see a large, two-story house made from the same stone standing on its own on a small rise. There were patches of yellowing lichen on the walls, flaking, white-painted window frames, a deep lintel and a steeply pitched, gabled roof. Thin gray smoke emanated from a row of chimney pots at either end but was quickly snatched away by the wind. A dark green creeper had almost engulfed one end of the house, as if a creature were in the process of swallowing it whole.

"This is a most odd kind of place for a holiday," she said, turning to her husband, who was wrestling with a gate, remembering as she did that she had promised before God to obey him. Apparently that now included coming to the ends of the earth with him on what she could only determine was little more than a whim.

Theirs had been a marriage while not exactly of convenience then certainly of expedience, the product of postwar euphoria, a sense of possibility in the world again, but that the day should be seized lest it be lost forever. Her father of course had said that she was too young, but her mother—always the pragmatist—hadn't objected. Young men were thin on the ground, too many of them had perished on foreign soil, and Mother had warned that even beautiful, clever girls—especially clever girls—would find themselves without a beau if they weren't careful.

They met at a church social, his parish being only a couple of miles from hers. Esther was down from university for the holidays, and despite her preference to stay in and study *The Poetics*, a friend had persuaded her to tag along. She'd spotted John across the hall, his height and direct gaze in her direction marking him out among a homogeneous sea of heads. He had brought her a cup of punch, she remembered, apologizing for the lack of ice, as if it were somehow his fault. She was charmed, as much by his two left feet when they danced the jive (he apologized for that too) as by his ready smile and quiet manner, so different from the loud, brash men she had previously encountered. He asked to see her again the next day, taking her for a stroll in a nearby woodland and doing nothing more than holding her hand. "If we went to the pictures we wouldn't be able to talk to each other," he said. "And that would be a terrible shame." She experienced a small thrill at those words. Perhaps here was a man who wanted intelligent conversation from a woman, not merely a decorative accessory to hang on his arm and his every word.

That he was a banker held little interest for her but pleased both her parents no end. "A steady income," her mother had said. "A respectable job," chimed her father.

Esther had hesitated only briefly in accepting John's proposal after a few months of walking out together. They had both determinedly ignored the tiny chip— a mere splinter really—on his shoulder that while she was studying at Cambridge, he had gone straight from school into the city.

They were married the week after her final examinations in a simple ceremony at her parish church. Her father escorted her down the aisle and handed her to John like a parcel being transferred from one man to another. She went from being Esther Parkes to Esther Durrant in the blink of an eye.

She didn't attend her graduation ceremony, held in the autumn of that year: by then she was three months' pregnant and even being upright made her retch uncontrollably.

Esther found herself in a partnership that was, if not exactly exciting, at least solid and dependable. She'd sometimes wondered if there might not be more to a marriage than the gentle affection that existed between them, but the fact of an honest, good man who loved her was not to be taken lightly. John was never going to surprise her (to delight her was more than one could reasonably hope for), but she knew others fared worse. All things considered, she counted herself a fortunate woman.

Teddy had come along before they had even been married a year and there had been no question, even on her part, of her taking up employment, nor of continuing her studies past her undergraduate degree. In the first year after his birth, she had thrown herself into motherhood with all of the zeal she had once reserved for her studies, determined to be the perfect mother, the good wife. Teddy, and John, wanted for nothing from her.

She refused to countenance an unspoken fear that her brain felt as if it was turning into the mush she spooned so tenderly into Teddy's perfect waiting mouth. She found herself numbed by the routine of feeding and changing, and the daily outing with him in the large Silver Cross pram, pushing it around the hilly Hampstead streets. At the end of the day, when Teddy eventually went down to sleep, she was too exhausted to concentrate on anything very much. The words of even her favorite books swam in front of her.

Until today, she had only been apart from him once since his birth, and that was when his little brother arrived. Her breath caught as she was pierced by a memory and she swallowed, tasting ashes.

"Don't worry about a thing, my dear. We're here to meet an old friend of mine." John interrupted her thoughts, giving her a look that was meant to reassure, but instead only served to mildly irritate her.

"Why didn't you tell me this before we set out? I am not sure that I am disposed to call on people, especially strangers," she objected.

"But, I said, he is not a stranger," he explained in a patient tone. "And I think you will find him most agreeable company. He's been very generous to invite us to stay."

As they were quibbling over John's decision to bring them to such a place, the front door of the house opened. In the gloom, Esther couldn't make out much, but John strode forward confidently, leaving her no choice but to follow.

As she came closer, a heavyset woman, white hair pulled back from her face and a bright-patterned apron straining against her ample bosom, loomed into focus. "Ah, hallo there," her husband called. "Dr. Creswell is expecting us. John Durrant, and this is my wife, Esther." He glanced at Esther who was looking mulishly at him, her arms wrapped around her waist, huddled against the wind. She was cold and tired and didn't appreciate being dragged to the end of the country to meet complete strangers. The minute she was alone with John she would tell him so. It was the first flare of real feeling she'd had in months.

The woman—the housekeeper, she supposed—ushered them into the hallway, furnished with a tall grandfather clock that chose that moment to sound the half hour, its solemn brassy tone causing Esther to start in surprise. Recovering herself, she shrugged off her coat and eased off her gloves, noticing as she did that her fingers emerged bloodless and pale. She allowed the woman to take her coat and hat but held on to her handbag. The house, although dim, smelled of beeswax and damp wool, and it was at least warmer inside than out.

"Just through here, if you'd be so good as to wait. Dr. Creswell will be with you shortly." The housekeeper's vowels were rounded and friendly, much like her figure. She moved rather more swiftly than might be expected for one so large and fast disappeared, swallowed up by the gloom of the corridor.

They had been shown into the parlor, lit only by the glow of an oil lamp and a small fire burning in the grate. Esther sniffed, smelling wood smoke, a rich aroma that was infinitely preferable to the dusty, acrid coal that generally burned in London hearths. There was a large rug strewn with a faded flowered pattern and three wing-backed chairs upholstered in somber olive green arranged to face the fire. A mahogany escritoire was pushed up against one wall and a large window looked out over the path upon which they had arrived. In a corner, next to a chaise longue, sat a rather impressive-looking gramophone, its fluted brass horn a bright and shiny flower in the shadowy room.

Esther perched on the edge of one of the chairs, set her handbag on the floor but kept her gloves in her hands, twisting them tightly together. John took the chair next to her, saying nothing. The clock in the hall ticked loudly, counting out the seconds as they sat. Time seemed to stretch, but in reality it must have been only a few minutes before the door burst open.

The man who came into the room was tall, with thick wavy brown hair, the shade of which reminded her of a newly shucked conker, unruly eyebrows that matched his hair, and a strong, square jaw. He was wearing a tweed jacket that hung off his spare, lanky frame and his trousers were the baggy corduroys of an off-duty farmer. The bowl of a briar pipe was firmly grasped in one hand. His cheeks were ruddy, as if he'd just that moment come in from a walk and he brought with him the sweet smell of gorse and tobacco. "Ah, there you are. Durrant, old man. How good to see you. Sorry to keep you waiting."

It was his voice that captured her attention. Low and gentle, with a faint huskiness, like sandpaper. She'd never thought of herself as the kind of woman to be affected by something as simple as the timbre of a voice, but she could have closed her eyes and been lulled to sleep by it.

Esther and John both rose, and the man extended his hand to her husband. They shook hands with hearty familiarity.

"This is my wife, Esther," said John, a protective arm at her back.

"Indeed. Splendid," said the man. "A pleasure to meet you." He studied her as an art critic might examine a painting, his searing gaze quite at odds with his soft voice, and she felt almost flayed at his careful regard of her, as if he could see the blood pulse in her veins, could penetrate the dark, empty heart of her. She looked away, studying the floor.

"Darling, this is my old friend Richard Creswell. We were at Radley together." John was unusually buoyant. She suspected it was to make up for her poor mood.

"Rather a long time ago now, eh?"

Esther looked up and noticed that the doctor's eyes—a light shade of blue that reminded her of swimming pools—crinkled at the edges when he smiled and his teeth were white and even.

She briefly touched her fingers to his—the lightest of contacts—and then huddled her arms tight around herself again, though they offered little protection from his unsettling gaze. She hadn't had an appetite for society nor polite conversation for some time now, and had hardly spoken to a soul save for the daily woman, John and Teddy, and Nanny of course, for the past several months. She didn't appreciate this situation being foisted upon her.

"Welcome to Embers."

"Embers?" she said faintly.

"The house. It gets its name from the island. It was built around, oh, seventy years ago now. Apart from a couple of cottages on the westward shore, it's the only dwelling. Must have been something of an effort to get the materials here and construct it, though it's likely that some of them were the result of shipwreck bounty. Rumor has it that, in years past, islanders used to attach lanterns to the necks of their cows so that passing ships might mistake them for boats at anchor and be lured onto the rocks."

"A deadly harvest," said Esther, noting that he, however, appeared to relish the anecdote.

"I suppose so. Apparently the original owner lived here by himself. A hermit of sorts," he continued. "Mad old fellow." Dr. Creswell boomed a rich, deep laugh that was, Esther imagined, honed on schoolboy rugby fields and cavernous dining halls. It bounced off the room's high ceilings, giving her the impression of boundless bonhomie and a welcome as warm as the fire. She relaxed her grip on her gloves. Perhaps this would not be the ordeal she imagined.

"And is there a Mrs. Creswell?" Esther was shocked at her outspokenness and her curiosity; it seemed that she had lost her ability to make polite conversation, to interest herself in the superficial. She rather thought, however, that he wouldn't be the kind of man who would mind.

"Not one that would put up with me," he said with a generous smile that went some way to contradict his comment.

"Richard has been here, what . . . nearly three years, didn't you say, old chap?" John interjected.

"About that," he replied, not explaining what had brought him there, nor what kept him on this bleak, windblown isle. "Now how about some tea? I expect you worked up something of a thirst on your walk up here, not to mention a chill. It'll warm you right up." He clapped his hands together with enthusiasm. "There's no sugar to spare, I'm afraid, though we do have Darjeeling—a gift from a grateful patient," he explained. As he was speaking, the door to the drawing room opened, and the housekeeper bustled in with a tray. "Ah, thank you, Mrs. Biggs," he said as she set it on the table before them.

Esther wondered idly what kind of patients would come all this way to see him. Or perhaps he had a practice on one of the larger islands they had passed on their journey here?

"Shall I be mother?" His voice interrupted her musings and Esther flinched.

"Oh, I do beg your pardon." The doctor looked mortified and Esther felt almost sorry for him. "Slip of the tongue."

She smiled thinly and felt a pang of longing for Teddy again, for the satin feel of his skin, and the way his thick blond hair lay flat to his scalp after a bath. He'd become quite a chatterbox in recent months, and spoke with a delightful lisp that charmed everyone who came across him. She still couldn't understand why they hadn't been able to bring him with them. It would be a very long week without him.

Dr. Creswell busied himself pouring tea and then handing yellow-and-white flowered cups and saucers to John and herself. There was a matching plate on which three plain biscuits rested, but she had no desire for one. Her hand shook as she raised the china cup to her lips and she had to concentrate to avoid spilling it.

Dr. Creswell and John began to reminisce about their school days and Esther was free to let her gaze wander about the room. It was spare, no extraneous decorative touches that the lady of the house might perhaps have brought, but scrupulously clean: not a mote of dust had been allowed to rest on the polished escritoire nor on the windowsills. Stacked next to the gramophone were a number of vinyl records. She recognized Prokofiev, Schumann, Delius, Satie. She had enjoyed concerts at the Royal Albert Hall, the London Symphony Orchestra, the summer Proms series, but there had been no such outings in the summer last gone by. Once, music had been a pleasure, filling the rooms of Frogmore, accompanying her afternoons, the background to quiet evenings at home after Teddy was in bed, but that had been many months ago, before . . . before . . .

She was wrenched back to the present by the realization that Dr. Creswell had asked her a question, had repeated it several times judging by the furrow between his eyebrows. "I beg your pardon," she said, the barest hint of apology in her voice. "My attention was elsewhere."

She noticed John and the doctor exchange a look of understanding. Their complicity rankled, but good manners meant that she let it go unremarked.

"No matter, Mrs. Durrant. I was merely asking if you had a pleasant journey."

"Oh, oh, yes, I suppose." She glanced at her husband for confirmation. "The sleeper was more than adequate, though the boat journey left something to be desired," she said dryly. She put her cup down on the table and stood up. "A little air, if I may. I'm sorry, I feel rather dizzy all of a sudden." She walked toward the window and raised the sash. A gust of wind blew toward her and she leaned into its chilly embrace, taking several deep breaths. After a moment she lowered the frame and turned back to them both, seeing Dr. Creswell crumpling up a small piece of paper in his hand and depositing it in the pocket of his jacket. John didn't seem to have noticed; he was looking at her with a mix of sorrow, regret, and what seemed like relief. Even in her numb state, she was attuned to the way her husband treated her differently now. He said he didn't blame her for what had happened, that it wasn't her fault. Over and over he had said it, but she knew better than to believe him. After all, she blamed herself, so why shouldn't he?

"Finish your tea, darling. Before it gets cold."

Esther nodded, but as she was about to return to her chair an old map, framed and hung on the wall, caught her eye. It showed a scatter of islands and at the bottom left a small boat being rowed by a serpent, and the words *There Be Dragons* in flowing script.

"Oh, take no notice of that," Richard laughed. "The dragons here became extinct a long time ago."

Esther raised an eyebrow but sat down again, taking a deep draft of the now lukewarm tea. The dregs felt chalky on her tongue but that was nothing unusual— kettles coughed up limescale unless they were regularly cleaned. Perhaps the housekeeper wasn't as efficient as she looked.

Dr. Creswell and John moved on to the topic of the increasing London fogs and she sat back in the chair, letting the conversation swirl around her once more.

Unaccountably sleepy, she leaned her head back against the antimacassar and her eyelids fluttered closed. She felt almost as if she were in a fog herself.

As she drifted toward unconsciousness, her mind flickered back to the doll, muddy and abandoned, that she'd seen on the path. Should she have picked it up? Was there a child crying somewhere because they had lost their favorite toy? How could that be, on such a wild and remote island where no one save for the doctor and his housekeeper appeared to live? It was very curious indeed. She must remember to ask John about it.

Chapter Five
London, Spring 2018

The shopping cart had a faulty wheel and Eve yanked it sideways, narrowly missing a display of turquoise baked bean cans. She could imagine the fuss if she knocked over the towering pyramid: the apron-clad supermarket assistants would come running, possibly the manager, shoppers would tut judgmentally and any small children in the vicinity might scream. She could do without any of that today, thank you very much, and breathed relief as she passed it without incident.

She consulted her list again, and checked the contents of the cart. Milk, bread—"the soft stuff, none of those chewy grains if you please" her grandmother requested—bananas, oatmeal, ham, tomatoes, green beans, and broccoli, sparkling water and a trio of prepared meals. That was everything. She pulled the bothersome cart toward the checkout, noticing as she did, buckets of bright yellow blooms. Daffs. Grams's favorite. A couple of bunches of those might cheer her up. On impulse she shoved them into the cart and then reached into her jeans pocket for her bank card.

It was past noon by the time she had battled the traffic back to the house, and her stomach growled in hunger as she pulled up. The yeasty aroma of the loaf she'd chosen from the baker's wafted toward her from the shopping bag that swung from her elbow and reminded her of how long it had been since breakfast. Eve juggled her phone and the keys, looking for the one that would open the door to her grandmother's house.

"Hello!" she called into the echoing hallway.

No reply.

Halfway along, a steep set of stairs led up to the first floor, and she noticed with annoyance the stack of overdue library books at the bottom. Damn. She had meant to take them back that morning. Sitting on top of them was a pile of folded clean washing and a pair of well-worn hiking boots with cherry-red laces rested on the step below. It would be a long time before her grandmother wore those again, but they had sat unmoved at the bottom of the stairs for months. Eve had at first wondered whether to tidy them away but had decided in the end to leave them be and so they'd stayed there, gradually acquiring a layer of dust and taunting her with their memories of paths long ago explored together.

A long, tiled corridor stretched past the stairs to the back of the house, where the kitchen looked onto a pocket square of a courtyard. Her grandmother's room was what used to be the dining room, off the corridor on the left. Grams had moved there last month, after a couple of weeks in the hospital, when it became obvious that her injuries precluded access to her bedroom on the floor above.

"Grams!" Eve called out again. "I'm back." She put the shopping bags on the floor outside the room before tapping gently on the door. Opening it a fraction, she peered in. The curtains were still drawn and she could just make out a humped shape under the covers. No movement. She must still be asleep. Eve retreated from the room and made her way to the kitchen, stowing the shopping in the fridge and cupboards before pulling out a board, butter dish, and the bread to make lunch for them both.

She filled the kettle, flicked it on, and while it was boiling she assembled a tray. Linen napkin, china cup and saucer—"never a mug, thank you very much"—

and a matching plate. She sliced the bread as neatly as she could, scraped on butter, added ham and some cucumber and cut the sandwich into triangles. She rummaged through the cupboards and found a vase for the daffodils, then tiptoed into the bedroom and placed them on the bookcase opposite her grandmother, where she'd see them as soon as she woke up.

Eve had taken her last bite of sandwich when she heard the cry. Swallowing hurriedly, she raced into the bedroom to see her grandmother sitting up in bed, eyes wide, long silver-gray hair a lion's mane about her face. She had the almost translucent, papery skin of the very old, and though it drooped in folds from her neck, her fine bone structure gave a clue to what an arresting-looking woman she must once have been. "Where did you get those?" she said, her eyes focused on the vase of flowers.

"When I went to the supermarket, Grams. I thought you might like some daffs to cheer you up."

Her grandmother leaned back against the pillows, closing her eyes. "Oh. I thought the ones in the garden had bloomed already. And actually, they are narcissi."

"Okay, narcissi then." Eve determinedly kept her tone upbeat. "Though I'm not sure there's much of a difference," she muttered. Then, more loudly, "And the ones outside are barely poking through the ground. It's still freezing out there. Forecast says we might get snow—in March! In London! Can you believe it?"

"Snow?" Her grandmother perked up.

"Anyway, I reckon these must be hothouse ones," Eve said.

"Or flown in from somewhere warmer."

"Perhaps. They smell gorgeous though, don't they?" For a moment, when Eve had pulled them from the bucket of water in the supermarket the thought that this might be the last spring her grandmother saw crossed her mind and she'd had to blink back a sudden rush of tears, leaning on the cart to steady herself. She'd always thought Grams indomitable, but seeing her in the hospital after her fall had changed her mind; she'd thought she might lose her. Although Grams seemed to be making a steady, if slow, recovery, Eve knew that things could change in the flutter of an elderly heart. A cold could lead to pneumonia, could lead to . . . she did her best not to dwell on it.

"Yes, they do. Thank you darling. Perhaps you might bring them closer."

"Are you hungry? I made a sandwich."

"Oh, if it's not too much trouble."

"Of course not. I said, it's already made."

"Oh yes, well then, that would be lovely." Her

grandmother was making an effort, Eve could tell, just as she herself was. Grams was frustrated by her inability to do much for herself anymore and Eve bore the brunt of her occasional burst of bad temper by biting her tongue and trying not to retaliate, reminding herself of the alternative.

Eve returned with the tray, setting it on a side table, and eased her grandmother forward so that she could adjust the pillows and make her more comfortable. When she was satisfied, she placed the tray in front of her, being careful not to slop the tea in the saucer. She'd receive a ticking off for such a transgression.

"Do you think you might be up to some work after lunch?" Eve asked, as she had done almost every day since she'd moved in. Eve was helping her grandmother write her autobiography, a manuscript that was due at the publisher's later that year. It had originally been planned to coincide with her ninetieth birthday but it now looked like that date would come and go before she'd even written a word of it. Lucky her publisher was patient.

True, there were sheaves of notes and a stack of indecipherable scrawls on scraps of paper, but each time Eve had asked if she wanted her to transcribe them, or for her grandmother to dictate to her, the answers had been a firm "no," a "perhaps tomorrow," or a "stop pestering me, darling. I'll get to it in my own good time."

Eve was taking a gap year. Just not the one she'd planned on. She'd graduated from UCL the summer before with little idea of what she wanted to do with her life. An offer to spend a few months with her boyfriend building a primary school in Africa, to do something that she could feel good about and put off getting a real job for a while longer had seemed like the answer, at least in the short term. But then her grandmother fell, breaking her hip. There had been no one else near enough to care for her—her uncle lived in New Zealand, and couldn't leave his farm. Eve's mother, who had moved to the South of France in pursuit of a sailing career years before, had died when Eve was a teenager, racing a sportscar on a winding road between Saint-Tropez and Ramatuelle. Eve's brother was in New York and only managed to fly back for the occasional weekend. There was really only Eve.

She couldn't bear the thought of Grams having to stay in the hospital for weeks on end, or worse, go into a home. Without even a second thought, she abandoned her plans—and David, who had made known his disappointment in her in no uncertain terms—and moved back in to the top floor of her grandmother's house.

This was a different act of service than building

schools, she told herself, though it had been hard to remember that when David's occasional emails pinged in her inbox and told of heat and dust, making bricks and raising walls, bare feet and joyous singing. She knew he was doing his best to make her jealous, and she couldn't help be aware that he was getting a tan and drinking beer with a foreign label while she bought prepared meals at Waitrose and massaged her grandmother's pale, chilly feet. She tried not to mind too much, but it had made for a very long winter.

She saw her grandmother eyeing the flowers again. "Actually, Eve, I think we could. It's time we made a start."

"Okay then," she said evenly, keeping the surprise out of her voice. She knew her grandmother was capricious enough to change her mind in five minutes' time and pretend that Eve had misheard her. She went over to the window to open the curtains and let what little light there was into the room. "How about you finish your lunch and I'll get my notebook?"

Editors had stalked her grandmother for years, petitioning to publish her memoirs, for, frail as she might appear now, she was once an Amazon of the climbing world, bagging summits with apparent ease, a better athlete than most men. In the 1950s and '60s she, and a small handful of women like her, had pushed the boundaries of possibility with every peak they climbed, putting paid to the notion that women were the weaker sex when it came to endurance and strength of mind. They had paved the way for a generation of noted British climbers and made it possible for women anywhere to believe in their own strength and ability.

Though she'd stopped expedition climbing in her early fifties, her grandmother had been in demand as a motivational speaker and tour leader ever since, and even now there were several invitations awaiting her return to health. It was hard to reconcile this frail old lady with a woman who had once been at the pinnacle of physical fitness, though the fire in her eyes still burned bright.

"I think it's time I got out of this damned bed too," said her grandmother, finishing her tea and holding out the tray, with its plate now bearing only a few crumbs, to Eve.

"Are you sure? The doctor said not to rush things."

"Pfft. What does he know? Let me be the judge of my own body. I've been in more pain than I am now and survived it."

"Tough as old boots hey, Grams?" Eve smiled. "There's a fire in the living room, so just let me get a few things sorted for you and we can work in there."

Her grandmother could be stubborn—Eve had inherited the same streak of obstinacy—and so Eve was quietly pleased that she was getting up of her own accord. Six weeks was too long to spend in bed, even if you were a shade under ninety. Grams would normally have chafed against being bedridden, but Eve was aware that this accident had scared her more than she was prepared to admit. It scared Eve too. Her Grams had been more of a mother to her than her own mum, taking her and her brother every holiday, often collecting them from boarding school at the end of term. Grams's home was as much Eve's, and she'd only left when she went to live in halls of residence at university. She would be completely untethered if she lost her.

The accident had been the smallest of things. Apparently, Grams had been on her way out to the local shops when she'd skidded on the tiled floor and come crashing down. She'd lain there, stranded, for nearly twenty-four hours before her cleaner, Agata, arrived. "I might need a bit of a hand," Grams had apparently said quite calmly, when the Polish girl had found her sprawled by the stairs the next morning. "I can't seem to get up." Agata had acted quickly, covering her with a blanket and calling for an ambulance. Grams had broken her hip and several ribs, and the paramedics who came and took her away chided her for not possessing an alarm button. "Living on your own, you really should have one," one of them had insisted. When Eve visited her in the hospital, her Grams recounted this, as if to imply that he was being ridiculous. "A seniors' medical alert pendant? Really? He obviously had no idea who he was talking to," she'd said dismissively.

Eve had gone out the next day and bought one.

After Eve helped her grandmother into a dressing gown, she held her arm out. Grams put her swollen-knuckled, liver-spotted hand on it, levered herself off the edge of the bed, and together they made halting progress out of the bedroom and along the corridor. Eve knew she must mind this reliance on someone else very much, but she uttered not one word of complaint, made not even a groan.

When they reached the front living room, she settled her grandmother on the sofa and stoked the fire, then took a seat on the chair opposite and turned the page of a brand-new notebook she'd bought in anticipation of this moment. She reached for the dictaphone that lay on the table next to her and switched it on. She planned to record her grandmother's memories and transcribe them later. The notebook was for any questions that might arise as she spoke.

Grams cleared her throat and launched straight in. "I suppose I was an accidental mountaineer, for I never really intended it. Women in those days didn't dream of abandoning their families to go in pursuit of their own goals." She paused. "But it was the making of me really. I see that now. I had to do what was needed in order to survive, to put one foot in front of the other and just keep going."

Eve had always known there was a core of steel running through her grandmother but the hairs rose on the back of her neck at the determination in her grandmother's voice.

"Pen y Fan. As you well know, it's the highest peak in South Wales, a shade under nine hundred meters, little more than a hill really. You remember we went there one October, you must have been about eleven or twelve—shocking day it was, thought the wind might blow you all the way to England. Anyway, where was I? Oh yes, your grandfather suggested it, though I still for the life of me have no idea why. It was the first time we'd ever walked anywhere. We left your mother and uncle—they were still little—with my parents for the weekend and joined a group from the local hiking and climbing club." She paused, thinking. "That's right, someone your father knew from work was a member, so that's how we came to be there. Anyway, it was a glorious day and the view down the valley and across to Bristol was spectacular. The sky seemed almost close enough to touch. We went on several walks that weekend and I learned to read a compass, and more important how to keep on going even when I thought I couldn't take another step. Who would have thought that would be the catalyst, the start of it?"

Eve glanced up from her notebook at her grandmother, who was looking at her as if daring her to deny the last statement. Eve had never heard her grandmother talk about her early climbing days before, but there was something about the tone of her voice as she said it, the cloud that passed fleetingly across her eyes, that told Eve that Grams wasn't speaking the entire truth, that the hiking trip to Wales wasn't really where it had all begun. She wondered what it was that she wasn't telling her.

Chapter Six
St. Mary's, Spring 2018

The sharp cries of seagulls tore at the morning peace. Almost exactly a month after she had left the balmy South Pacific, Rachel found herself sitting at a quayside café in Penzance, wrapping her hand around a mug of weak coffee and guarding a muffin from the marauding gulls that hovered overhead. The *Scillonian III*, her final transport, was waiting, its white bulk looming over the stone quay.

Living in tropical heat for so long had reduced Rachel's ability to cope with temperatures any less than twenty-five degrees Celsius, and in London it had been close to freezing. Even with her new thick woolen sweater, socks, leather boots, and a down jacket firmly zipped up to her chin, she had shivered her way about her errands. Snow had begun to fall as she left, thick flurries that muffled the sounds of the city, blurring its hard edges. Radio announcers warned people to stay indoors, not to venture out unless absolutely necessary.

But here, down south, it was warm enough for her to sit outside—albeit with her thick jacket on—and the day was calm, only a light onshore wind to ruffle the gulls' feathers.

She had stayed at a bed and breakfast to the north of the quay the previous night and her landlord had told horror stories of seasickness when the shallow-bottomed boat got under way in anything more than a slight swell. She was happy to see flat conditions that morning for the two-and-a-half-hour voyage.

As per her brief, she would map the locations of the venus clam (Rachel preferred not to think of it as warty, it was merely bumpy, with pretty frilled rings, rather like a crinoline petticoat, judging by the photographs she'd studied), noting the differences in numbers and size on the larger islands compared to the more remote ones. There would almost certainly be a difference—she well knew that small marine creatures such as these were some of the first indicators of the effects of global warming and pollution. She would then compare her data with that of the study that had been undertaken five years previously.

Dr. Wentworth had given her a list of locations where

the previous observations had been carried out and she had studied them before she left London. Tooth Rock, Droopy Nose Point, Monk's Cowl, Darrity's Hole, Paper Ledge, Bread and Cheese Cove . . . the names sounded delightfully, eccentrically English and she looked forward to exploring them, even if she was less certain about Hell Bay and Cuckold's Carn.

When she had arrived in Penzance, she'd made her way to a dive shop and fitted herself out with a dry suit and a new mask and fins. She didn't expect to be doing much diving, but would certainly need it for snorkeling. She had also purchased waders, an incongruous rubber apron-and-boot combo that made her laugh at herself in the mirror when she tried them on.

Glancing at her watch, Rachel saw that she had about fifteen minutes before she was due to check in. She finished her drink, paid the bill, hauled her backpack onto her shoulders, and lifted the new suitcase bought to accommodate her recent purchases.

After checking her luggage and boarding the ferry she found herself a seat on deck, staring at the slate roofs of the mainland and feeling the throb of the engines beneath her as they got under way. The light was soft, the colors muted, as if someone had turned a dimmer switch down. It was a far cry from the golden haze of the South Pacific, the rich greens of the taro leaves and the brilliant colors and intoxicating fragrances of the tiare flowers . . . cream and yellow frangipani . . . She squashed the thought that she might have been hasty in her decision to come so far, to the other side of the world where everything seemed so unrelentingly gray. She pushed her earbuds into her ears, pulled her beanie down over her hair, and turned up the volume. Unsentimental rock blasted through any lingering doubts.

When the ferry docked alongside the quay at Hugh Town, the main port for the Isles of Scilly on St. Mary's, which was also the largest island in the group, Rachel was surprised. The journey had passed without incident, she'd not felt the slightest twinge of nausea. In fact she'd been on rougher trips on the Manly ferry, which plied its way from her northern beaches home across the harbor to the heart of Sydney.

She hadn't been able to see much of her surroundings as, almost as soon as they had left the mainland, a light misty drizzle had begun to fall, obliterating the landscape. She had no idea in what direction they were traveling. Despite the weather, she had remained outside—the only passenger crazy enough to do so— and tipped her face to the elements, feeling a little rain drip inside her collar and snake its way down her neck. The thrill of a new adventure quickly displaced her earlier misgivings.

As she disembarked, she noticed a number of smaller fishing vessels at anchor in the bay. The ferry had docked behind a bright yellow and green catamaran with the word *Ambulance* emblazoned across its hull in enormous letters. She could see a man and a woman in green uniforms loading a patient onto the wharf and into a wheelchair and stopped for a moment, intrigued by the sight. A water ambulance. Of course. It made perfect sense in such a place.

Gathering herself and her belongings, she pulled up the hood of her jacket and walked along the main street. As she wound her way east, she stopped in the lee of a small shop and pulled out a piece of paper from her pocket. *Shearwater Cottage. Church Street. Green gate and front door. Key will be under the flowerpot,* it read. Trouble was, she couldn't see a sign for Church Street. Then a thought struck her and she looked up, turning around to survey the small town. Sure enough, a little farther ahead she spied the steeple of a church, and then another. It stood to reason that was where Church Street would be.

It was only later that she realized she could have checked the maps app on her phone, but she had never been in need of it on Aitutaki, even when she first arrived there, and so wasn't in the habit of using it.

As it turned out, finding the cottage and the key was easy and she pushed the door open, the width of her backpack causing her to ricochet off the walls of the narrow hallway. Dr. Wentworth had been correct: there were just two rooms downstairs, a small living room furnished with a floral sofa and a couple of armchairs, and then the kitchen. She could make out a blur of garden through the wavy glass panes of the back door. She also noticed that someone had turned on the radiators and left a plastic-wrap-covered plate of food and a container of what looked like soup on the kitchen table.

Rachel rested her backpack against the wall, shucked off her jacket, and picked up a note that was resting against the soup. It was succinct and to the point: *The Bishop and Wolf. 7 p.m. Ask for Janice.*

She unwrapped the plate and picked up the sandwich that had been left there. Sea air always made her hungry and the cold weather even more so. She took a huge bite, put the remainder back on the plate, and then walked upstairs to explore.

There were two quaint bedrooms. The main room was papered in a delicate flowered pattern and furnished with a comfortable-looking bed made up with a thick duvet. Several rose-pink woolen blankets lay folded at its foot. There was a large pine chest of drawers and an upholstered chair near the window, which overlooked the street. It wasn't exactly her taste, but she'd never been that fussy about her surroundings as long as they were clean and kept out the drafts. Next door, a bathroom—with a large tub, she noted—and then the other bedroom, which contained a single bed and a desk. Excellent. She would make that her study.

Later that day, having eaten, unpacked her few possessions and soaked some warmth back into her bones in the bathtub, Rachel decided to go for a walk to explore the island. She'd spent so much time on airplanes, trains, and buses in the past month that opportunities to stretch her legs had been few. The earlier drizzle had stopped and a weak sun was doing its best to shine through the clouds. Taking her jacket in case the rain returned, she laced up her new hiking boots, wiggling her toes at the unaccustomed constriction. On Aitutaki she'd been mostly barefoot, and although she'd worn the boots a few times in the previous few weeks, they still felt heavy and cumbersome.

Janice—at least she presumed it was her—had also left a map of the island on the table and she pocketed that before heading out.

Rachel had done her research before leaving London, and so she knew that the main island was slightly less than two-and-a-half-square miles. She reckoned she should be able to walk around it in about four hours, but as it was after three o'clock she decided to aim for a quarter way around and then she would turn back. She didn't want to be caught out when the light went. Sunset was later here than on the mainland, but she wasn't taking any chances on her first day.

She headed south, picking up a path that wound its way along the rocky coastline toward a place on the map called Piper's Hole. The visibility was considerably better than when she'd arrived that morning and a sharp climb rewarded her with a vista of several smaller islands, lying long and low across the milky green water. As she reached the top, she sat down on a wide, flat rock to catch her breath.

A sense of lightness, something she hadn't felt since being on Aitutaki, overcame her. She felt as if she could breathe again, fill her lungs, her chest expanding, ribs spreading outward. The cool, pure air smelled of seaweed and salt, wet wood and green, growing things.

She remembered drawing maps of islands as a child, fascinated by their possibilities: secret springs, hidden forests, buried treasure. Now she was older, she loved them for the sense of isolation that they brought. Self-

Chapter Seven
Little Embers, Autumn 1951

Esther awoke to the deep, brassy bong of a clock chiming. She swallowed, feeling the pull of her tongue across the dry roof of her mouth. She must have fallen asleep with her jaw hanging open. A seam of light escaping heavy curtains that had been drawn across a window came into focus and she raised her head to fully appraise her surroundings. She had no idea where she was. Beneath her, an eiderdown, on top of her a blanket, though she was still clothed. She tried to move her arms but found that they were securely wrapped around her waist. A coarse fabric chafed at her neck. She rolled to one side in an attempt to free her arms, but it was in vain. She had been bound. The design of the garment was such that it could not be torn, could not be loosened. She'd heard of such things, but never actually seen one: a straitjacket. The realization sliced through her and she cried out without thinking, a whimper at first and then louder. "John!" she called out. "John. Help!"

Silence.

She rolled herself awkwardly to a sitting position, threw her legs over the bed and onto the floor. She stood up and staggered to the window, pushing her head through the gap in the curtains and blinking at the brightness. Nothing in front of her save rippling grasses, steel-gray ocean, and the soughing of the wind as it caught on the walls of the house. A desolate landscape. The island. The house. Embers. Memories flashed back to her now, like the card game she sometimes played with Teddy. She tried to match them up. Scarlet poppies on charcoal serge. Jaunty flags atop a fishing boat. An olive-green armchair. A ruddy-cheeked face. Chestnut hair.

Had she perhaps fallen asleep—such an event was entirely possible, given her habits of the past few months—and then been helped upstairs to rest? But that didn't explain the binding.

Esther went to the door but, with her hands useless, she could not turn the Bakelite handle. She knelt instead and attempted to peer through the keyhole, but there was a key on the other side of the mechanism blocking her view. She called out again, bending down and putting her mouth to the hole, and then straightened up and kicked the door, hard, with her foot, ignoring the pain it caused her stockinged big toe. "Help!" she bellowed, as loud as she could. "Help me! Someone! John! Where are you?"

There was only the answering sound of the wind as it gusted around the thick-walled old house. She collapsed against the door, her knees buckling underneath her as she slid to the floor. As the truth of what had happened began to dawn on her, the words *puerperal insanity* swam into her head. She'd first heard them spill from the doctor's lips—another doctor, one who had visited in the days after the baby was born, the same one who later prescribed ("for your nerves, my dear") the red pills that brought such blissful oblivion. Schoolgirl Latin meant she knew the word *puer* meant boy, and *parere* to bring forth. But she was confident that she was not insane by the mere fact of childbirth.

True, after everything that happened, she had struggled to get out of bed some days, had lost interest in all the things that she normally enjoyed, even, to her horror, becoming short-tempered with Teddy, but nevertheless, that was perfectly understandable given the circumstances . . . But now . . . They were on holiday, weren't they? Could John have brought her to a virtually deserted island in the middle of the Celtic Sea, to a strange doctor, for some other reason? Esther had never imagined him capable of subterfuge but was now forced to consider the possibility.

As she sat, there was a heavy tread outside the room, the click of a key turning and the rattle of a door handle.

"Mrs. Durrant, is that you?"

A female voice, a clipped accent. It was not the housekeeper then; Esther remembered her. She shuffled away from her position against the door, far enough for the person attached to the voice to push it open and see her sitting there. "Oh my goodness." A woman with tightly curled brown hair bound by a starched white cap, a spotless apron covering a sky-blue dress, looked at her with concern. "Mrs. Durrant. I expected you would sleep for longer and that I would be here when you awoke. Well," she said. "This all must be a terrible mystery to you, I suppose."

"What am I doing here? And where is my husband?" Esther glared at her, suddenly furious.

"Please stay calm." The woman's voice was soothing but Esther was not interested in being placated. "Your husband is only considerate of your welfare, you must understand that. It was necessary to sedate you, I'm afraid; Dr. Creswell thought it for the best. Your husband has assigned the care of you to us for the time being. This is a place where we heal those who are sick, not in body but in mind."

"What? What on God's earth does that mean? How can he even do that? And who exactly are you?"

"My name is Jean Bardcombe; I'm a nurse, but you probably gathered that." The woman touched the cap that indicated her position. "You are unwell and it is our job to help make you better again. The binding is because your husband said that you scratch yourself. Without being aware of it."

Shame washed its ruddy tide over Esther, making her shrink away from the nurse. It was true. Ever since the baby had gone she'd woken up every morning with rusty bloodstains streaking the bedsheets and long, angry welts across her forearms and torso, her thighs . . . She had no idea how it happened, for she slept each night as if she had tumbled into a dark well.

Deep in the marrow of her was the thing she'd been trying to avoid, brought to the surface by this strange new place. She was bad, rotten at the core, not fit to be called a mother. What was worse was that she had brought this on herself. She probably deserved it. That was why he'd been taken from her, her sweet baby, her second son. That was why she was here, locked up.

Still, some part of her refused to give in. "Where is

John? Is he downstairs? I *demand* to see him. John—"
Esther's voice rose and she shouted through the open
door to make herself heard.

The nurse shook her head. "Your husband has returned to London."

Esther was dumbfounded. He'd left her there? She'd
heard of husbands committing their wives to insane
asylums—for she was under no illusion, now, that was
what this godforsaken place must surely be—but had
never imagined John would do such a thing to her,
despite everything that had happened. She'd always
believed that he loved her, depended on his kindness.
Would he have really thought this the most appropriate
course of action?

"Exactly how long will I be here for?" She still
couldn't comprehend that she was a prisoner on this
desolate island. Marooned miles from home, miles from
Teddy, her fate surely no better than the shipwrecked
sailors from the captain's story.

"That really depends on you, Mrs. Durrant. If it
helps, try to think of it as a convalescence if you like.
You've been through a great deal."

Esther railed at the patronizing tone. She was in-
censed. How dare John discuss their private matters
with strangers—no matter if they were a doctor or
nurse—without telling her?

A tall figure appeared behind the nurse and Esther recognized Dr. Creswell.

"Ah, Mrs. Durrant, there you are. I trust Nurse Bardcombe has explained matters satisfactorily?" He gave her a smile that momentarily brightened the dim room but Esther did not return it.

"I'm afraid there's been a dreadful mistake—" she began.

"Shush now, don't upset yourself," he said. "Perhaps you might like some breakfast? We grow quite a few of our own vegetables, the chickens give us eggs, and Mrs. Biggs is a fine cook."

"I don't think you heard me," she insisted through clenched teeth. She didn't give a damn about chickens or vegetables. "My husband would *never*—"

"I'm afraid he did," Dr. Creswell interrupted. "But we're here to help you, Mrs. Durrant."

Esther's shoulders slumped, not wanting to believe it but hearing the ring of truth in the doctor's words.

"As I was saying, a boat comes once a week with other essentials. So you'll see we manage rather well."

Once a week. Esther began to calculate rapidly. At worst, she'd be here for no more than seven days; if she managed to escape the confines of the house, that was. But if she did escape and make her way home, would John not simply send her back, believing it was the best place for her? Where would she go instead? Her parents? Or would they defer to her husband's authority and insist that she be returned, like an unwanted package, to this windblown, pitiless place? And what about Teddy? Nanny couldn't look after him all by herself— what about on her day off? Even as she thought this, she acknowledged that Nanny had been looking after Teddy for months, forfeiting any leave owing to her, working around the clock to see to his needs because Esther had been unable to. Her mind whirled as she tried to make sense of her situation, to find a way out.

"Now, some breakfast, Mrs. Durrant?" the doctor asked again as if she were a welcome guest. "We will, of course, unbind you." He said this as if it were nothing out of the ordinary to wrap a person up in thick calico so tightly they could barely move.

Esther threw him a withering look.

Chapter Eight
St. Mary's, Spring 2018

Rachel had passed a couple of pubs on her way to the cottage earlier that day. The Mermaid, with its brightly painted sign of a round-bosomed maiden combing her hair, was next to the wharf, its footings in the sand, practically in the water. The other, the Bishop and Wolf, was on the main street and she found it easily.

It was warm and cozy inside and a fire crackled in the grate. There was a low hum of people chatting, and an occasional metallic clatter and shout from the back of the pub, where she assumed a kitchen must be. She walked up to the bar, ordered half a pint of the local ale, and then asked the girl serving if she knew anyone called Janice.

She smiled at her. "You must be the new research scientist."

Rachel was a little taken aback that even the barmaid knew who she was. It was a small island, but not that small surely?

"Janice is my mum," the girl explained.

"Oh, right." Rachel smiled back at her. "She left me a note. I'm supposed to meet her here."

The girl placed her drink on the bar in front of her and nodded in the direction of a doorway. "In the back bar. You won't miss her. I'm Lucy, by the way."

"Rachel. And thanks."

Lucy had been right. Janice was the only woman in the small timber-lined room but Rachel wouldn't have missed her had there been a sea of other females. She was a symphony in teal, purple, and copper. She would have out-peacocked a peacock had there been any in the vicinity.

"Hello, love. You must be Rachel." Her loud voice boomed in the small space. She stood up and shook Rachel's hand enthusiastically, her beaded earrings jangling, and then waved her toward a seat opposite.

"So where were you before here?" she asked as Rachel sat down. Rachel explained her last assignment and Janice's eyes rounded. "Ooh, that sounds very exotic. Heck of a sight warmer than here, that's for sure."

"It'll get better in summer though, won't it?" Rachel asked hopefully.

"Eventually," Janice laughed, jangling again with a musical tone. "For at least a couple of weeks. But the islands will grow on you, mark my words. You'll find it hard to leave. Almost everyone does."

Rachel decided that now was not the time to disagree and she took a sip of her beer.

"I hope the cottage is suitable," said Janice. "We had to scrounge around for some new furniture. The last resident did something dreadful to the sofa—best not to ask," she said, as she caught the look of alarm on Rachel's face. "But it was a stroke of luck that we were able to get a replacement from one of the guesthouses here; they've recently updated theirs. You'll find that nothing goes to waste on the islands if we can help it."

Rachel nodded. "It's lovely, thank you. And thanks for the sandwich and soup—they were very welcome."

"No problem, my dear. You'll find the supermarket farther along the street here, and there's a bakery and a greengrocer's. A deli too, if you fancy something gourmet. The pâté's really good, just make sure you ask for the pork and cognac one."

As Janice was telling Rachel about a weekly yoga class in the church hall—"It's a great way to meet people," she insisted. "We don't bite."—a group of men barreled into the room, taking over the last empty table. Wearing heavy fishermen's sweaters and boat shoes, their hair windblown and crisp with salt, they had the healthy, raw complexions of those who spend a lot of their time outdoors.

Rachel noticed them noticing her but kept her attention firmly on Janice. Most of the time she tied her long, dark hair back, but this evening she'd left it out and it fell like a waterfall almost to her waist, thick and glossy. Though she generally dressed for comfort rather than aesthetics, it didn't seem to make any difference when it came to being noticed by the opposite sex. "I swear you must give off some sort of pheromone," Mel, one of her friends at university used to complain. "How can they tell that you're up for it?"

"Probably because I am," she had laughed.

Perhaps, though, they could tell that she was a loner? Some of her lovers had found that a challenge. "You march to the beat of a different drum," one had complained, only half-joking. A few had tried to pin her down, but sooner or later she had tired of them and slipped away, mercury in their grasp.

She took another sip of her beer and glanced under her lashes at the men. One of them was looking directly at her and she finally returned his curious stare with a curve of her lips and a question in her eyes. He dropped his gaze. Janice—who had been in the middle of an anecdote about the local dentist and a recent wisdom tooth extraction—noticed and stopped talking. So did the other men at the table. In fact, the whole room went suddenly quiet.

The man who had been staring stood up and came over to where they were sitting. "Hey, Janice. How's the pottery going?"

Rachel knew he was fishing for an introduction. He was tall, and broad-shouldered, with a pleasing huskiness to his voice and she liked the way his hair sprang away from his face, as if it had a life of its own. He wasn't her type though: he was at least her age, if not a few years older, and more likely to be either a) married, b) looking for a wife or, c) had already found and lost one and was dragging his baggage with him. Younger men were generally far less complicated in her experience. He did, however, look familiar, as if she'd seen him somewhere before.

"Not bad, thanks, Jonah. And yourself? Heard you had a call-out this morning?"

"All good. Mrs. Henderson over on Bryher turned an ankle. We got her over to the doc's and fixed up. Even gave her a ride home again." He smiled, revealing a set of perfect white teeth.

"Rachel, this is Jonah. He's one of the islands' ambulance officers, on the *Star of Life*," Janice explained. "Rachel's our new scientific research officer."

That was where she'd seen him before—unloading a passenger at the quay as she arrived.

"Pleased to meet you, Rachel," said Jonah, extending a hand and directing his smile at her. "Glad you've joined us. Perhaps I can show you around when you've got some time?"

Janice coughed and lifted her glass to her lips to hide her smile.

"Do you hike?" he added.

Rachel nodded. She definitely preferred walking to yoga. "The best way to get an idea of a place."

"Then I'll take you exploring if you like."

"Let the poor girl settle in, won't you, Jonah?" Janice protested.

"It's fine, really," said Rachel. "That'd be nice."

His smile widened and she noticed a faint fanning of lines at the corners of his eyes that only added to his rugged appeal.

"But I do have a lot of work to do, and I'll be fairly busy with that for the foreseeable future," she added, giving him an apologetic grin.

His face fell.

"Well, perhaps a drink sometime then?" He wasn't giving up.

She inclined her head. "Sometime," she echoed.

There was a not-so-subtle cheer from his companions across the room. Rachel could have sworn she saw a blush rise up his cheeks, but he turned away and went back to his seat. She heard him telling his mates to "give it a rest" and grinned inwardly.

"Oh, I almost forgot," said Janice, interrupting her thoughts. "There's a dinghy for you to use. I'll show you where it's moored tomorrow if you like."

"Excellent." Dr. Wentworth had mentioned a boat.

Chapter Nine
London, Spring 2018

E ve had grown up in awe of her grandmother. By the time she was old enough to remember, Grams had retired from mountaineering, though she still led groups of climbers, more often than not decades younger than her, on hiking tours of the Swiss and French Alps. Eve remembered one summer holiday she and her brother spent with Grams in the Valais. She must have been about twelve. Their pockets filled with barley sugar, they barely had time to stop and gaze in awe at the Matterhorn towering above them as Grams scampered along the track with all the speed and agility of a mountain goat, her hair in two silver plaits that gave her the look of an elderly Heidi. They scrambled after her, following the yellow signposts, Grams's blue backpack a mere dot in the distance. More often than not, Eve and her brother would arrive, exhausted, at the hut that was to be their resting place for the night to find Grams bouncing from foot to foot, impatient for their arrival. "Come on slowcoaches," she would tease, before rewarding their efforts with slabs of milk chocolate studded with hazelnuts.

She always had a seemingly inexhaustible supply of chocolate.

Grams taught them about the mountains, how to read the weather and tell when a storm was brewing by watching the light, high clouds that sometimes sat at the top of the jagged peaks, and which streams to collect icy, clear drinking water from. At night she taught them the names of the constellations and awed them with stories of climbing the famous peak that dominated the landscape. "The Matterhorn," she would whisper, as if it were something sacred. "Did you know more than five hundred people have died attempting it?" Then she'd add in a louder voice, in her no-nonsense tone, "Of course, like any mountain, climbing it is the easy part. It's descending where you can really get into difficulties. Time it poorly, or get stuck out there too long and you're asking for trouble."

Eve also remembered other half-term holidays, in the Brecon Beacons, or, when they were older, getting the train to Scotland to bag Munros—summits over three thousand feet. Her last visit, when she had been sixteen and her brother more interested in his new girlfriend than chasing their grandmother up mountains, had been to Ben Nevis. Via the easier Pony Track than the cliffs of the north face. The highest mountain in Great Britain. They'd gone over the May bank holiday weekend—"too early in the season really," Grams had said as they set off, "but beggars can't be choosers"— and were pelted with hailstones as solid and unforgiving as ball bearings. Hard-packed ice on their way to the summit made the going treacherous. "Just as well we've got our Gore-Tex on," Grams had shouted into the wind that threatened to blow Eve sideways. They were hours from the top and Eve's feet and fingers were frozen blocks of ice but Grams had a look of gritted-teeth determination that gave Eve the strength to keep going. There was no way she would quit if Grams wasn't going to. It wasn't until half an hour or so later that her grandmother noticed how much she was struggling. "Eve, darling, I think perhaps it's not our day," she called out. Even now, Eve could recall the reluctance in her voice. "Come on, let's get out of this miserable place." As they scrambled back down the unstable scree, Eve privately vowed that it would be her last such adventure, though she didn't know how she would confess it to her grandmother.

"It's as much a mental challenge as a physical one. You have to put your icy boots back on and get out of the tent, even when it's the last thing you want to do." Grams's voice brought Eve back to the present. "Of course, then our oxygen tanks weighed more than eighteen pounds—that was pretty much all we carried on the push for the summit. No fancy backpacks, no space for emergency rations. Even our ice axes weighed far more than they do now. Here—" she pointed over to the corner of the room. "Pass me mine, will you, darling?"

Eve got up and retrieved the old-fashioned steel and wood axe that had been resting against the wall. It felt solid and heavy in her palm.

"Hello, Socius, old friend." Her grandmother caressed the worn handle lovingly. "My partner—for that's what it was. I'd be long dead without it. It saved me from hurtling into a crevasse, never to be seen again, on more than one occasion. I wasn't certain I'd ever make old bones."

"Weren't you ever terrified, Grams?" Eve asked.

"Almost always," she said brusquely. "But most of the time I didn't have the luxury of being able to think about it. My old boots are somewhere in the house as well, aren't they? *Fortitudo*—courage, for that's what they gave me when I laced them up. We didn't even have proper harnesses—just a rope around our waists. If one of us were to fall there was nothing to take the strain and you'd be lucky not to fracture a rib, or worse."

"Did you ever fall?"

"Of course," she said. "But I was lucky never to break anything. A bit of frostbite is the worst I've had to put up with. I suppose," she said, suddenly pensive, "anyone would say that I was extremely lucky." She shifted in her seat and Eve half-rose to see if she could make her more comfortable, but her grandmother plowed on. "We wore wool underwear, a down jacket and pants, and then a windbreaker. We tied twelve-point crampons to our boots with string and our canvas tents were a darn sight heavier than today's lightweight ones. I remember one storm where the wind tore a hole in my tent. Now when was that . . . ?" She leaned back, lost in the memories. Eve checked that the voice recorder was still working and waited.

"Did I ever tell you about the time I was stalked by a snow leopard in Nepal? I think that was on the same expedition," she said with a wink. If Grams had been any other old lady, she would have sworn she was making it up, but she'd heard even taller stories over the years and didn't doubt the veracity of them, however outlandish, for a minute.

Her grandmother sighed. "I'm getting ahead of myself . . . Back to the beginning. Now, not long after Wales, we spent a few weeks one summer in the Lake District, left your mother and uncle, who were only small, with a local woman while we went off tramping about. It was the first time either of us had ever done anything more than a scramble, and we were faced with a slab of sheer rock. Well, your grandfather didn't think I'd manage it and had even arranged for me to be escorted back to the cottage where we were staying by a chum of his. He made the mistake of telling me this before we roped up, so of course I wasn't going to back down, no matter how terrifying it might have been. After that first proper climb, I was hooked. I even learned to belay rather well actually, though I could scarcely flex my hands for days afterward and my palms had no skin left on them." Her grandmother glanced ruefully at her knotted, arthritic fingers. "We used to try and get away for as many weekends as we could. In fact, I think our love of climbing helped mend the holes in our marriage. Especially after everything that happened . . ." A look of regret swam across her grandmother's lined face, making her seem suddenly tired and vulnerable.

Eve blinked. She'd always assumed Grams and Gramps had a rock-solid partnership, right up until her gramps's death nearly fifteen years ago, though at the time she wouldn't have been old enough to be aware of much if anything had been awry. It was disconcerting to discover this hadn't always been the case. What *had* happened?

Before she could probe further, Grams continued. "We'd meet outside the Park Lane Hotel on a Friday night for the bus to North Wales and stay in farmhouses in the valleys. Sometimes one of the other wives and I had to stay in the barn, as the men were all inside. We didn't care. As long as we got to climb."

Eve was astonished. "It was really that sexist?"

"Oh yes. That wasn't the half of it. Climbing has long been the preserve of males. One of my favorites, the Grepon, in the French Alps, was climbed by two women, Miriam O'Brien Underhill and her partner, Alice Damesme, in 1929 if I remember correctly. After that some ridiculous French mountaineer—male of course—was reported to have said, 'Now that it has been done by two women alone, no self-respecting man can undertake it. A pity, too, because it used to be a very good climb.' Can you believe it? It made me absolutely furious when I heard the story. The prejudice even then was astounding. Women weren't supposed to have the mental fortitude for high Alpine climbing, let alone the physical strength. But we proved them wrong."

Eve heard the satisfaction in her voice.

"I remember my first summit of Mont Blanc. It was the hardest climb I'd ever attempted, and I certainly didn't feel ready, but then I don't think one ever does. Well, I never did anyway. We'd spent two nights acclimatizing at a local hut. I wished I had thought to bring earplugs—some of the men snored horribly, so any sleep I did manage was fitful at best, but at least the food was good. Though I would have eaten anything you put in front of me, truth be told. Climbing sharpens the appetite.

"We descended to Chamonix for a night and prepared for the summit. As usual, we began the climb in darkness, to get as high up the mountain as possible before the sun softens the snow too much. As we reached the Grand Couloir, a snowstorm blew up and we couldn't see where we were going. It was like iron filings on my cheeks. Our leader asked if anyone wanted to go back down, but everyone voted to keep going. We climbed through the couloir and then had a scramble upward for nearly half a mile. By this time it was beastly cold, but we kept on. There was a nasty cornice, I remember; I was worried it would collapse on top of us. Then, the storm disappeared as suddenly as it had arrived and the most glorious dawn broke. Orange and crimson tinged with gold." Her grandmother coughed, wiped her hand over her mouth and continued. "I've seen more than my fair share of sunrises, let me tell you, Eve, but I've never forgotten this one. There were mountains as far as you could see, their peaks like needles piercing the sky. It was unbelievably, brutally beautiful. There was once a time in my life when I'd thought I'd never find beauty again." Eve's ears pricked up—what was her grandmother referring to? She was dropping hints like bread crumbs, but never elaborating. She didn't have the chance to ask, as her grams continued.

"We got to les Bosses, a ridge of ice just before the summit and I was forced to take a breath with every step, the air was so thin up there. I remember being terribly thirsty, but there was no time to stop to make a drink. Eventually we were there, the whole of Europe spread out beneath us. Majestic is the only word I can think of to describe it, and that doesn't even come close. It was quite literally breathtaking. The stillness up there, the quiet. The snow and ice dampen the sound. All you can hear is your own heart racing.

"I'd been my father's daughter, my husband's wife, a mother . . ." She halted for a moment. "But never someone in my own right. Not until then."

Eve saw her grandmother close her eyes, letting out a slow breath.

"Are you tired, Grams? Would you like to stop?" she asked.

The old woman's eyes flew open. "Not a bit." Her voice was determined. "Now, where were we?"

Eve glanced down at the notes she had made. "At the summit of Mont Blanc," she replied.

"Ah yes. Now, it had taken us longer to get there than planned and it had gotten late so we had to glissade some of the way down."

"Glissade?"

"When you take off your crampons and slide down the slope, trying to use your ice axe to steer. If you find yourself going too fast you have to roll over and dig the point of your axe into the snow. When you've never done it before it's quite terrifying."

Eve listened, fascinated, as her grandmother continued to describe their descent into the valley. She didn't find it hard to picture her slip-sliding down a glacier.

"Old age is a curse, Eve darling," her grandmother said, changing tack again. "Almost everyone is gone now. And you've only the company of younger people, who get impatient when you can't do things," she added.

Eve started to protest.

"Don't try and tell me otherwise. It's true," she said. "But then I'd be impatient with me right now. Blasted fall."

"You've had a life larger than many, Grams," said Eve. "And you'll get better again, even the doctor said you were a living marvel."

Her grandmother scoffed at this last remark.

"Lucy Ambrose," her grandmother blurted out. As she slipped from one anecdote to another, Eve could tell that her grams's memories were becoming jumbled. She would do her best to make sense of them later. "One of the best. We used to climb together whenever we could. She became one of the country's finest climbers. For a while we were known as the 'housewife explorers,' which of course ticked us off no end."

"What happened to her?"

"Died on the descent from Sasso delle Dieci in the Val Badia. The Dolomites. 1981. She was forty-eight."

"Oh gosh. How did you cope with that? Did it make you think twice about continuing to climb?"

"Climbers die all the time, Eve; it's one of the risks you take every time you make an ascent. And I was no stranger to death by then. I thought of those I'd lost every time I stepped on a mountain, they walked beside me, never left me."

"Oh, Grams." Eve immediately thought of her own

mother, of the times that she imagined her close by even though she was no longer alive. "Did it help you cope when . . . well, when Mum died?"

The old woman rested her head against the back of the sofa. "Not really. Losing a child, no matter how old they—or you—are is different. Far, far worse. Always heartbreaking."

"Like losing your mother," said Eve quietly.

"Yes, my dear, as bad as losing your mother."

Eve squeezed her grandmother's hand, feeling the fine bones beneath the thin skin. "We're lucky we've got each other, hey?" she said, swallowing the lump in her throat.

"For now, darling," her grams sighed. "Then all you're left with at the end are the memories. Good and bad. But you've got to go out and make them, no matter what risks there might be."

Eve didn't feel as if she were making any particularly exciting memories, not at the moment anyway.

"Oh, I know you're stuck here with me, watching the days pass by—" Eve went to object. "And I do appreciate it, Eve; I really do. I know what you've given up, to take care of me."

"If you mean David, I'm not certain it was ever going to be a long-term thing anyway," Eve admitted.

"There's plenty of time for love in your life and when

you meet the right person, you'll know in an instant—but promise me that as soon as I'm well again you'll go and have adventures, make use of that degree of yours—one of my great regrets is that I wasted mine. And then come back and tell an old lady all about it."

"Of course, Grams," Eve reassured her. "Though I haven't a clue what I might do with myself actually."

"Something will come along, you'll see."

They sat for a moment in easy silence.

"Did you know?" Eve asked, thinking again of David. "That you'd met the right person? Right away?"

"I'm afraid I did," her grams said and Eve heard an unmistakable sadness in her voice. "But by then it was far too late."

Chapter Ten
St. Mary's, Spring 2018

S he's seen better days, but she's seaworthy enough. I had the boys down at the boatshed check her over. They gave her a clean bill of health." Janice patted the hull of the aluminum runabout affectionately.

It was the next morning, and they had arranged to meet down at the quay, near the Mermaid, at low tide.

Rachel looked dubiously at the small craft. White paint flaked from its sides and the name on one side was almost worn away. The *Soleil d'Or.* "Golden Sun," said Janice, seeing her looking at it. "It's a type of flower that grows on the islands, a narcissi. The season's almost over—it's much earlier here than on the mainland—but you'll see a few rogue late bloomers if you look carefully."

Rachel rolled the boat from one side to the other

and as far as she could tell there were no obvious weak spots. The outboard motor looked in okay condition. She'd piloted worse. "All right then, let's take her out for a spin," she said.

"I'll leave you to it," said Janice, handing her the keys. "I've got a date with a firing kiln."

After leaving the pub the night before, Rachel had spent several hours familiarizing herself with the nautical charts of the islands that her supervisor had provided. It would take weeks to plan out an observational strategy, but for now she simply couldn't wait to get out on the water and start to explore.

"There's plenty of fuel," said Janice before she left. "And a spare tank in the boatshed." She indicated a small wooden shack farther along the beach, past the slipway. "You can keep her moored here too."

"Cheers," said Rachel. "I reckon I'm all set."

"Have fun." Janice waved her good-bye.

Rachel pulled the tinny off the sandbank and out into the water. She'd taken the precaution of wearing her new tall rubber boots and as soon as the little boat was afloat, she hopped onboard, nimble as a cat that didn't like getting its paws wet. The day was a fine one, though a crisp westerly blew the water into frothing whitecaps. Rachel's hair whipped about in the wind and she regretted not bringing a beanie to keep it in check. She didn't let that oversight stop her though and started the outboard. It coughed throatily into life and she opened the throttle, expertly steering out of the harbor and into the channel between St. Mary's and the other islands.

She knew from her reading that the Isles of Scilly were made up of more than a hundred and forty islands. Some were wildlife sanctuaries, home only to populations of torpedo-shaped puffins, cormorants, kittiwakes, and gulls. Only a handful were inhabited, and the total human population was around two thousand people, though that number swelled considerably in summer with a seasonal influx of tourists who came to camp and hike or stay in one of the many guesthouses on the larger islands.

Rachel whizzed past a colony of seals basking on large gray-brown boulders, and thick splinters of stone that tumbled toward the shoreline. Then a red-and-white-striped tower loomed. The St. Martin's Daymark. She remembered it from her study of the maps. As the boat puttered along, she thrilled to the feeling of salt spray on her face, the freedom of being at the helm, completely in control.

Slowing eventually, she drew closer to the shore of St. Martin's and saw the figure of a white-bearded man dressed in a long mustard-colored duster coat, looking for all the world as if he was waiting for an old-fashioned motorcar to drive. He raised his arm at her from where he stood on a small cement quay and she gave a cheery wave in return, wondering why he didn't appear to be feeling the cold as she was. A little farther along she saw what she thought must be black rabbits, startled and hopping through hedges at the buzz from her engine. It was all new and fascinating to her.

The tinny's draft was shallow, but there were sand-bars lurking beneath the glass-green water, waiting to ground the unwary, so she steered the boat away from the shoreline and continued on, toward the Eastern Isles, passing Tresco and St. Martin's, with their green fields and low hedges. There were glimpses of bright yellow among the green and she remembered Janice's comment about the narcissi. The island's low slopes, bare of trees, looked like sleeping giants part-submerged by the water and she almost fancied she could see a head, shoulders, and arm of one. Eyes tearing from the wind, she wiped her face and blinked, smiling at her wayward imagination.

Heading closer to shore once more, she saw perfect crescents of startlingly white sand, and the water turned from bottle green to turquoise. They weren't dissimilar from some of the beaches on Aitutaki, the only difference being that the water here was likely several tens of degrees colder than the balmy, bathlike conditions of her last posting.

She puttered steadily across the water, past Teän Sound and then seeing what she thought was Ragged Island, then Great Ganilly, Little Ganilly, Great, Middle and Little Arthur and Nornour. Truth was, they were so small that it was hard to tell them apart. But she had a knack for geography and she'd soon learn.

Then, just as she was about to turn back, she saw one final island—Little Embers, if she was correct. It was long, narrow, and T-shaped, two humps of land with a sandy neck at the top of the T.

A large stone house stood halfway up one of the hills. Its gray-brown walls and slate roof gave it the appearance of one of those ancient stone effigies. It looked almost as though it had been part of the landscape forever. Had *endured*, undaunted by wild winds or seas or storms. Did anyone really live there, in such isolation? Smoke drifted from its chimney, so it appeared that they must.

Rachel had been under the impression that all of the islands out this way were uninhabited, so made a mental note to ask Janice about it when she next saw her.

As she motored on, she saw the ruins of two cottages

on the other side of the island, their roofs caved in and walls tumbling down. She checked her watch. A couple of hours had passed since she set off and her stomach was beginning to rumble. Perhaps it was time to head back.

She hadn't bothered with a trip to the island's small supermarket earlier in the day—she'd been impatient to get to the slipway—and breakfast had been nothing more than a cup of black coffee, made from the scant supplies that she found in a kitchen cupboard. By the time she got back to St. Mary's and had tied up *Soleil*, she was too hungry to waste time shopping.

The Mermaid stood right in front of her, beckoning. She'd lay bets there was a fire blazing inside too. She was numb from her nose to her toes and once the thought of a fire had snagged in her brain, it was impossible to resist.

The pub was quiet, just a handful of customers sipping on pints, and she took a menu from the bar, settling into an armchair by the fire.

"Fancy running into you again. How are you getting on?"

Rachel looked up from the menu to see Jonah's cheerful face, noticing again the laughter lines fanning out from his eyes. He was in uniform, a high-vis waterproof hung open to reveal dark green twill trousers. His shirt, of the same material, was emblazoned with a gold badge. There was a faint but reassuring smell of liniment about him, reminding her of grazed knees and Band-Aids.

She grinned back. The exhilaration from her boating expedition had put her in a good mood. "Better now I'm starting to warm up," she said. "I can't remember the last time I was so cold."

"This?" he laughed. "Count yourself lucky you weren't here a few months ago. You do know it's spring now?"

Rachel shuddered, holding her numb fingers out to the fire to warm them. "I'm sure I'll get used to it," she said, though her teeth were still chattering.

"How about a drink?" he asked. "That is, if you're not meeting someone else? I've got an hour's break."

"Thanks. Lemonade perhaps? I've got work to do this afternoon."

"We can do better than that. They do a good spiced cider here. That'll warm you up from the inside."

She nodded. "Perfect."

He came back a few minutes later carrying two glasses of cloudy, golden liquid and a plate of pork pies. "You look like you might be hungry too."

"Oh really, you didn't have to," she protested.

"Nonsense. Go on—help yourself. I can't eat all of them."

"Okay, if you're sure." She cut into one of the pies and took a bite. "How long have you been a paramedic?" she asked after she swallowed her first mouthful.

"Nearly fifteen years—" he reached across and wiped a stray crumb from her cheek. The gesture was intimate, assured, and Rachel felt a spark at his touch, as if there was too much static electricity in the air.

"And have you always lived on St. Mary's?"

"Born and raised. Went to the mainland to study of course. But I couldn't wait to come back. Why wouldn't you when there's all of this here?"

"I suppose."

"Let me fill you in on the place," he said. "One of the islands is said to be the resting place of King Arthur. Another story is that there was a tsunami in the eleventh century and the islands are tips of old mountains. Some people still believe that there are churches and houses down there, stretching all the way to Land's End. Fishermen have said they can hear bells tolling at night . . ."

She looked incredulously at him, finding the story hard to believe.

"These days, people say that eventually St. Mary's

will be cut in two," he continued. "Hugh Town is on the narrowest part of the island—there's Town Beach on one side and Porthcressa on the other, but there's not much that separates them. It'll only take a few meters' rise in sea level and half the town would be underwater. Global warming and all that. The island's highest point is at Telegraph Road, a hundred and eighty-seven meters above sea level. For now anyway." His eyes danced at her.

"You are well informed. And can you tell me about this place?" Rachel raised her head and looked around. She was intrigued by the old pub. It reminded her a little of one of the bars in Aitutaki—both were filled to the brim with sailing memorabilia.

"It was originally a warehouse, but it's been a pub since the 1950s I think. The décor hasn't changed much since then either," he said ruefully.

"I guessed as much. I like it though. There's a nice sense of history." Rachel wiped the crumbs from her hands with a napkin. "Luckily, the pork pies are considerably fresher."

She was rewarded with his loud, rollicking laugh. Surprisingly, it warmed her almost as much as the fire.

"So what do you do for fun, Jonah?" She took a sip of her cider and fixed him with a deliberately wide-eyed, innocent gaze, teasing him. She was gratified to see him confused as to her meaning, but he chose not to take the bait.

"Well, in summer there's gig racing. Rowing boats, that is. Wooden, with six oars. A bit like your surf lifeboats I think—I saw a TV documentary about them once. Everyone comes out to watch—it's exciting."

"I'm sure it is," Rachel said. She liked the idea of watching muscled young men wrestling with a wooden boat.

"But tell me more about you—you didn't get that tan by spending two weeks in Spain."

"No," she agreed. "I've been living in the Cook Islands. Aitutaki, to be exact, for the last couple of years."

Jonah whistled. "I can see why you'd be less than impressed with the weather here then."

Rachel gave him a stoic grin. "I'll get used to it."

"And what is it exactly that you're doing here? Local gossip has it that you're studying clams."

She nodded. "Yep. Clams."

"What's the deal with them? I wouldn't have thought they were that exciting, so I'm hoping you can enlighten me as to otherwise." He delivered this sentence with a grin and Rachel wasn't entirely sure if he was taking her seriously or not.

"It's part of a study to determine if levels of sea

pollution are changing around the islands. We're so far from the mainland here that there's always been a flourishing population. My job is to see if numbers have altered since the last survey five years ago, and if their locations have altered in any way. Then, if they've changed shape or size."

"So essentially you're here to count clams."

"The *Venus verrucosa* to be specific," she said.

"That sounds like a Harry Potter spell," he laughed. "And just how long is that going to take?"

"Well, I've got to make a survey of the areas that were studied last time and provide an initial report in two months' time. And then if that all looks fine, I'll get counting, as you say, and measuring, over the next three or four months."

"And after that?"

"Who knows?"

"It doesn't bother you?" he asked.

"Bother me?"

"Such short-term work. Not knowing where you'll be in a year or so's time? If you'll even have a job?"

"I'd be more bothered if I could see the whole of my life stretching out in front of me, with no surprises," she said.

Jonah shook his head. "I don't know if I could live

with that kind of uncertainty. I like knowing I'll be in the one place for as long as I want to be. Besides, staying put doesn't mean life is boring."

Rachel remembered the jolt of electricity at his touch, but chased it from her mind. They were never going to see things in the same way, even though she liked him. "Fair point," she said, though she didn't exactly agree with him.

Chapter Eleven
Little Embers, Autumn 1951

He would always remember the moment he first saw her, as if it were etched on his memory as a photographic negative onto silver. Her profile was classical—straight nose, strong brow, high forehead, a determined chin. Indeed, her stillness made him think she could easily have been carved of marble. Richard could also see that she was painfully thin, but her skin was the perfect ivory of an English rose, her hair, though disheveled, the rich brown of polished wood, and her lips as plump and luscious as a midsummer strawberry. She was tall, nearly on a level with him, straight-backed, long-limbed, and fine-boned. Her hands were large, with long, slim fingers that were, at present, clenched into fists that made her knuckles quite white.

She reminded him of a sleek, tremulous grayhound and he had known as soon as he looked into her startling violet-gray eyes that accepting her as a patient had been a terrible mistake. A mistake to invite a woman into what, with the exception of Mrs. Biggs and Nurse Bardcombe, was an all-male enclave. He had been expecting a frumpy housewife, not this. Even her voice was a delight—melodious and clear as a treble bell.

Unfortunately, it was too late to change his mind—she was here now, her husband had departed, and there had been no plausible reason he could summon for turning her away.

The look on her face was at odds with her careless beauty; it was as contemptuous a scowl as had ever been directed at him. She was rigid with fury, the slight shake of her shoulders a clue to her controlled emotions. The straitjacket had been a sensible precaution, but he couldn't keep her bound forever, and she didn't appear, for the moment anyway, to be hysterical.

He was about to explain things to her when a loud wail caught his attention and he moved to the window to determine the cause of it.

Robbie Danvers, former Wing Commander of 149 Squadron, who had piloted Wellington bombers over German-occupied France on too many missions to count, was standing outside in his pajamas. He had lost his doll again. It wasn't strictly speaking Robbie's. In actual fact it was Robbie's niece's—she'd given it to him before he came to Embers, telling him the doll would watch over him, but Robbie was often so distracted he kept putting it down and forgetting it and then causing a stink when he couldn't find the wretched thing. The doll was also filthy from being left outside in all weather and somewhere along the way had lost its dress and sunbonnet. Despite Robbie's neglect, it was nevertheless obvious that he derived much comfort in having something, even an inanimate object, that was his and his alone. Just as a young child might be unable to sleep without their favorite teddy bear, Robbie was inconsolable when he lost the doll, and so Richard continued to indulge him in this. The poor man had suffered so greatly that he wasn't about to take anything that soothed him, however unlikely, away from him.

"Wait here a minute," Richard said. "I'm afraid that's another of our patients. He's lost Susie again."

"Susie?"

He shrugged apologetically. "His doll."

"A doll?"

"Yes, I'm afraid so."

"We saw one as we arrived. Not far from the jetty."

He noticed that she appeared annoyed at the admission, as if she were cursing herself for speaking. "Oh, excellent. That could only be her. Thank you." Richard raised the window sash and called out. "Robbie. Try down by the jetty."

There was a pause in the wailing.

"Yes . . . the jetty. But put some clothes on first, old chap, or you'll catch your death." Richard withdrew his head from the window and turned to face Esther. "Come on then, let's unwrap you." She stood, unmoving, as he undid the buttons at the back of the gown and his fingers fumbled slightly as he noticed the curls of hair at the nape of her neck. There was something vulnerable about the way she bent her head to give him better access and he was reminded of undressing another woman in very different circumstances.

Marianne: a nursing sister at Northfield with whom he'd had a brief romance during the war. They'd had six months together, stealing time whenever their shifts allowed it, before she had been posted to Hong Kong. They wrote, of course, and he'd even considered proposing though they were probably both too young, but then a day had come when a small envelope, addressed to him in an unfamiliar hand, arrived. Her sister, who wrote with news of a bomb hitting the hospital. Marianne had been at the center of the impact. A new influx of patients at Northfield the same week meant that there had been little time to mourn her.

He caught the scent of Esther's perfume, something delicate and floral, and cleared his throat, retrieving his focus. "There you are. Jean can give you some ointment for those scrapes later. Best if you come with me now and I'll introduce you to the chaps. There are three of them at the moment. Robbie lives in one of the cottages. He's been with us for nearly six months. Then Wilkie—Colonel William Cooper-Jones—he's a relatively new arrival. And finally, Captain George Menzies. They should all be at breakfast, that is if Robbie has found Susie."

"And did you bind them when they first arrived?" Esther asked, her expression grim.

"It has sometimes been necessary, yes," Richard admitted. "But I've found that it's seldom for long. Most of our guests quickly adjust to the regimen here. In any case, I'll give you a full briefing after we've eaten." He had finished unbuttoning her and loosened the fabric that bound her arms, reaching for her wrist. "I'll take your pulse while we're here."

He felt her blood throb in her veins where he pressed.

"Hmm. Sluggish," he said to himself before abruptly releasing her arm. "There's some water in the ewer on the table over there—cold, I'm afraid—and soap and a towel next to it. Jean will show you everything else. Come downstairs when you've changed and into the kitchen—it's at the back of the house, just follow the smell of toast—you'll find we don't stand on formality."

Richard left the room, though he found himself unable to shake the aroma of the woman's perfume, which seemed to follow him along the corridor, and could not erase the image of the scowl that had twisted her face but failed to mar its beauty.

He went downstairs, where Wilkie was sitting at the kitchen table forking up scrambled eggs and George spreading blackberry jam on a hunk of homemade bread. He bade them a warm good morning and then took a seat himself. "Now then, chaps, we have a new guest staying with us. You may have seen her arrive yesterday. Mrs. Durrant is here at the behest of her husband. I trust you will treat her with respect and kindness."

"A female of the species?" asked George as he bit into his toast. "I say, things are looking up."

"Steady on there, Captain. Mrs. Durrant has suffered a great tragedy, no less than you fellows. You will do well to leave her be."

Robbie, who had just entered the kitchen, the missing doll under his arm, caught the tail end of the conversation. "Roger that, Doc," he said with a salute.

Chapter Twelve
St. Mary's, Spring 2018

Rachel left the pub after her lunch with Jonah and made her way back to Shearwater Cottage. He had extracted a promise from her that she would meet him later in the week to go to a party that was being held by friends of his. She might enjoy her own company but that didn't mean she turned down all invitations to socialize, especially when she was new in town.

She stopped along the way at the small supermarket and loaded a basket with breakfast cereal, milk, teabags, chicken, assorted vegetables, and a net of oranges. She popped a packet of chocolate biscuits on the counter just as she was about to pay.

"That'll be thirty pounds and twenty-five pence, thanks, love," said the woman behind the till as she rang up the items.

Rachel passed the woman her bank card without flinching. She was used to the higher prices of almost everything on islands. Her salary for this job was adequate, and in any case, her general living expenses were never great. The cottage came with the job. She didn't buy expensive clothing or eat out at fancy restaurants, and living on islands generally meant that entertainment, when it was available, was never extortionate. It was a simple life, but she never once felt as if she lacked anything. She had, however, been happy to hear from Janice that the island had a library, which was a definite improvement over Aitutaki.

It was the middle of the afternoon by the time she returned to the cottage and she left the groceries on the kitchen table as she went about lighting the fire. Janice had told her that there was plenty of wood in the store at the back of the house and, when she checked, she was also pleased to see kindling, newspaper, and fire lighters.

It had been several years since she'd had to get a fire going—on Aitutaki it rarely got cold enough to need long sleeves, let alone any form of heating—but she'd learned as a teenager while living in Pittwater. Nights there in winter could be chilly, and their house had been heated solely by a wood-burning stove in the living room.

The timber was dry and it caught within a few minutes and she knelt by its warmth, holding out her hands to the flames. Eventually, when it was blazing and kicking out a fair bit of heat, she brewed a cup of tea and snaffled a couple of the biscuits from the packet she'd left on the table.

She retrieved the folder containing the original report from her daypack and sat back on the small couch opposite the fire to reread it.

The fire crackled as Rachel turned the pages, absorbed in the summary of its findings. She hadn't had time to give it more than a cursory glance when her supervisor handed it over, and she intended to spend several days familiarizing herself with it before mapping out her own plan of action. Rachel loved to read, even screeds of dry data, for they too told a story of their own if you looked carefully enough. She paused in her efforts only to throw another log on the fire and it was several hours before she finally put the report down.

For the rest of the week, the weather was fine and Rachel spent her mornings out on the water, piloting *Soleil* around the islands. She got to know the currents and tides, where the clear channels were, and where to avoid submerged rock ledges. In the afternoons, she continued to read through the folders that Dr. Wentworth had given her, jotting down notes and thoughts as she went.

She didn't run into Jonah again, and welcomed the lack of distractions. She was emailing a brief report of her activities to Dr. Wentworth late on Friday afternoon when her phone beeped. She'd swapped numbers with Jonah and it was a message from him reminding her about the party he'd promised to take her to that evening. He'd call by at 7 p.m. *Dress casual.*

Just as well. Rachel didn't own a skirt or dress.

She washed her hair, combing it out and letting it fall down her back, before pulling on a pair of clean jeans and a turquoise cashmere sweater that she'd splurged on in Selfridges before she left London. It made her think of the lagoon in Aitutaki and brought out an aqua color in her eyes.

Jonah arrived just as she was taking a bottle of red wine that she had bought earlier that day from the small rack in the kitchen. She handed it to him and turned around to put on her coat, beanie, and a thick scarf. Even though the party was only a few streets away, it was cold out as far as Rachel was concerned—though Jonah seemed perfectly comfortable in a light sweater.

"What's that?" he asked, pointing to a large map

that Rachel had pinned up on a wall next to the kitchen table.

She raised her eyebrows at him.

"Yes, I know it's a map of the world, but what are all those dots?"

The map was scattered with a series of red spots like a rash, most of which appeared to be floating in the middle of various oceans.

"Everywhere I've been. Right from when I was a kid."

"Wow. I'd only have about five or six to put on my map. A couple for here, and Cornwall, the odd one in Greece and France, and that'd be it. Kind of makes me feel unadventurous."

"It's there for the taking," she said.

As they approached the house, Rachel could see light streaming out from an open door and hear the beat of music floating toward them.

"Hallo!" A voice called out as they approached. "Come in, come in." A bearded young man, his long hair drawn back, ushered them into the hallway. Rachel clocked a tight-fitting T-shirt that emphasized broad shoulders and a pair of long, muscular legs encased in a pair of jeans. "You must be Rachel. Jonah mentioned he'd invited you. I'm Luke," he said. He took her coat and led them toward the back of the house, a large open kitchen and dining area that was filled with people chatting and drinking. The muffled thump of a drumbeat added to the background hum. "I'd introduce you, but I'm not sure they'd hear me," he apologized. "Would you like some of this?" He indicated the wine, which Jonah had handed over together with a six-pack of beer that he'd brought.

Rachel nodded. "That'd be nice, thanks."

"Jonah?"

He pointed to the beers and Luke passed one back to him. "I'll just grab a glass, won't be a sec."

"I'll lay bets that he won't return anytime soon," said Jonah once Luke had left.

Sure enough, Rachel saw that he had been waylaid by a tall, fair-haired girl as he ventured farther into the room.

"Come on," he said. "Let's go and grab one ourselves. This"—he held up the beer bottle—"needs an opener, in any case."

They pushed their way through the throng of people and reached a kitchen table laden with bottles, glasses, and a few half-empty bowls of chips and nuts. "Here," Jonah held up a glass, triumphant. A few seconds later and he had located a bottle opener as well. He led her toward Luke, where he relieved him of the wine, opened it, and poured some for Rachel.

She took a grateful sip.

"So who would you like to meet?"

"Who do you suggest?" said Rachel, thinking she wouldn't mind getting to know Luke a little better, although he seemed to be caught up in an intense conversation with the blonde.

"Well, selfishly I'd like to keep you to myself all evening, but . . ."

Jonah was flirting with her. Without a doubt.

". . . you should meet a few of the locals. Andrew! Emily!" He called across to a couple standing near the window and beckoned them over.

"Come and meet Rachel. She's new to the islands. Andrew's a chef at the Star Castle, and Emily teaches at the primary school here," he explained as he introduced them.

Rachel shook hands with Andrew, but Emily embraced her in a hug. "Welcome," she said, with a broad smile. "You must have come from somewhere exotic, look how healthy you look compared to our pasty faces." Emily, in fact, was pink-cheeked and bright-eyed and, although pale, didn't look at all pasty.

Rachel explained what had brought her to St. Mary's.

"You're an Aussie, yes?"

Rachel nodded. Changing schools every few years when she was younger and then moving jobs so often meant that she was well-practiced at fitting in to new situations. An Australian accent generally worked wonders too and she was soon caught up in a conversation about Sydney with the couple, who'd visited on their honeymoon.

Jonah drifted away to chat to a few other people, but she was aware of him looking back at her every so often, checking she was okay. The last time she caught him doing so, she raised her glass at him and smiled, silently reassuring him she was doing just fine. She had lost sight of Luke in the crowd.

An hour or so passed, and Emily introduced her to a few more people before she found herself back by Jonah's side. "Another drink?" He raised the bottle he was holding.

She shook her head. "I think I've had enough thanks. Too much booze doesn't suit me—I get shocking hangovers."

"You and me both," he said, putting the bottle down on a nearby table. "I'm on call tomorrow too. There's nothing worse than being out on a boat when you're feeling a bit shabby."

Rachel suddenly remembered what she'd been going

to ask him. "I went over to the Eastern Isles earlier this week."

"Oh yes?"

"From what I'd read, they're all supposed to be un-inhabited. But I could have sworn I saw smoke rising from a house on Little Embers Island."

"That'd be Leah."

"Leah?"

"Strange lady. Bit of a hermit really. One of the local boats drops supplies to her once a week and she almost never leaves the island. We check in on her from time to time, but she doesn't much care for visitors. Swore at me last time we came ashore actually. I think she might be a bit mad, to be honest."

"I'd better keep my distance then."

"Only from her," said Jonah, "You'll find that the rest of us are pretty friendly."

The meaning of his words was obvious but she shied away from the invitation in his eyes. He wasn't her type at all—she preferred them young, sweet, and very sexy—and he was merely sweet. Okay, maybe a little bit sexy, but not enough for her to break her self-imposed rules. "So it seems," she said, laughing off the comment. The party had thinned out as they'd been talking and Rachel was ready to leave. "I'm going to head out now," she said.

"Of course, it's getting late. Let me get your coat."

"Don't worry, I can see myself out," she insisted. "It's just down the road."

To his credit, Jonah hid his disappointment well, though she could tell that he would have been more than happy to go home with her given the slightest encouragement.

"If you're sure?"

"It's hardly far, and unless I'm mistaken these aren't exactly mean streets." She gave him a smile and he took the hint.

"Good point. All right then, well thanks for coming and I'm sure I'll catch you around." He gave her a mock salute.

"Thanks for inviting me; it was nice to meet a few new people. I really appreciate it." She looked around but couldn't see their host. "Can you thank Luke for me?" She stepped forward and gave Jonah a hug, breathing in his warm, male scent. Salt, sandalwood, and liniment. It was oddly comforting.

Chapter Thirteen
Little Embers, Autumn 1951

Esther flung the wretched straitjacket onto the bed, wincing as the edge of it caught a particularly savage scrape that hadn't quite healed. She'd soon be out of this dreadful place, all she needed was some time to plan her escape. What did John think he was doing, banishing her like this? How dare he? No matter what he thought she'd done, this was the last place on earth she ought to be. She should be in London, in Well Walk, Hampstead. In her bedroom at Frogmore. If she'd been there now and the weather had been better, why she might even have felt up to a walk on the Heath. She conveniently ignored the fact that she hadn't left the confines of her home for several months. It wasn't that she couldn't, she told herself; it was that she hadn't wanted to. In any case, she couldn't bear the concerned looks of her neighbors, the prying glances. Some of them had actually—Mrs. Campbell-Jones from number 51 was one—crossed the road to avoid her, as if she might lay a witch's curse on their own babies.

She spied her suitcase—and, strangely, John's as well—in a corner of the room. Picking it up, she hauled it onto the bed and pushed aside the buttons keeping the locks closed. The metal flaps flew open and she raised the lid. There, neatly packed between layers of tissue paper were her clothes. Blouses—viyella, cotton, and chiffon—tweed skirts, a couple of cardigans, lisle and silk stockings, and another pair of shoes. She shook out a blouse and threaded her arms through the sleeves, automatically doing up the pearl buttons down its front. When she had tucked it into her skirt and pulled on a cardigan, she went over to retrieve John's suitcase, curious to see what was inside. She opened it and gasped. Yet more clothes. But they weren't John's—they were hers. "Heavens, really?" she said aloud. For inside that case was a good deal of her summer wardrobe—lightweight Liberty lawn shirtwaisters, knee-length cotton skirts, two pairs of sandals, even a shirred and boned bathing suit. She was as horrified to realize that her husband clearly expected her to be at Embers well into next year as she was shocked that he imagined she might contemplate something as frivolous as swimming.

As she riffled through the garments, her hands struck an envelope. Thick cream Basildon Bond. She'd recognize the paper, and the handwriting, anywhere. Her husband's slanting script. She tore open the seal and unfolded the sheet inside.

"*My dear Esther . . .*" it began. "*My heartfelt apologies for duping you like this, but I felt I had no choice. I had no idea how you would react if I told you our true purpose in coming to Embers. You have been entirely absent from all of us for the past several months, not without good reason I admit, but I find I am at my wits' end to know how to help you. Richard is an exceptional doctor and I was—we are—very lucky to secure his services. I have every confidence that he will make you well again, but you must try and cooperate with him.*

"*Please know that I do not blame you in any way for what happened, and my only wish is for your recovery and safe return to me, as the woman I married, the woman you truly are. All my love, John.*"

Esther refolded the paper carefully and sank down next to the suitcases. She'd been correct. It was an utter betrayal. He'd presented her with a fait accompli. Frustration, sorrow, and, finally, a kind of blank nothingness that rendered her incapable of moving engulfed her. She had no idea how long she'd been sitting like that, but when she was disturbed by a knock on the door, pins and needles had invaded the leg folded underneath her. "Mrs. Durrant?"

Him. The doctor.

"Are you coming for some breakfast? The chaps have saved you some, but I can't vouch for how long it will last if you don't turn up soon."

How could he sound so bloody cheerful? Didn't he realize he was running an asylum? "Actually, I don't think I am particularly hungry," she replied. "I may stay here awhile." Cooperating was the last thing she was prepared to do, added to which she could imagine the curious stares that would be inflicted upon her if she did make an appearance at the breakfast table.

"Right you are then." The reply was neutral, not judging.

When she was sure he had gone, she went to her handbag, which was sitting on a chair by the window. As she searched its depths, she held her breath against a dark, spiraling terror that threatened to engulf her.

Her fingers encountered something soft and she pulled it out. Pale blue and knitted by her mother. A winter cap of Teddy's. She held it to her nose, remembering the dear smell of him. Her face contorted and her mouth trembled as she fought back the sudden rush of tears, missing him desperately in that moment, swamped by the knowledge that she had let him down. She had let everyone down.

After a while, she put the cap to one side and collected herself. Her fingers closed around the pillbox in her handbag. Taking a glass and filling it from the ewer on the nightstand, she washed one of the shiny tablets down with a gulp before lying back upon the bed, willing unconsciousness. It was not long in coming. As she drifted off she felt as if she were at the bottom of a deep well, and that, no matter how loud she might shout, no one would hear her. But then no one would come to bother her either, and that was a most welcome thought.

When Esther woke it was nearly dark and it was a few moments before she remembered where she was. She caught sight of the letter, abandoned on the bed, and recalled its message. Barely able to comprehend her husband's perfidy, she swung wildly between outrage and self-recrimination. Should she take another pill perhaps? Her doctor had instructed that she take no more than one a day, but such circumstances as she now found herself in demanded extreme measures.

She had just clasped the pillbox when there was a

knock on the door and the housekeeper bustled in, carrying a tray covered by a linen cloth. Esther closed her fist tightly around the box, slipping it into her pocket as inconspicuously as possible.

"I thought you might like some tea, Mrs. Durrant." She set the tray down on a dressing table and as she removed the cloth, the smell of baking wafted into the room. Despite herself, Esther felt her mouth begin to water. "There's a couple of my scones there." Mrs. Biggs looked as if she wanted to add something, but pressed her lips together in a firm line and left as swiftly as she'd arrived.

Once she was sure the housekeeper was not going to return, Esther roused herself and poured some tea. She was terribly thirsty. After drinking several cups, she carefully sliced a scone in half, gathering up the crumbs into a small pile on the plate and pushing them around with the tip of her finger. She looked at it for a long time before taking a bite.

Later that evening, the nurse reappeared and wrapped her in the straitjacket again, her swift and practiced movements catching Esther by surprise before she had a chance to resist or get away. "It is for your own good, Mrs. Durrant," she said firmly. Esther was more horrified by the fact that she was now rendered incapable of taking her pills than she was by the indignity of being bound. After the nurse had gone, she lay wide-eyed and sleepless, tossing and turning as much as the binding would allow, only dropping off as the birds began to chirrup and chatter.

This continued for three more days. Each morning, the nurse would knock on her door, help her loosen the ties of the straitjacket and invite her to breakfast, and each morning Esther would decline, swallow a pill, and sleep the day away. Finally, on the fifth morning, without really knowing why, she answered differently.

"Give me a moment," she said. "I'll come down." The nurse simply nodded her head and closed the door. As she dressed, Esther examined the tracks along her forearms. They were beginning to heal. The straitjacket was doing its job it seemed, and she must be scratching less even when she wasn't bound. It was something at least. Squaring her shoulders, she prepared to leave the room.

The sight that greeted her upon her arrival in the kitchen took her by surprise. There was the doctor, of course, then three other men also sat around an oval table, one of whom—Robbie she surmised—was cradling the doll she'd stepped over when she arrived. He was pretending to feed it toast and the others were either completely oblivious or feigning ignorance. There was a scraping of chairs on the slate floor as they registered her presence and rose to greet her. "Ah, Mrs. Durrant. So pleased you could join us. Menzies, George Menzies." A small man with the dark good looks and mournful expression of a gypsy violinist extended his hand to her. She gave him a faint smile and took his hand. His grip was surprisingly strong and belied his slightness.

"Colonel William Cooper-Jones, ma'am. Wilkie to those who know me well." The colonel was several decades older than the others, with a shock of white hair. He was wearing a collared shirt and regimental striped tie but Esther noticed that his pullover was worn clean through at the elbows and his trousers bagged at the knees.

"And this is Robbie," said Dr. Creswell. "You helped him recover his doll the other day." The third man put down his toast and gave her a wave. He had a long face, with hair that grew high on his forehead and of a shade that made her automatically think of carrots. Cinnamon-colored freckles dotted the milk-pale skin of his face and hands and his ear, the one she could see at least, for he was standing sideways to her, made her think that he must, at some point, have suffered the nickname "jugs" or "wing nut."

It was only as he turned his head toward her that she noticed a mass of scar tissue to the left of his cheek and where his ear should have been was nothing but a small round hole. The left-hand corner of his mouth pulled down like a torn pocket. She'd seen similar sights in London, but never at such close proximity and was instantly ashamed to feel slightly nauseous. She looked at him gravely, trying not to let the pity show on her face. "Pleased to meet you all." Politeness, drummed into her from girlhood, thankfully came to the fore.

"Scoot along now, chaps, make some room for Mrs. Durrant." Richard pulled out a chair next to him, indicating that she should sit.

"Please, it's Esther," she said as they all resumed their seats. "I'd much rather you call me Esther."

"Right you are then, Esther," said Robbie. "Here on a furlough, are you?"

Esther wasn't sure what he meant.

"Go easy on her, old chap," said Wilkie as he sipped from his cup. "She might not appreciate your sense of humor."

Dr. Creswell pushed a crock of yellow butter toward her, and indicated the toast rack in the center of the table. "We've one cow on the island—Bella—at the moment it's George's job to milk her. Mrs. Biggs churns it."

"She's a beauty, I'll give her that," said George. "No disrespect to Mrs. Biggs of course, but our Bella's got a better set of pins than Betty Grable." The other men were obviously used to George's jokes, for no one laughed. Only Robbie grinned, but his eyes were lowered and Esther wasn't sure if that was at George or the jam that he was slathering generously on his bread.

Esther wasn't the slightest bit hungry, but took a knife and placed a knob of butter on the side of the plate in front of her. She reached for a piece of toast and cut it into triangles. The knife was blunt.

"There's jam," said Robbie, indicating the jar in front of them. "Blackberry. Scrumdiddlyumptious."

Even Esther raised a smile at this. She took an unenthusiastic bite of the toast and was surprised to find that it didn't stick in her throat the way so much food had recently. In fact, it was rather nice. She took another bite.

"It doesn't seem like a madhouse, does it?" asked George.

Esther nearly choked on her mouthful. "Um, er. I suppose not," she said, swallowing a lump of toast.

"Quite the holiday camp, in fact. Isn't that right, old man?" George was being facetious.

"Well, while I'm not sure that's exactly sincere, I'm

glad to hear you appreciate it, George," said Dr. Creswell evenly.

"Oh, don't mind George," said Wilkie to Esther. "You'll get used to him. We're all queer old coots, one way or another." He gave a throaty cough and then another and Robbie stood up to thump him on the back.

"Damned mustard gas," he spluttered.

"Wilkie fought in the Great War as well," George explained, calmly eating his eggs. "Awarded the Victoria Cross. Valor in the face of the enemy. Doesn't like to talk about it much."

"That's enough," said Wilkie when he'd finished coughing. "Ancient history now."

Esther finished her toast and reached for the teapot, pouring herself a cup. She saw George glance at the scars that weren't covered by her cardigan and she put the pot down and self-consciously pulled the sleeves over her wrists.

"How are you getting on setting up the darkroom, Wilkie?" asked the doctor.

"Rather well actually," he replied. "It won't be too long before I can start developing in there."

"Wilkie's a keen photographer," explained Dr. Creswell to Esther. "But supplies of paper and chemicals have been hard to come by."

"I see." She finished her tea and set down her cup.

"Now then Mrs. Durrant—sorry, Esther," the doctor addressed her. "As you're up and about, why don't we spend some time in the front parlor after breakfast? There's a nice fire in there. The men will get everything shipshape here. We all muck in; Mrs. Biggs can't be expected to do everything."

Esther didn't think there was any point in objecting and rose from her seat. The officers rose too, amid another scraping of chairs.

"Gentlemen," said Dr. Creswell.

"Doc," they chorused.

The doctor ushered her into the parlor where she and John had been received earlier in the week. If she looked carefully enough, she fancied she could see the indent in the cushions.

"Please, do take a seat, Esther." He indicated the chair she'd occupied previously before going over to the fire and prodding the banked embers into life. Sparks rose as he threw on a fresh log and it hissed and spat as it began to catch.

He sat opposite her, crossed his legs, and folded his hands over one knee, as if he were settling in for a cozy chat. "I expect you're wondering how this all works."

Esther said nothing.

"Your husband thought I might be able to help you and I'd certainly like to try. My methods, however, are somewhat unconventional. I spent the war as a junior doctor attached to a military psychiatric hospital, in the Midlands. Some of what I experienced there inspired me to establish my practice here. I have a firm belief in the benefits of a simple life, the peace and quiet of nature, group support, activities such as taking care of livestock, gardening, fishing . . . everyone contributes here."

"A veritable Utopia."

"If you like," he said, ignoring her sarcasm. "We'll ease you into it. Everyone is allowed to take their time. I meet with each of my patients every day, individually. Sometimes we talk, but it can be about anything really. Not always about their state of mind or what's happened to them. Everyone has to take some exercise, unless it's really pouring out. Fresh air and a tired body work wonders for the spirit, I've found. We also hold a brief service on Sundays, but attendance is entirely voluntary."

"You'll have to excuse me on that count," she said. "I'm having a hard time believing in Him just now."

"Of course."

"And are all your guests mad?" she asked.

"It's not a term I like to use. Combat fatigue is generally the best way to describe it."

"And exactly how is this meant to be suitable for my situation? I mean, I can see why men who've faced the horrors of war might need this, but me? I am hardly in requirement of your services."

"Your husband . . ."

Esther flinched at the mention of John. She was still furious with him, couldn't believe he'd tricked her so blatantly, had such little regard for her. In the days she had spent in the room upstairs she had come to view him in a very different light. He wasn't perhaps the kind, diffident man she believed him to be. "I'm afraid there has been a terrible mistake," she insisted once more.

"Let me be the judge of that. John has given me the authority to treat you, initially for three months, with the possibility of extending it to six, if required."

"Six months?" This was worse than she had even imagined. Her mouth hung open in shock.

The doctor held up his hand. "Now then, please don't distress yourself. As I said, initially it will be three months. Let's work with that for now. You know, you might even come to enjoy your time here."

"But this isn't my home. I belong in London, not

on this ridiculous speck of land in the middle of the bloody sea! Don't I get any say in it at all?" Her throat constricted and she gulped in air. "And what about Teddy? My son? I cannot be away from him for that long. A child needs his mother." Esther felt rage course through her like lightning, swiftly chased by a sickly tide of remorse. She hadn't exactly been the best of mothers recently. She wanted to run to the jetty as fast as she could, to get back to Teddy. But that would be futile—there wasn't a boat for another two days.

"Esther, I think you know as well as I that you are not, how would we say it, not quite yourself," he said. "Don't fret about the time away. John assured me that your son will be well looked after—you have a nanny, I understand?"

But there's no substitute for a mother, she wanted to rail at him. Instead she bit her tongue, recognizing that it was pointless to argue. She would save her outrage for future battles.

Chapter Fourteen
St. Mary's, Spring 2018

Rachel woke early. The night before, she'd walked the short distance home underneath a night sky awash with stars, and as the noise of the party receded, she had become aware of an absolute stillness, the quiet that she had never been able to find in cities or towns and had come to crave like a drug.

This morning, however, the raucous cries of gulls shredded the air, calling her to get up and get moving, for the tide waited for no one. She stretched and looked out of the window, spying blue skies. Even though it was a Saturday, she rarely observed weekends. She worked when she could and took time off when she felt she needed to and it all seemed to even out.

She was also conscious that the run of good weather she'd experienced since arriving on St. Mary's could change at any moment and wanted to embark on her study without delay. Her first official report was due to Dr. Wentworth in a few days and, as yet, she had little to account for her time.

She sprang out of bed, pulled on her jeans from the previous night and a warm sweater and hurriedly brushed her hair. There hadn't been much in the way of food at the party, so she set about making herself a large omelet. She intended to be out on the boat for most of the day and didn't want hunger to distract her from her observations, so a good breakfast was in order.

She grabbed her waders and a clam gauge: a pair of calipers designed especially for measuring the length and width of the shells. She had also brought her camera with her, encased in waterproof housing, intending to photograph some of the clams up close in order to compare them with those taken five years earlier and she planned to take samples at one or more of the sites previously identified. Such was her rush to get out on the water that she forgot to check the forecast before leaving.

Her first destination was the curving sweep of Great Rock Beach on Tresco and she reached it easily, shooting across the water in the light little boat, the breeze ruffling her hair. Either the air temperature had warmed by a few degrees or she was acclimatizing to the weather, but for the first time since arriving, she wasn't bothered by the cold. She cut the engine and coasted in on water as clear and aquamarine as a gemstone. Reaching the beach, she hopped into the shallows, pulling the *Soleil* up onto the white-sugar sand. The tide was ebbing, but she dragged it above the high-water mark just to be sure.

She consulted one of the maps that Dr. Wentworth had provided and compared it with the beach in front of her. At one end was a series of rocky shelves. Crab's Ledge was where she needed to begin.

When she reached it, she shrugged off her daypack and removed the calipers, her notebook, and a pen. The water was calm here. Drawing closer, she could see bright green weeds floating like a mermaid's tresses in the current. Carefully, she stepped into the water, her waders keeping her feet and legs dry. As she ventured deeper, the water pressed in on the rubber, sucking it against her legs. There were dog whelks, cockles, goose barnacles, sea snails, and limpets all crowded onto the rocks. She concentrated her gaze and was eventually rewarded with her first sighting. The *Venus verrucosa* in all her ridged glory. She was pleased to see a fair-sized colony, several larger ones and a collection of babies, uncovered by the low tide. She got out her calipers and set to work, measuring and recording. She'd slung her camera around her neck and when she'd taken the measurements she needed, she began to photograph the colony, placing a small plastic ruler next to them for scale.

All of this took more than an hour and as she worked the tide began to turn, submerging the clams once more. When she eventually straightened up, she was sore from bending over and arched backward, stretching out her spine. She glanced up at the sky. While she'd been working she'd been vaguely aware that the sun had gone in, but hadn't thought anything of it, so absorbed was she in her task. Now, however, she saw that dark gray clouds had begun to roll in from the north. They definitely looked to be carrying rain. The wind had picked up too, flecking the previously glassy water with peaks of foam, as if they were whipped egg whites. She was fast learning that the weather here could change in an instant. She made a mental note to be more circumspect about checking the forecast next time, but wasn't especially worried; she'd been out in far rougher weather and lived to tell the tale.

She waded back to where she had left her backpack, stowed her gear away, and returned to the *Soleil.* Her camera still around her neck, she looked up at the sky again, calculating whether she would make it back to Hugh Town before the storm.

She'd always been a gambler.

Dragging the tinny back to the water's edge, she pushed it clear of the sand and climbed in, lowering the outboard and getting under way.

Unthinking, she turned the boat toward the Eastern Isles, instead of south back to St. Mary's. Later, she wouldn't be able to explain why she had done so. A momentary lack of concentration, tiredness from her late night and morning's work perhaps?

It was to prove a costly mistake.

Chapter Fifteen
Little Embers, Autumn 1951

Richard regarded the woman before him. Her eyes were blazing and her brown hair, which looked as soft as eiderdown, curled riotously about her face. Bright spots burned in her cheeks. Her chest rose and fell as her breath came in sharp bursts. He could see that her hands were shaking and she was struggling to hold them still. He needed to do something to soothe her, to ease her agitation.

"Do you like music, Esther?" he asked.

"Do I what?" Despite her distress, her tone was glacial.

"Like music? Classical?" He pointed to the gramophone.

"Actually, as it happens, I do. But I don't see how that will solve anything."

"Indulge me if you will." Richard went over to the gramophone, removed a thick shellac-coated disc from its brown paper wrapper and placed it on the turntable. He wound up the machine and then gently placed the needle on the record. Immediately the delicate strings of Vaughan Williams's "The Lark Ascending" filled the room. Esther's eyes widened but she leaned back into the chair, eventually closing her eyes as the music swelled. Her body, until then taut as a violinist's bow, slackened slightly. She was completely still and he was able to look upon her without fear of being caught staring. Her mouth was wide and generous, her cheekbones prominent, her forehead broad, and her chin determined. He noticed the purple shadows under her eyes, the shell-curve of her ears that were revealed as her hair fell away from her head, the graceful line of her neck, the deep hollow where it met her collarbones. For several minutes there was no sound in the room save for the soaring music and the crackling of the fire. Richard stood utterly still, watching as a single tear escaped her lashes and traced its way down her cheek. He felt like an intruder on her private grief.

The music finished and she didn't move. Had she fallen asleep?

No. She stirred.

The pooled sorrow and regret in her eyes as she

opened them and met his gaze sliced into him like a lancet. Once again he cursed himself for accepting her as a patient.

Richard had never intended to become a psychotherapist. Before going up to Oxford to study medicine, he'd been set on a surgical career, but then, in the final year of his degree, he returned home after the Hilary term to find that his mother, suddenly and without any apparent cause, had gone mad. Stark, raving mad. His father explained somberly that he'd done his best to keep her safe, but that when he'd returned from work on not one but several occasions and found her wandering the village muttering to herself and bothering the local shopkeepers, he had been forced to act. "Dr. Nancarrow insisted it was for the best. We shall just have to muddle along without her for the time being," his father explained.

For as long as Richard could remember, Hannah Creswell had dressed differently from other mothers, been louder and more forthright in her opinions, had hugged him fiercely and often. She'd always been what his father described as "highly strung," but he had put her violent mood swings down to an exuberant, if somewhat tempestuous, personality. He'd never had an inkling that there was anything seriously the matter; she'd simply been his flamboyant, loud, loving mother.

That summer changed his life. She was locked up in Foster Hall, at the Cornwall Mental Hospital, on the edge of Bodmin Moor. Visiting was allowed on Sunday afternoons between the hours of two and four. Richard made the two-hour meandering bus journey from their small village every week without fail, only to find her drugged, glazed and unresponsive, completely unaware of his presence. On each return journey, he stared out unseeingly at the ripening wheat fields, frustrated at his inability to help her and vowing not to return, but the next week found him making the trip again. His father rarely joined him. "I don't think it makes any difference, us visiting her." He wasn't sure if it was his father's unyielding resolve or his own helplessness that broke his heart, but either way Richard wouldn't let his father see his distress. He was ashamed of the relief he felt when it was time to return to his studies.

Esther reminded him too much of his mother, before she became ill. The intelligent light in her eyes, the depths of fierce passion lurking beneath the surface, the barely concealed anger. He had no idea if he was going to be able to help her. Unlike the war-traumatized men he treated, making Esther Durrant well again, figuring her out, would be a very different task.

"Well. Aren't you going to play me some more?" Esther had wiped away the tear from her cheek and was staring up at him with clear eyes.

"Did you like that?" he asked.

"For a moment I felt as if I were sitting in a meadow on a warm summer's day." She sounded surprised at herself.

"Indeed," he said with a smile. "It does rather transport one, doesn't it?"

There was a pause as they both recalled the dying strains of the music.

"Let me tell you a story instead," he said. "Of a man called Darius, the king of all of Asia. He was utterly bereft at the death of his beloved wife. Nothing could console him. He went to Demokritos, a god, for help. He said that if Darius could find the names of three men untouched by grief and inscribe them on his wife's tomb, then he would return her from the dead." He had her full attention.

"Darius had his men search the length and breadth of his kingdom but couldn't find anyone. He had been mourning as if he was the only person to have experienced so great a loss. None of us has lived without sorrow, Esther. You are not alone."

"Do you mind if I ask a few more questions?" Esther was blunt, declining to comment on his story.

"Fire away." Her curiosity could only be a good sign, he told himself. John had reported that she had simply stopped taking an interest in anything, could scarcely be persuaded to rise from her bed in the morning, so this was promising.

"Why here?"

He considered the question. "My aunt is a friend of the wife of the current leaseholder. He's a London insurance broker who's never ventured farther west than Reading and the place had been empty for a while. She knew I was looking for somewhere to set up a facility."

"A facility?"

"To treat ex-servicemen. After the war I wanted to continue to help them, to create a therapeutic community of sorts. To try and even up the balance sheet in however small a way for the injustices they had suffered." He gave her a small smile. "I suppose I am drawn to broken things. As a boy I loved to fix, to repair and restore. The same goes for me now, except it is people not toys."

"But why here?" she asked again.

"There's peace and quiet and we lead a simple life: shared daily tasks and physical labor, with plenty of time to talk. We're cut off from the mainland and I do believe the isolation helps."

"I see. Does it work?"

He inclined his head modestly. "I like to think it does. My first patient, a captain, late of the Coldstream Guards, arrived clutching a wooden replica of a Lee Enfield rifle and would not release his grip, even at mealtimes, even when asleep. But one day, a few weeks after his arrival, I came across him in the henhouse, holding Bess, one of our Black Orpingtons. He was crooning to the bird, stroking its feathers, and the replica gun was lying, discarded, several feet away. It was nearly a month before I could get more than a few words from him, but he went on to make enough of a recovery to leave the island nearly six months later. There have been more since."

"Impressive. And have you ever treated women here?"

"I confess I have not." He didn't add that he had doubts as to the wisdom of doing so, but that he owed a debt to her husband and had been unable to refuse him.

As a schoolboy, Richard's unfortunate nickname had been Shrimpy. With the mixed blessing of a thin, high-pitched voice that choirmasters loved and no amount of studied effort could deepen, he was, of course, mercilessly teased for it. It wasn't until he turned seventeen when he suddenly shot up by more than a foot and his voice dropped by an octave that the taunting had ceased. John had been one of the few to be kind and had shielded him from the worst of the older bullies.

Richard also foresaw a time when the stream of war-traumatized patients would eventually dry up and he would need to look to other patients—and that would include women—if he were to continue to practice at Embers. Besides which, her story intrigued him.

"I see. And how do you stand it here?"

"What do you mean?"

"We're in the middle of nowhere—don't you ever feel trapped? Marooned?"

"I can't say I do," he said, surprised. "I like knowing every inch of the island: where the terns nest, where the foxgloves bloom in late summer, all freckled and pink, the sound of the wind in the reed banks, the purple of the heather, and the green of the sea kelp that washes up on the beach." He paused, thinking of the beauty that island life brought him. "The best place to find clams, what time of year the mackerel bite . . . the seasons bring change to the island, and the summers especially are something to behold."

"Are you from the islands?"

He shook his head. "No. The mainland—a small village near Lostwithiel."

"What a charming name. Lostwithiel," she repeated, stressing the "Lost." "I've no idea where that is, I'm afraid. I've rarely left London."

"Well, that will explain why you're unused to country life," he said. "I suppose I could as equally ask you if you do not feel hemmed in by so many buildings, crowded by so many people and assaulted by noise . . ."

Esther inclined her head. "Point taken. But how do you survive? What do you live on?"

"It wasn't easy at first—before we were able to milk Bella and we had dug the vegetable garden. I'm a better fisherman now than I once was. We catch a fair amount of bass, mackerel, sometimes garfish. I'm hopeful for our new lobster pots. Then there are always limpets, though that's only when we're desperate," he grimaced. "Our needs are simple, and you can grow almost anything here. We have strawberries and gooseberries in summer, cabbages, rutabagas, turnips, onions, and potatoes in winter, apples and plums from the orchard. What little meat and dry goods we need come from St. Mary's."

"Water, electricity?"

"There's a freshwater spring, and as you've seen we manage with oil lamps and candles."

"But books, newspapers, company, conversation?"

"Oh, we make do," he laughed. "And the news is seldom good, so not having the papers is a luxury as far as I can see."

"And what am I supposed to do while I am incarcerated here?"

"Please, it is not an incarceration—"

"So I am free to leave then?"

"Not exactly," he said, sitting back. "But don't dwell on that. While you are here you are welcome to do as you please—at least initially. If you are tired, you may sleep, although I do recommend at least an hour's walking a day. In summer we swim . . ."

"Oh, I shall certainly not be here come summer," she said with conviction.

"Very well then." There was no sense in debating that point with her. "Some of the men have taken up hobbies—Wilkie has his photography, George his bird-watching. Perhaps you might like to help out in the garden?"

Esther appeared to consider this. "We had to turn ours over to an allotment during the war. Mother insists that the roses will never recover," she said with a wry twist of her lips.

"We will also spend at least an hour a day together, beginning now." He clasped his hands together and leaned forward. "How about you tell me why you think your husband wanted you to be here? What has been ailing you?"

"There's nothing so very wrong with me, I'm certain," Esther replied.

Despite her assertion, Richard noticed her shoulders rise up toward her ears, her hands grasp her elbows, her eyes harden.

"Had some rotten luck, that's all," she continued. "No more or no less than anyone else has had to put up with. Only trouble is, I can't seem to dig myself out of it. Must try harder, soldier on, stiff upper lip, you know." She compressed her mouth as if trying to contain her emotions. "Exactly what nonsense did my husband fill your head with?"

Richard was unconvinced, saw how she had folded in on herself. "Come on now, Esther," he said gently. "You don't have to put on a brave face for me."

She gazed out of the window, her expression opaque. "It's really not necessary for you to be kind. In fact, I would much rather you weren't. I'm not sure I can stand any more kindness."

"Duly noted."

"When we are finished here, I think I should like to go for a walk," she said, changing the subject.

Richard had no intention of pushing her too hard, at least not to begin with. "Of course. We have covered enough for our first session anyhow. It is rather blustery out there, so do be sure to wrap up warmly. There's little chance of you getting lost, but perhaps you might allow me to do the honor of showing you the sights, so to speak."

"Oh, I am sure I am perfectly capable of finding my own way around."

"I insist." His tone brooked no argument. Until he was certain she wouldn't go and do something stupid, he, or one of the others, would accompany her whenever she left the house.

She lifted her chin, but didn't argue further. "I might go and see if my husband packed suitable footwear. It appears he thought of everything else."

The bleak look on her face was back, but he remembered her instructions not to be kind. "Excellent," he said. "It seems we understand each other perfectly."

Several minutes later, he met her at the foot of the stairs. She was wearing a tightly belted trench coat and a pair of sturdy, flat-soled brogues. Her hair had been tucked into the rather unfortunate hat she had been wearing on her arrival several days before and she carried a pair of leather gloves. Richard wasn't sure why it gave him such pleasure to see that she hadn't applied lipstick, but it did. He had always hated painted faces, and had never much cared for the slippery feeling of kissing Marianne, who had favored a particularly garish shade of red.

He chastized himself for thinking of Esther Durrant and kissing in almost the same breath. It would not do at all. "Come on then, let's be off." Annoyance with himself made him more abrupt than he would have liked, but she didn't appear to notice. He unhooked a bucket and a shovel that hung by the front door and set off.

They took the path that led down to the jetty, but before reaching it, he indicated that they should follow a narrow track, barely a foot wide, that wound its way through the seagrass, following the shoreline west. He soon noticed that Esther was struggling to keep up with him and so he adjusted his pace accordingly. "Look, out there!" he cried, stopping so suddenly that she almost bumped into him.

"What? Where? There's nothing but endless sea."

He pointed in the direction that he had been looking, toward a group of rocks that stuck up out of the frothing water like obsidian. Some of the rocks appeared to be moving, cleaving and launching into the sea. "Seals."

"Oh yes, there they are." Like sudden sunlight on

an overcast day, the flash of her smile, her face briefly lighting up, transformed her. Warmed him too, if he was honest.

"Come on, it's nearly low tide. Let's go down and see if we can find some clams. Mrs. Biggs makes a rather good soup from them."

She followed him toward the beach, hearing the hiss of the waves as they struck the shore, and watched as he dug in with the shovel. He sifted through the up-turned sand until several long, thin shells were revealed. "Razor clams. Absolutely delicious, I guarantee it," he said with satisfaction. "Grab them for me, before they bury themselves again. Here—" He handed her the bucket he'd brought.

Esther removed her gloves, stuffing them in her coat pocket and gingerly picked up one of the shells, brushing off the sand and holding it high to examine it. "Are you sure we can eat them?" She wrinkled her nose.

"Well, we're not doing this for the hell of it."

Chapter Sixteen
Isles of Scilly, Spring 2018

As Rachel piloted the small boat out into the open water, she could see that the storm brewing on the horizon was moving faster than she had anticipated. It would almost certainly be upon her before she could make it back to St. Mary's and safety. She glanced backward. Tresco was behind her now, not worth heading back to. As she read the shapes of the islands on the starboard side, expecting to see Samson and the gray-brown buildings of Hugh Town, she had to check twice. They didn't look like the islands she had been expecting to see at all. Unless she was mistaken, these were Great, Little, and Middle Arthur.

A sickening feeling took hold in the pit of her stomach. She must have taken a wrong turn when she left Tresco. There was no time to go back now. The visibility was closing in fast and the wind, which had picked up, began to lash at the small boat, making it rock from side to side. She looked around again. The storm bore down, almost upon her now, and she felt the first fat drops of rain splash on her face and ping off the metal boat. It was as dark as an eerie twilight. A jagged bolt of lightning split the sky and then, only seconds later, an almighty boom of thunder, as if a bomb had been dropped.

Rachel had seen her fair share of dramatic tropical storms while living in the Pacific, and as a result had developed a healthy respect for their damaging power. She certainly didn't like being out on the water in a small boat in such a storm with nowhere to hide from the lightning, but she forced herself to remain calm. She steered onward, trying not to panic and over-rev the engine. Going too fast in such conditions would be a mistake: the chop was heavy and she didn't want to take on any water and risk having to stop and bale out.

She remembered the old house on Little Embers and, despite Jonah's words about the hermit who lived there, calculated that it was her best hope of shelter. Just able to make it out on the horizon, she opened the throttle, riding the knife edge between speed and control in order to get there as quickly as possible.

There was another almighty crack and Rachel reflexively ducked, even though it would make no difference if the lightning did decide to strike her. Water slapped over the side of the little dinghy and the bow wave came dangerously high but she continued, urging the motor on.

The shoreline of Little Embers came into view just as the outboard sputtered, lost power, and then cut out completely. The boat wallowed in the sudden lull and Rachel nearly overbalanced. She steadied herself and pulled the starter cord, trying to spark it back into life. She pulled it again, and again, but it stubbornly refused to restart. It was dead. She let forth a torrent of expletives and slammed her hand against the plastic casing. She was screwed.

Marooned.

Drifting fast away from the land.

The rain had begun to pelt down now and within a few minutes a puddle formed at her feet. The words "sitting duck" echoed in her head. One thing was certain, there was no point in remaining at the stern of the boat doing nothing to help herself.

She took her camera from around her neck, unclipped the straps of her waders and pulled them down to her waist, then, lying as flat as she could, wriggled out of them, removing her jeans at the same time. She stripped off her sweater and T-shirt for good measure:

they would only weigh her down. She'd been caught out once before in a storm on Pittwater and she was a good swimmer, so she wasn't ready to panic, not yet. But the water in the Scilly Isles was considerably colder and she risked hypothermia unless the currents were kind to her.

Wearing just her bra and knickers and soaked through from the rain, she calculated that there were about five hundred meters between her and the shoreline. No big deal on a calm day in warm water, but a different story in the middle of a torrential downpour with limited visibility.

As if to urge her over the edge, a forked bolt of lightning lit up the sky, the thunder rolling in milliseconds behind it. The storm was almost overhead.

She crawled forward to the front of the boat and grasped the line attached to the bow, tying it over one shoulder and across her body. Her plan, sketchy as it was, was to swim the boat into the shore.

She stood up in the rocking boat and before she could change her mind, leaped overboard.

Jesus. It was freezing. The icy water forced the air out of her lungs and her brain felt as if a tight metal band was cinched around it. Gasping as she came to the surface, she found a sightline on the island—a clump of trees that she could just see through the gloom—and struck out for them.

It was harder than she had imagined to tow the boat behind her, and when she looked up again after a few minutes of swimming, she didn't appear to have made any progress at all. Flipping onto her back, she began to kick, giving her arms a rest. As she did so, a wave washed over her and she swallowed a mouthful of seawater. Not such a good idea. Coughing and spluttering, she turned back on her front and began to swim again, counting her strokes in lots of fifty to keep herself going.

She felt as if she'd been at it for hours, but it was probably only minutes. Her arms were burning from the effort of swimming, the muscles working hard against the tide. She had lost all feeling in her fingers and toes and she had to clamp her lips together in order to stop her teeth from chattering and swallowing more water.

A choppy wave broke over her and she ducked, holding her breath until she deemed it safe to surface again. Feeling considerably lighter in its aftermath, she realized that the line attaching her to the boat had come loose. *Soleil* was now drifting away from her at a fast rate of knots.

Perhaps jumping out of the dinghy hadn't been the smartest thing. In fact, it was probably right up there with leaping into a blowhole when she was a teenager (her parents still didn't know about that one). She was deciding whether to keep swimming for shore or go back and try and reach the boat, when her hands struck something solid. She barely felt the grazes to her knuckles as they hit bare rock.

The decision had been made for her. She abandoned all thoughts of the dinghy. Saving herself was the priority. She staggered to her knees as another wave washed her shoreward, tumbling her over the rocks. She tried to get a purchase with her fingers, but the rocks were slippery with weed. Another wave washed over her and she felt her arm bend under her, fingers catching in a crevice.

Stuck.

Willing herself not to panic, she held her breath and fought to wrench her hand free. It was wedged between two immovable slabs of rock. As she pulled it this way and that, stars sparked beneath her closed eyes and bubbles burst from her mouth as she screamed into the water, swearing against the pain and her own stupidity.

Chapter Seventeen
London, Spring 2018

That evening, Eve cooked supper with Radio 4—
"the wireless" Grams insisted on calling it—
burbling in the background. She paid far less attention
to the news reports than usual, for her grandmother's
stories were still swirling in her head. What did she
mean when she said that she thought she would never
find beauty again? It seemed such a desperate thing to
believe, especially for someone who had been so young
at the time. And what about her comment that she had
found love, but that it was too late? That was even more
perplexing.

The pips sounded the hour and Eve turned off the
grill but not the radio. It was the accompaniment to
their days. In the early hours of the morning, the so-
norous tones of the shipping forecast woke Eve, the

never-changing list of names, as familiar as a prayer: Forties, Cromarty, Tyne and Fisher, German Bight, Humber, Fastnet, Fair Isle, and Scilly summoning her to her duties, for her grandmother still needed help reaching the bathroom.

Before lunch, Grams liked to listen to *Woman's Hour*—"They've had me on a few times, you know," she told Eve one day as they listened to a female astronaut talk about her life and work.

Late at night Eve could often hear the low-pitched tones of *Book at Bedtime* floating up the stairwell, for her grandmother liked things at high volume.

Eve was twenty-three. She should have been at the movies with a group of girlfriends, watching a play or listening to a band, or enjoying a well-earned cold drink in the dust of Gunjur with David, not listening to the latest installment of *The Archers* and heating up a prepared meal. She tried not to mind too much. As she sliced two lonely carrots into rounds and shook frozen broccoli into a saucepan, she wondered what exactly she *was* going to do with her life once her grandmother was better, whenever that might be. Surely there had to be something as breathtaking as an alpine sunrise in her future. In the London dark it seemed hard to imagine.

The next day was warmer and the previous week's snow and slush had melted away, leaving the streets cleansed. When Eve stepped outside she could feel the faint breath of spring in the air. Almost overnight, trees were misted with green and snowdrops poked their delicate heads from among the blades of grass. She walked on the Heath in higher spirits, lifting her face to the sun that shone weakly overhead. The almost imperceptible change of season gave her the feeling that things might be about to alter elsewhere, that the long winter of her grams's recuperation might nearly be over. Certainly she had been more animated yesterday than Eve had seen her in months and she took it as a good sign. She hoped that they might make more progress that day.

When she returned, after kicking off her muddy boots and leaving them at the door, she brewed a pot of tea and went in to Grams's room. Placing a cup and saucer down on the dressing table, she noticed that a small jewelry box stood open. It was generally firmly shut, fastened with a tiny gold key that Eve had never turned.

Her grandmother's eyes were still closed and her breathing was the slow, rhythmical sound of someone fast asleep. Eve's eyes flicked over to the box again and she risked a glance inside, noticing a pretty silver brooch decorated with flowers. She'd never seen it before, certainly never seen her grandmother wear it. At the center of each flower was a tiny red stone—a ruby she thought. A half-forgotten Bible verse floated through her mind: "Who can find a virtuous woman? For her price is above rubies." She reached inside and picked it up, turning it over in her hand. There was an inscription on the back: "To the Lady E from her friend R. As a testimony of his esteem. *Ex tenebris lux*." What did that mean? And who was R? Not Gramps, that was certain. She remembered her grandmother's comment the previous day about meeting the right man too late. Was this another clue? Checking on her grams's still-sleeping form, she wondered about the stories her grandmother had yet to tell her and if she would divulge them all.

She was returning the brooch to the box when she heard the rustle of bedsheets, her grandmother stirring. She walked the few steps to her side, hearing a gasp and drew closer, leaned down, her eyes searching her grandmother's face. It had lost the calmness of sleep, was scrunched up, lips pursed, a deep furrow between her eyebrows. She was shaking her head from side to side, as if fighting something off. Under the blankets, her legs jerked.

"Robbie. Robbie. The orchard . . . can't breathe. No air . . ."

A flash of alarm arced through Eve. Was her grandmother having a turn? She wondered if she should summon help.

Then, as suddenly as it had come over her, she was still again, her expression relaxing, the folds of skin settling around the bones of her face.

Eve waited for several minutes to reassure herself that it had been nothing more than a bad dream.

Eventually, she left the room. Tea could wait. But who was Robbie? It wasn't a name she'd ever heard before. Was he the "R" who'd given Grams the brooch?

Chapter Eighteen
Little Embers, Autumn 1951

Esther's motives for getting out of the house were not simply the need for exercise. She wanted to reacquaint herself with the jetty, for she had been counting the days until the boat would call again. After digging for clams and filling the bucket that they had brought with them, they walked onward, the hard sand and tidemarks of dark seaweed crunching beneath her shoes. At the far end was the jetty. "So there's no boat on the island?" she asked.

"I must confess, I never learned to sail. Bit of an oversight, all things considered," Richard replied.

"So you are as stuck here as we are?"

"Well, I wouldn't put it like that exactly."

"And the supply boat comes once a week?" she said, stopping to catch her breath.

"That's right. Every Friday. Except in really bad weather."

"In the morning or afternoon?"

Richard looked sideways at her. "Depends on the tide—she needs high tide to be able to dock at the jetty. Why? Is there anything you particularly need?"

"Oh no, nothing really. Idle curiosity." She wasn't sure he believed her, but she had the information she needed, for now.

When Esther woke on Friday she went straight to the window to check on the weather. For the first time, the nurse had not wrapped her in the straitjacket the night before. The weals on her arms and torso had healed well, and she noticed no new damage as she pushed aside the curtains. To her relief, the sun shone faintly through a thin layer of clouds. The boat would come; she just had to make sure she didn't miss it.

The day before, she had asked the doctor for some notepaper and a pen, saying she wanted to begin to write down her feelings about the events that had brought her to Embers, that it might help. It had been a lie. She used the paper to write to John, to insist that he come and get her. She wrote, her hands flying over the pages, telling him how much she missed both him and Teddy, and that Teddy surely needed her. She implored him in the strongest possible terms to allow her to come home, promising that she was quite better and ready to be a wife and mother again. When she was finished, she folded the note carefully, wrote the address on one side and sealed it with several drops of wax from her candle. The letter was her only hope of escape from this infernal place.

In the days since her arrival, she had become fond of the other men, and even Robbie's ruined face no longer shocked her as much as it first had. In turn, they treated her with politeness and respect, and were rather amusing company at mealtimes. Robbie, in particular, had been kind. One morning, she had ventured to the vegetable garden—a large rectangle that featured orderly rows of cabbages, purple heads of broccoli, spinach, leeks, Brussels sprouts and the golden tops of onions, their green shoots tied off for winter—and watched him digging potatoes from the dark, loamy soil. He began to tell her what had brought him to the island. "I flew Wellingtons, a nice big kite, but do you know, when I crashed all I felt was the sheer relief of not having to fly the damn thing anymore. I don't know how we got out of the plane—I was unconscious and the bloody thing caught on fire. Broke my tibia, fibula, mandible, not to mention melting half my face . . ." He said all of this without a trace of self-pity. "We were over France and it was tremendously cold, the day before Christmas Eve actually. There was snow on the ground when we landed. The Germans found us and took us to a field hospital in Valmont. That's where my rear-gunner—he didn't survive the crash—was buried. I found out later that they dug two graves that day." He jabbed the ground with his garden fork. "They didn't expect me to make it either, but somehow I did. Then I was moved to Rouen, to another hospital, had numerous operations, nearly lost my leg, and eventually ended up in Stalag Nine. That's when things got a bit rough. Still, nothing lasts forever, does it?"

Esther was astonished. She had heard about prisoner-of-war camps of course, but to actually meet someone who had been in one, well that was a different kettle of fish entirely. "How on earth did you survive?"

"We lived on acorn coffee, potato bread, and occasionally a bit of stew. We were all thin as rakes."

She hadn't meant what they lived on, rather how they got through it, but she didn't interrupt.

"There was a Prussian doctor, he loved to do minor operations without an anesthetic. He took the wire out of my jaw without one."

Esther tried not to look shocked.

"It was four years before I was repatriated. The day I'd dreamed of, the moment that had kept me going through all those dark times. But when I arrived back at HQ they invalided me out. Out of the air force forever. I tell you, I've never felt so low as I did that day. All I'd been through and then they turned around and said they couldn't have me, didn't want me." He pushed his hair off his face until it sat even more wildly. "Rough trot, don't you know? After everything I'd put up with. They tossed me aside like a broken toy. What was it all for anyway? That's the thing I don't understand. King and country?" He laughed, a hollow sound that was fast snatched away by the wind. "They didn't repay the sacrifice. Not one bit."

"Oh, Robbie, that's just awful." Esther could barely comprehend what he, and the others, must have had to go through. She felt even more of a fraud for being at Embers at all. These men needed the treatment Dr. Creswell was offering; she really didn't. "But what brought you here, if you don't mind me asking? The war's been over for a while."

"I had what I suppose you'd call a breakdown. My sister found me outside hiding under a bit of corrugated iron, clutching T. S. Eliot. Wouldn't come out no matter what she tried." He shook his head ruefully.

"T. S. Eliot?" She was curious.

"The Hollow Men . . ." He intoned the words. "I was pretty much catatonic apparently. It was coming here or a lobotomy. Thank Christ my sister found this place; it's made all the difference. The doc, he gets me to talk about it in a way that I can't to anyone else. Makes it a bit easier to bear somehow; and digging up this—" He poked at the soil again. "Seeing things grow takes away some of the frustration somehow. There's something, however small, that's good and right about it."

Esther murmured in agreement.

"Though I'm still not sure if I'm better off than those who didn't come back," he added.

"Especially being in a different kind of prison," said Esther.

He looked up at her, surprised. "It's hardly that. Not for me anyway. I *want* to be here. What scares me most is the thought of leaving."

A little after noon, she saw George and Robbie heading off down the path to the jetty, George pushing a rough-hewn cart with old bicycle wheels on either side. Esther hurriedly pulled on her walking shoes and ran after them, her stockings catching on the sharp grass that lined the way, the pungent reek of seaweed pricking her nostrils. "Mind if I come too?" she asked breathlessly when she caught up with them.

"Looking for something to do?" George asked.

"I suppose," she replied, feigning nonchalance.

"It's a bit like that at first. Best if you can find yourself something around here, help take your mind off things." His voice was kind and she knew he meant well, but the only thing on Esther's mind was escape.

As they neared the jetty, she could see a small boat in the distance. She felt for the letter that she'd hidden in her pocket, her fingers closing around a shilling in the other. She had no stamps and so planned to appeal to the captain to buy one on her behalf when he reached the main island. She hoped there was a post office there—surely there had to be?

The three of them stood at the end of the jetty, listening to the slap of the waves against the timber and watching as the boat hove into view and then came alongside. The captain threw a couple of lines to Robbie and George and they lashed them to posts on the jetty. The boat sat low in the water, with several sacks weighting the stern. The captain killed the engine, and then, with an agility at odds with his tubby stature, made his way toward them. Hefting a sack effortlessly, he passed it to the waiting men.

Esther watched as the boat was unloaded, her heart drumming as she waited for her chance. She couldn't risk one of the men seeing her; they would surely inform the doctor. As they turned to haul the cart back up the path, she saw her chance. "I'll help cast off," she said. "You chaps go on ahead and I'll catch you up."

"Sure you can manage?" George asked.

"Yes, yes, of course," she insisted. "I know what to do." *It couldn't be that hard,* she muttered under her breath.

They set off back up the path with a wave to the captain.

Thanking her good fortune that they had left her on her own without an argument, Esther waited until she was sure they were out of earshot. She began to undo the knots holding the lines fast to the jetty and then waved to the captain, beckoning him to come closer. "Do you think you can post this for me?" she implored, retrieving the envelope and the shilling from her pockets and holding them out to him.

The captain looked uncertain. "Mail usually goes once a month. The doctor, 'e passes it on to me."

"Oh please, would you mind? I'd really be terribly grateful." Esther gave him her most winning smile, doing her best to charm him. "It's a drawing for my little boy, you see." She crossed her fingers at the lie.

The wind had started to come up and the captain was anxious to be on his way. Giving him no choice, she pressed the paper and the coin into his hand and went to finish untying the lines. The captain shrugged and put them both in the pocket of his sou'wester while she threw the last line aboard.

As the boat pulled away, she felt relief that her plan—so far at least—had worked. The captain had looked reluctant, but he'd taken the letter and she was sure he would do as she'd asked. With a sudden burst of enthusiasm, she sprang up the path to catch the men. She began to calculate how long it might be before John would come back for her . . . a week? Perhaps two. She steeled herself to cope with that.

Chapter Nineteen
Little Embers, Spring 2018

The crackle and snap of twigs as they caught alight . . . the stutter of rain on a windowpane . . . and somewhere a low whistle. For a moment Rachel believed she was back at Shearwater Cottage, having fallen asleep over her folders.

Her eyes fluttered open and she saw peeling wallpaper with an indeterminate, mottled effect that could have been water damage as much as an intentional pattern. Beneath her was a scratchy sofa. Moss green, with the roughness of coarse wool.

"So you're awake." The voice was croaky, rusty almost, as if it hadn't been used in a while.

Rachel swiveled her eyes in its direction and focused on the slight woman standing in the doorway. The light was dim; a single oil lamp cast shadows over her face but she could make out a snarl of thick, curling auburn hair loose to the woman's shoulders. She was wearing baggy corduroy trousers in a murky shade of mustard that were held up by a ratty leather belt and a darned, knitted sweater spattered with shades of green, brown, and gray, as if she'd been using it as an artist's palette. She looked older than Rachel, but younger than her mother—mid to late forties if she'd had to hazard a guess. Her gray eyes fastened on Rachel's with an unflinching gaze.

"Saw you out there as the storm came in and wondered what you were up to. No idea why you decided to swim for it though. You're not from the islands, are you?" she said, as if that offered some sort of explanation.

Rachel shook her head imperceptibly and swallowed. Her throat was raw, most likely the aftereffect of swallowing a bucketload of saltwater.

"Good job I got to you in time, or you'd have been feeding the fish. You were a lovely shade of Prussian when I pulled you out."

"I . . ." Rachel didn't know where to begin. A memory of being stuck in the rocks surfaced. "My hand. It was caught. I would have made it otherwise." She was defiant.

"As I said, lucky I was there, eh?"

"Where am I?"

"Little Embers."

"My tinny . . ." Rachel went to sit up but slumped down again as a wave of dizziness and pain washed over her. Her right arm throbbed.

"Lost at sea, I'm afraid."

"Oh Christ." How was she going to explain that to Dr. Wentworth?

"Not sure he had much to do with it. I'm Leah, by the way."

"Rachel," she said weakly.

The woman grunted. "I'll go and put the kettle on; a cuppa will help warm you up."

Leah disappeared into the recesses of the hallway and Rachel took the opportunity to assess her surroundings. The room was chaotic, with books and papers strewn across every surface, in untidy piles on the flowered rug and propping open the door. Ragged curtains were drawn across two long, rectangular windows and she was lying facing the fire, a thick blanket covering her and several hot water bottles packed against her torso, legs, and feet. From somewhere came the smell of cooking—something rich and savory.

She raised her left hand to her hair and found it was still damp. Then she remembered that she'd only been wearing her underwear when she jumped overboard and looked down, seeing that she was now clad in a loose, paint-daubed T-shirt that might once have been white. Leah must have put it on her.

She was attempting to sit up again when Leah reappeared with two mugs.

"Ah. I wouldn't try to move too much. Your hand is somewhat the worse for wear."

"What do you mean?"

"I reckon you've broken a finger or two and I may have sprained your wrist in trying to wrench it loose from the rock." Leah said this matter-of-factly. "It's a bit swollen but I'm sure it'll be right as rain in a day or two." She put down the mug she was carrying and lifted a corner of the blanket. Rachel craned her neck and could see that her right forearm, lying across her chest, was twice the size of the other, the wrist thick and puffy. Two of her fingers were also swollen and had turned a fetching shade of purple. As she looked at her hand and gingerly tried to move her fingers, pain flooded through her once more and even though she was still freezing, sweat beaded on her forehead. "Ow! Fuck, it hurts."

"Yeah, I wouldn't recommend that." Leah opened a blister packet of tablets and held two out to her. "These'll take the edge off."

Leah had placed the tea on a small table next to her

uninjured side and Rachel sat up awkwardly, biting her tongue as she jostled her swollen arm in reaching for the mug. The tea was sweet and strong and as she sipped it, she started to feel her natural optimism reassert itself. She hadn't drowned. She was in one piece—well, sort of. She thought briefly of her camera, her phone, and the day's observations. She was sorry to lose the camera, but the phone she could claim on insurance, and at least the obs were only a day's worth. The boat, however, was a bigger problem. How was she going to explain that to Dr. Wentworth? He would, without doubt, think her the biggest idiot on the planet.

He wouldn't be too far off the mark.

Leah reappeared, a rusty tin box in her hands. She set it down on the coffee table and pulled open the lid, which came away with a screech of complaint. "I thought I'd wait until you woke up before strapping your hand," she said, rooting around inside the box.

"Oh, thanks." Rachel wasn't sure that had been the best idea.

"I'm not much of a nurse." Leah pulled out a grayish bandage. "This stuff's been here for years, but it should do the trick."

As Leah sat down next to her on the sofa, Rachel smelled wood smoke and the slightly sour odor of old clothes rarely washed. Leah's hands were small, square, and strong: capable hands. The nails were rimmed with a murky khaki color, but apart from that they looked fairly clean.

"Hold out your arm."

Rachel did as she was asked, moving it carefully toward her.

"So, Rachel, why don't you tell me exactly what brought you all the way to the Eastern Isles in such atrocious weather?" Leah began to wind the bandage along the lower part of her arm. "You're a long way from home."

"Not really," she replied, a defensive note in her voice. "I'm living on St. Mary's. I'm a research scientist. Ow!"

"Sorry. It might hurt just a little. No, I meant Australia. That's where you're from, aren't you?" Leah's hands moved quickly and efficiently as they unrolled the bandage.

"Originally. But I've lived all over. Cooks, Maldives, Guam . . . Southern Hemisphere or equatorial islands mainly."

Thunder rumbled outside the window. "We don't often get storms as bad as this so late in the season," Leah said, glancing up. "But when we do, it's not safe for man or dog out there."

"I wouldn't have set out if I'd realized," she said, Leah's words making her feel foolish. "I don't make a habit of such stupid mistakes."

"You don't say," she said, fastening the bandage by tucking it neatly in on itself. "That should help."

It did, though the ache was still there.

"Dinner's on. Hope you like mutton."

Leah disappeared again and Rachel was left wondering who exactly she was. Jonah had said that she was a hermit, but there had to be more to it than that. Who in their right mind would choose to live such a lonely existence?

She was on the point of dozing off again when Leah reappeared carrying tin plates and two forks. "You might be more comfortable on the sofa tonight—it's warmer in here than anywhere else in the house. I'll pull out some spare linen for you tomorrow, but it's all in the attic and I'm not going up there until it's light again."

"Surely I'll be able to get back to St. Mary's by tomorrow?" she asked.

"I wouldn't be too certain of that. This storm looks set to hang around for a day or two," Leah said, handing her a plate. As if to back her up, a clap of thunder sounded, making the windows rattle in their frames.

Rachel balanced the plate on her lap and then took the fork Leah held out. "But you'll be able to take me back then?"

"Well, I would if I had a boat."

"What?"

"I said I would if I had a boat."

"Yes, I heard that, but what do you mean?"

"Exactly what I said," Leah said with exaggerated patience. "I don't have a boat."

"You're kidding. How do you get around? Get supplies? Food?"

"I rarely need to leave the island, and Tom from the co-op on St. Mary's sends out a delivery once a week."

Rachel was astonished. She knew a fair bit about living remotely, but this was on another level.

"When's the next delivery due?" she mumbled through a mouthful of stew.

"Let's see . . ." She thought for a while. "The last one was two days ago. Yes, that was it."

"So next Thursday," said Rachel.

"I don't exactly keep track of days, but if you say so."

"Do you at least have a phone?"

Leah looked at her as if she'd asked for a direct line to the moon. "Nope."

That meant it would be another five days before anyone came. Five days. She was due to contact Dr.

Wentworth on Monday. He would be unimpressed if she missed her first check-in. Mind you, he was hardly likely to be happy about the news she had to give him. She put it to the back of her mind: there was nothing to be done about it right now.

"Don't you get lonely here?" Rachel had never been good at subtlety. "I mean, only seeing someone once a week at best? Not being able to contact anyone?"

Leah looked at her with a mix of irritation and resignation. "I've been lonelier in big cities, even in small towns. No, this suits me just fine."

Without thinking, Rachel moved her injured wrist and winced again.

"Those painkillers doing any good?" Leah asked.

"A little," she replied, not wanting to complain.

"You might not have the best night's sleep tonight."

"I'm tougher than I look."

"I'm sure you are." Leah reached for the plate, which Rachel had scraped clean as they spoke. "We don't run to dessert in these parts I'm afraid."

"That was delicious, thank you. And thank you for taking me in, for rescuing me."

"I was hardly going to leave you out there to drown, now was I?"

Chapter Twenty
Little Embers, Autumn 1951

Richard often started his therapy sessions with a piece of music, taking care to select something soothing that might suit his patient. It helped to achieve a calm state of mind so that he could begin to probe deeper into the events that brought them to Embers in the first place. For Esther, he chose the Vaughan Williams again, having seen how it affected her the first time he played it. It didn't hurt that it was also one of his favorite pieces.

Nearly ten days had passed since her arrival and the presence of a woman on the island hadn't been as disruptive as he had initially feared, at least as far as the other patients were concerned.

Robbie in particular had taken a shine to her. He had seen them both in the garden, Robbie leaning on his shovel, seemingly engaged in earnest conversation, and Esther holding her hair off her face as the wind tried to grasp it. He had noticed how the fresh air brought pinkness to her pale complexion and that she had begun to eat a little more at each meal. He was aware that she had a small supply of Seconal—John had given him details of the medication she'd been prescribed—but he had preferred to let her finish them rather than distress her further by taking them away. He would not be prescribing any more, however. His aim was to wean his patients off all sedatives and stimulants as their condition improved. A small dose of valerian, if they were plagued by nightmares, was the most he would allow.

In their daily meetings he could see that she had slowly begun to trust him, telling him small details of her life in London, how she loved to walk on the Heath in spring, her favorite place to swim in summer. True, they had only talked generally, and he had not broached the subject of her recent past yet. It would take time before she would be able to unburden herself. One morning, they had been talking of the bathing ponds when he dared to ask the question.

"Tell me about your children, Esther."

She blanched, but recovered herself quickly. "Well, Teddy is nearly two and a half and a bit of a handful—John likes to call him Teddy the Terror in fact. He's mischievous, but such a happy little chap, and so loving . . . I'm afraid I'm not always a terribly good mother to him." She lapsed into silence.

"What makes you say that?" he asked gently.

"Well, I'm here, aren't I? I should be at home, looking after him, like a proper mother would be."

"Now don't blame yourself for that; it can't be helped. And you're here to get well again, so that you *can* be a good mother again."

"But I'm perfectly well. I've just been a little out of sorts, that's all." She brushed imaginary crumbs from her skirt and shifted in her seat. "A bit blue, that is if I was forced to admit to anything."

He smiled inwardly at the understatement. "Are you sure about that, Esther? What about your other child?"

"My other child?"

He deliberately left a long silence. It was one of the oldest tricks in a psychologist's book. You had to leave space for the patient to go inside themselves, to let the silence stretch until they filled it with what had often been buried deep. Esther was stubborn though, self-contained, and the silence stretched and stretched, all while she remained perfectly still.

The dong of the grandfather clock in the hall announced it was time for lunch and he reluctantly drew their session to an end. "Let's chat some more tomorrow, shall we?" he said, as if nothing untoward had happened. "Why don't you go on to the kitchen and I'll tidy up a few things here?"

Esther got to her feet, an economy of motion that was graceful and fluid. It pleased him inordinately to watch her: tramping along the seashore, sipping tea at breakfast, the way one side of her mouth curled upward in wry good humor at something Wilkie or Robbie said. It probably wasn't right to be so affected by her presence, but he found it impossible not to be.

She gave him a brief, questioning glance as she left the room and Richard felt himself color, as if she had been able to read his thoughts. She closed the door and he reminded himself once again of his professional obligations.

He went to his study and sat at the desk there, moving aside a sheaf of papers to reveal his diary. The year, 1951, was stamped in gold on the front and a thin ribbon marked the place. November, the dying month. A scant few weeks until Christmas, he noted without a great deal of enthusiasm. As a boy, the day had been a highlight in an otherwise uneventful existence. There had been presents—a train set, a football, and one memorable year a black bicycle with a shiny bell that he loved to sound loudly as he rounded corners, surprising unsuspecting pedestrians. There had been the tantalizing aroma of turkey roasting, crunchy potatoes, and the taste of sweet oloroso sipped in the drawing room. His mother, full of girlish excitement at the present opening, then claiming exhaustion and retreating to her bedroom long before it was time to retire for the night. His father disappearing behind the *Times*, leaving Richard to play with his toys by himself.

During the war his taste for ceremony, gifts, and festive food had waned and he generally preferred to work on the days that most wished to relax on. Since arriving at Embers, there had been two Christmases, celebrated quietly, though Mrs. Biggs had on both occasions managed to rustle up a goose and the patients inveigled him in games of charades and hunt the thimble, the thimble in their case being requisitioned from Mrs. Biggs's sewing case. Both occasions had been surprisingly agreeable and had boosted morale, despite his patients receiving sometimes heart-wrenching messages from their loved ones. The hand-drawn cards from their children were the hardest for all to read.

Richard picked up his fountain pen, opened the diary to that day's date. "E.D. Session five," he wrote. "Patient appears in measurably better humor, but refuses to acknowledge the events in her recent past." He then put the diary aside and inserted a piece of paper into the squat typewriter that also sat on his desk. The keys clacked in a staccato rhythm as he recalled their conversation, Esther's mood, her physical health, even her body language. Little went unnoticed or unnoted. Eventually, after nearly half an hour and several pages, he pulled the last piece of paper free of the cartridge and placed it in a manila file before securing it in a cabinet.

To an outsider it might have appeared that he was making little progress, but his work had shown him the value of patience and gentle persistence in all things.

Chapter Twenty-one
Little Embers, Spring 2018

Leah had been right. Rachel slept fitfully, kept from deeper slumber by the pain in her arm every time she moved, as well as the sound of the wind swirling around the old house and the scattershot of rain on the windowpane. The fire had long died down and she shivered under the blanket, reliving the panic she'd felt when her hand was stuck. She'd done some pretty foolish things in her thirty-five years, but deciding to swim while towing a tinny behind her in a raging storm had to be right up there among them. She could just imagine the look on her older brother's face when she told him.

To distract herself she lay on the sofa trying to work out how she was going to get off the island before the supply boat came, and exactly how she would explain the missing tinny to Dr. Wentworth.

Sometime in the early hours, Rachel's thoughts turned to Jonah. If anyone were to notice that the *Soleil* had gone missing it would most likely be him. Would he perhaps organize a search party? No one in their right mind would set out in such a storm though. And even if he did, there was a lot of ocean and so many islands; it would be like searching for a needle in a haystack.

As a dim light began to filter through the curtains, Rachel was struck by the sudden silence. The rain had stopped and the wind no longer howled. As she was lying there, contemplating the peace, she heard a series of creaks as someone came down the stairs and then the metallic clang of pans being placed on a stove. Leah must be awake.

Sure enough, about ten minutes later, Leah opened the door and appeared with two mugs in one hand and the packet of painkillers in the other.

"Get any sleep?"

Rachel gave her a weak smile. "Not a lot."

"Thought you might want a cuppa. I hope you don't mind it unsweetened. Used up the last of the sugar yesterday. There's milk though. I keep a cow on the island. Margaret. Named after one of your country-women in fact." Leah handed her the mug and Rachel took it with her good hand.

"Margaret?" Rachel was puzzled.

"Olley."

"Oh, the painter. I love her work." Rachel smiled, pleased at the fact that they might have something, however tenuous, in common.

"Bingo."

"And do you paint?" she asked, remembering the multi-colored stains on Leah's clothes.

"I used to. Wasn't too bad once. But now . . . now I just dabble and try not to mind that somewhere along the way my talent deserted me." Her tone was light, but Rachel sensed an undertone to the throwaway comment.

She took a sip of tea. It was hot and comforting. "I see."

"I doubt you do, but never mind that. I won't have anyone feeling sorry for me."

"I'll do my best not to," she said firmly.

"Good. As we're going to be stuck with each other for the next five days . . ."

Rachel gave a loud, involuntary sigh as she thought again of the time she would lose.

"May I continue?" Leah fixed her with a glare and she nodded mutely.

"I've not had a houseguest before, but there will be certain rules if we are to get along—I am probably rather too used to my own company. I suggest you stay right here for the day." Leah held up a hand as Rachel started to protest. "That's a nasty sprain and you look like you could do with more rest. Then, you're welcome anywhere in the house, with the exception of my studio upstairs. That's strictly no entry. I'll be in there most afternoons, but in the mornings I milk Margaret, see to the vegetables, and generally try and do a bit of maintenance about the place. If you do decide to go for a walk, just let me know, as I don't fancy scouring the island for you if I can't find you."

Rachel was about to say that she rarely got lost, but then remembered how in fact she'd ended up on the island and thought better of it.

"I'd welcome some help in the kitchen, if you think you can manage it, as the one thing I do get sick of is my own cooking," Leah continued.

"How do you like tuna pasta?" Rachel asked with a grin.

"I like it just fine. You'll find the ingredients you need in the pantry. I'd also better give you the guided tour at some point today." Leah had shown her the bathroom the night before, but the rest of the house remained a mystery. "I'll dig out some clothes for you, but I'll get the fire lit first. Can't have you getting cold again."

Once the fire was going, Leah disappeared and Rachel heard the scrape of something being drawn across the ceiling, followed by a thump and a loud bang. "Everything okay?" she called out uncertainly.

"It will be," came a muffled reply from somewhere above her.

More banging, another thump, and then Leah re-appeared. In her arms was an old-fashioned suitcase, dark brown leather, with rusted brass locks. Her forearm flexed under its weight and Rachel could see that her muscles were well-defined. Leah might be slight, but she was strong. Just as well, thought Rachel, or she probably wouldn't be sitting there.

Leah placed the suitcase on the floor next to her with a heavy clunk. "There's a few things in here. They might not be your style, but beggars . . ."

"Where did it come from?"

"The attic. Before that, buggered if I know. It's been here since I've lived at Embers. I had a quick look a while ago, but when I saw the clothes would drown me,

I left it where it was. You're welcome to anything you like."

"Who lived in the house before you?"

"No one permanently, well, not for about fifty years anyway—the place was almost a ruin. I got it on the condition I did a bit of fixing up. Which is a never-ending job."

Leah bent down and popped the latches, which gave way with a rusty click.

Rachel peered inside. It was lined in emerald-green moiré silk, faded in places, and her nose wrinkled at the pungent smell of mothballs that wafted toward her. Neither moths nor silverfish would have stood a chance. She could make out a dark wool jacket—or possibly a coat—with a curled black collar and a rather crushed mousy-brown felt hat.

"I'll leave you to have a look if you like. Got to see to Margaret. She's in the cow shed, but the roof's not the best and the storm last night could have spooked her."

Rachel eased herself forward on the sofa, nursing her sore wrist, and began to explore the contents of the suitcase with her good hand. She lifted the hat and coat off the top of the pile and placed them in the lid. Below them was a layer of tissue paper, browning at the edges and crumbling at her touch, and then a neatly folded pistachio-colored twinset: a short-sleeved sweater and matching cardigan adorned with pearl buttons. She spread the cardigan out and reckoned it would probably fit. Below these were some pleat-fronted, cuffed tweed trousers and a pair of sturdy flat shoes. Then, folded into more tissue paper, several pairs of silk underpants that looked a bit like shorts, a camisole, and a strange lacy contraption with strips of elastic hanging from it that she vaguely recognized as a garter belt. It was confirmed when she uncovered a pair of pale silk stockings. The clothes were in almost mint condition, but it was clear they came from a much earlier time.

She discarded the T-shirt she had slept in and gingerly eased the camisole and the sweater over her injured wrist, doing her best not to twist it and cause more pain. Then, the trousers. She managed the metal zipper with one hand, but the top button was beyond her and she left it undone. Eventually she stood up, smoothing the sweater down. The trousers crumpled slightly at her ankles, but apart from that, they fit fairly well. She could tell just from looking that the shoes would be far too narrow for her broad Aussie feet so didn't bother with those.

She knelt down again and rummaged through the rest of the things, finding a thin brown leather belt, another sweater, and a sheer, short-sleeved blouse in sunny yellow. Who had these clothes belonged to? How old had she been? What must her life have been like? Maybe she came here on a holiday? The fabrics were good quality, the sweater almost certainly cashmere and the clothes well made, but beyond that there were few clues.

Just as she thought she'd seen everything the suitcase contained, Rachel felt the hard corner of something in a side pocket. A book? She pulled it out. Yes. An old copy of Daphne du Maurier's *Rebecca*. She'd read it once, years ago, for school. The pages of this copy were well worn and as she flicked through them several pale blue envelopes, the flimsy airmail type, fell out from among the pages.

She read the address on the front of one of them. *E. Durrant, Frogmore, Well Walk, Hampstead, London NW3.*

Was this a letter, written by the owner of the clothes? To her mother, a sister, or a friend perhaps? First, however, she looked at the other envelopes. Six of them. All addressed to E. Durrant. Stamped, but unsent. How odd.

The envelopes hadn't been sealed, the flaps simply tucked inside and she was about to open one when she heard Leah coming along the corridor. She felt unaccountably guilty, as if she'd been caught peeking at

Chapter Twenty-two
London, Spring 2018

"Who was Robbie?" Eve asked her grandmother. She had gone into her room an hour or so later and found her grandmother sitting up in bed.

"Robbie?"

"You were talking in your sleep . . . something about an orchard?"

Esther sighed. "Really? Talking in my sleep?"

Eve nodded. "Do you have dreams like that very often?"

"Not anymore, not for years actually." She paused. Sighed deeply. "I don't suppose there's any shame in you knowing, darling."

"Knowing what, Grams?" Eve asked.

"Once, a long time ago, when Teddy was quite little

actually, I wasn't very well. John—your gramps—took me away, to a place where he thought I would get better."

Eve's eyes widened. She'd never heard about this before. "Go on."

"It was an island. Quite, quite remote. I don't even think it's inhabited today."

"Like the Scottish Highlands or something?"

"South, darling. Off the coast of Cornwall. The Scilly Isles."

Eve had certainly heard of them—Scilly was one of the names on the shipping forecast. "Isn't that where daffodils come from, the early ones, I mean?"

"Yes, darling, it is. It's beautiful there too. Though at the time it was the last place I wanted to be."

"So what happened? Why did Gramps take you there? How long were you there for?"

Her grandmother held up her hand. "Slow down, Eve. Are you sure you want to hear this?"

"Yes—but should we put it in the book? Should I get the recorder?" Though Grams had begun their notes for the book with her first experience of climbing, Eve hoped that whatever her grandmother was about to reveal might help the reader understand what drove her to scale mountains, to endure the cold and the altitude when she could have been comfortably at home looking after her two small children like any normal housewife would have been doing in the 1950s and '60s.

"I'll tell you what happened and you can decide, for it will affect you too."

Eve didn't know what to make of that comment, but kept quiet, letting her grandmother speak.

"A long time ago, when I was a young woman, I did something unforgivable. A crime in many people's eyes. Certainly a sin."

Eve could scarcely imagine it. Her grandmother had always been the embodiment of respectability and honor. A woman who was as steadfast as the mountains she loved to climb. She found it impossible to believe that her grams was capable of a criminal act, let alone one that had remained a secret for decades, and how could it have consequences for her? She wasn't even born then. Were her grandmother's memories becoming muddled again? However unlikely such a statement, Eve did her the courtesy of not dismissing it out of hand. "Sins can always be forgiven, Grams," she said gently.

Her grandmother gave Eve a wan smile, then continued. "I didn't know it then, but I was suffering from what they call postnatal depression. John—your gramps—knew something was wrong. Of course there were pills, but they only did so much."

Eve's eyes widened even further.

"Your grandfather tried everything to help me, believe me, he did. Then he took me away. To Little Embers. And left me there."

Chapter Twenty-three
Little Embers, Autumn 1951

Two weeks had passed since Esther had first woken at Embers, bound and confused, and she found herself surprised by the return of her old energy, the energy she'd had before the exhaustion of motherhood overcame everything. She spent her days largely unbothered by the cloud of dread that had hovered over her in London, her eyes were brighter, and her appetite had recovered itself, with the result that her skirts no longer swung loosely about her hips. It would likely be a couple of weeks more before she heard from John, but she comforted herself with the thought that her letter must surely have found its way to him by now and he must be planning her return at that very moment. She tried not to miss Teddy too much, but still slept with his woolen cap under her cheek. She had nightmares that he was calling to her, but when she went to hold him her hands would not stretch to meet his; he was always out of reach. It was only first thing in the mornings, the moment before her eyes snapped open, that she felt dragged down by loss again, when she remembered why John had brought her to Embers in the first place.

One morning, waking earlier than normal, she had gone outside for some air and in the fog she almost convinced herself that she heard something—a half-strangled, bleating cry. A shadowy form loomed out of the mist and her breath caught in her throat. It looked like the figure of a young boy. Teddy? As she raced closer, a shrub emerged and her heart slowed its thunderous beat. She was seeing him everywhere, her mind playing tricks.

She'd fallen into a routine, breakfasting with the men and then helping Robbie in the kitchen garden when the weather was fine. The repetitive act of weeding and digging and the sheer physical exhaustion was working a subtle magic, keeping her focus in the present and with little opportunity to rake over the past, during daylight hours at least. The grimness of the previous months faded from her memory, as if the dawn was finally breaking after a long, dark night.

She had even come to trust the doctor, disarmed by

his charm and steady good humor. She was surprised to find herself laughing, more than once, in their sessions together. She enjoyed sparring with him about the future of the Catholic Church in England, discussing postwar Europe, the Korean War, and public education. She never knew quite where their conversations would take them. He certainly gave her opinions far more weight than John had ever done, was prepared to listen and debate with her at length.

Despite his skills, however, he hadn't managed to get her to reveal anything about the events that had brought her there, for she knew if she uttered the words out loud that she would have to own up to her part in the tragedy.

About three weeks after she had arrived, on a Friday at noon, the tide was reaching its zenith. She practically scampered down the narrow path to the jetty, leaving Robbie following some way behind her, dragging the cart. They arrived in plenty of time to meet the boat—they could see the wide-beamed vessel as a speck on the horizon—and settled on the jetty's end to wait. The sun had come out from behind the clouds and Esther tipped her face to its warmth, swinging her legs and feeling a bubble of expectation well up inside her. Surely there would be a message from John by this boat? It had better come soon, for the bright, glossy pills were almost finished. She'd been rationing them, taking one every other night, but they would be gone within a week and she didn't know how she would cope after that. She didn't want the doctor to know she was taking them—she couldn't really explain why—but if John didn't send for her soon, she might be forced to ask him for some more. She couldn't manage without them.

"The place has grown on you, hasn't it?" said Robbie. He'd left the cart where the jetty met the land and come down to sit beside her, the unblemished side of his face closest to hers.

She looked sideways at him. "I'm not sure what you mean."

"You look almost happy. Quite different from when you first arrived."

"Perhaps I'm well enough to be leaving soon?"

"Perhaps." He didn't sound as if he believed her.

"Anyway, I have to go home soon. My son needs me."

"How old is he?"

"Two and a half. His name's Teddy." Her eyes misted over and she blinked to clear them, staring ahead of her. "How long have you been here?" she asked.

He brushed his fair hair out of his eyes. "Nearly six months I reckon. You should see this place in summer—

there's nowhere I've ever been that's quite like it. Hard to believe it's still England. Gorgeous for swimming."

"Well, I shall have to take your word for it, for I do not expect to be here come summer." Her tone was certain but she could tell from the look on his face that Robbie didn't believe her.

She cast around for a change of topic. "Tell me about your family. If it's not going to upset you that is," she added hurriedly.

"Oh no, not at all. My parents died in the Blitz. Now there's just my sister, a brother-in-law, and a niece with the sweetest smile you ever saw." The undamaged corner of his mouth turned upward at the memory.

"No wife? Children?"

He shook his head. "Didn't expect to survive the war, so it hardly seemed fair to leave someone stuck with mouths to feed and no breadwinner."

"Indeed. But how about since the war ended?"

He laughed bitterly. "I'm not exactly a pretty boy anymore, am I?"

"Do you know," she admitted, "I was a bit taken aback by your face when I first met you, but now—well now, I hardly notice it. It'll be the same for the right girl, I know it will. You've the kindest, biggest heart, Robbie."

"Very sweet of you to say so, old girl, but I'm not

much good to anyone at the moment. I doubt there's anyone alive who wants to lie next to me when the nightmares come."

"But love would change that; the right woman, and I'm sure there is one, someone who will love you."

"If only it were that simple," he said, not quite meeting her eyes.

"But you're getting better, aren't you?"

"I suppose. The doc seems to think so anyway." He got to his feet and began to wave at the boat, which was fast approaching the shore. Esther's anticipation grew as the skipper threw the engine into reverse and the boat came alongside the jetty. He tossed a line to each of them and they tied her up securely. "Ahoy there!" the skipper said, passing across a crate stamped with the Hugh Town Stores name and then another of mail.

Esther registered the brown paper parcels with excitement but stepped back out of the way as Robbie took the crate from the skipper and deposited it on the jetty next to them. She leaned forward to peer into it, optimistic that it would contain word from John. It was all she could do to stop herself from riffling through it there and then.

"Expecting something?" asked Robbie, noticing her darting eyes.

"Oh I hope so," she said. "My husband . . ."

She watched as the skipper handed two more crates and a sack to Robbie and then prepared to leave. "Gotta get a move on," he said in a thick Cornish accent. "Fearful storm brewing from the north."

"Time and tide wait for no man," said Robbie with a salute. "See you next week, Captain."

"God willing."

Esther helped untie the lines holding the boat fast to the jetty and they waved the captain off.

"Would you like to check before we set off back to the house?" asked Robbie kindly.

She nodded, barely able to speak, and knelt down, not caring that the damp timbers of the jetty soaked the knees of her lisle stockings. "Oh, a parcel for you, Robbie!" she cried, handing him a large rectangular box. "And one for George . . ." She riffled through the remaining packages, coming to a slim envelope with a North London postmark. Her heart leaped as she recognized the writing and she leaned back on her heels and tore the envelope open. As she slid the paper out a sudden gust of wind ripped one of the sheets from her hand and it sailed away, over the jetty and into the water. "Oh no!" she cried, scrambling to her feet and following where it had landed.

Before she could do anything further, Robbie had stripped off his heavy pullover and leaped into the sea, the splash sending a shower of salty water onto the jetty.

He scooped up the errant page, held it clear of the water, and began stroking the few yards to the shore with his other arm.

"Are you quite mad?" she called as she ran down the jetty to meet him, realizing as she said it that her choice of words might have been better. "It's freezing in there." But she couldn't help but be thankful that he'd saved it for her.

He emerged, spluttering, holding the paper triumphantly. "Your letter, madam," he said with a bow as water streamed off him, pooling on the sand. He looked ridiculously pleased with himself.

Esther laughed at the absurdity of it all, but then covered her mouth with her hands: his teeth were chattering with cold. "Oh, Robbie, you really shouldn't have. But thank you." She leaned forward and gave him a quick kiss on his good cheek then turned to look at the letter. She still held the second, dry page, in her hands and the writing was bold and clear. Unfortunately, despite Robbie's efforts, the ink had run so as to make the message on the first, sodden page almost indecipherable. She peered at it, trying to make sense of the waterlogged words.

"*My darling Esther—*" she read. The rest of the page was a washout, and the ink swam before her eyes. She blinked and turned to the page in her other hand. A single paragraph. "*I hope you have by now settled in and are feeling better. Richard is a wonderful doctor and I have every confidence that, in time, you will make a full recovery and return to us. Teddy sends a kiss. Your loving husband, John.*" Esther let out a low moan, the mention of her son lancing her with fresh agony. Her husband hadn't paid any heed to her pleas to return home—if indeed he had received her letter at all.

"Bad news, old chum?" Robbie asked.

"I suppose so," she said, unable to quell the tremor in her voice. "It seems I shall not be returning home as soon as I had hoped." She screwed the pages into a tight ball and hurled them into the sea. "I'm sorry you had to get wet. It appears that the letter wasn't worth rescuing after all."

"Come on now, it can't be that bad."

"Can't it?" she rounded on him. She had to take her anger out on something, someone. "Do you know what it's like to be away from your child? A small child who needs his mother? What it's like to lie awake every night wondering if he's eaten his supper, if he's warm enough, if he's sleeping peacefully? To be hundreds of miles away from him, hoping he isn't missing you, isn't crying out for you?"

Robbie said nothing but stepped forward and took her in his arms. Caught off guard, Esther submitted to his embrace, not caring that he was soaking wet. He smelled of tobacco, earth, and salt, a comforting mix that enveloped her, made her feel unaccountably safe. She found herself clinging to him, reveling in the strong feel of his shoulders beneath her hands. It had been months since John had touched her, and even longer since she had felt desire for anything or anyone. Its sudden flare, sending heat coursing through her and causing her to turn her lips toward his, took her by surprise. As their lips met, she came to her senses, jerking herself away violently and turning to run back up to the house before her wayward body could betray her any further, before Robbie had a chance to say anything.

Chapter Twenty-four
Little Embers, Spring 2018

Leah handed Rachel a rolled-up ball of socks. "There are a few pairs of boots by the front door. They'll likely be too big, and some of them have been here since before I arrived, so the rubber might have perished, but it's the best I can offer I'm afraid. Not that you should be going out today though."

Rachel bit her lip and allowed herself to be told what to do. She was a guest of Leah's, she reminded herself.

Leah watched her struggle, one-handed, with a sock and then knelt down in front of her. "Here, let me."

Rachel felt momentarily embarrassed that an almost-complete stranger was putting socks on her bare feet, something even her mother hadn't done since she was little, but she relinquished them and let Leah slide each one on. They were huge, and sagged around her ankles, but they would keep her feet warm.

"Breakfast is ready. Porridge. I usually eat in the kitchen, but it's warmer in here so I'll fetch yours for you."

Rachel didn't even have time to mutter a thank you before Leah left the room. She eyed the suitcase again. She was itching to see what the letters contained but didn't know how long Leah would be gone.

"Like I said, I'm all out of sugar until Tom comes again," Leah said when she returned after only a few minutes, setting a tray on Rachel's lap. Rachel looked at the steaming bowl of oats and milk and took a tentative spoonful.

"It's delicious," she said, and to her surprise it was. Rich and creamy and just a hint of salt. She wolfed it down and looked up to find Leah watching her with the barest twitch of her lips.

"More?"

She nodded. "Yes please."

After breakfast, Leah disappeared, the back door that led from the kitchen slamming shut behind her. Rachel reckoned on her being gone for a fair while: she remembered Leah had mentioned a number of chores to be done every morning about the place, so as soon as she'd left, Rachel shuffled forward on the sofa and reached into the suitcase again. Her fingers closed on the book and she pulled it out from under the clothes, placing it beside her on the sofa. She rested her elbow on one of the envelopes and used her good hand to pull out the pages it contained. They had been folded in half, and she carefully smoothed them flat. "*My darling E. . . .*" it began. She glanced at the top of the sheet. "August 1952," she said aloud. Hoo-eee. The letter had been written more than sixty years ago. After the Second World War. Before the Vietnam War. Before man landed on the moon. Before the fall of the Berlin Wall. Before mobile phones. Before the internet.

When her mind had stopped boggling she read on. "*I count the days since you left, and wonder how it can be that the sun still rises and falls, that your heart beats so far away from mine. I am filled with despair when I wake and know that I will not see your secret smile, the one I like to imagine that you reserve only for me, that I will not hear your laugh, walk with you to the jetty or the beach, never wrap my arm around your waist again. Your absence tears at me until I can no longer breathe and I scarcely have the strength to get up every morning. It is only by writing that I feel you anywhere nearby, even though I know you are far away from here. I am bound by the (mis)fortune of loving you until the end of my days. My only solace is in writing these letters to you, for they bring me closer, as if you were here beside me once more, if only for the time I spend writing them.*"

Rachel had never been a great believer in romance, but something in these words moved her. How wonderful—and heartbreaking—to be so loved and so lost. She read on.

"*I tell myself that you cannot be missing me half as much as I do you, and I am happy that you do not feel the same agony as I do, for I would not wish that for you in all the world, my dearest. My fervent hope is that you therefore think of me only occasionally, but always fondly, and that your life will be a joyful one.*"

Rachel's heart twisted.

"*It is the season of shooting stars here, and I had so hoped to watch them with you. Great showers of light are spread across the night sky and I imagine them as a spangled bouquet in tribute to your beauty. I wonder if you can see them from where you are?*"

Rachel liked the idea of watching meteor showers with someone you loved. She'd seen them when she was living on Aitutaki, and had indeed been entwined in the arms of her then lover, but she wasn't sure she'd ever been *in love*. Certainly not in the desperate, all-consuming way this writer was.

She carried on reading. The letter told of daily walks, collecting clams, of the way the sun caught the water and reminded him of the light in E's eyes. At the bottom, the letter "R" as a sign-off, the curve of it finished with a flourish.

She was taken aback. Who could have written such a heartfelt, soul-baring missive, licked the stamps on the envelope even, and then not bothered to send it?

She'd never imagined the kind of love that the writer of this letter felt, had never wanted to be so beholden, so dependent on another for happiness. What would it be like to be the object of someone's unwavering adoration: would she feel cherished or claustrophobic?

She opened the next envelope. This letter was dated July 1952. "*My dearest E. . . .*" it began again. "*Another month has passed since you left and though I do my best to keep my spirits up, I must confess that your absence haunts me still. There is a hole where my heart once was, as if a cannon had been shot clean through me. It is a terrible irony that I fear missing you will send me mad.*"

Rachel read on, wondering if the intended recipient was a man or a woman, deciding that it must have been a woman as she read: "*I dream of your tender lips and creamy skin but every morning awake to find my heart cut out once more. I enter empty rooms and imagine the smell of your perfume in their quiet corners. I breathe it in from the clothes you left behind—please don't think me strange for that, for it is all I have. They taunt me with your absence. The memories of our days together, and these, for now, sustain me. Know that I hold you in the highest regard, and will do so always, no matter what fate may have in store for us."*

She read through the next three letters, one dated May, then June and September. May, the first letter, told of the writer's shock at the departure of E, of their desolation at being without her, and how after only a few short months of knowing E, the writer could no longer comprehend a world without her in it.

One remained. October. It began in the same manner as the previous five, addressed to "Dearest E," but consisted of only a single sheet of flimsy paper.

"I cannot continue," the bald typed words said. *"I am the bearer of too great a grief and there is only one way I can release myself of this burden."*

Rachel found herself caught up in the story now. What did the writer mean to do? As she was pondering the letter writer's fate, the door slammed. Leah was back. She hastily gathered the letters and tucked them between the pages of the book, lying back and pretending to read the novel just in case she came in.

She held her breath. A second slam of the door

meant that Leah must have found what she'd come in for and gone out again. She sat up, reached for the final letter, and continued reading. "*I shall write no more. I must put you out of my mind, for it is the only way. Of course, you came to this sensible conclusion far sooner than I. We can never be. Our lives must—and do—go on, but separately, and I must make the best of it, not wallow in grief. Know that not a day will go by that I will not think of you. My darling, my heart will be forever yours. I like to think that someday you might read these words and understand. R.*"

Who was this E. Durrant of Hampstead, and who, here on this island, had been writing to her? And why had the letters never been sent, but were instead tucked away in a suitcase full of clothes? Rachel let the paper rest against the blanket and pondered the possibilities. She felt suddenly melancholy, infected by the lost hope of the last letter.

Seized by a sudden urge to get off the sofa and away from the cloying sadness, she stood up, folding the final letter between the pages of the book with the others, returning them to the suitcase and closing the lid. It was time to explore the rest of the house. Perhaps it might yield further clues?

Rachel tiptoed along a narrow flagstoned hallway, past the bathroom and the stairs—the upper floor was where Leah's studio was and where, presumably, she also slept—and through to the kitchen at the back of the house. This was as chaotic as the sitting room. A large dresser was heaped with what looked to be mostly junk: fishing reels, an old flowerpot, scissors, a couple of hardback books, jam jars filled with an assortment of nails, an array of mismatched china stacked in teetering piles . . . Their breakfast things sat in the sink, the porridge pan soaking in water. Rachel spied a kettle to one side of a wood-burning range and other cooking utensils hung from a pole suspended from the ceiling. There was no sign of a fridge, or toaster, or any other of the usual modern conveniences, but then that was hardly surprising as the island wasn't connected to the electricity grid. She was struck again by how isolated it was.

It would be a long five days before she could return to St. Mary's, though at least Leah didn't seem too unwelcoming, nor especially loony, despite what Jonah had told her. A little bossy and rather remote, but then who wouldn't be, living by themselves for years on end?

Leah reappeared briefly at lunchtime and cut a few slices from a loaf of bread and a hunk of cheese, taking it up to her studio, indicating with the minimum amount of words that Rachel could help herself to whatever she found.

After chewing on a slice of bread, Rachel spent a good part of the afternoon sleeping, but then as the sky began to darken, got up and made herself useful in the kitchen, finding boxes of pasta and canned tuna in the pantry, cheese and milk in a kind of cool store fronted with chicken wire. She'd managed to open the boxes and cook one-handed without having to call for assistance, though it had been more of a challenge than she expected and by the time she had finished she was quite exhausted. As she was doing her best to clean up, Leah had emerged once more, hands covered in paint, another layer of dark green and white flecks on her sweater and a streak of carmine through her long auburn hair.

"What flowers are they?" Rachel asked as Leah cleared the table of some of its detritus and placed a jug containing a few sprigs of a prickly yellow-flowered plant. Rachel knew a great deal about biology, but considerably less about botany, particularly European species.

"Gorse. *Ulex europaeus.* Supposed to represent the darker qualities one needs to survive the journey of life, to give you the energy you might need to make difficult decisions. In Scotland it's associated with the Cailleach, the Divine Hag, or the spirit of winter."

"Oh," said Rachel. "Right. The spirit of winter." She'd only asked its name.

"It's also not bad in gin," said Leah, with a cackling laugh.

"So what brought you to Embers?" asked Rachel as they sat down to eat.

"Pretty bloody direct, you Aussies, aren't you?" said Leah through a mouthful of pasta. "If you must know, I'd been living in the Highlands of Scotland. But it was too bloody cold there in winter, even for me, so I started looking for somewhere down south. A friend of mine knows the leaseholder of this island, a doctor, I believe, and he let me have it on the condition that I keep the place from completely going to wrack and ruin."

"But why an island? And you the only inhabitant?"

"That way I'm in control, you see. I get to decide who comes, and mostly it's no one, which is just fine."

"Unless they shipwreck themselves on your doorstep," Rachel said wryly.

"Yes, well there is that unforeseen interruption."

Rachel couldn't imagine why anyone would want to be so cut off from the world, entirely on their own, the only company a cow and a few chickens. Yes, she'd lived in some pretty remote places, but there had always been other people around. "Don't you miss things?"

"Like what?"

"I don't know . . . conversation, someone to share a sunrise or sunset with, the occasional glass of wine . . ."

"Don't really drink," Leah said bluntly, cleaning her plate with a slice of bread. "Not bad having another cook around the place for a change though."

That was the most thanks Rachel was going to get for dinner.

Chapter Twenty-five
Little Embers, Autumn 1951

Richard, who was making notes at his desk, glanced up to see Esther flying up the path from the boat, her arms dangling at her sides like a loose-jointed marionette, a stricken expression on her face. He put down his pen and went to meet her, catching her as she arrived at the front door. He had been anticipating this. He'd seen the alacrity with which she volunteered to meet the weekly boat and guessed that she was waiting for news from her husband.

"It's all right," he said, holding up a warning hand and standing in her way. "It's all right, Esther," he repeated. "Why don't we go inside and talk about it?"

Esther went to move past him, shaking her head, refusing to speak to him, but he stepped to one side, preventing her escape. "I think I know what's going on."

He steered her into the drawing room and she looked up at him, her eyes a stormy violet. "I don't know that you do."

He blinked to keep his focus. "You had a letter from John. Am I correct?"

She nodded.

"And he is telling you that it is best if you stay here for the time being."

"How do you know?"

"Because I advised him before he left that it would take some time before you were truly well again, no matter what you might communicate to him."

She narrowed her eyes, scowling at him. "I see. Clearly you both know better than I what is best for me. You collude with each other; I should have known." Agitated, she turned away from him, her fists clenched by her side and her whole body quivering.

"Come on now, Esther. We are all on the same side here. John cares deeply about you and I'm here to help you, if you'll let me."

There was silence and then the fight went out of her, her shoulders slumping. "I suppose you are."

He closed the door and indicated that she should

take her customary seat opposite him. It was time to broach the subject that they had been skirting since her arrival.

"Do you blame yourself for what happened?" he asked once they were settled.

"What do you mean?"

"For what happened to Samuel?" It was the first time he had mentioned the baby by name.

She hesitated, but then began to speak. "He died," she said in a flat tone. "And yes, of course I am to blame. I was his mother; I should have known that something was wrong, very wrong."

"Why don't you tell me exactly what happened?" he said gently. "You have to tell someone, at some point. Why not me? I shall not think any less of you, that I can promise."

She took a deep breath and gripped the edge of the chair, her knuckles white against its dark green fabric. Richard could see that she was battling to control the pain she held folded inside herself. "You can trust me, Esther, always," he reassured her. "You can trust me with anything."

She looked at him, blinked several times, and then began to speak, her voice quavering with barely suppressed emotion. "He was only six weeks old. He'd had a bit of a sniffle and been fussing, but he took my milk and settled quickly when I put him down to sleep." She stared out of the window. He followed her gaze and saw Robbie coming up the path with the cart.

"Go on."

"He slept through. I'd not had a full night's sleep in weeks—I insisted that Nanny wake me for all of Samuel's feeds—and I was exhausted. When I woke early, I knew immediately that something was wrong. The house was quiet, too quiet. He'd never slept through the night before. I got up and ran to his room—it was at the other end of the corridor from ours—and went to his bassinet." She gave a sharp sob. "He was so cold. Like marble. Teddy was there—he'd been trying to wake his baby brother, and it was all I could do not to scream and frighten him. Nanny came as soon as she heard me talking to Teddy. Together we tried to revive him, to blow our breath into his lungs, but it was too late. Too bloody late." She fixed her gaze on the rug between them. "After that nothing really mattered anymore; there didn't seem to be any point in getting out of bed in the morning, carrying on. Any point in anything actually."

Richard reached for her hand, to offer what comfort he could. "Thank you for trusting me with that, Esther, but I must confess that I don't understand why you blame yourself."

"Don't you see? I should have known. I should have stayed awake; I had an inkling that something was not quite right, but I ignored it in favor of my own sleep. How could I have been so selfish? A terrible, selfish human being, not fit to be a mother."

She raised her eyes to meet his, and he nearly lost himself in their depths. He could feel the pain that shimmered from her and it was all he could do not to take it on himself. Why did this woman affect him in a way that no other patient had? "It's so desperately sad to lose a child. But you should not blame yourself. No one blames you, Esther."

"Oh," she said with a bitter laugh. "I think John does. He's not been the same with me since then."

"You've both suffered a great loss; it's not surprising that things are different between you. But I know he does not blame you—he would not have gone to the trouble of sending you here if he did, surely you can see that?"

"He wants to be rid of me, can't stand me the way I am now, I am sure of it. I've tried, believe me I've tried, for Teddy's sake, but I'm in a hole so unfathomably deep I can't seem to see a way out of it. I don't think I'll ever be the person I once was. Happy, carefree." She gave him a wry smile. "I don't deserve to be."

"Yes you do, Esther, and that's what I'm here for. Together we can do this. I am good at my job."

"I don't doubt it," she said softly.

"Good, then we have a basis on which to start. Why don't you tell me what happened after you discovered your baby had died? I know it is painful, but it will help to talk about it."

Esther's mouth worked, as if she were deciding where to begin. "John woke up and saw us trying to save Samuel. He ran down the stairs to the telephone to call an ambulance. I heard wailing, almost like an animal in pain; it was a while before I realized that it was me. I couldn't seem to shut myself up. I held Samuel, wouldn't, couldn't let him go. John was downstairs waiting for the ambulance. It was an age before anyone came, but then I remember someone prying my arms from Samuel's body. John had called our doctor too, and I remember a syringe, and then . . . nothing." She took a sharp intake of breath. "They must have taken him away from me. I still don't know where he went. I never saw him again, never even got to say good-bye." She twisted her hands on the chair. "There wasn't a burial and I was in too much of a fog to ask why not. It was only later that John told me they had taken his body to the hospital. To see if they could find out what had happened to him. He let them do that, to his own son!" She spat the words out. "They never gave him back."

"Oh, Esther, I'm sorry," he said. Hearing her tell the story, even though John had told him some of it already, made his heart ache for her.

"There's no grave, no way of sending his soul to heaven, no way of telling him how sorry I was, how I had let him down, that it was all my fault, that I hadn't loved him as a mother should."

"What do you mean by that? You cared for him, did you not?"

Esther slumped. "In the sense of seeing to his needs, yes."

Richard watched her carefully. There was still something she was keeping hidden. He hoped that she would reveal it, given time.

"You have every right to be as angry as you are," he said. "No one should be denied the chance to say farewell to their child."

"I . . ." She hesitated. "I began to wonder if I had in fact gone completely mad. I couldn't think clearly, everything was as hazy as the London air, I had trouble remembering even the simplest things." She gave a shuddering sigh. "Am I? Mad?"

"No, Esther, I don't think you're mad, or bad . . . just terribly sad, that's all."

"Sometimes it seems as if it's all I can think about; I can't get out of my own head. Does that make any sense?"

He nodded. "Yes, it does. We all have to battle demons from time to time—and the ones of our own making are the most fearsome adversaries. But I can reassure you that it will pass. This isn't the way things will always be."

"Is that a promise?" She didn't sound as if she believed him.

"It is. It'll be all right in the end."

"How do you know?" Her eyes flashed at him. "How can you say that with such confidence?"

"I have faith in you, Esther. You are stronger than this. It will not beat you." He spoke more forcefully than he had intended. Had he really raised his voice? He had wanted to shock her out of her self-doubt. He couldn't remember the last time he had lost his cool, but Esther affected him in a way no other patient had. It would not do, he needed to regain control of himself.

"You may well go on to have other children. Life will be whole again," he insisted.

"No," she said. "Never. I shall never have another child. What if . . . ? What if the same thing happened again? I could not bear it. No. I do not deserve to be a mother."

She was beginning to get worked up once more, tapping her foot in agitation against the floor, her leg jerking and shaking. "All in good time, Esther. Do not trouble yourself with such thoughts." His voice had returned to its normal volume. "Shall we stop now, listen to some music perhaps? It might help."

"All right," she said eventually. "But not the bloody Vaughan Williams again."

"I thought you liked it?"

"I do, but that doesn't mean I want to hear it all the time."

He chuckled, pleased that even in this moment she was able to jest with him. "Indeed. Let's try something different then." He stood up and went over to the gramophone, riffling through the LPs stacked on the shelf beside it. He selected one and placed the needle on the record. Immediately, a smoky-sweet sound filled the room. "I'll Get By."

Esther gave the ghost of a smile and began to sing along, a husky alto, and Richard knew that it was a sound he would remember forever.

Chapter Twenty-six
Little Embers, Spring 2018

Rachel elected to sleep on the couch again. The rest of the house was arctic and she hadn't fully recovered from her near-drowning; her bones still held the water's chill.

Leah had found some sheets and as she shook them out the smell of lavender wafted toward her. She wondered briefly if that was the perfume that the letter writer referred to before reminding herself that the scent would hardly last for more than fifty years. There was a pillowcase for the lumpy pillow, a thick down-filled quilt, and the blanket she'd used the previous night. Before retiring, Leah stoked the fire, adding a couple more logs. "That should stay in till morning." Their conversation over dinner hadn't been exactly sparkling, but now she was even more parsimonious with her words and Rachel decided against mentioning the letters she'd found, at least for the time being.

She went to the bathroom and washed herself as best she could with one hand. The water was icy and she was as quick as she could manage, taking just enough time to rinse her face and rub a finger over her teeth, which were by now feeling decidedly furry. Leah had left her the packet of painkillers and she chugged back another two of them with a mouthful of water. Her wrist had begun to ache again.

"See you in the morning," Leah said as she reappeared in the doorway. She kept early hours then.

"Sure thing." Rachel had napped earlier and wasn't particularly tired, so once Leah had left she pulled out the book that had been in the suitcase and settled herself on her makeshift bed. A candle gave just enough light to read by. Propping the book on her knees, she turned the first page, reading the inscription. "*For my dear Esther. Christmas 1951.*" Esther must be the "E" to whom the letters were written. Esther Durrant: the name was familiar somehow, hooking a memory that for the moment eluded her.

Did the letter writer give Esther the book as well, the year before?

As Rachel turned the pages, a small square black-and-white photograph fell out. She held it up and saw that it was of a group of men and women. They were bundled up in coats and hats and standing in front of a stone house—the same one she was now staying in, she realized with a shock. She flipped the photo over to see if there was anything written on the back. "*February 1952.*"

One of the women was wearing a cloche hat and a coat with a thick round collar. It was the same as the hat and coat in the suitcase. Was this Esther perhaps? She pored over the image, but it was indistinct and grainy.

She couldn't shake the nagging feeling that she was intruding on someone else's life. She felt like an interloper: wearing the woman's clothes, reading letters written to her—love letters no less—and now, judging by the well-thumbed pages, reading what must have been one of her favorite books. She scanned the faces of the men and women in the photo: was one of these the person who was in love with Esther, the person who had written the letters, or was it someone else? What had they all been doing here? Was it a holiday? If it had been summer, she might have suspected that, but in winter? Somehow they didn't look like close friends—their body positions were awkward and each was standing just a little separately from the next. There were no arms slung casually around each other's shoulders, no sisterly encircling of the waist. True, one of the men was resting a hand on the shoulder of another, but it looked awkward somehow. The picture was certainly very different from the selfies that everyone took these days. After a while, she put the photograph down and returned to the book.

The house was quiet. She'd seen a grandfather clock in the hallway, but it no longer tick-tocked away the seconds or sounded the hours. It had stopped at a quarter to twelve, but who knew when—it could have been months ago, but was more likely years. Leah apparently had little use for timepieces. But then why would you, when the rising and setting of the sun told you all you needed to know?

The scrape of the pages as she turned them and her steady breathing were the only sounds and they helped to quiet the chatter in her mind. After a while, her eyelids began to drift downward and she was almost asleep before she suddenly jerked awake. She had forgotten the candle. It could be disastrous to leave it burning. She sat up awkwardly and blew it out. Smoke curled up toward the ceiling and the smell of the molten wax reminded her of long-ago birthday parties. She felt an unexpected pang of homesickness. Wondered what her mum and dad might be doing right at that moment. She vowed to call them as soon as she got back to St. Mary's. Wouldn't go into detail about her misadventures though—she didn't want them to worry about her.

It was pitch dark when Rachel woke again. She was certain she'd heard a noise and lay completely still, her heart pounding as she listened hard.

Nothing.

She moved her hand across her pillow and encountered dampness. She blinked. Her eyelashes were wet. The full force of her dream came rushing back to her. She'd been struggling against something that had her in its grip. She was searching for something, something that meant a great deal to her, that she longed for, but now that she was awake again she couldn't figure out what it was. A line from one of the letters floated back to her: "*there is a hole where my heart once was.*" She let out an involuntary sob while at the same time scarcely believing that she was crying over a few sixty-plus-year-old letters. Blinking rapidly to stanch the tears that were threatening to brim over once more, she gave herself a stern talking-to. Rachel Parker didn't cry over nothing. Certainly not over people she'd never even met. What was wrong with her? Had a near drowning had more of an effect than she thought?

She closed her eyes and tried to dismiss her fanciful imaginings, telling herself it was nothing more than delayed shock, but they swirled around in her brain, giving her no peace. As she was on the point of falling asleep, the thought occurred to her that she had spent her whole life avoiding the kind of connection that the letters told of so poignantly.

When Rachel woke late the next morning, it appeared that Leah was long gone, judging by the lukewarm porridge she found in the pan in the kitchen. She helped herself to what was left and contemplated the bandage on her wrist. Her natural inclination was to remove it and take a look. It no longer ached so fiercely if she kept it absolutely still, but the slightest movement and she recoiled in agony, gritting her teeth to keep from yelling out. Realizing that if she took the bandage off she would never be able to wrap it up again, she decided against it. Seeing what her wrist looked like wouldn't change anything. Perhaps there was a way to bind it to her, stop herself from knocking it?

She remembered seeing a scarf in the suitcase and sure enough, tucked away in an elasticized pocket on the side of the case was a large olive-green and brown satin square. Try as she might though, she was unable to tie it in a knot to make a sling. She needed Leah's help.

After the laborious process of getting herself dressed,

Rachel pushed her feet into a pair of oversize boots that lay abandoned at the front door and went in search of her rescuer.

She tramped around to the back of the house, being careful not to trip in the too-big boots and found an old orchard, trees with wizened apples hanging from their branches. To one side, a few chickens scratched at the scrubby grass and she could see a brown-and-cream–colored cow in the pasture beyond standing in front of a ramshackle stone building.

She shivered as a gust of wind blew off the ocean. "Hey . . . ," she called. "Leah!"

There was no answer aside from a deep baritone "moo" from the cow. She went over and watched her mulch grass between her rubbery lips, grinding the green pulp in a continuous, ruminant cycle. "Margaret, old girl. Any sign of your mistress?" she asked.

The cow continued chewing, completely ignoring Rachel.

"Thought so." Rachel was just about to turn back to the house when a flash of something red in the long grass at the side of the cow shed caught her eye. She moved closer for a better look: a spade, rusted and disintegrating at the edges, the wooden handle thick and splintered. She stepped away and the toe of her boot encountered a solid object. She glanced down. A bottle.

In fact, she saw as she went closer, probably more than fifty of them, hidden by the overgrown greenery that snaked its way up the brick wall. Their labels were torn, faded, gin and possibly vodka judging by the shape and color of the bottles. All empty.

Having found no sign of Leah in the immediate vicinity of the house, Rachel took a narrow path that led toward the beach, being careful not to jostle her arm too much. She felt the sand crunch under her boots and noticed small wavelets rippling toward the shore. She recognized the shoal of rocks on which she'd foundered during the storm and shuddered at the memory. A brace of gulls screeched and carried on, squabbling over the bloated carcass of a fish.

She scanned the water in the vain hope that she might spy a passing boat, but water traffic was rare this far out among the islands and the ocean remained resolutely empty. To her left was an old wooden jetty; a figure was sitting at the end of it wearing an old raincoat and holding a fishing rod.

As Rachel walked toward her, Leah turned around, a finger to her lips. "Quiet, or you'll disturb the fish."

"Okay," she whispered back, treading carefully now. "I was wondering if you might be able to tie this in a sling for me," she said as she reached her, holding out the scarf.

Leah grunted but put the rod down on the jetty and got slowly to her feet. Rachel pulled her hair to one side while Leah folded the scarf into a triangle and wrapped it around her neck, tying the two ends in a firm knot. Up close, Rachel could see the deep grooves on either side of her mouth and the crow's feet that fanned from her eyes. She'd initially put Leah at about mid to late forties, but exposure to the elements could have made her look older than she was. She was certainly weathered, though that, contrary to Leah's earlier statement, might have been as much from booze as the passage of time.

"Thanks," she said when Leah had finished. "That's a big improvement."

"No bother." Leah returned to her fishing.

"Caught anything?" Rachel asked.

"Not yet." Her back was still turned away.

Not exactly in the mood for a chat again. "Okay, well, I'll see you later then."

Another grunt.

Rachel retraced her steps along the jetty and wondered what to do with herself. She wasn't used to being inactive and unproductive. There was always the book to return to, but she'd had enough of being stuck indoors and the prospect of exploring the island was more appealing, so she turned right when she reached the sand and began to walk along the beach. The sand was fine and white as sugar and littered with seashells. She picked up several particularly fine *Trivia arctica*—cowrie shells ridged like gnocchi on their undersides—that were hidden amid dark tranches of dried seaweed. The sharp, sour smell of iodine and salt prickled her nose and made her feel at home. A couple of seagulls pecked at the weed, flying off as she approached, complaining in noisy squawks at being disturbed.

When the beach came to an end she scrambled up a rocky bluff, stumbling as she almost lost her balance. By the time she reached the top she was completely out of breath, but the views, across the whole island and out to sea, were astonishing. It was a clear day and she could see the other islands in the group, small treeless hummocks on the horizon separated by a silver-blue ocean. Their presence brought her some comfort and reminded her that she would, in a few days' time, be back on St. Mary's, safely at Shearwater Cottage.

She continued, forcing her way through swaths of rusty bracken and brambles that tore at her borrowed trousers, snagging the fine wool. Reaching a low, lichen-covered drystone wall, she saw the ruins of a couple of old cottages, heaping piles of limpet shells nearby. They looked desolate, empty and hollow. At the first one, the door hung on one hinge and she tentatively pushed it open. She nearly jumped out of her skin as something fluttered inside and a large blackbird flew out, just missing her ear. The air was dank and musty. There were two rooms and when she went into the second, which was furnished with an old metal bed frame and a torn and stained mattress, the hair on the back of her neck stood up. All of a sudden she felt as if the wind had been knocked out of her; she couldn't breathe. She stumbled out of the house, taking deep lungfuls of clean air as she emerged. She wasn't tempted to enter the second cottage.

Deciding she had done enough exploring for one day, she walked back in the direction of the main house, leaving the bracken behind and passing bright yellow gorse and banks of heather. She eventually found herself on the far side of the orchard and plowed her way through the long grass in between the old apple trees. The temperature here was cooler than out in the open and her skin prickled again, as it had at the old cottage. There were the beginnings of blisters on her heels from the borrowed boots, and her wrist, even though it was resting against her chest in the sling, was starting to ache again. Fighting the feeling that she was being watched, she hurried to the back of the house, kicking off her boots at the door before going inside.

Leah was in the kitchen when she got back, and was holding something. Rachel recognized it immediately. Her camera. Bulky in its waterproof housing.

"Oh my God!"

Leah gave her a grudging smile as she reached for it. "Found it washed up by the tide as I was on my way back from the beach."

"That's wonderful, thank you." Rachel checked it over. It was intact, undamaged by its watery adventure. The camera had been a graduation gift from her parents more than a decade before and she was delighted to have it returned to her. She had assumed it was gone forever.

"I don't suppose there was anything else?" she asked, ever the optimist. "No sign of my boat?"

Leah shook her head.

Even though she knew the answer, Rachel felt disappointment curdle in her stomach, followed closely by hope that someone—Jonah if she was truthful—might by now have noticed the boat missing and would come looking for her, then guilt as she thought of the time they would spend searching, the worry she might have caused. She kicked herself for her impetuousness once more and wondered exactly how she was going to break the news to Dr. Wentworth of the delay to the project, not to mention the abandoned boat.

"Lunch?" Leah interrupted her thoughts.

"Yes please. Can I do anything to help?"

"All under control."

There was a large stockpot of water boiling on the stove and Leah held up a basket that contained a couple of fair-sized khaki-green lobsters. "We've got ourselves a feast." She looked pleased with herself.

When the crustaceans were ready, scarlet and steaming on a plate, Leah cracked the shells with an old hammer and they dove in. She thoughtfully cracked most of the shells, so that it was easy for Rachel to get at the meat one-handed. The lobster was possibly the best Rachel had ever tasted: sweet and juicy, and they dipped it in melted butter as they ate. She groaned when they had finished, her stomach full.

"Not bad," said Leah, butter glistening on her chin.

"We have this great dish at home that my mum sometimes makes—chilli mud crab—until now I'd thought it was the best way to eat shellfish, but this is incredible," Rachel said.

While they were eating, Rachel—who was an inveterate observer of things and also people—had been studying Leah covertly, looking for signs that years of boozing might have left. But her eyes were clear and her hands steady. Perhaps she'd given up, as she'd said earlier? Either way, Rachel knew better than to mention the empty bottles by the cow shed.

She was still wondering about it when Leah looked at her and Rachel colored, aware that she'd been caught staring. "What did you run away from?" Rachel blurted out before she could censor herself.

Leah looked at her in astonishment, as if she hadn't heard her correctly. "Curiosity killed the cat, you know," she said.

"Good thing cats have nine lives," Rachel shot back.

Leah hesitated and then roared with laughter. "Who said I was running away from anything?" she asked, wiping a tear of mirth from her cheek. "Perhaps I was running toward something."

Leah stood up abruptly, her empty plate in her hands, and Rachel knew she wouldn't get more of an answer from her than that.

After lunch, Leah went to her studio and Rachel was left to her own devices once more. Her frustration at being stranded was growing, more so for not being able to communicate or get on with her work than the actual isolation of the island. She relished her own company, but when there was nothing to occupy her, time dragged.

She decided to reread the letters. On her walk that morning, the words had kept returning to her, echoing in her head as her mind tried to guess at the story behind them. She had thoroughly searched the suitcase the previous day, even going so far as to pat down the lining in case anything had been slipped inside, but there were no more clues to be found.

She retrieved the envelopes from the book and spread them out again. Six of them. And then, nothing. They spoke of a love unlike anything Rachel had ever known. Did it really burn that fiercely? And why had they never been sent? Would the two people concerned both still be alive? She desperately wanted to know and it began to dawn on her that she wasn't going to be able to leave the matter unresolved. She still hadn't decided whether or not to mention the letters to Leah. Their friendship—if you could even call it that—was a tentative one, forced by circumstances and Rachel had no idea what Leah's reaction to the letters might be. She wanted the chance to find out more before raising the subject.

She stood up and paced about the small living room, running her hands along the backs of the old-fashioned olive-green armchairs and nearly tripping on the holed, faded rug. The place looked as if it hadn't been touched for years and a thought suddenly struck her: perhaps it might be hiding other secrets? Over in one corner was a gramophone of a type that she recognized from black-and-white movies and she looked at it curiously, wondering if it still worked. On a shelf nearby was a dust-laden stack of old records, their sleeves faded and torn in places. She picked one at random, slid it out of its paper covering, and placed it on the turntable.

She found a handle on the side and cranked it carefully. She wasn't sure how she knew, but she remembered that you had to place the needle onto the record and she lifted it, balancing it carefully on one finger. A hiss of static and a crackle and then the music floated over her, filling the ruined house with sound. She stood and listened for a while, transported back to a sultry afternoon in the school music room, where the sound of the violins competed with the cicadas outside, and the high notes roused a yearning in her for something that she couldn't put her finger on. The record finished and she shook her head to clear the feeling.

She glanced about the rest of the room. Below the shelves was a cabinet with a carved facade and two wrought-iron handles. She tried one and then the other. They didn't budge. She cast about looking for any sign of a key. It would be almost impossible to find in this room, drowning as it was in curios, books, and papers, but she looked anyway, peering behind the sofa, feeling between the cushions, on the bookshelves, in various small lidded pots, in ashtrays, underneath a tarnished brass ship's bell . . . Aha! There was something underneath the bell. A small iron key with a silk tassel looped around it.

The key slipped into the lock as if it had been kept well oiled, and the doors swung open. Unlike the rest of the cluttered room, there was only one object inside. A slim catalog. The words *Leah Gill: Recent Works* stamped in gold on the front.

It didn't look like there were going to be any clues about Esther and her mysterious lover in the cupboard, but her heart skipped a beat nonetheless.

Chapter Twenty-seven
Little Embers, Autumn 1951

At supper that night, Esther made a limited contribution to the conversation and avoided discourse with Robbie in particular. He gave no indication to her, or the others, that anything untoward had occurred, though he too appeared quieter than usual. She was embarrassed and ashamed of her actions down on the jetty, but was at a loss as to how to broach the subject with him. He had only been trying to comfort her, but she had taken advantage of that for reasons she couldn't begin to fathom. The memory of it swirled around in her head, making it pound and forcing her to pinch the bridge of her nose at the pain. As soon as she finished eating, she excused herself from the table with a genuine headache.

Later, she went in search of Jean. She had something to ask her.

She came across the nurse in the doctor's study, tidying papers and files that he had left strewn over his desk. "I wonder if I might have a word?" Esther said.

Jean straightened up to face her. "Of course. What can I do for you, Mrs. Durrant?"

"Well, I–er . . ." Esther hated the groveling tone in her voice but pressed on. "I wonder if you might be able to give me something . . . something for my nerves. I didn't want to bother the doctor, you see. I thought you might be able to help."

"I see."

"Yes, I've run out. Damned nuisance, I know."

"Unfortunately, Mrs. Durrant, we have no such medicines on the island." Her tone brooked no argument.

"Oh, I see. Very well then. Thank you." Hiding her shame at having had to ask, Esther retreated to her room, cursing herself for having swallowed her pills like sweets when she had first arrived, and cursing John again for abandoning her in such a far-flung, desperate place. She knew, deep down, that he had likely only been doing his best for her, but it didn't make things any easier.

Mrs. Biggs had laid a fire and left a hot water bottle under the sheets and this small act comforted her. She lay down, holding Teddy's cap against her cheek and closed her eyes, remembering the way her son's hair shone like spun gold as it caught the light, the pearls of his teeth that were revealed when something pleased him. For once the nightmares kept themselves at bay.

Rising early the next morning, she dressed swiftly, stepping into houndstooth-check trousers and a wool twinset. After the previous day's conversation with the doctor, she felt clear-headed. It had felt good to finally tell someone, though she pushed down the knowledge that she hadn't recounted the full story. Some of the burden she had been carrying seemed miraculously to have been lifted, however, and she was anxious to do something useful. She had been wallowing in self-pity for too long and it was time to make amends, however small. She would seek out Robbie and apologize to him as soon as she had an opportunity.

The tide would be out and clamming was one of the few activities she could think of to occupy herself with, for the garden was as thoroughly weeded as it could ever be. The last time they'd collected clams, Mrs. Biggs had steamed them with some cream and parsley and they had been as delicious as promised. She tiptoed downstairs, pulled on a jacket and boots and took the shovel and bucket from their place just inside the front door. There was enough light to guide her footsteps without mishap and she was down at the beach, watching as the day—destined to be a bright, clear one by the looks of things—began. The sun was barely up, with only a thin orange visible at the horizon and she stood for the best part of an hour, enjoying the expanding, crystalline light, the gentle suck of the sea and the solitude. The dawn held so much promise; a fresh page on which to make a mark, the blots of the previous day washed away. She felt more like herself than she had in months. A growing regard for the doctor hovered on the edges of her consciousness, but she deliberately pushed away the thought of the warmth that bloomed inside her whenever they spent time together. Nevertheless, she found herself thinking of him in idle moments, even now, wondering . . .

"I say! Is that you, Mrs. Durrant?" A voice rang out across the beach and carried toward her. His shout took Esther by surprise and she started, looking up to see Wilkie bearing down on her. He carried a large tripod under one arm, a camera in his other hand, lurching from side to side as he covered the uneven ground.

She straightened and waved at him, pausing in her collecting as he came closer.

"You're up early," he said, huffing with the effort of carrying the camera equipment over the uneven ground.

"Getting some clams in before the tide comes up."

He grunted. "Good idea. Thought the light might be a cracker for some photos. I say, would you mind if I took your picture?"

Self-conscious, she tucked an errant strand of hair behind her ear. "I'm hardly presentable," she protested, crossing her arms and looking down at the trousers that she'd stuffed into a too-large pair of Wellingtons.

"Nonsense," he said. "Dead ringer for Katharine Hepburn according to Robbie. And he knows his actresses."

Esther colored, wondering what exactly they'd been saying about her.

"I won't take no for an answer," he continued. "Just let me set her up. You keep on digging; I'll get one of you in action."

She turned back to face the shore, glad of something to do. Esther had never been one to enjoy posing for photos, even as a girl. Her wedding picture, showing a more carefree young woman framed in silver, rested on the piano at home. It was a rare portrait.

She sliced the edge of the shovel into the sand, placed her foot on its shoulder, and stepped down hard, then leaned back to get her weight underneath it and turn the whole thing upward, hopeful of revealing more buried clams. She soon became reabsorbed in her task, enjoying the feeling of her muscles working and the satisfaction of uncovering the shellfish. She forgot about Wilkie being there and was caught unawares as she straightened up, shielding her eyes from the rising sun and staring directly into the camera.

"Oh brilliant!" he called out. "The light's just perfect. Say what you like about the Huns, but they make bloody good cameras." He clicked the shutter and wound the film on before coming closer. "It's a Leica. Got it when I was in Italy, from an RAF reconnaissance chap. Doesn't require a great deal of technical know-how, so it suits me to a tee."

She picked up her bucket, resting the shovel over one shoulder, a worker at the end of a shift. Wilkie refocused, clicked the shutter again and then wound the film on to the next frame. "Much obliged, Mrs. Durrant." Of all the men, he was the only one who insisted on formally addressing her, despite her insistence that he do otherwise. "It makes a welcome change to have such a pulchritudinous subject. I have to confess I am a little bored with birds and wildflowers. And you catch the light far better than they."

"You mean those?" She pointed toward the sea

campion, the delicate white petals of which dotted the grasses that rolled down toward the beach. "But they are quite pretty are they not?"

"*Thou art more lovely and more temperate*," he said with theatrical flair.

"Oh come now, Wilkie, you do but flatter me beyond the point of reason," she laughed.

"Madam, I think you mock me," he replied, getting into the Shakespearean swing. "But seriously." His voice returned to normal. "It's all about the light."

"What do you mean?" she asked.

"I've noticed. When you think no one's watching you. I can see that you're trying to find the light, just as fiercely as you were digging for those clams. But you know the real trick is to contain the darkness."

She knew he wasn't talking about photography.

"You have to make it a place that you can return to, but—and this is the key—one that you can leave," he said. "Make it a shadow room in your mind if you like. Put all the sadness, the anger, the sheer impotence there. Otherwise it'll take over your life, poison everything."

"But that's not what the doc does."

"No, he walks into the room with us." There was a long pause and Esther noticed a shadow pass over his face. His eyes took on a far-off gaze and it seemed as if he were somewhere else.

Eventually, he began to speak. "The first war. Nineteen seventeen. Passchendaele. Heavy rain and mud. So much blasted mud. Couldn't get any of the artillery close to the front, too damned boggy. I was only a second lieutenant. Still wet behind the ears, too young to be scared until it was all over. Captured an enemy pillbox that was giving us some jip. Shot two gunners and forced the rest of the poor buggers to surrender—ten of them. They had to find me a new uniform after that—it was shredded with bullet holes but somehow they all missed me. Still get the nightmares. There's never been anything as bad as that since."

Esther murmured her sympathy. "How do you keep on going?"

"Beauty."

"Beauty?" she echoed.

"Even when it seems there is none to be had, you must seek it out. Find a way to dream again, to believe, believe in the beauty of life, however fleeting."

Esther wasn't sure she could ever achieve this. "Is that what brought you here?"

"Not really. I spent over three years as a prisoner of war. Changi. They reckoned if you were there for more than three years you went around the bend. I guess ending up here is proof of that." A short bark of a laugh escaped him. "It's easier for those with actual physical wounds. People think we should just snap out of it, or that we are two wafers short of a communion, or malingerers, or even worse . . . cowards." The word hung in the air between them.

Wilkie drew a packet of cigarettes from his pocket and offered her one. She shook her head. He tapped one out, lit up, took a long, satisfied drag, and then coughed throatily before taking another. "Chronic bronchitis. Suppose I should give these up, but what can one do?"

Esther pulled her hair back from her face, watching him.

"Had a nervous breakdown, I suppose you'd call it, like some of the other blokes here. I'd been home for nearly five years. Having a marvelous time actually—wine, women, and song. Then out of the blue I couldn't see the point in going on. Nothing in life held any value anymore. The doctor—the one who referred me here—said it was a delayed reaction. According to him, severe malnutrition can have that effect on the nervous system. I can't vouch for that, but that camp certainly affected something in me. The dirt, the disease—those bloody Japs let men die through sheer neglect if you can believe that. They had no respect for life. They treated us like animals . . ." He coughed, remembering she was there. "The good thing is that I don't take anything too seriously anymore—not authority, nor convention, not even death—well, apart from my own perhaps. Nothing is really worth getting that worked up about when you stop to think about it."

"I suppose you're right," she admitted.

"People like us have to find a way to live with our sorrow, for it can never be banished forever, that's where modern medics—with the possible exception of our esteemed doc—get it wrong, they think they can make it all go away and never come back."

"And are you successful in this endeavor?"

"Sometimes." He sounded wistful. "On certain days—and increasingly more of them, I am happy to report. Take today for instance. A beautiful beach, a lovely woman, morning light, and the only shooting that's going on is with my camera . . . You have to learn to be grateful, Mrs. Durrant. For the small things."

"I still think it'd be easier if we could take something like nepenthe," she said.

"What?"

"Nepenthe." Esther swung the bucket, slopping

sand and water over the brim. "The drug in the *Odyssey*. A drug for forgetting, for banishing grief. Medicine for sorrow."

"Perhaps the doc does have it?" He arched an eyebrow and looked across her to where the sun had climbed in the sky.

"Perhaps he does," she said with a smile.

"Come on. Let's get back. It's time for rations."

"Do you reckon Robbie's burned the toast again?"

"Indubitably."

Chapter Twenty-eight
Little Embers, Spring 2018

Rachel retrieved the catalog from the cupboard and returned to the sofa with it, setting it down next to her. There was a single, arresting image of a child's face painted in thickly layered oils on the front. The child had the gorgeous fat cheeks of a toddler, full lips, curly copper hair, and a far-off expression in its gray eyes—the same expression she'd seen sometimes on Leah's face.

Rachel opened the catalog at the first page and came to a short introduction, which she scanned briefly, not knowing how long she would have before Leah herself descended the stairs.

In it, the writer hailed Leah as one of the most promising up-and-coming British portraitists of her generation, comparing her to Francis Bacon and Lucian

Freud. Rachel was astonished. It made Leah's choice to live on this remote island even more perplexing.

She leafed through the thick, glossy pages and studied the plates—reproductions of oils of men and women, often nudes or semi-clothed, their flesh by turns careworn or luminous, but sensual and so real she felt she could almost reach out and feel skin beneath her fingertips. There was one of a woman lying naked, the curve of her back like the body of a violin, her long hair spilling on the floor next to her as if it was ink.

The same child who was on the cover was featured several more times throughout: there was one of him or her sitting, naked and straight-backed, turned slightly away from the artist, with rolls of flesh on dimpled thighs and soft-boned arms.

These paintings in particular were tender, confronting in their intensity, and an inexplicable longing twisted through Rachel. She had never allowed herself the luxury of imagining children of her own, didn't think she'd ever be settled enough, too selfish for sleepless nights and school runs. She read the caption of one. "*Tabitha. The artist's daughter. 1994.*"

Leah had a child. She did a quick calculation. The painting was done almost twenty-five years ago, so the daughter would be a woman now. Where was she? Was she aware that her mother was living as a virtual hermit? Rachel didn't know much about art, but even to her untrained eye the pictures were revelatory. Their intimacy seemed to lay bare the relationship between the painter and the subject. She turned back to the introduction. It had been written by a Max Erwin, of the Erwin Gallery, Cork Street, London.

Footsteps sounded on the stairs, so Rachel quickly closed the catalog. She had just replaced it and shut the cupboard door when Leah called out, "Cuppa?"

"Yes, thanks," she answered, feeling slightly shaky at her subterfuge.

There was a clank and then the rush of water. A kettle being filled. Then, something Rachel hadn't heard since being stranded on the island: the sound of singing, a bluesy, soulful melody.

Rachel was still sifting through the implications of Leah being a famous and very talented painter, when she strode in, two mugs in her hand, and placed one on the table next to her. "How are you doing?" she asked, fixing her with a piercing gaze, almost as if she were studying her.

"Erm, fine thank you. Just . . . er . . . just reading," she indicated the copy of *Rebecca* which lay beside her. That was odd. It was the first time Leah had asked how she was, and she appeared to be in a rather strange mood. If she'd had to hazard a guess, Rachel would have said she was actually cheerful.

"Glad you're not getting bored here."

"Oh, I'm pretty good at amusing myself."

"How's the wrist holding up?"

She looked down at the sling. "Much better now I don't keep jarring it."

"Just as well, 'cause there aren't any more painkillers I'm afraid."

Rachel nodded. "That's fine. I don't really like taking them unless I have to."

"Sensible girl. Right, I'd better get back to it," she said, turning to leave.

"May I look at your work sometime?" she asked, emboldened by Leah's good mood.

"Oh, I just dabble. It's nothing much—amateur stuff really." Her tone was dismissive.

Having seen the catalog, Rachel knew Leah was lying to her. But why?

Rachel could hardly concentrate for the rest of the afternoon as the two mysteries—Esther's and Leah's—chased themselves around in her head, giving her no peace. Leah had clearly once been a highly regarded artist, her star on the rise, so what had happened?

Had there been a husband as well as a child? Was it something as mundane as divorce that had driven her here? Was it because of her drinking or did that come after? Something dreadful must have happened to cause her to hide herself away, shun the world.

Unable to quell her restlessness, Rachel shrugged the thick coat from the suitcase around her shoulders and took herself back to the beach. She nursed a vain hope that she might see a passing boat or yacht and be able to attract the attention of those onboard. Even if she saw nothing, it was better than staring at the four walls in front of her. The wind had come up again and, as she stood on the end of the jetty where Leah had been fishing that morning, she scanned the choppy waves, becoming mesmerized by their ever-changing pattern. Not a vessel in sight. For the first time since her arrival on St. Mary's, she began to doubt the wisdom of her decision to come to the Scilly Isles. The problem was, she wasn't sure where she belonged anymore; she'd been on the move for too much of her life. It had never much bothered her until then, but all of a sudden she felt very much alone and a long way from those who loved her.

After a while, the light began to fade and Rachel returned to the house. "Thought you'd gotten lost," said Leah as Rachel entered the kitchen.

"I went down to the jetty, wanted to see if there might be anyone passing," admitted Rachel.

Leah scoffed. "Fat chance of that."

"I know, but I couldn't help looking anyway."

"The time will pass soon enough; it always does," said Leah, sounding resigned.

"Who is Tabitha?" asked Rachel, the book she'd found still very much on her mind.

"Who told you about her?" Leah's voice was sharp.

"No one. I found a book, a catalog actually," Rachel admitted.

"You had no business rummaging through my personal things." Leah glared at her, gripping a tea towel between her hands as if she intended to use it as a weapon.

"I'm sorry. I didn't mean to, I was bored . . . I shouldn't have opened the cabinet, but I found the key, and then, well, I couldn't help it. But you . . . you are an incredible artist."

"You know so little." Leah's voice was withering.

"I'm really sorry," said Rachel, trying to convince Leah of her sincerity. "If I'd known it was going to upset you, I wouldn't have mentioned it."

"Humph." Leah was not easily mollified.

"Your work . . .", Rachel began.

"I was pretty good once, wasn't I?" said Leah, her mouth curving upward.

"More than just 'pretty good' I'd say."

"Not so much anymore though."

"Really?" Rachel found that hard to believe.

"I only paint for myself these days, and only because I can't seem to stay away from it. Sometimes I think it's only paint that holds me together," she said with a wry laugh. "But stop digging, Rachel; leave well enough alone. I'm not interested in talking about my work."

Rachel let the silence between them grow as Leah began scrubbing the sink with determined vigor.

"If you must know, we've lost touch," Leah said, not pausing in her buffing. "Tabitha and I . . . ," she added, prepared to answer Rachel's original question if nothing else, it would seem. "Things weren't exactly easy when she was a teenager. Got caught up in a bad crowd. Drugs. Fights. Police involved. Being a mother isn't always a picnic, you know, even when you think you're doing your best. I haven't seen her for years. I've no idea where she is now, to be honest." She said this quickly, baldly, as if she'd not told anyone, at least not for a long time. Her face twisted in anger, or was it pain? Rachel couldn't tell. Then before she could say anything, Leah threw down the scourer, opened the back door, and stomped out.

Oh Christ. After a moment, Rachel went after her, worried that she might have stormed off, upset by her questioning.

She found her bringing in laundry off a makeshift washing line.

"Here," Rachel said, unpegging a threadbare towel and starting to fold it with difficulty. "Let me help you."

Leah grunted.

"I'm really sorry, Leah, I had no idea."

Chapter Twenty-nine
Little Embers, Winter 1951

Before Esther had much time to think about it, Christmas Eve was upon them and a howling nor'easter blew across the island, making venturing outside all but impossible. "Gale force, I reckon," said Wilkie at breakfast. Robbie fretted about his brassicas being flattened and the spinach being ripped to shreds, and Mrs. Biggs dared not peg out the linen for fear of it being blown halfway to Spain. The doctor stayed in the parlor with each of the men entering at intervals for their daily counseling session.

Stuck inside, Esther kept to her room. She found herself counting the minutes until it was her turn for an hour with the doctor, going over their previous conversations in her head, remembering the keen intelligence in his eyes, the fall of hair over his forehead, the almost boyish excitement with which he greeted her. Shortly after lunch he summoned her and she settled herself on her now favorite chair. He sat opposite her, a little way across the room. "I don't think we should talk of home today," he said quietly.

In the weeks since she'd told him about Samuel, he hadn't brought it up again, but she nodded, grateful once more for the reprieve. It would have been too difficult to countenance on such a day, a day when it was all she could do not to spend every moment imagining what Teddy might be doing. What might he be hoping for from Father Christmas—a train set or some toy soldiers perhaps? She wished for him to be caught up in the excitement of the celebration, and not missing her. "What, then?" she asked.

"The book. Tell me what you thought of it."

The week before he had loaned her his copy of *The Kon-Tiki Expedition.*

Esther's eyes lit up. "Astonishing. I can't begin to imagine how they could be so single-minded, so brave."

"To set out on the Pacific Ocean on a raft made of little more than balsa wood. For a hundred days. It beggars belief, doesn't it?"

"How does one even begin to believe that something

like that could even be possible I wonder? I know he did his research, but even then . . ."

"One thing's for sure, they must have been damned sick of the taste of fish by the end of it."

She laughed at his words, enjoying the lightness that bubbled up from her chest. It felt good to think about someone else's life for a change. They carried on talking until, before she knew it, the hour was almost up. "It has to be an act of faith, doesn't it?" she asked, considering the book again.

"What does faith mean to you, Esther?" he said, suddenly serious.

Her thoughts swam before her. "That's not an easy question to answer. I'm not sure I've a great deal of faith in anything anymore. Especially in myself."

"That's why you're here. To learn to have faith again."

He held her gaze until she could bear it no longer, looked away before he could see the tears begin to form in her eyes. In that moment she almost believed it possible.

The supply boat had called the day before with a delivery of mail and a shoulder of pork from the Hugh Town butcher. "That's lovely, that is," Mrs. Biggs had said when she took charge of it, carrying it as triumphantly as if she'd won first prize in bingo. "It'll roast up fair with some applesauce on the side," she said before hefting it onto the kitchen counter with a loud thud.

Esther smiled at the prospect of crackling and gravy.

"A feast," Jean agreed.

That morning, Wilkie had retrieved a driftwood branch from the beach and Richard had unearthed a box of decorations from the attic. Shiny red and green glass baubles hung on cotton threads from the bleached timber and they had propped it up in a corner of the hallway. By common consent they had all decided to delay the mail opening until Christmas Day itself, placing the parcels and letters that had arrived earlier in the week under the salvaged tree. Esther could see there was one for her from John, but, unlike the days before the letter that had arrived previously, she held out little hope of a summons to London this time.

In the fortnight before Christmas, she had conceived of a way to extend an olive branch to Robbie, for it bothered her that he might have taken offense at her actions that day on the jetty, and they still had not spoken about it.

She'd found Susie, his doll, abandoned in the kitchen one morning and taken swift measurements. A scrap of sprigged muslin from a drawer in the chest in her room was just large enough to fashion a new dress, with a simple sleeveless bodice and a gathered skirt. A flowered remnant stolen from the hem of a summer frock and a short length of ribbon from her suitcase became an accompanying sunbonnet. Mrs. Biggs had supplied a needle and thread to facilitate the endeavor. When she had finished, Esther had folded them as carefully as if they were her own garments and wrapped them up in brown paper. The small parcel sat with the others under the tree.

After supper that night—a thick barley and vegetable soup that had simmered tantalizingly all day on the stove—George had produced a penny whistle and piped the opening notes of "In the Bleak Midwinter." Jean sang along, her voice a surprising clear and sweet soprano. Esther glanced around the table at the faces lit by candles and united by misfortune and sorrow. They were a motley band, but despite this, she felt a growing kinship with them: Wilkie, stoic and observant, his camera never far from reach; Robbie with his ruined face and kind heart; George with his beanpole figure and haunted eyes; Mrs. Biggs, a woman in perpetual motion, cooking, cleaning, and washing for them all. And of course the doctor, who never tired of listening, talking, and who fiercely loved his music and his books. It was only Jean who she could not warm to, could find no common ground with. Indeed, the woman seemed to resent her, not that she had ever said anything exactly, but it was just a feeling that radiated from her, especially since she'd refused Esther the tablets when she asked for them. She suspected that Jean did not approve of her being there, taking a valuable place away from a far more deserving serviceman, someone who really needed their help.

Despite Jean's unspoken reproof and missing Teddy desperately, Esther went to her bed that night warmed by Christmas spirit and thinking that the world was not such a harsh place as she had once believed it to be, that there might be a light at the end of a very dark tunnel. Surely she would be home soon.

When Esther woke on Christmas Day, however, the heaviness that had followed her around for months returned. The storm had not abated. Noisy rain lashed the windowpanes, making them rattle, and water pooled on the sill, leaking in from the gaps between the frame and the mortar. The fire had gone out in her room and she shivered as she dressed herself in as many layers as she could find. Even several cups of Mrs. Biggs's strongest tea failed to warm her more than a couple of degrees. Wilkie, though, was uncharacteristically chipper, whistling as he and Robbie cleared away the breakfast dishes.

Robbie, however, was much more subdued than usual, and he seemed to be somewhere else. Esther caught a distant look in his eyes as he wiped the dish towel over the plates. Who or what was he missing? She didn't feel she could press him for the information. She'd overstepped the mark and there was now an unspoken tension between them that she wasn't able to dispel.

Before breakfast, Wilkie had presented Esther, Jean, and Mrs. Biggs with a sprig of sea holly. "Close as we'll get to the real thing," he said as he bent over and carefully pinned the spiky leaves to Esther's cardigan. "Mind you don't prick yourself now."

Mrs. Biggs, who was rubbing the pork rind with mustard powder, turned to George, who had at that moment been almost blown in the back door. "Did you manage to find some scurvy grass for me?" she asked.

He held up a bunch of glossy dark green, spear-shaped leaves, triumphant.

"Oh wonderful. Pop them in the sink, will you, there's a love."

Esther looked at them, curious. "Scurvy grass?"

"Full of vitamin C," said Mrs. Biggs. "I'll fry it up with a bit of butter. Now, do you think you might lend a hand with those spuds?" She indicated the bowl of muddy potatoes at the far end of the kitchen. "There's a peeler here somewhere. An apron too, if you need one."

Esther rose from the table and located the peeler in a drawer. With the weather as miserable as it was, there was no chance of venturing outside, so she was glad of a task to keep her busy and stop her thinking too much of Teddy, who must surely be up and unwrapping presents in the drawing room at Frogmore, or perhaps running home after the service at St. John's in Church Row, skipping along the Hampstead pavements in anticipation of gifts to come. She worried that he would be wrapped warmly enough, that he should not catch a chill.

"Lunch will be at one sharp," Mrs. Biggs said as Esther finished the potatoes and rinsed her hands. "Mind you're not late."

"I wouldn't dream of it," said Esther, drying her hands.

They gathered in the front parlor a little after noon. The doctor had produced a bottle of dry sherry and poured a small glass for each of them. Esther was surprised that the mood was jolly and found herself un-expectedly buoyed up by it. "A toast," Richard said, when everyone had a glass. "I know you are all far from your families and loved ones, and I pray that you will be returned to them before long. In the meantime, let us celebrate what we have. Merry Christmas." They drank—Robbie and George a deep draft, draining their glasses, Esther and the doctor a more temperate sip—and then attention turned to the parcels under the tree. Esther was astonished to see the small pile had grown exponentially overnight, with a number of large, in-expertly wrapped boxes augmenting those already under the tree. She was wondering exactly where they had come from, when the doctor handed her an oddly shaped, bulky package. She couldn't begin to guess what it might be. "Secondhand I'm afraid," he said, "but they should fit."

"Oh. Golly. Thank you." She was flustered. "I'm afraid I did not think to contrive a gift for you."

"And I had no expectation of one. Anyway, as I said, it is nothing new."

"Come on then. Open it and put us out of our mis-ery, Mrs. Durrant," Wilkie urged.

Esther placed her sherry glass on a side table and pulled at the wrapping. A pair of brown leather walk-ing boots with jaunty scarlet laces emerged.

"You have feet nearly as large as mine," Richard explained. "And these were a little small for me. They're Austrian—the best—and hardly worn. I thought they might be suitable."

"Oh, but I am sure they will be. I must confess, my shoes are not exactly up to the terrain here, so these will be most welcome," said Esther gratefully.

"Indeed. I have seen that you are often in danger of slipping."

She blinked, touched that he had noticed. "Thank you. That is most thoughtful." She looked across the room to see that Robbie had retrieved the small parcel she had left for him and was reading the label she had attached.

"For Susie!" he cried as he opened it, beaming with delight.

"About time she was decent," laughed Wilkie, who snapped a photograph of Robbie holding up the bonnet.

"Thank you," Robbie said to Esther, looking her in the eyes, at last.

"It was nothing. My needlework skills aren't exactly those of Monsieur Balmain or Madame Chanel, but hopefully the dress will fit."

"She will be the best-dressed baby on the island," he said, coming over to embrace her. She squeezed him tight as he held her, feeling the bones beneath his sweater. He'd lost weight in recent weeks, she was sure of it.

More presents were handed out and gifts exclaimed over. Between them, the doctor and Mrs. Biggs had managed to find something useful for each of the patients—for George a pair of binoculars. "T'were my late husband's," she said as George unwrapped them. "But I've no need of them."

"You are a woman of infinite kindness," said George with a gallant smile.

For Wilkie, a book on photography, for Robbie a new spade and several packets of seeds—"Cucumbers!" he exclaimed—and for Jean a pretty box of soap. Esther opened a slim envelope to reveal a print of one of the photos Wilkie had taken down at the beach a few weeks earlier. In it, she was staring straight at the camera, her hand shielding her eyes, her hair blown by the breeze. "I look rather fierce," she said as she took it in.

"You are a warrior, Mrs. Durrant," Wilkie replied.

"Hardly," Esther retorted. "But that is most kind, thank you, Wilkie."

He had made another print for each of them, showing the six of them standing in formation outside the front of the house. It was a picture he'd cajoled them into a week previously. The doctor and George were standing behind the others and George's hand rested lightly on

Robbie's shoulder, with Esther and Jean flanking him and Mrs. Biggs standing slightly off to one side. Robbie held his doll in the crook of his elbow, and all of them had managed a semblance of a smile, though they didn't exactly look like carefree holidaymakers. "I shall treasure it," said Richard with sincerity as he looked at the print.

George had shyly presented Robbie with a slim volume of poems and Esther noticed a wave of color rise up from his collar as he read the inscription on the flyleaf. Before she could begin to wonder at what it might say, a parcel with a London postmark was thrust into her hands. Her fingers fumbled with the paper as she began to open it. She turned away from the group toward the window, desiring privacy. A box of barley sugar, its amber twists catching the light, and a new book, a novel. There was also a letter. "*My darling Esther . . .*" it began. "*I hope by now you have begun to forgive me and that you are much improved in spirits. I received a report just this week from Richard, who says you are making splendid progress, of which I am so glad to hear.*" Her eyes scanned further down the page. "*. . . Teddy misses you but he is looking forward to the pantomime,* Jack and the Beanstalk, *which his aunt Clementine will take him to in the company of his cousins. The arrival of Father Christmas is antici-*

pated with much excitement, as I believe he has begun to understand what it all means—plenty of presents for him." Esther stared at the drizzle that was snaking its way down the windowpane. She could not believe that she was missing her son's third Christmas.

"Everything okay?" The doctor was beside her.

She nodded, not trusting herself to speak.

"It's a difficult time of year, especially hearing from home like this. Try not to dwell on it."

"I'll be fine," she said bravely. "After all, I won't be here for too much longer, will I?" Esther looked at her forearms, where no evidence of her former scourging could now be seen.

A beat of silence and the doctor cleared his throat. "It's possible you will be well enough to return home before too much longer. We shall see how you progress in the coming weeks."

Esther felt a small, but unexpected balloon of optimism well up within her; his words were perhaps the best gift she could have wished for. "You are so kind to give me hope, Richard." She addressed him by his first name, worrying as she did so that she might be overstepping the boundary of doctor and patient. She was immediately abashed. "Come. Let's rejoin the others and put our best foot forward, shall we," she said, her tone sharper than normal.

Chapter Thirty
Little Embers, Spring 2018

Rachel crept up the stairs. It was the third day since she had been shipwrecked on Little Embers, and, as with every other day, Leah had gone out early to see to Margaret and tend her vegetable patch. Rachel was running out of things to keep herself busy, and walking on the island gave her an eerie feeling, making her realize the extent of her isolation. She preferred, now, to keep to the house, planning to only venture once or twice to the jetty to scan for passing boats.

She hadn't believed Leah when she had said her work was no longer any good and, curiosity getting the better of judgment, wanted to see for herself. She conveniently ignored the fact that Leah had specifically forbidden her from entering the studio.

As she reached the landing at the top of the house,

she was faced with a narrow corridor, along which five doors were spaced. She turned the handle of the nearest, feeling a twinge of misgiving as the latch lifted, but nevertheless peered around the door. A dusty room, the curtains faded and drawn against the light. A single bed, a dresser, and a small rag rug on the wooden floor. She ran her finger along the top of the dresser, seeing the line it made in the dust. It clearly had not been occupied for some time. She retreated, closed the door gently, and approached the next door.

This room was large and light, with windows that looked out over the front of the house, offering a view to the sea. It must have once been the main bedroom, though it contained little furniture now. Unlike the rest of the house, it was neat and orderly, with a large easel set up in front of one of the two rectangular windows.

Canvases were stacked in a corner, and along one wall a long cabinet housed tubes of paint, trowels, and brushes.

She walked over to the canvases. "Oh!" Rachel let out an involuntary gasp as she saw the first of them. It was a landscape, all clouds and water and light. Completely unlike the paintings in the catalog in terms of subject and composition, but Rachel could see there was a similar style in the way the paint had been applied.

She looked through the others—there were at least thirty of them in varying sizes and all eloquently captured the milky light of a wintry islandscape. Melancholy and lucid, they spoke to Rachel of loneliness, a solitary existence that she recognized immediately. She knew without a doubt that Leah had been wrong about her talent having deserted her.

She didn't linger. Instead she hurried back downstairs, for a thought had occurred to her. She found her camera where she had left it in the living room and hastened up the stairs, back to Leah's studio. She was interfering, but ignored the voice of reason, snapping a few shots of the larger canvases. Art this good deserved an audience, one way or another. As she was about to leave, she went over to the window to see what Leah was currently working on. Her mouth fell open when she saw what it was.

A portrait.

It was her, unmistakably her. Lying on the green sofa in the borrowed twinset, her dark hair swirled about her, her eyes closed. The vintage clothes made her seem like a woman from a different time, but Leah had captured Rachel's likeness exactly. Rachel stood and stared at the painting, didn't know what to think.

Eventually, she took another quick snap of the half-finished portrait and hurried out of the room, not wanting to risk being caught. Did she dare confront Leah about the paintings? She wasn't supposed to have been in the studio in the first place, but really, now that she knew, she had to do something about it, even if it meant interfering . . . work like this shouldn't be hidden away.

After she had left the studio, Rachel threw on the black-collared coat and went outside to try and give herself time to think. She walked down to the jetty once more, though there was no sign of Leah fishing this time. Sitting down and swinging her legs over the end, she wondered what to do. Should she confront her? She was so lost in thought that she didn't at first register the bright yellow and green catamaran speeding toward her. The boat she'd been hoping to see most of all.

When eventually she did spot it, she jumped to her feet and began to wave her good arm manically, yelling out to the boat. It didn't matter, it was headed straight for her.

Delight and relief flooded through her like a drug as she saw Jonah's cheery face behind the windshield. He waved back at her, calling out her name. She'd never been so happy to see a familiar face in her life and she continued to wave excitedly until the boat pulled up alongside the jetty. Before it had even tied up, he hopped out of the boat and landed a few steps away from her.

"Rachel!" Jonah went to wrap her in a hug, but stopped as he saw the sling. "I thought I'd never find you. What happened? Are you okay?"

"Slight argument with a few rocks, nothing serious," she said, feeling suddenly bashful.

He raised a disbelieving eyebrow at her.

"But Leah pulled me free and has been looking after me. I'm fine, really," she said.

"I'll be the judge of that in a minute."

"How did you know where to find me?"

"Janice and I were worried when we realized the *Soleil* was missing after the storm and you weren't at the house . . . I imagined the worst—"

"I should have checked the weather," she interrupted. "But I'm okay. Though I could do with getting off this island and back to work. I need to report in to my supervisor."

"So where's your boat?"

"Um, yeah, well, about that . . ." She kicked at a loose board, too embarrassed to look at him. "I lost power to the motor so I decided to swim it in to shore. Turned out not to have been the smartest decision I've ever made."

"No kidding," he said, an incredulous expression on his face. "What on earth did you think you were doing?"

Rachel held up her good hand. "It's okay, I don't need you to tell me anything I don't already know."

"And your arm?" he said, eyeing the sling.

"It's a little sore," she admitted. "But I'm sure it'll be fine in a few days." She'd never been one to make a fuss about things.

"Yes, well, we'll see about that. Hello, Leah," he said, looking past her.

Rachel turned around to see her rescuer coming down the jetty to meet them. She must have heard the sound of the boat.

"I see you've found her then," said Leah.

"We've been searching since the storm, but I didn't think she would have been this far east. It was only on a hunch that we came out this way today. Rachel says you rescued her. That's very good of you."

"No more than anyone would have done in the same situation."

"We'll take her off your hands now, get that arm looked at properly."

"Right you are then. Some peace around here would be good," said Leah brusquely.

Rachel turned to Leah. "I can't thank you enough

for everything you've done. I really am grateful." She stopped, remembering something. "Oh, I need to get my camera," she said, rushing past Jonah and Leah and running back to the house.

When she got inside, she went to the living room, found her camera and then saw the copy of *Rebecca* with the letters hidden between its pages. Before she could think better of it, she slipped it into her coat pocket.

She ran into Leah on her way back.

"Glad they found you, hey?" she asked.

Rachel nodded. "Thank you again, Leah. I'll come back and see you if I may? Once I get a new boat sorted out."

"Oh, there's really no need."

"Well, I'd like to return the clothes." Rachel indicated the coat, feeling a twinge of guilt as she remembered what she'd shoved into the pocket.

"No one here was using them; you're welcome to keep them. No good to anyone else."

"Well, I'll come and see *you* then." It was a promise she knew she would keep.

To her surprise, Leah leaned forward and engulfed her in a hug. "I suppose that'd be all right," she said gruffly.

They were interrupted by the blast of the boat's horn. "Sounds like your bloke's in a hurry."

"Oh, he's not my bloke," said Rachel. "Just a friend."

The horn sounded again.

"I'd better run," she said. "Thanks again, Leah!"

She ran back down the path.

"Sorry about that," said Jonah as she stepped aboard. "But the tide's turning and we need to be back by lunchtime. I'll have a look at that arm as soon as we get back, but you might need to see the doc as well."

"Yes, of course," said Rachel. "I can't believe you found me."

"I can't either," he said, giving her a grin that was three parts relief and one part amusement.

Rachel felt weak with pleasure. As much at seeing him again as the thought that there might be a hot bath waiting for her when she got back to her cottage. "Honestly," she said, "I don't mind admitting that I'm glad to leave there. It felt like an island of lost souls. Pretty eerie in places."

"I can imagine," he said. "Though I thought you liked a bit of isolation."

"Not like that," she admitted. "I'm so glad you found me. I can't believe you cared enough to come looking for me."

Jonah gave her a funny look. "Of course I care enough," he said. "I'd do it for anyone who was lost."

Jonah examined her hand when they got back to St. Mary's and sent her straight to the doctor, who diagnosed a Grade II sprain and a broken finger, which he set in a splint before restrapping her wrist. "There's some serious ligament damage there, but you're lucky the wrist isn't fractured. It'll be at least six weeks before you can use it again."

Rachel's spirits sank. How was she going to be able to do her job with the use of only one hand?

She was still feeling dejected when she returned to Shearwater. The first thing she did was go to her laptop and check her emails. Sure enough, there were two messages from Dr. Wentworth, the first reminding her that he was expecting her weekly report, and the second asking why she hadn't filed it. She took a deep breath and began typing, but her one-handed progress was frustratingly slow.

After she finished and pressed send, she sat back, glancing out of the window and seeing gray clouds hanging on the horizon, a low ceiling capping the sky. She remembered that she hadn't told Leah that she'd seen the paintings.

Chapter Thirty-one
Little Embers, Winter 1951

When Richard had seen Esther standing at the window, her shoulders hunched over the letter, he'd felt compelled to go to her. She looked like a frail bloom, her head angled toward the paper, tendrils of hair curling about her slender neck, and he was helpless in the face of her distress. He knew he was in grave danger of caring too deeply for her.

Their hour together had become the high point in his day and he found himself looking for ways to prolong the time. Esther was well read, well educated, and possessed a lively mind. In addition, her keen sense of the absurd, together with an underpinning kindness that showed itself more and more often, made her only more attractive to him. They talked of books, music, of poetry—she favored the metaphysical poets of the seventeenth century, he those of the First World War: Sassoon, Thomas, and Brooke—of philosophy and astronomy, of politics, history, and economics.

"But surely you can see that Churchill is a brutal imperialist?" she railed on more than one occasion. "As evidenced by his appalling treatment of the indigenous Kenyans?"

He tried to argue for the prime minister's nobler virtues and strong leadership, his stance against Nazi Germany, all of which she only reluctantly acceded to.

He loved that she wasn't afraid to disagree with him, but that despite their differences, they saw the world almost through the same eyes, held the same values dear.

He also spoke to her of his ambitions. "I am writing a paper on new and individualized treatments for patients, based on my experiences at Northfield, and also here. I hope to change the management of psychiatric cases, especially depression, to break new ground," he confided.

"For certainly there are better means than electric shock treatment or, God help us, lobotomy," she said with a shiver. "That does indeed sound like a worthy endeavor."

"I confess I have little spare time to work on it, but I am determined to complete it. It could help change the course of so many lives. Shining a light on better treatment, to help those poor souls who have experienced such horrors defending king and country, is the least I can do. I didn't go to war. I suppose this is my way of making amends."

"Making amends? Whatever for? No one thinks less of you because you did not fight, if that's what you mean. No one that matters anyway."

He smiled at the thought that she was counseling him.

"Tell me, what decided you upon this course of medicine?" she had asked one day. He gave her a brief sketch of his mother and she had looked at him with such sympathy that he felt afresh the wound of that long-ago summer. Had he been given cause to describe the perfect woman, he would not have imagined someone quite like Esther, but now that he knew her, no one else would ever come close. It was as subtle and as simple as the way she held herself, the sideways sweep of her gaze when something amused her, the low timbre of her voice that made him want to lean forward and listen even more closely to what she was saying. It was the way she entered a room, the light in her eyes as if she was about to recount something wonderful that she'd saved just for him. That she was the wife of an old school chum caused him even more anguish than the fact that she was his patient—for she would not be his patient forever, but she would always be married to someone else.

He found himself to be at the mercy of his own desires in a way that he had never before experienced. It disrupted his sleep, made him careless of the others. Despite the longing that plagued him day and night, he vowed that she should never know of his feelings. He owed that to her as her doctor.

It was ridiculous to hope, but when she called him by his Christian name before Christmas dinner it was as though she too acknowledged their deepening friendship. Such a small gesture meant everything.

The rest of that day passed in a blur for Richard. After the austerity of prior years the table almost bowed with the weight of food upon it and everyone ate heartily. Mrs. Biggs had boiled up a pudding, sweetened with honey and dried fruit, and he held it aloft as, doused in liquor, blue flames danced about its surface.

"There's a thruppenny bit in there for one lucky lad," said Mrs. Biggs, who had downed several more sherries by this point.

"Or lass," said Robbie, angling his spoon at Esther.

Try as he might, Richard could not keep his eyes from returning to Esther, caring less as the evening wore on and the level in the wine bottles grew lower, that anyone might notice. He watched the way her face glowed in the candlelight; how gentle she was with Robbie and his doll. As they ate the pudding, he saw her take a spoonful and a puzzled look appeared on her face. She raised her napkin to her lips and delicately spat into it and he worried for a moment that something was wrong.

"It appears I am the lucky one in this instance," she said, holding a coin up for all to see.

He caught a split-second look of disdain on Jean's face, as if she'd just at that moment thought of something unpleasant. He couldn't be certain, but it looked very much like jealousy. He dismissed the notion. Jean was an excellent nurse, even if she was at times a little humorless.

He returned his attention to Esther, who was beaming at them all, delighted by her good fortune. He hoped the coming year would prove luckier for her than the current one had—she, as much as any of the men under his care, deserved it.

Chapter Thirty-two
St. Mary's, Spring 2018

Rachel was soaking in a scalding hot bath, her injured hand hanging over the side, when there was a loud banging at her door. Scrambling to wrap herself in a towel, which was no easy task with only one usable hand, she went downstairs to see who it could be.

"Halloo!" A male voice boomed through the door.

Jonah.

"Come on in," she called out from the bottom of the stairs. "It's unlocked. I won't be a sec, just getting changed." She raced back up the stairs and awkwardly pulled on a pair of tracksuit pants and a sweater. It felt good to be back in her own clothes again. Pushing her feet into a pair of UGGs and drying her hair with a towel, she padded back down to the kitchen.

Jonah was there, filling the small space as he unloaded a large shopping bag. "Dinner," he said. "I thought you might appreciate the help. Hope you don't mind if I make myself at home in your kitchen."

She blinked. "Be my guest. And you're a star. Both for bringing me back to civilization and for thinking of my stomach."

"Actually, it was more the thought of you trying to do everything one-handed," he said. "Speaking of which, how is the paw?"

She looked down at her bandaged wrist. "I can't use it for at least six weeks."

"Bummer."

"Exactly. I've had to explain myself to my supervisor—I don't know what he's going to be more pissed off about—the fact that there will be a delay to the research or that I've lost the boat they've given me. Personally, I'm laying bets on the boat."

"Doesn't rain but it pours, eh?" he said, opening the wine. "Here, drown your sorrows in a glass of this."

She took a hefty slug, hoping it might anesthetize her disappointment and frustration with herself, now the euphoria of being rescued had worn off.

"Tell me something good, Jonah. I'm sick of wallowing in my own troubles," she said.

He glanced up from the chopping board, where he was dicing tomatoes, and grinned at her. "Okay. Well, this morning we answered a call about a suspected heart attack, but it turned out to be severe indigestion."

"Really? That's the best you've got?"

He shrugged. "Well, actually, this afternoon, after finding someone I'd been rather worried about . . ." He winked at her. "I got to visit the primary school and teach a class of ten-year-olds first aid. They loved it. Wanted to know how many lives I'd saved, whether I'd seen a dead person, and could they have a go on the defibrillator. One cheeky so-and-so tried to nick my stethoscope."

Rachel laughed. "You like kids?"

"Course," Jonah replied. "What's not to like?"

Rachel thought of her two nieces and three nephews, growing up so far away, and what she had missed out on. She looked at Jonah, imagining him for a moment as a father, two, or even three kids hanging off him. She knew instinctively he'd make a good one.

The smell of garlic and frying onions made her mouth water, reminding her of her mother's cooking, and she continued to watch Jonah as he stirred the pan, tasting, adding a few grinds of pepper. Eventually he put a lid on the pan and then picked up his wineglass, joining her at the table. "That'll take half an hour or so. Hope you like bouillabaisse."

"Smells like heaven."

"Good. So tell me about Leah. What's she really like?"

"Tough. Terse. Doesn't suffer fools. Independent. But then I guess you'd have to be, living on your own like that."

Jonah nodded.

"But she was nice to me. Bandaged me up . . . Did you know she was an artist?"

"Really? I don't think anyone on the islands knows her well—in fact, you may have found out more than most around here."

"I found an old catalog from an exhibition of hers from years ago," Rachel said, taking another sip of wine. "She said she only dabbles now, that her talent deserted her, but what I saw in her studio was more than that. I'm not sure why she doesn't exhibit anymore. Also, she has a daughter, but they're not in touch."

"That's sad. Did she say why?"

"Something about her being a difficult teenager— drugs, that kind of thing."

"Might go some way to explaining why she's living on Little Embers all by herself."

"Oh, and there was something else."

"What?"

"There was a suitcase. Mostly full of clothes—in fact, the ones I was wearing when you picked me up came from there. But I also found letters—love letters."

"Leah's love letters? Isn't that a bit of an invasion of her privacy?" He looked at her in astonishment.

"Oh God no. These weren't hers," she reassured him quickly. "They were written in the 1950s."

"Wow. Okay, now I'm interested. Tell me more." He leaned toward her, anticipation lighting his face.

"They were addressed to an E. Durrant, in London, Hampstead, and who I am pretty sure was a woman, from someone with the initial 'R.' But for some reason they were never sent—the stamps weren't postmarked."

"Well, that *is* odd."

"Do you know anything about the house on Little Embers? Who used to live there before Leah?"

Jonah shook his head slowly. "Can't say I do. But Janice is probably the best person to talk to about that."

"Janice?"

"She works part-time as a curator at the Isles of Scilly Museum. It's just up the street from here. If anyone knows anything about Little Embers in—when did you say? The 1950s?—it'll be her. I think she'll be there tomorrow in fact."

Rachel brightened. If she wasn't going to be able to

work for a few weeks, she might as well have something to keep herself occupied. Finding out more about who had once lived on Little Embers and what had happened there years before would be interesting. She drained her glass and Jonah stood up to pour her a refill, checking the pan on the stove as he did so.

"I reckon it's ready," he said, lifting the lid and breathing in the garlicky steam that billowed out.

Rachel found a couple of bowls and he carefully ladled the broth and shellfish into them before slicing a loaf that he had brought. She took her first mouthful and the taste of garlic and tomato flooded her senses. The thought that she could fall for a man who cooked as well as this flitted through her mind, but she pushed it away and took another hungry bite. As they ate and chatted, her mood improved, and the threat of losing her job began to fade into the background. Jonah was easy company, and they found plenty to talk about, moving from what island life had been like on Aitutaki, to who was going to be taking part in the gig races that summer, then from her experiences with giant clams to some of the best hikes on the islands.

When they had finished, he cleared away the dishes, insisting that she stay where she was. When the kitchen was clean, he folded the tea towel neatly by the sink. "I'd best be off."

She was surprised. "But it's early."

He glanced at his watch. "I know. Sorry. It's trivia night at the pub. I can't let the team down."

"Oh, I see," she said flatly.

He shrugged. "Boys' night."

"No, that's okay." She hid her disappointment that he was leaving so soon—she'd been enjoying his company. As a friend of course, nothing more, she told herself firmly. She had also been going to show him the letters, but he'd announced he was leaving before she had the chance to get them out. "It was really nice of you to make the time to come and cook for me."

"You're welcome. I don't like eating alone, in any case."

As they reached the front door, he leaned in and kissed her lightly on the cheek. "See ya," he said, and left with a wave.

She lingered there for a moment before closing the door. When she went back into the kitchen she noticed Jonah had left his sweater on the back of a chair. She couldn't shake the feeling that the house felt suddenly empty without him there.

Chapter Thirty-three
Little Embers, Winter 1951

"Mind if I join you?" Richard asked Esther as she sat on the stairs the next morning, lacing up her new boots. They'd all been cooped up in the house for two days because of the bad weather, and since arriving on the island, Esther had come to depend on her regular tramps across the dunes as if they were medicine; in fact, they most probably were. Initially, she had been escorted by either Robbie or George, but now she generally wandered unsupervised, sometimes spending hours out on her own, often circumnavigating the entire island several times. This was the first time Richard had asked to accompany her.

Esther had been fighting her growing attraction to him for some weeks, telling herself that it was the result of being in forced proximity, in an unnatural situation, that it was a friendship and should never be anything more. She had a husband; she had made vows of fidelity and constancy in front of God, and despite everything she did not cast such promises idly aside, even if He'd fallen out of her favor recently.

But it was the first time in her life that she'd known anything like *this*, this overriding desire to be with someone, to never want to leave his side, to feel thrillingly alive merely by being in his presence, and, she finally admitted to herself, to long for his touch. Her hours with Richard were some of the happiest of her life, and she found herself recalling the deft movement of his hands when describing the construction of a boat, the suddenness of his smile when she teased him, the wistful look on his face when he let his guard down, when he thought she wasn't watching. Time seemed to both speed up and slow down whenever she was with him, as if touched by a wonderful kind of magic, as if they existed outside time itself.

It had never been that way with John.

"Of course not. I was thinking of going up and over the other side," she said as she finished tying the laces and got to her feet. Her voice sounded unnaturally calm, belying the tumult inside her. "Usually takes a couple of hours, if you've the time to spare?"

"I do indeed. Sessions are canceled anyway—even

a doctor needs a few days off," he said with a lopsided grin.

"Especially the doctor."

"Do they fit all right?" he asked, indicating his gift.

"As if they were made for me."

"Excellent. Shall we be off then?"

After about half an hour or so of walking, they reached the highest point on Little Embers, a rocky bluff some fifty or so feet above sea level. From there, Esther could see the far-off slim white pencil of the lighthouse she'd spied on her voyage to the island. The tranche of shifting gray-blue sea lay like a hammered metal sheet between them, pockmarked with islets and swarming with seabirds hovering on currents of warmer air. She had sometimes wondered if she could swim to one of the nearer islands, but sensibly decided that even if hypothermia didn't get her, they were by all obvious appearances uninhabited.

Esther came up here often, never failing to be uplifted by the view. It felt boundless, especially after having been hemmed in by buildings when she'd been in London. Only on the Heath, on Parliament Hill, had she felt anything approaching this freedom and space, and even that was in a far more limited way than here. "Isn't it glorious?" she said, reaching her arms wide, a smile splitting her face. As she turned to face him she caught his expression, a tenderness that cut her resolve to ribbons. She could not look away.

"Esther, I do believe you are restored to the person you once were, before you became ill."

So that was why he had accompanied her up here. She felt a tiny stab of disappointment. A question formed on her lips. "Are you certain?" she asked eventually.

He nodded.

Esther, finally hearing what she had wished for, found herself confused by a mix of elation and sudden despondency. She stood, buffeted by the wind, feeling weightless. The shrieks of the birds, the roar of the ocean faded into the background. All she could hear was the insistent thrum of her heartbeat. She wanted to run, to burn off the adrenaline that surged through her, but she couldn't move, held fast by his gaze.

"I have to confess that I am torn," he said, and she saw his eyes darken, desire replacing tenderness.

He stepped forward and reached for her hand. "Esther—" he hesitated, searching for the right words.

She put a finger to his lips, a futile attempt to silence him. If she let him continue to speak everything would change forever.

"Esther, look at me," Richard entreated, as if he

could sense her confusion. "Tell me. Do you feel as I do?"

It was the simplest of questions, but it flayed her open. She raised her eyes to his and in that moment felt beyond reproach, beyond judgment, all other cares as remote as the distant lighthouse. "I fear I do." She saw relief flood through him and felt it in herself, a syncopated beat of acknowledgment.

He smoothed back her hair with infinite gentleness. Their breath mingled, vapor misting in the cold air. She smelled the scents of a forest, tobacco, and salt and her blood sang with the truth of him. She knew in that moment that she loved him, would always love him.

They stayed like that for a long time, then sat, side by side, perched on the slope, the sea in front of them. "I wish we could stay here forever," Richard said, taking her hand in his and turning it over. He traced the lines on her palm with an inquiring finger. "Is your future written therein?" he asked, a sad smile on his face.

"Past, present, and future perhaps," she replied. "Though I believe we make our own destiny. There are forks in the road wherever you look."

"Is this one?" he asked.

"I fear it is." Esther gripped his hand in hers. "Can't this moment last forever?" she asked.

"If I had but one wish to grant you . . .", he replied.

Eventually, though, the wind strengthened and Esther began to shiver. "You're cold," he said, putting an arm around her shoulders. "It's time to return in any case. Mrs. Biggs will wonder what has become of us if we're not back for lunch."

Esther got reluctantly to her feet and together they retraced their steps. Everything was different now, her world had tilted on its axis and her head was in such a spin that she could make no sense of it. The war and its aftereffects had turned so many moral compasses away from true north, why should she not follow the pull of her own? For, as she had discovered, it might all end tomorrow. "No one must know," she blurted out as they approached the house.

Richard stopped and looked back at her. "We must be circumspect. Act as if nothing has changed."

"*Everything* has changed. I cannot believe this."

"Neither can I. But I cannot imagine it could have ever been another way. If it helps, look at it as a sincere friendship, a communion of souls that were destined for each other. Can there really be anything wrong in that?" There was such an earnest expression on his face that Esther felt her regard for him grow even larger, her heart a balloon pressing against her ribs.

"Do you really believe that?"

"I have to. There can be no other explanation for my impulses. I risk everything in inviting such a . . . such a *close* friendship, but to be without that . . . well, I should be bereft."

Esther waited a minute before replying. "I fear I too would be lost."

They were nearly back at the house. As they came around to the back door, Esther saw the twitch of a curtain at an upstairs window. The shadow of a cloud passed over the glass, revealing the face of a woman behind the curtain, a white cap. Jean. They would have to be careful.

A few days later, Esther stood at the sink, peeling the skin of the cooking apples into long thick strips. It was a Saturday afternoon and sometimes Mrs. Biggs made a pudding or a crumble for their supper. Esther had wanted to make herself useful and offered to prepare it. Earlier she had measured out flour and butter and the precious sugar, rubbing the ingredients to form a pleasing rubble. She didn't hear the footsteps behind her and jumped as she felt a gentle hand on her shoulder, the blade of the peeler jabbing into the fruit.

"Esther," he whispered.

"Richard," she scolded, concerned and thrilled all at once. "Anyone might see us."

"Hush," he soothed. "The men are all on the beach and Mrs. Biggs is out collecting eggs. We are safe. For a while in any case."

She put down the apple midpeel and turned to face him. "Well, you had better hold me, for I can hardly stand up when you do that."

He smiled and wiped away a smudge of flour from her cheek. "You grow more dear to me by the day."

Esther had never been especially vain, but even she had noticed that since coming to the island she had lost her London pallor and the dullness in her eyes was a thing of the past. She saw herself now, reflected in his eyes, in his tender regard, as beautiful.

Neither of them heard the creak of a door handle.

Jean Bardcombe stood in the doorway. A gasp escaped her, jaw slackened.

Esther leaped away from Richard as if scalded.

"Ah, Jean, there you are," Richard said, pretending that nothing was amiss. "Esther was just showing me how she gets this perfect peel." He held up the curling strip that was on the chopping board. "Quite a skill, don't you think?" His voice sounded entirely normal, as if this were a regular conversation.

Jean pursed her lips as if she'd tasted lemons and bristled past them. "Don't let me interrupt, Doctor. I was on my way to my room in any case."

"That's torn it," said Esther, looking in horror at Richard after Jean had left. "What are we going to do now?"

"Don't worry too much about her," he said.

Esther couldn't believe how unconcerned he sounded.

"There was nothing to see," he insisted.

"Will you say something to her?" Esther couldn't shake a nagging doubt that no good would come of Jean knowing of their . . . their what? Was it a romance? A love affair? Could she really have fallen for a man she had never even kissed? It wasn't as if they'd done anything strictly wrong.

But even as she thought this, she knew that she was lying to herself.

Chapter Thirty-four
St. Mary's, Spring 2018

Setting her glass of wine next to her laptop and pulling out the letters again, Rachel decided to use the rest of the evening to see if she could track down Esther Durrant of Frogmore, Hampstead. If she was still alive that is.

First, she found the suburb on a map, and was then able to zoom in on the street, and then on a photograph of the house itself. It was an imposing brick building, with a white portico and white-painted windows. A black wrought-iron fence separated it from its neighbors and a large tree took up one side of the front garden.

Then she googled Esther Durrant. As soon as the search results came up, she figured out what had been nagging at her. She remembered reading a book about female mountaineers a few years earlier. Esther Durrant had been one of them. The first woman to summit a handful of Himalayan peaks in the late 1960s and '70s. There was even a Wikipedia page, which Rachel combed through. No mention of a husband, or children, though she was referred to as the "housewife who climbed the Himalayas" in one article. No mention of her death either as far as Rachel could tell. So there was a good chance she was still alive. Was it even the same woman though? She did a quick calculation of the dates. They fit. Even so, there might have been more than one Esther Durrant living in Hampstead at that time. She tried not to get her hopes too high.

Rachel was about to shut her laptop down and head upstairs to bed when she had one final thought, a hunch really. There had to be a telephone directory online. There was even the possibility—rather remote though, she admitted to herself—that Esther Durrant still lived at the house, Frogmore.

She typed "Durrant" and the initial "E" into the search function of the online phone directory and waited. A stream of names came up. There were dozens of E. Durrants in North London alone. Gradually she narrowed it down to those in NW3. There were four. One of whom was in Hampstead.

She opened a maps page and searched for the address. It was only two streets away from Well Walk, where Frogmore was. It was a long shot, but nevertheless Rachel felt hopeful. She made a note of the phone number and checked the time on her computer. After ten. Probably not the best time to call out of the blue. She would have to wait until morning.

When she woke up, Rachel saw the pale green cardigan that she'd left folded on the chair at the end of her bed, and her first thought was of Esther Durrant and the number she'd written down the night before. It was still too early to call though, and so she padded downstairs to make herself breakfast. Jonah had put the rest of the bread back into a paper bag, thoughtfully slicing it for her before he left, and so she grabbed two pieces and shoved them in the toaster.

After she'd eaten and dressed, it was still early, so she decided to go for a walk and check what time the museum opened. Jonah had said it was on Church Street, on the way back to Hugh Town, and she remembered passing it on her way to the quay.

It was a bright, sunny morning and the streets were empty. As she walked, the smell of frying bacon drifted toward her from an open window, the sound of a radio burbled from another, and a trio of speckled-wing butterflies danced in the breeze.

Rachel found the museum easily and was checking the opening time when Janice materialized beside her. "Rachel, my love, I heard you were shipwrecked," she cried, her bracelets jangling and the bright purple and orange tunic she was wearing billowing as she waved her arms. She looked almost like a butterfly herself. "We were all so worried. Jonah had half the town looking for you."

He hadn't mentioned that.

"We were *so* relieved to hear that you'd washed up on Little Embers."

"Thanks, Janice," said Rachel when she could get a word in edgewise. "I'm sorry to have caused so much concern."

"And the boat? *Soleil?* Any sign of it? Jonah said you'd sunk."

Rachel shook her head. "Not exactly sunk, but it's definitely gone. I'm not sure how I'm going to go about getting another one—or if anyone will trust me with a boat again. I'll certainly be checking the weather forecast before going out next time." She gave Janice a wry grin.

"Oh, never mind that," Janice replied, reassuring her. "You'll be fine, something will turn up. I'll ask around, see if you can't rent something until the insurance is sorted. You've reported it to the police, yes?"

Rachel nodded. "And thanks, I'd appreciate that. In any case, I'm out of action for a few weeks." She indicated her wrist.

"Oh you poor love. I guess that means you won't be able to make yoga tonight either?"

"I guess not." Rachel smiled apologetically.

"Now, what brings you here so early in the morning?"

"Actually, I was looking for you. I had some questions about Little Embers and Jonah tells me you're the fount of all local knowledge."

"Oh, I can certainly tell you a few stories," said Janice.

Rachel's heart beat a little faster. So there *was* something unusual about that island. She knew it.

"I'd be glad to have a yarn with you. We don't open for another hour or so—I thought I'd come in early and sort out some paperwork, but I'd far rather sit and chat." She gave Rachel a conspiratorial smile. "Why don't we grab a coffee from up the road and we can talk there?"

"Sounds good. It'll be my treat," said Rachel.

The café was almost empty and they settled themselves at a corner table and waited to be served. When their coffee arrived, Rachel began. "What do you know about the island before Leah lived there?"

"Well, let me see . . . the people who lived there at one time are said to have starved to death. A bitterly cold winter did them in."

"What? When was that?" Rachel was astonished.

"In the early 1900s or thereabouts."

Not when the letters were written then. "What happened after that?"

"Well, it was uninhabited for a while. I think there was a family from the mainland who rented it in the 1930s and used to come and visit occasionally. Summer holidays, that sort of thing."

"How about later, in the 1950s?"

"Oh, well, it became what you'd call a kind of respite house nowadays I suppose. Soldiers traumatized by the war—the Second World War—were sent there. If they'd had a breakdown, or . . . shell shock. That's the word I'm looking for."

"What a strange place to be sent to. So far away from everywhere."

"It was set up by a doctor, I think. Not sure of his name. I can probably find out if you like."

"Were there ever any women there?"

"Do you know, I did hear that there was once a female patient."

Rachel's eyes lit up.

"There was something of a scandal there at one

point I think," Janice continued. "My father used to be on the force. I remember he had to go over there."

"The force?" Rachel interrupted.

"The police."

"What kind of a scandal?" Rachel wondered if it had anything to do with Esther.

"I'm afraid he never did tell me exactly what happened, but not long afterward everyone left and the place was hardly used after that, just the odd holiday visitor. I reckon Leah's the first person who's lived there in decades."

Rachel stirred sugar into her coffee. Was Esther Durrant, the mountaineer, the woman who had been there? Somehow she had a feeling she might have been.

Janice didn't have much more to add on the subject, but did have questions about Leah. "Did she seem all right to you?" she asked.

"I guess," said Rachel. "Why?"

"I worry about her, all on her own out there. If something should happen . . . if she fell, or hurt herself . . . Well, no one would know, would they?"

"I suppose not. But that's not a reason not to live the life you want to. I think for the most part, she's . . . well, not exactly happy . . . content I suppose you'd say."

"What would you think about keeping a bit of an eye

on her? You know, when your wrist is better? You'll be out that way a fair bit, won't you?"

"I suppose so. That's if I can organize another boat and not lose it again. *And* if I still have a job." Rachel gave a hollow laugh.

"It'll all come out in the wash, you'll see," said Janice, patting her arm.

Rachel wished she had her confidence.

There was a package sitting on the front step when Rachel returned to the cottage. A plastic bag wrapped around something. She picked it up and peered inside, finding a note and an old mobile phone.

She'd mentioned to Jonah over dinner that she'd lost her phone and wondered aloud how she would replace it without going back to Penzance.

"*It's got about thirty quid's worth of credit on it,*" the note said. "*Hopefully enough to last until you can organize a new one. My number's in the contacts. J.*"

Rachel smiled. He was being so nice, and yet he didn't seem to want anything from her in return. Sure, he'd seemed interested at first, but if the previous night had been anything to go by, he'd clearly had second thoughts.

She let herself inside, found the phone number she'd written down the night before, and dialed.

The voice on the end of the line was female, young. She gave her name as Eve. Not exactly what she'd been expecting. Rachel dithered; had she gotten it right? "I was wondering if I might speak to Esther Durrant," she said.

"I'm afraid she's not awake yet. She sometimes sleeps in in the mornings, especially since the accident. Perhaps I can take a message? I'm her granddaughter."

"The accident?" Rachel blurted.

"Who exactly is this?" The voice became suspicious.

"I'm sorry, I should have said. Esther won't know me. My name is Rachel, Rachel Parker, and I'm calling from St. Mary's on the Isles of Scilly. I think I might have found some things belonging to your grandmother and I'd like to return them to her. Did she ever live in a house called Frogmore, in Hampstead?"

"Er, yes, she did actually," said Eve. "But it was a few years ago now."

Rachel punched the air. She'd been right. "Then they're definitely hers. Listen, I've got a photo. Perhaps I could email a copy of it to you?"

"Sure." Eve gave her an email address. "Can you—"

"Thanks, Eve," said Rachel, a sudden blast from a foghorn in the harbor drowning out Eve's last remark. "I really appreciate it."

Rachel clicked on her phone to end the call and turned to her computer. There was likely to be an email from Dr. Wentworth waiting for her and she had been putting off checking. She drummed her fingers on the kitchen table as it loaded—she still hadn't gotten around to setting up the second bedroom as an office. Yep, there it was. Her fingers hovered over the keyboard. She'd never been one to shy away from difficult circumstances, but this email could have a disastrous effect on her immediate future. She wasn't ready to leave the Scilly Isles just yet.

"*DEAR RACHEL* . . ." He'd written in a random mix of all caps and normal sentences, and almost all of the message was in the subject line of the email. She was sure it probably wasn't deliberate, but it was unsettling nonetheless, as if he was shouting at her. "*I WAS DISTRESSED* . . ." He went on to say that he was thankful that she was okay, but that it was *MOST UNFORTUNATE THAT THE BOAT SANK.* The capital letters made her wince. "*YOU WILL NEED TO MAKE A FULL REPORT.*" He expressed his doubts that his superiors would be sympathetic—"*AS YOU HAVE ADMITTED NOT CHECKING THE FORECAST and ABANDONED SHIP.*"

Rachel fumed. She did not "abandon ship" as Dr.

Wentworth put it. She'd been towing the damn thing to land due to a defective outboard. She growled in frustration and read on.

"*As to being unable to work for six weeks, I will need to consider WHAT CAN BE DONE. To that end, I would like you to REPORT TO ME here at the museum first thing Monday. 9 a.m. sharp. That should give you time to make the necessary travel arrangements. Regards, C. WENTWORTH...*"

Rachel puffed out a breath. Well, he hadn't sacked her; nor had he asked her to stump up for the cost of a replacement boat, so that was something to be grateful for. She still wasn't looking forward to a meeting with him, though. For all she knew, he was saving the dressing down she doubtless deserved for when he saw her in person.

There was one light in the darkness, however. A trip to London would mean that she could take the letters to Esther Durrant and deliver them herself. Perhaps she might even find out who wrote them to her and why they were never sent. She was curious to find out what had happened, and if Esther had any clue that the mysterious "R" had been so desperately in love with her.

She grabbed her camera to take a digital photo of

the black-and-white print so that she could email it to Eve, and remembered that she'd snapped a few of Leah's paintings. She flicked back to look at them and was struck again by how remarkable—"luminous" was the word that sprang to mind—they were.

Chapter Thirty-five
Little Embers, Winter 1952

New Year's came and went. They toasted the early minutes of 1952 with a finger of whiskey each. Richard would have liked to linger with Esther, but in spite of his dismissive words in regard to Jean, he was careful not to give anyone further cause to question their relationship. As far as the men were concerned, she was another of his patients and was afforded no special treatment.

January was a bleak month, but he was warmed by Esther's company and conversation and dreamed at night of her lips on his, what the feel of her skin might be. They still met every day for their hour together, although he wasn't strictly treating her any longer for she had made close to a full recovery from the depression that had beset her, as far as he could tell. He found himself longing for her and desolate when their time was up. When he gazed upon her face, felt the pleasure of making her laugh, seeing the light sparkle in her eyes, nothing else mattered. When they were alone together, on occasional snatched walks on the far side of the island, he could pretend that she wasn't his patient. They were the most precious moments of his life.

He made his fortnightly report to John Durrant, ignoring his conscience as he wrote of only small improvements and the need for Esther to remain at Embers for some months to come. That John had entrusted his wife to his safekeeping caused him no small agony and he finished each missive with the resolve to end things between himself and Esther, to tell her that he had sent word for her to return home. It was a resolve that melted as soon as he saw her again.

Esther, however, showed less and less desire to leave the island; she spoke infrequently now of her life in London and of John and Teddy. It was as if she had placed them in a box and put it on the top shelf of a cupboard, something to pack away for a season. She appeared to be happy, content to tend the garden, hike for hours, and was as avid for his company as he was for hers.

One afternoon they contrived to be at the beach together. They walked out of sight of the house and

Esther was laughing at something he'd said, skipping along the sand in front of him, when suddenly she turned, grasped his hand and drew him close, closer than they had ever been before. He shuddered as she ran her chilled hands under his sweater, her eyes widening at him as she encountered his bare skin. When he thought he could bear it no longer, she raised her face to him, offering her lips to his, meeting him tentatively at first, then deeply, passionately. In that moment he nearly lost all reason.

He lay awake that night, torturing himself with the knowledge of the sins he was committing, the damage to his professional reputation if it were ever to be known. Things could not continue as they were. Jean was definitely suspicious and he sometimes caught her regarding him with faint distaste, as if she had smelled something unpleasant, though she was quick to assume a mask of detached professionalism and was always deferential to his requests.

Richard felt as if he was out in no-man's-land, far from safety on either side. He didn't know whether it was best to continue forward or try and venture back.

One day in mid-March, the supply boat brought a letter addressed to him with a Cornish postmark and a typed address. Richard tore the envelope with his fingers—no letter openers were used at Embers; even knives were accounted for, locked away by Mrs. Biggs after every meal. One couldn't be too careful. He scanned the flimsy sheet enclosed. It was from his father. "*Son, I regret to inform you . . .*" The words blurred as he read. Guilt washed over him as he remembered when he had last seen her. A week before he left for the island. She hadn't even recognized him, asking constantly for his father, who never visited. He hadn't stayed long.

"Is everything all right?" Esther asked as they tramped up the island's highest hill later that day. "You're awfully quiet."

"Am I?"

"Come on, out with it. It helps to talk." She threw him a sideways glance, mocking him.

"A letter from my father . . . about my mother."

Esther reached for his arm. "It was bad news?"

He nodded, unable to speak for a moment.

"She died last week. You know you rather remind me of her."

"Really? I'm not sure I like the sound of that. If you know what I mean."

"Not in *that* way," he said. "God no. No, in the way that she lit up a room when she came into it; when you were with her—when she was well anyway—she made you feel like the most special, most interesting person. It was exciting just to be around her."

"Oh, Richard, I am so sorry." Esther's eyes, dark violet in the bright sunlight, filled with sympathy.

"Actually, it's rather a relief. Am I allowed to say that? She'd been unwell for years and there was nothing anyone could do to reach her."

"Even you?"

"Especially me." He laughed bitterly. "Ironic, isn't it? A psychiatrist with a barking-mad mother?"

"Not at all, darling. It actually explains everything. Will you have to go to the mainland?"

"I must." His father's letter had given details of a funeral service for a week hence and that he hoped Richard would be able to attend. "I will just be able to make it if I take next week's boat. That is, if the weather holds."

"I shall miss you."

"And I you. But I shan't be gone for long. And everyone here is doing splendidly. Jean should be perfectly able to keep things running while I'm gone."

Chapter Thirty-six
St. Mary's, Spring 2018

Late that afternoon there was a knock on her door and Rachel heard Jonah call out to her. She put down the book she'd been reading and went to answer it.

He was standing there in his uniform, his hair curling in the fine mist—mizzle, as he'd described it to her—that had enveloped the islands once again. "Rachel." His eyes lit up as he saw her. "Wanted to check you got the phone."

She nodded. "That was really thoughtful of you. It'll be a great help. I'll return it as soon as I've sorted myself out with a new one."

"No rush."

"Fancy a cuppa?" she asked. "I've just put the kettle on."

"Only if you're sure."

"Course. Come on in." She walked down the hall-way and he followed.

"How's the pain now?" he asked, noticing as they reached the kitchen that she was holding her arm against herself.

"On a scale? About a five. The doc gave me some fairly decent painkillers, but I'm trying to have them only at night; they make me pretty dozy."

"Anti-inflammatories?"

She nodded.

While she made tea, he looked about the room. "My sweater," he said, spying it on the back of the chair. "Wondered where that got to."

"I was going to return it," she said with a grin on her face. "Honest."

"Tell me these aren't the letters you mentioned." He had spotted the slim pile of envelopes she had left on the kitchen table.

She looked at him as innocently as she dared.

"You didn't say you'd taken them."

Rachel flushed. "Leah said I was welcome to any-thing in the suitcase . . ."

"Really?" He clearly thought she'd been wrong to remove them.

"Actually, I may have found the woman who they were written to. In fact, I'm going to give them to her in a couple of days' time. I think she'll want to read them."

Jonah's eyes widened. "Hoo-eee. You don't waste any time."

His next question took her by surprise; she'd been expecting more of his condemnation, not his curiosity. "Mind if I have a look?"

"I won't tell if you won't," Rachel said. "Just be gentle, they're rather old and I'd hate for them to be damaged before I've had the chance to deliver them."

"I'm not sure . . ." Jonah hesitated, good judgment clearly battling with intrigue. "It seems an intrusion. Exactly how long ago did you say they were written?"

"About sixty-five years ago."

"Okay, I can't resist a peek." He picked the first envelope from the pile and opened it carefully. "*My darling E. . . .*" he read. He fell silent, his eyes skimming the paper. Rachel studied him as she added milk to both of their mugs. He was absorbed in the letter, his hands smoothing the sheets flat against the table.

She placed one mug down on the table at a safe distance from the letters and returned to the kitchen bench to clean up her lunch dishes. Jonah read on, finishing the first letter without comment and moving on to the second.

It was only after he had read all of the letters that he looked up at her, his eyes soft, and let out a long breath. "He really loved her, didn't he?"

"You never know, it might have been a she . . . ," Rachel said. "But yes, whoever wrote these truly did. And suffered for it."

"But the writer made something so beautiful out of their suffering. Have you ever been in love like that?"

Rachel shook her head.

"I think it would be a great sadness never to find the someone who truly understands you, and you them. Even if you can't spend forever with them."

Rachel shrugged. "She never read these though, did she?"

"Yes, but she must have known how he felt. No one writes letters these days, which is a shame, when you consider how beautiful—and lasting—they can be," Jonah said, holding up the final pages.

"Yeah, nowadays you're lucky if you get a text," she laughed.

"And you say you're taking these to her? Who exactly is she?" he asked.

"She's nearly ninety. And once upon a time she was an accomplished mountaineer."

"Wow. I can't wait to find out why the letters were never posted to her."

"Me too." She smiled at him. Jonah looked at home in her small kitchen and she found she liked having him there.

Chapter Thirty-seven
Little Embers, Spring 1952

Esther was quick to notice the first hints of a changing season. Spring came early to this part of the world, and almost overnight the landscape was awash with narcissi, their heady perfume and cheerful orange and saffron-yellow petals dancing on the breezes that swirled around the island. When they were fishing one afternoon, Richard made her a present of a bunch of them and laughed when she buried her nose deep in the trumpets and emerged with it dusted with pollen. "I swear they have a scent unlike any other," she declared. "Utterly divine."

"They are also known as the Lenten lily," he said.

"The what?"

"A symbol of the end of Christ's time in the wilderness. Rebirth. Renewal. New beginnings."

"New beginnings?" she echoed.

"The scent of narcissus will forever remind me of you," he said, folding her in his arms.

She didn't mind that he crushed the petals as they clung to each other.

They were interrupted from their embrace by a sharp tug on the line, almost causing the fishing rod to be lost to the sea. "Whoops," cried Richard, running after it. "Nearly got away." They worked in unison: Richard grabbed the rod and began to wind the reel in as fast as he could while Esther stood by with a large net, ready to catch the slippery fish as it emerged from the waves. She stumbled in the soft sand and landed awkwardly on one elbow, her skirt soaked by the saltwater.

Richard took one look at the expression on her face, threw his head back and burst out laughing.

"It's not funny, you know," she said as she got to her feet and attempted to brush the wet sand from her legs, giggling back at him nonetheless.

"Of course not," he said between gasps, "I'd help you up, but this fish is rather more important. I can't let it get away."

"Is that right? You'd save the fish before me?" she said in mock annoyance, hands on hips.

"Well, we've got to eat. Have you still got the net?" he asked. "Come on, look sharp."

After a few minutes' effort there was another mackerel to add to the two writhing in the bucket on the
sand. "Mrs. Biggs will be pleased," he said as he removed the hook from its mouth. "Her stargazy pie is
legendary, or so she tells me."

"A man who's driven by his stomach."

"Among other things."

Later, they tramped back to the house, the bucket
containing five large mackerel and a couple of small
fish swinging between them. "Careful!" Esther cried
as the bucket swung perilously close to her. "You'll get
seawater all over me and I've hardly dried out."

Richard flashed her a grin and she smiled back
at him.

"Is it wrong to suddenly feel so happy?" Esther
asked. "It's just that I haven't felt like this for months,
years even."

"Well, then how can that be a bad thing?"

Though she felt as if she were basking in perpetual
sunlight, Teddy was never far from her thoughts, and
guilt nipped at her with the sharpness of a razor clam.
She missed him most at night, yearned for the soft velvet
of his skin against hers, the sight of his ruddy cheeks and
the sound of his voice when he called her "Mummy."
She reasoned with herself that he was probably better

off without her, that he was thriving with the attentions of Nanny and John, that he was too young to be missing her very much. She still slept with his cap next to her, though the smell of him had long gone from it.

From time to time she thought of John, but though he pricked at her conscience, she quickly pushed such thoughts aside.

As they arrived at the front door, Richard left the fish outside before going to the shed to lock the fishing gear away. "I'll see to those later," he said. "But first I've got an hour with Robbie." He looked at his watch. "Oh heck, the time ran away with us. I'd better not keep him waiting any longer."

Richard kicked off his boots and bade Esther farewell, risking a kiss as he left.

Esther pulled off her own boots, tucking the laces out of the way and placing them neatly outside the back door. She walked into the kitchen, touching the place where Richard's lips had been, and ran slap-bang into Jean. The nurse eyed her suspiciously.

"Fishing with Dr. Creswell?" she asked.

"Yes actually. Mackerel for supper tonight." Esther's reply was smooth, her face calmly innocent.

"Indeed." The nurse looked at her closely. "I'd be careful if I were you, *Mrs.* Durrant."

Esther chose to deliberately misunderstand her. "Oh, I doubt there is anything to fear from catching our supper," she said lightly. "There's nothing dangerous out in those waters."

"I wouldn't be too sure," Jean replied.

When the time came for Richard to leave the island for his mother's funeral, Esther found herself at something of a loose end. The days dragged and she did her best to fill the empty hours with longer and longer walks. Her legs were strong now, the muscles in her calves and thighs defined in a way they had never been, and she felt as if she could carry on forever. Often she packed a sandwich or a couple of apples from the orchard—"red rollers," Mrs. Biggs had called them, and they were delicious, sweet, crisp, and juicy—with only the fading light forcing her back to the house.

Sometimes she managed to persuade Robbie and George to join her. Robbie had stopped carrying Susie everywhere with him. In fact, Esther didn't think she'd seen the doll since shortly after Christmas. She hoped that was a good sign.

"Do you think you'll be going home soon?" she asked Robbie one day as they walked along the water's edge together. George was a few yards ahead of them, but they had lingered to collect the smooth stones that lay scattered on the beach. The day was a fine one and so she cast off her hiking boots and socks and rolled up her trousers, enjoying the sun on her skin and the grit of the sand beneath her bare feet.

"Probably," he sighed. He didn't sound particularly enthused.

"Don't you want to leave?"

He shrugged. "If I'm honest, I'm dreading it. What if nothing has changed? What if I go back to the way I was? What if it's only being here that makes every-thing all right? What if here is the only place I feel that I belong anymore?" With a practiced flick, he tossed a flat pebble into the water, making it skip across the wavelets.

"But what about the people you love—your family? Don't you want to be with them?"

He flicked another stone. "The person I care about more than anything in the world is right here."

Esther stilled, then noticed him gazing ahead at George.

"It's different for you. You have your husband, your son . . ."

"Yes," she acknowledged, "I do. But you know, one of my sons died. After Teddy, I had another little boy."

She made herself say his name. "Samuel. For a long time I thought it was my fault. That I should have been there, should have known something was wrong."

"Really?"

"I don't think so now," she said slowly. "Not any-more. Ri— the doctor, I mean—has helped me to see that it was an inexplicable accident, that some babies forget how to breathe and no one knows why. That it wasn't anything I did or didn't do."

"Esther, I couldn't imagine you ever hurting a fly," said Robbie.

As she heard his words, she knew that wasn't true. A decision had to be made, and she would hurt some-one, sooner or later. "Show me how to do that?" she pleaded, breaking the intimacy of the moment.

"For you, Esther, I will reveal my secrets," he said with a mock bow. "First you have to find your pebble. As flat and smooth as you can."

"Okay." She cast around the shoreline but could see nothing but shells, bleached white by the sun.

"The best ones are over there," he said, indicating a spot farther away from the beach, where the dunes met the path.

"How about these?" she asked as she returned, clutching a handful of shale.

He examined them carefully. "They'll do. Now, it's

all in the wrist. Here, like this." He covered her hand with his and snapped it toward the water. Esther, however, forgot to let go until too late and the stone sank into the water with a loud splash.

"Have another go. You can't expect to get the hang of it on your first attempt."

Esther selected another stone and did her best to copy the action she'd seen. This time the stone gave one skip before disappearing into the sea.

She gave a small whoop of excitement and noticed George turn back at the sound.

"That's better. Don't give up; you'll soon get the knack," said Robbie.

"We can't give up, can we?" she asked, suddenly serious. "Even if it takes more courage than we think we possess."

"I suppose not," replied Robbie.

She gave him a squeeze. "It'll be all right, Robbie, it'll be all right, you'll see."

She said it to reassure herself as much as him.

Jean, however, used Richard's absence to confront Esther, rounding upon her one day when Esther was digging up carrots from the vegetable garden.

"Mrs. Durrant, I think we need to have a talk," she said.

"We do?" Esther was confused. Was this about her treatment?

"I know all about you. Your little secret. Think you're Mrs. Perfect, don't you? Well, you might have fooled Dr. Creswell, but you can't fool me."

"I'm sorry?" Esther stood up, the trowel hanging loosely from one hand.

"How dare you take another man when you've one of your own waiting for you at home? They're thin enough on the ground as it is. God help your greedy little soul." She shook with the force of her anger and Esther noticed a stray bead of spittle at the corner of her carmine-lipsticked mouth.

Somehow, Esther had known something like this was coming. "I don't suppose you've ever been in love," she replied calmly, facing her down. She would not be bullied or made to feel ashamed.

"Love? Love? I lost a man who died fighting for his country. What would you know about that? You've led a sheltered existence, haven't you? A princess in your grand house, I bet. Never having to lift a finger."

Esther's mouth hung open. The ferocity of the woman's attack stunned her.

"And what about your little boy?" Jean seethed. "What about him? Call yourself a mother? You're not fit for it. Not fit at all."

Esther could summon no defense against Jean's accusations.

"It's not right," she continued. "I hope you rot in hell for what you're doing. Dr. Creswell deserves so much better than you." Her piece said, the nurse stormed off back to the house.

Jean is in love with Richard. The thought hit her with the ferocity of a speeding bullet. That explained her animosity, her digs about Esther's responsibilities at home. It suddenly all made sense. Esther went, in that moment, from being irked by Jean to feeling compassion for the woman. She understood what hopeless love felt like.

Esther might have denied it, but she knew some of what Jean had said was true. What she and Richard had done was wrong, even if it amounted to little more than a few stolen kisses. Her place was at Frogmore, with Teddy . . . and John. For better . . . or for worse.

She worried about what Jean might do—if she wanted, she could ruin both of them with a few well-chosen words. She could only hope that Jean's regard for Richard would persuade her to remain silent, but there was no guarantee of that.

As she lay awake in the small hours, she formulated a plan. She had to convince Richard of the need for her to return home as soon as she could. To persuade him that theirs had been a joyous, but brief, friendship, nothing more. No matter what her heart desired, what her body cried out for, she had to put an end to it. If she allowed things to continue, they would both overstep the boundaries and it would bring nothing but misfortune to them all.

If she wanted her son back—and oh, how she longed for him—then her only choice was to return to her husband. She knew there was no way that John would let her take Teddy and leave him. In any case, no court would agree to it, not with her history, and, she reluctantly admitted, he deserved better than that.

Silent tears soaked her pillow as the first light of a new day began to dawn.

Chapter Thirty-eight
London, Spring 2018

Hampstead was a sea of cherry blossoms and as Rachel wound her way from the station up along the edge of the Heath and toward the High Street she stopped to admire the delicate pompoms, many of which had showered the pavement like confetti. After just a short time on St. Mary's, the crowds and the noise and the dirt of the Underground came as a shock to her, and she was happy to be out of the crush and closer to nature again, even if it was bounded by buildings. The suburb was a tangle of brick houses set on a series of undulating hills and she enjoyed the uphill tramp to Esther's house.

She stopped and checked the map on her phone again and worked out that she was only a few streets away from her destination. In fact, Well Walk was just around the corner. Curious, she detoured to see it for herself.

Frogmore didn't look much different from the Google image that she'd found: tall and solid, with a series of square-paned windows at the front. The tree in the garden was also a cherry, adrift with blossoms. A panel of buzzers was fixed to the left of the front wall: the house had been turned into flats. She wondered exactly how long ago Esther had moved out.

She had emailed the copy of the photo she had found at Embers to Eve, asking at the same time if she might come to visit, telling her that she was going to be in town later in the week. Checking her watch, she saw that it was just after two o'clock, the time that Eve had suggested in her reply. Taking one last look at Frogmore, she began to walk in the direction of Esther's present home.

The house was narrow and part of a terrace, but still imposing, with a spiked black-painted front fence and windowboxes overflowing with scarlet geraniums. She let herself in the gate and lifted the heavy iron ring of the doorknocker. The sound of it banging on the metal echoed in the quiet street.

"You must be Rachel," said the girl who answered the door. She was slim, with long fair hair and a healthy, rosy complexion completely at odds with those of every other Londoner Rachel had so far encountered. Her eyes were an arresting gray-violet. She was dressed in an old pair of jeans, a pale pink sweater, and embroidered leather slippers, and a tiny diamond twinkled on one side of her nose. "Eve." She held out her hand for Rachel to shake.

"Thank you for seeing me. I hope it's not too much of an inconvenience," said Rachel, grasping her hand.

"I'm terribly sorry," said Eve, "but Grams had a bit of a turn last night and she's not up to visitors just at the moment."

"Oh." Rachel was disappointed. She had been excited at the possibility of finding out who had written the love letters, and what had happened all those years ago. "I'm sorry to hear that."

"She might be better, perhaps later next week . . . ," Eve offered.

Rachel shook her head. "I'm only up for a few days, while I see my supervisor. I suppose I should give you these." She fumbled in her daypack and brought out the book and the photograph. The letters were still tucked inside the book. "The book has her name in it as well." Rachel hadn't yet mentioned the letters to Eve, thought that possibly Esther Durrant might want to see them first, indeed might even want to keep them to herself.

"Thanks. I'm helping her write a memoir at the moment, so this might come in useful," said Eve, looking at the photo. "She was beautiful when she was young, wasn't she?" Eve turned the picture toward Rachel and pointed to the young woman on the left of the frame.

"Did you show it to her when I emailed it through?" Rachel asked.

Eve nodded. "She looked at it for a long time. And then the next day, she wouldn't get out of bed at all. Said she felt dizzy. She doesn't have a temperature, and the doctor can't find anything specific, but she seems rather shaken."

"Oh, I do hope I haven't been the cause of it," said Rachel, contrite.

"She's a tough one," Eve replied. "She's climbed the highest mountains on three continents. I doubt that a photo would faze her that much."

"Well, do let me know if there's anything more I can do, or if you need anything from Embers, anything at all."

"Of course," Eve smiled. "I've got your details. Thank you for coming all this way. I'll make sure she sees it as soon as she wakes up."

Rachel walked back across the Heath to the train station and tried to forget all about Esther Durrant and the mysterious letters. She'd done her bit by getting them—finally—to her and she really didn't need to have any further involvement. But not knowing much more than when she'd first found them nagged at her. She knew she'd have a hard time letting it go. She supposed she could always email Eve in a week or so's time, use the excuse of inquiring about her grandmother's health. That thought made it a little easier to walk away.

The rest of the day was Rachel's to spend as she liked. The weather was fine and so she decided against getting back on the tube, making her way on foot back toward her hotel, which was near Green Park, instead. She checked the map on her phone and worked out a rough route, one that would take her down through Regent's Park and into Mayfair. She brightened. She'd treat herself to tea at Fortnum & Mason and try not to think too much about her meeting with Dr. Wentworth on Monday.

She was nearly there when she looked up at the street sign to check her progress: she was standing at the entrance to Cork Street. She'd been preoccupied the entire hour and more that it had taken her to walk from Hampstead, but she'd half-known where she would end up when she'd seen the street name as she was looking at the map.

She saw a sign hanging from a shopfront a little way down the street: Max Erwin Gallery. The same name as in the catalog she'd found at Little Embers. She quickened her steps and reached the gallery seconds later. She stood outside, looking in through the large plate glass window. There was an exhibition of Aboriginal art and, before she knew it, she was pushing the door open and inside the white-walled space.

"May I help you?" A blond-haired woman walking toward her swiveled her eyes the length of Rachel, taking in her jeans, sneakers, backpack, and wrist in a sling. Rachel knew she didn't exactly fit the image of a prospective customer.

"I was wondering if Mr. Erwin was around?" Rachel felt distinctly out of place in the cool, sterile surroundings, but she stood her ground.

Again the judgmental gaze, the flick of the eyes. "I'm afraid he is otherwise occupied at the moment. May I inquire as to who is asking?"

"Oh, he won't know me, but you can tell him I'm here about Leah Gill. My name's Rachel Parker."

The woman's eyes widened for a nanosecond, then she turned and disappeared into a back room. Rachel stood, admiring the swirled and dotted paintings in the gallery as minutes ticked by. She was reminded of ocher dirt and azure skies and gulped down the homesick feeling, glancing at her watch. Was the icy blonde even going to bother returning?

Rachel was just about to give up and leave, when a small, balding man in a dark suit scurried through the door, panting, as if he'd just run a mile and wasn't in the habit of such exertion. "Ms. Parker?" he asked, giving her at least a more welcoming look than the blonde had. He blinked at her and his mouth widened, lips stretching over his teeth and reminding Rachel of a small, amiable frog.

"Yes," she replied. "Mr. Erwin?"

"Indeed, that is me. Welcome to the gallery."

"Thank you."

"I understand you're here about an artist I represent? Actually, I should say *represented*. She no longer paints, more's the pity."

"Yes, Leah Gill. She saved my life," Rachel admitted.

A spark of interest lit up his dark eyes. "Do tell me more."

"I was pretty much shipwrecked near the island where she lives. I got my hand—" Rachel indicated the sling—"stuck in between some rocks during a storm. She pulled me out. I would most likely have drowned had it not been for her."

"Well, what a tale," he said. "Good for her—and you of course. But what brings you here?"

Rachel explained about finding the exhibition guide

at Leah's house and that she'd remembered his name from the introduction. "And then here I was outside this gallery. I had to come in."

He raised a suspicious eyebrow.

"Her work is amazing," said Rachel. "And she *is* still painting. She just won't show anyone." As she spoke, she noticed a flash of interest spark in the art dealer's eyes.

"Are you sure? She always insisted to me that she'd given up."

"See for yourself," she said, unzipping her bag and getting out her camera. She turned it on and flicked through to the snaps she'd taken of Leah's land- and seascapes.

He exhaled slowly, a low whistle. "Well, I never. She's been holding out on me."

"Oh, I don't think it's like that," said Rachel quickly. "She honestly doesn't think she's any good anymore. She's lost all confidence, but have a look at this one . . ." She showed him the half-finished portrait of herself. "It's amazing, isn't it? Even as a sketch."

"It is." Max pressed a finger to his lips. "How do I get ahold of her?" he asked. "Judging by these, it's about time I talked some sense into her."

"She doesn't have a phone, or even an address really. Though if you wanted to write to her, I could take a letter," Rachel suggested. "I'll be back there in a few days' time, and she gets a regular delivery to the island."

"I'll do better than that," he replied. "Tell me again how to find her."

Chapter Thirty-nine
London, Spring 2018

Eve closed the door on the tall woman with the Australian accent and held the photo up to the light. Even though she'd seen it on the scan that Rachel had sent through, it was fascinating to see the actual print. The faces in the picture looked wary, haunted even, as though they had seen far too much in their young lives.

Now Eve had seen this photograph, taken when Grams was at Little Embers, it made her story so much more real. As she turned to walk down the hallway, still engrossed in the photograph, the book Rachel had given her slipped from her fingers. Eve stared for a moment as it lay splayed on the floor. The pages had come loose and flown off in several directions as the binding split, the old glue cracking. As she scrambled to pick them up, she noticed a number of flimsy pale blue envelopes caught among the pages.

She flipped one over. It was addressed to Grams, at her old house, Frogmore. How peculiar. Grams hadn't lived there for more than twenty years, not since Gramps died. Eve noticed that the envelopes weren't sealed; though they had stamps on them, old ones too by the look of things, for they bore a price of 2½d, whatever that amounted to. Did she dare to take a look? She was tempted, but then decided that her grams should probably be allowed to read them first. They were addressed to her, after all.

She hesitated outside the door to her grandmother's bedroom, before gently turning the handle and creeping in.

The curtains had been drawn and the room was dim. Grams was lying in bed, the covers pulled up around her chin so that only her head was visible. Her eyes were closed, but fluttered open as Eve came closer.

"How are you feeling?" Eve asked, smoothing her grandmother's hair back from her forehead.

"Better I think. Who was that at the door?"

"You heard? Sorry if it woke you."

Her grandmother blinked. "Doesn't matter."

"It was the woman who emailed the photograph. She dropped it off, and this as well." Eve showed her the book in her hands.

Grams's eyes widened. "I remember that," she said, pleasure lighting up her face.

"Grams, there were some letters in the book. Addressed to you."

"Oh?" Her grandmother blinked in surprise.

"Would you like to have a look at them now? Are you up to it?"

"Well, help me to sit up, darling, won't you?"

"Of course." Her grandmother sat up as Eve rearranged the pillows until she was more comfortable, before going over to the window to open the curtains and let the daylight in.

"My spectacles?"

"Right here." Eve handed her the reading glasses and the slim bundle of letters. Her grandmother's hands shook as she took them from her and peered at the writing on the first envelope.

"Who are they from, Grams?"

Her grandmother hesitated and when she spoke there was no mistaking the tremulous excitement in her voice. "I can manage from here, thank you, Eve." Her lips set, unyielding as the seam of a clam.

It was a dismissal. Fair enough. Let her read them in

peace; there wasn't much privacy left to her these days. "How about I go and make some tea?" Eve asked.

Esther didn't answer; she had already begun to read.

When Eve returned to the room, her grandmother was sitting very still, staring straight ahead, and Eve worried at first that something dreadful had happened. As she came closer, she saw that tears had tracked down the old lady's sunken cheeks, leaving damp splotches on the front of her nightgown. She looked worn out, every one of her eighty-nine years showing in her expression, her defeated posture. "Are you okay, Grams?" Eve asked gently, perching on the bed next to her and taking her hand. It felt warm and birdlike in hers, thin skin covering fragile bone.

"I'm not entirely sure." She held out the letters with her other hand. "But you might as well know the whole story. My unforgivable act."

"Unforgivable? Really?" asked Eve softly, taking the pages from her, but keeping her eyes on her grandmother.

"I had another child. Two years after Teddy and before your mother. Samuel. He was a beautiful baby, but I'm afraid I was a terrible mother. I couldn't seem to love him as I did Teddy. I thought there must be something dreadfully wrong with me, that I'd failed. Some days it was impossible to even rock him in my arms; I couldn't bring myself to be near him, to touch him."

"What happened to him?" Eve couldn't help interrupting.

"One morning. The fifteenth of September. The leaves on the trees were turning . . . I remember, there was an orange and yellow carpet of them on the lawn in the back garden. I went into the nursery. Teddy was standing by Samuel's cot; he'd been trying to wake his baby brother. It wasn't until I got there and went to pick Samuel up that I realized he was cold. Stone cold."

"Oh, Grams," Eve's hands flew to her mouth. "But that wasn't your fault. It was SIDS, right, or something like that?"

Esther nodded. "But I was convinced that it was my fault, that I didn't love him enough, that was why he died. After that, well, nothing else seemed terribly worthwhile anymore. I could hardly look after Teddy. Your grandfather was so worried about me, though it was a long time before I realized that."

"Some women don't always feel that rush of love for their child, even I know that, and it certainly doesn't make you responsible."

"But at the time I believed it was, you see. Part of me always has. I didn't love him; I neglected him. And I was his *mother.*"

Eve reached across to hug her. "Hasn't anyone told you that's just not true?"

"Someone did, once."

Eve thought awhile. "So that's why Gramps took you to Little Embers?"

"Yes."

"And that's where the woman—Rachel—found the letters and the photo."

"Yes."

"But I still don't understand why he did that. It seems so . . . I don't know, so *extreme* I suppose."

"I think he thought I'd gone completely mad. Barmy. It seems harsh now, especially to separate me from Teddy, but I imagine he was at his wits' end. He was doing the only thing he could for me. And I did eventually get better. After a fashion."

"How?"

"There was a doctor. That's him in the photo. Dr. Richard Creswell." Esther pointed to the tall, dark-haired man at the back of the group. "And some lovely chaps—all damaged by the war. They'd been through far worse than I had."

"Are they the other people in the photo?" Rachel asked, picking it up from where it lay on the bed.

"There's George, and Wilkie, and that was Robbie," Esther's voice cracked and she pointed to the fair-haired one of the bunch. Eve saw her gaze linger on him. "And Jean—Nurse Bardcombe, miserable so-and-so. She didn't approve of me. One way or another we'd all suffered. Too much."

"It was an asylum?" Eve asked.

"Not exactly."

"You were locked up?"

"Not exactly."

Eve looked at her disbelievingly. "Oh, Grams. How long were you there for?"

"Four months, three weeks, and two days."

Eve was silent, considering the fact that her grams remembered to the day how long she'd stayed somewhere more than sixty-odd years ago.

"How could Gramps have done such a thing? Locked you away as if you were a madwoman?"

"Darling, in those days it was perfectly acceptable behavior by a husband. He was the head of the family. He only did what he thought was best." She sighed.

Eve couldn't begin to imagine it.

"It wasn't all bad," Esther continued. "But it changed everything. A few years after that I started climbing. It was the only way I could escape. When I was on a mountain, I forgot. It took everything I had in order to keep going. There was no energy left over for anything else."

"Being depressed isn't being weak, Grams. Surely you know that now?"

"That's not what I meant." Esther lay back against her pillows.

"Well, it's a testament that you didn't let it define you," said Eve.

"Didn't I?" her grams asked tiredly, closing her eyes. "I think it defined everything about me forever afterward actually."

"Do you want to include this in the book?" Eve asked after a while.

Esther waited a long time before opening her eyes and answering. "That will mean telling the whole story."

"There's more?" Eve asked, incredulous.

"I'm afraid there is, but I'm not sure I can do that unless I know if he's still alive or not."

"If who is alive?" Eve asked.

"The man who wrote me those letters."

Chapter Forty
Little Embers, Spring 1952

Richard stood on the foredeck of the sloop, feeling the wind in his hair and the spray on his face. It had been a strained and claustrophobic week in the company of his father and aunt and he was glad to be returning to the island. His mother's funeral had been brief, attended only by a handful of mourners from the village who remembered her in better days, his father, aunt, and himself. He laid a bunch of narcissi on the heaped earth and whispered a few lines from a favorite poem.

His aunt had left a few days after the service and Richard spent the remaining time quietly, venturing into Truro for a few much-needed supplies—notebooks, ink and paper most urgently—and accompanying his father to the village pub for dinner and a pint or two in the evenings. Their conversation was stilted, and when they did speak it was of inconsequential things, trivia. There was little to reminisce over.

While he was in Truro one morning his attention was caught by a local jewelry shop. Esther had been very much on his mind. On a whim, he entered the shop and glanced around. Trays of rings, small stones glittering, fine-link necklaces, charm bracelets, watches all arrayed for him to inspect. There was nothing that fit exactly what he had in mind and before he knew it, he found himself inquiring whether it might be possible to fashion a bespoke piece. It was perfectly possible, the jeweler replied once Richard had explained what he had in mind, but would take a little time. He checked as the jeweler wrote out the inscription that was to be engraved on the back of the piece. "If you can send it to Little Embers posthaste, I should be most grateful," he said as he settled the bill and gave the address. He hoped it would be beautiful, that she would like it.

Now, as the boat approached the jetty, his heart swelled. He had come to love this island and the patients he treated there, and, of course, there was Esther. He could scarcely see beyond the fact of holding her in his arms once more.

Jean met him at the dock and as they walked to the house, she reported that nothing untoward had occurred in his absence. Once he had fortified himself with a cup of tea, he saw each of his patients in turn. All the while he was checking up on them, another part of his mind was wondering where Esther was, what she might be doing, and how sweet it would be to see her smile spread across her face again. Time seemed to crawl along and though he did his best to concentrate on Wilkie, Robbie, and George, he couldn't wait to be done. He had deliberately saved his meeting with Esther until last, wanting to savor the moments they would share.

He noticed the worried expression on her face as soon as she entered the parlor. "Something's changed, what is it?" Rising to meet her, he stopped himself from pulling her into his arms and settled for holding her hands in his.

"It's Jean. She knows." Though the door was shut, Esther spoke in a whisper.

"Really?" He was surprised. "She gave no indication of it to me."

"Oh, believe me, she does. She took the opportunity of your departure to confront me."

Richard paused, considering the implications. "I

don't think we should be too concerned," he said eventually.

"Underestimate her at your peril," Esther warned.

"Come now, my darling, I fear you worry too much. But let us not talk of such unpleasant matters."

Esther would not look him in the eye and a thread of apprehension snaked its way through him. "Is there something else?"

She nodded, finally raising her eyes to meet his. "I have had some time to think and I believe this to be a mistake. You . . . me . . . us. It cannot end well, we both know that."

He went to interrupt her but she raised a hand.

"Please. Let me finish or I shall be unable to say what I have to say." She released her hands from his and went over to stand by the window, gazing at the landscape. "It is time for me to return home. As you have admitted, I am much recovered, and my son needs me."

She turned back to the room, facing him, tears welling in her eyes. He could see that it had cost her greatly to make the decision, to utter the words that would bring an end to everything. His buoyant mood at returning to Embers was dashed, but he knew she spoke the truth. He could not argue against it, could not distress her further.

"Very well," he said. "I shall send word immediately."

"Thank you. And for not trying to dissuade me, for I could not have borne that."

They held each other's gaze for a long time before Richard asked, "It wasn't our time, was it?"

"On the contrary, my darling, it *was* our time."

Before long Richard became aware that there were other lovers on the island in addition to Esther and himself. Late on the day after his return to the island, he was sitting on a chair at the back of the house, feeling impossibly low as he scraped the scales from a large wrasse. It was the bounty of that afternoon's fishing expedition and destined for the dinner table, but it gave him none of his usual pleasure. Out of the corner of his eye he noticed a movement in the orchard. The sun had dipped below the horizon and the light was dim, but the wind had dropped and so the disturbance and rustle of the trees was a sudden, out of the ordinary sound.

Curious, he put down his knife and rested the fish on top of a nearby stone wall, straightening up to get a better look. He had taken only a few steps toward the orchard when he saw the couple. The figures were in shadow, with their backs to him, but he recognized George's distinctive fisherman's cap right away. They were locked in a tortuous embrace, George pressed up against the bark of a tree, Robbie behind him. The force of their movement was causing the tree to shake and groan as if it were about to splinter. The few remaining fruit on its branches thudded to the ground to join other windfalls. Richard looked on at the inexplicable scene, too shocked to say anything; the two men were oblivious to his presence, caught up in their own urgent desire. He slowly retreated, returning to the wall where he'd left his catch. With a grim expression on his face, he picked up the knife and began to gut the fish, making a clean cut from cloaca to gills and letting the guts spill out onto the grass.

Richard said nothing at supper that night, but watched the two men carefully for any sign that might give them away. If he hadn't seen them with his own eyes, he would have doubted there was anything untoward between them, but he could not shake the scene; it flashed back at him like a silent film, the images flickering in his memory.

He turned the problem over in his mind. On the one hand, who was he to deny them, let alone judge them? Did he perhaps share some of the blame for this, locking them away in such a remote place with nowhere to turn for comfort but to each other? Was the torture they'd

Chapter Forty-one
London, Spring 2018

Rachel's phone buzzed and she turned it over. A message from Eve.

Not sure how long you'll be in London for, but Grams is feeling better and would really like to meet you. She wants to ask you about the letters.

She was due to see Dr. Wentworth that morning and had woken early, anxious about what he might have to say to her. In the few short days she'd spent in London, she had found herself missing the cool gray skies and low islands and, disconcertingly, a certain charismatic water-ambulance officer. She didn't want her supervisor to sack her before she'd scarcely begun the study.

Her train back to Cornwall was due to leave that evening—she'd booked the sleeper, which would get her into Penzance early the next morning and in time for the daily ferry to St. Mary's. She thought a moment before texting back.

Can we make it this afternoon?

As she pulled a brush through her hair and twisted it in a messy bun, her phone buzzed again.

Four o'clock?

She would just have time to spend an hour or so there before returning to the station for her train. She sent a thumbs-up emoji and then grabbed her bag before heading off to her meeting.

"So, Rachel. Perhaps I might hear this sorry story from the beginning?"

Charles Wentworth looked at her disapprovingly over his glasses as Rachel began to explain, his expression darkening as she described her decision to try and tow the dinghy to shore.

"I must say, I find myself somewhat at a loss. Less than a week into the job and you've lost your only mode of conducting this research. It's all extremely UNFOR-TUNATE," he said with a heavy sigh.

Rachel could hear the word as if it were capitalized like his emails and she felt what little optimism she had brought into the room evaporate. "I'll replace it, of course," she said, knowing that the cost would prob-ably wipe out her savings. "If the insurance doesn't come through that is."

"Yes, well, we'll have to see about that. You said the outboard quit?"

"It did."

"It was supposed to have been serviced before being handed over to you . . . I'll check on that. Leave it with me," he said abruptly. "You brought the police report?"

Rachel handed it over.

"Now, as to your ability to continue the research . . ." He looked pointedly at her arm.

"It'll heal soon," Rachel said quickly. "And I'll work extra days to catch up, when I'm back on board that is. And I'm sure I can find a boat to borrow too."

He made a steeple of his fingers and looked at her with an expression that Rachel struggled to read.

"I believe that when we last met, I raised the fact that funding hadn't been signed off on," he said.

Rachel's spirits sank even lower. Was the project to be abandoned before she'd even properly begun?

"The good news is that it's been approved—in fact, we've managed to secure funding for the project for the next five years."

"Five years?"

"One of the bigwigs at Ag and Fish caught wind of it and gave it a leg up in the committee hearing."

"Ag and Fish?" she asked.

"Ministry of Agriculture, Fisheries, and Food. And then the Department for Environment, Food, and Rural Affairs got involved. Best not to ask exactly why, but the upshot is that we're expanding the scope of the project. However," he paused, "in light of recent developments I'm sorry to say that we will be looking for someone else to run it."

"What?" Rachel was astonished. "But why . . . ?" He held his hand up to silence her but she plowed on regardless. "I'm ideally qualified for this and my references are excellent. Please, I would ask you to reconsider. Why waste more time trying to find someone else when you've got the best candidate already in place? I know I am the right person for the job." Rachel was surprised to find herself arguing so vehemently for a posting that would mean staying in one place for the next five years.

"You would need to commit to the entire project. I noted from your previous experience that you don't tend to stay anywhere longer than a couple of years. Can you assure me you would be there to complete the project?" It was as if he were reading her thoughts.

She nodded. "Of course."

There was a long silence. She felt like a specimen squirming under a microscope but held his gaze, did not back down.

"Very well then," he said. "I will discuss the matter with my superiors, but remember that I'm going out on a limb here for you. We can't afford to have any more such incidents in the future."

"Yes, absolutely." *No more near drownings or wrecked boats.*

"I only hope I'm making the right decision."

So did she.

Esther Durrant was a very old woman. That was Rachel's first thought as she stepped into the living room of the house in Hampstead she'd visited a couple of days ago.

"Grams," Eve said loudly. "Grams, Rachel is here, you know the lady I told you about, the one who brought the photo."

Esther was sitting on a chair facing a vase of daffodils. She was frail-looking, with hair that flowed over her shoulders like a silver river, and a deeply lined face. Her shoulders pulled across a cardigan like a coathanger, and impossibly slim wrists extended from the sleeves. Her legs too were long and thin as sticks and her feet were set at an awkward angle on a small footstool. Her eye sockets were deep and the eyelids hooded, but beneath them Rachel could see that her eyes were the same color, if a little more faded, as her granddaughter's. She might be old, but Rachel could see that she must once have been a striking woman.

"Hello, Mrs. Durrant," Rachel began.

The woman waved her closer. "It's Esther, please. And come and sit where I can see you. My eyesight's not what it once was. Nor my hearing, I'm afraid."

Rachel sat on a chair that had been thoughtfully placed next to Esther's, putting the daypack she'd been carrying down on the carpet beside her.

"Eve, darling, perhaps we might have some tea? You would like tea, my dear?"

"Oh yes please, thank you." Rachel had skipped lunch and hadn't even brought water with her.

"And some of those flapjacks too," Esther called out as Eve left the room.

A few minutes later, Eve reappeared carrying a tray laden with a teapot, cups, and a china plate stacked with the requested flapjacks. "Here you go Grams. Would you like me to pour?"

Esther waved her away. "We can manage, darling. I'm sure Rachel can help."

"All right then, just let me know if you need anything else. I'll be upstairs."

"Poor girl," said Esther when Eve had left. "It must be tedious for her to be here looking after me. She was supposed to be in Africa, helping to build a school with her boyfriend. Instead, she's been stuck here all winter. Now, where were we?"

"Eve said that you wanted to see me about the letters that I found."

"Tell me again where exactly they were."

Rachel explained about the suitcase that Leah had brought down for her.

"I'm afraid I left the island in rather a hurry," Esther said. "A suitcase of mine was supposed to be sent after me, but never was. I still don't understand how the letters got there."

Rachel shrugged. "I'm afraid I can't help on that front."

"There is something you can help me with. If you're willing?"

Rachel looked at the old lady. Was she going to find out the story of who had written the letters?

"I wonder if you might help me track down the author?"

"Of course. But do you think he—or she—is still alive?" Rachel said doubtfully. "Those letters were written a long time ago. Sorry if that comes across as harsh, but I am just being realistic. I'd hate to get your hopes up."

"Who's going to get her hopes up?" said Eve, entering the room.

Esther sighed. "You might as well hear this too," she said. "After all, you'll know soon enough."

"Know what?"

"The name of the person who wrote the letters."

Rachel and Eve looked at her expectantly.

Chapter Forty-two
Little Embers, Spring 1952

Jolted awake by a scream that shredded the air around him, Richard shot out of bed, reaching automatically for his dressing gown. Early morning—or middle of the night, for that matter—disturbances were not uncommon, but there was something about the tone of this cry that was different.

Terrified.

Urgent.

Shrill enough to curdle the blood.

It propelled him down the stairs, through the kitchen, and out of the back door before he even had time to consider the fact that he was barefoot.

He looked around frantically. Nothing seemed to be untoward. The first rays of the sun glowed through the damp mist that cloaked the trees and shrubs. There wasn't a breath of wind and a curious stillness overlaid the island. Even the birds, which should have been tuning up for the dawn chorus, were silent. The orchard, not a hundred yards from where he stood, was an army of shadows, each one a soldier marching as if in battle formation.

Richard rubbed his eyes and warned himself against such fanciful imaginings—it must have been the claret he'd drunk last night in an attempt to dull the fact of Esther's decision. His head pounded in time with his pulse and his tongue was thick in his mouth. He was about to turn back, thinking the heartrending sound must have come from inside the house, when someone screamed again. This time there was no mistaking the owner of the sound, nor the direction from which it came.

He ran toward the orchard, his heart in his mouth. "Esther! Esther, is that you?" he cried. "Where are you?" He stumbled on a tussock of grass, oblivious to the fact that the bottoms of his pajamas were now soaked with dew, and ran on, toward the sound. He imagined her hurt, injured, certainly in pain: what catastrophe might have befallen her?

Within a few seconds he was at the edge of the orchard, and then, by Esther's side. He noticed that she held a shovel in one hand and that the empty clamming bucket lay on its side on the ground next to her. Her eyes were as dark as pansies in her pale face, her body shaking with violent spasms. She didn't seem to register his presence, didn't seem to see him at all, staring off into the distance, her eyes glazed over.

He grasped her firmly by her forearms, trying to still the shaking. "Esther," he said. "Esther, it's me, Richard. What's wrong? What's happened?"

She collapsed into his arms, not speaking for several minutes while he continued to hold her. Eventually, she spoke, but he could barely make out her words. "It's Robbie. Poor, poor Robbie," she sobbed before uttering another wild, keening cry. In all the time he'd been treating her, Richard had never seen her lose her composure like this. It scared him more than her screams had.

"What?" He shook her, as if the action might bring her to her senses. "Esther, what is it?"

"Robbie . . ." She gulped again. "He's over there." She pulled away from him, turned and pointed into the thick of the orchard, where the old trees grew close together, their branches so intertwined that it was impossible to tell where one ended and another began. Then her knees buckled and she sank to the grass, the shovel abandoned, her face in her hands.

Richard walked toward the knotted trees, glancing

back several times to check that Esther was still there. She hadn't moved an inch. As he walked farther into the orchard the mist became thicker and he struggled to see more than a few feet ahead. Then, all of a sudden, the dark shape of a man loomed in front of him.

The first thing he noticed was his shoes. Unlaced, as if he'd been in too much of a hurry to tie them properly. And only then that they were suspended a few inches above the long grass, a pile of flattish stones lying in disarray beneath his feet.

The soldier dangled from a thin noose that had been tied to an upper branch of one of the apple trees, his head at an unnatural angle.

Richard had no idea where Robbie would have obtained the cord. He had always been careful to keep such items—knives and skewers too, anything that might be misused—carefully locked away.

His face was bloated, eyes bulging, tongue lolling out of his mouth. Richard felt a wave of nausea roll over him and he recoiled from the sight, staggering a few footsteps before retching bile onto the grass, heaving until there was nothing left in his stomach.

Wiping his mouth on the back of his hand, he returned to the body that swung ever so gently, as if it were a metronome marking out adagio time. Richard had seen his share of harrowing sights, had imagined himself immune to them, but this, a man he had come to care for . . . it was unthinkable.

Why had this happened? How? He'd had a brief conversation with Robbie just yesterday and nothing seemed to be amiss. How could he not have foreseen this? He kicked himself for having been so intent upon Esther in recent weeks that he failed to notice any warning signs. He had counseled suicidal men before and once, at Northfield, a colleague's patient had used a razor blade in the bath, but this was the first time someone under his care had chosen to end his life.

After a while, he turned away and retraced his steps. There was nothing more he could do for Robbie, at least not in this moment, but he hoped, at least, to comfort Esther.

He found her where he'd left her, sunk to her knees and oblivious to the seeping damp. She was still shaking, her body quivering and her teeth chattering.

"We should return to the house."

She looked up at him with fear in her eyes. "I should have known. He tried to tell me," she said. "Last week, on the beach."

"Tell you what?"

"That he was in love with George."

Richard remembered a conversation he'd had with George just before his visit to the mainland. He had spoken of contemplating suicide while he was a soldier. "I had been living in such bitter cold and was utterly miserable," George said. "I got to the point where I didn't really care what happened to me. One day I was cleaning my gun and the thought floated to me—a click of the safety, a tug of the trigger, and it would all be over. Blissful escape. My fingers were trembling as I forced myself to put the safety catch back on. I didn't want to kill myself, at least I don't think so, but after that I was afraid. Afraid that I was going to do it on impulse, and that if I did that, I'd be letting everyone down, especially my men." Richard had warned Jean to keep a close eye on George while he was away, but it hadn't occurred to him to worry about Robbie.

He had believed the man was making solid progress and would have been ready to return to the mainland within weeks. In fact, they had discussed just the day before what his life might be like when he left Embers and Richard had confirmed that Robbie's time on the island was drawing to a close. Could that have been the trigger?

Richard put his head in his hands.

The police would have to be summoned; his practice would be scrutinized, perhaps even suspended, but he didn't have time to worry about that now. His first concern was for Esther and his other patients. He could well imagine the effect on them, that months of recovery might be lost as they were plunged into uncertainty and their own private despair again. Suicide would have a devastating effect on all of them, but George would take the news especially hard.

"Come on, darling, let's get back to the house." He held a hand out to Esther and helped her up.

Chapter Forty-three
London and St. Mary's, Spring 2018

"His name was—is—Richard Creswell." Esther's voice shook as she said the name, as if it was one she'd not allowed herself to say for the longest time. "He was the doctor at Embers. We didn't mean to fall in love. We were the best of friends . . ."

"But he was your *doctor*. You were his *patient*. You were ill, *vulnerable*," Eve interrupted, a look of astonishment on her face. "And you had been committed by your *husband*."

"Don't judge me, Eve," said Esther. "Not without knowing how it was. To begin with I was as angry as you. I couldn't fathom that John would send me away, away from Teddy and my home, without my consent. But it wasn't as black and white as that—"

"But—" Eve interrupted again.

"Let me finish, darling. And please . . . I've judged myself harshly enough."

Eve bit her lip, chastened.

"We were the best of friends. We talked. I mean *really* talked. About politics and psychology, music, art, literature . . . and he listened, valued my opinion. Do you know how rare that was in my day? Well, it was, let me tell you. He saw me as more than a housewife, more than a mother. It was incredibly attractive. I suppose I was vulnerable, but it wasn't like that. He saw me, me, exactly who I was and who I could be."

"So what happened?" Eve asked.

"I got better and I came home. I had responsibilities here—your grandfather, Teddy of course."

"That must have been hard," said Eve. "I mean to leave a man you were so in love with, to know that you would never see him again."

"It was," said Esther. "But it would have been hard either way. I loved Teddy so much, and I knew that if I chose Richard I would never have been able to keep Teddy with me. Your grandfather would never have countenanced it. I had to make the best of it. I always thought one day . . . one day he might turn up, or I might find him again." She sighed. "You never forget that kind of love."

Eve's mind flashed to David, who she had once

imagined herself so in love with and now barely gave a second thought to. "Did you look? After Gramps died I mean?" Eve asked.

"It didn't seem right, not straight away anyway. And then I thought that he had most probably married, gotten on with his life, and I didn't want to be the one to disturb that. It could have stirred up more trouble than it was worth. Anyway, he might not have wanted to hear from me, not after what I said to him."

"Oh, Grams," said Eve. "What did you say?"

Esther shook her head, her mouth firm. "I thought I was being kind, but really it was unforgivably cruel."

"But what about now?"

"Read the letters," Esther said, holding them out to Eve. "And then you'll know why I have to try and find him. If, that is, he is still alive."

"We'll help," said Rachel. "If he's still alive, we'll find him, I can promise you that. It's such an incredible story; it deserves—you deserve—to find out, to see him again. I only hope we aren't too late."

"So how did you get on?" Jonah asked when Rachel returned to St. Mary's.

"Good . . . and bad," replied Rachel.

They were sitting on the wall of the quay, eating ice

creams. The weather had taken a sudden warm turn and when Rachel had run into Jonah as she was disembarking the ferry, he'd suggested the treat. It felt good to be back among the islands; she had grown to love the gentle light and the peace of the place.

"Tell me the good first."

"Well, I still have a job. As long as I can rent a boat for a while," she said.

He grinned at her, raising his hand for a high five. She went to slap it in return but he caught her hand in his and held it, curling his fingers around hers and squeezing them. This simple action made her heart contract uncomfortably and she felt a bolt of warning flash through her. It wouldn't do to get too fond of him, nothing could come of it, she told herself, and she liked him too much to hurt him.

"So what's the bad?" he asked, releasing her hand.

"The project's been extended."

"But that's a good thing surely?"

"I had to make a commitment to stay here for the next five years."

He said nothing.

"You don't understand. I never stay anywhere longer than two at the most."

"Why on earth not?"

She hesitated. "It's just always been easier that way. Life's too short and there's too much world out there to see. I hate the idea of being tied to a single place."

"Or a single person?"

"I didn't say that."

"You didn't have to. I know your type."

"And what would that be?" she asked warily.

"Women like you chew men up and spit them out before breakfast."

"I beg your pardon?" He sounded like he was joking, but there was an edge to his voice that she'd never heard before.

"You're a law unto yourself. Answer to no one, do exactly as you please."

"And that's a problem for you?" she fired back.

"I haven't made up my mind yet," he said with a mock-serious expression on his face.

She looked down at her ice cream and then out to the ocean, a deep sapphire blue that stretched forever. Jonah saw through her as if her skin were tracing paper and it threw her off balance. A line from one of the letters came to her: "The memories of our days together warm me at night . . ." She knew with sudden certainty that she would always remember *this* day, *this* hour, simply sitting on a quay licking salted caramel ice cream with a man who made her feel unsettled and at home all at once.

"Oh, and I met Esther Durrant," she said. "I looked her up online and tracked her down to a house in London. She's very old, but still got all her marbles."

Jonah raised his eyebrows.

"And this is where it gets really interesting . . . she's asked me to help her find the person who wrote the letters to her. She never heard from him again—it was more than sixty years ago. He was a doctor—Richard Creswell."

"Do you think she still loves him?"

Rachel scoffed. "Can love really last that long? I mean, without seeing someone?" It was such an abstract idea; she found it hard to imagine.

"Of course. Why not?"

"You are a hopeless romantic, Jonah, did you know that?"

He crossed one arm over his heart. "Owning it."

They were both laughing and so didn't notice a marauding seagull, keen for the last of Rachel's ice cream, swoop down on them until it was too late.

When Esther had told Rachel and Eve about Richard Creswell, Rachel thought privately that the chances of him still being alive were slim. But the old lady had looked so hopeful that she hadn't wanted to disappoint her and promised she'd do her best to try and track him down.

Starting with Google, Rachel whittled down the possibilities. There were plenty of Richard Creswells, but none of the right generation. Then after nearly an hour of searching, she came across a mention of his name in an obscure academic paper on treatment of shell shock during the Second World War. Bingo. That had to be him. She read the abstract, which led her to a hospital in Birmingham called Northfield. She searched again, but found that it had closed in 1995. There was little hope then of finding their records; she would have no idea where to start looking.

Esther had said she didn't know where he might have settled after leaving Little Embers. "To be honest, I didn't allow myself to wonder. I had my own life to get on with and looking backward would have only prolonged the pain," she had said.

Rachel started with logic. Where had the doctor lived before Little Embers? Where did he grow up? She sent a quick text to Eve, to see if she could find out from her grandmother anything about Dr. Creswell's background.

An hour or so later, her phone pinged. Eve had responded.

Cornwall. "Lost" something or other, and not far from Bodmin. She can't remember any more than that.

It wasn't much to go on, but Rachel was up for the challenge—it wasn't as if she had anything better to do until her wrist healed.

Another search yielded a town called Lostwithiel. That looked promising. There was a local library and she looked up the phone number. She was just about to call to see if she could speak to someone when there was a loud knocking on the door.

Janice was there, holding a plate covered with a tea towel.

"Hello love. I thought you might like a bit of cake. Baked fresh this morning. Can't eat it all myself."

Rachel stood back to let her in.

"So Jonah tells me you found some letters." Janice had taken a seat at the kitchen table while Rachel put the kettle on. Her eyes were alight at the prospect of a juicy story. The cake had obviously been a pretense, not that Rachel minded.

"I did," Rachel admitted, explaining that they'd been in the suitcase of clothes that Leah had given her to wear on the island. "And I found the woman to whom they were written."

"Ooh, do tell," she said, leaning forward on her elbows as if she didn't want to miss a single detail.

Rachel recounted how she had gone about finding Esther, adding, "And now she's asked me to help her find the writer—a Dr. Richard Creswell, the one who was at Embers all those years ago."

"That name rings a bell," said Janice.

"He's got to be in his nineties by now, and might not even still be around, but I have to find out—I couldn't really say no to her, not after reading them."

"Why not?"

"They were the most beautiful love letters I've ever come across. Not that I've read many, but you know what I mean."

"Ooh," said Janice, taking a large bite from the slice of cake that Rachel had placed in front of her. "I don't think anyone's ever written me a love letter."

"Me neither," said Rachel, feeling a sudden yearning for something she'd never had.

"So where did you start?"

"Google."

"Any luck?"

"Not really. People that old don't generally have much of a digital footprint. All I've got to go on at the moment is the name of a town near where he lived when he was growing up."

"Can I help? The museum's got some pretty good search options."

"Sure, have a go at it," Rachel shrugged. "The more the merrier. After all, we might not have much time."

"Or we might be entirely too late."

"True. But I think it would put Esther's mind at rest—you know, to find out what happened to him. I think she might still love him."

"Oh, I'm a sucker for a love story," said Janice, the bracelets on her arm jangling as she bit into her cake again.

Late that afternoon, as the sun was beginning to set, Rachel walked past the slipway near the pub, feeling a pang as she noticed the mooring where *Soleil* had once been tied up. She was fretting over her assurance to Dr. Wentworth that she would see the project through, that she would stay on the island for another five years.

"Halloo!"

She looked up to see a now-familiar figure a little way along the causeway.

"Leah, what are you doing here?" she asked when

the woman came closer. "I thought you never left Embers?" Rachel's mind scudded back to her meeting with the art gallery owner in London.

"Never say never," she said. "Anyway, I thought it was about time I got out and about a bit. Join me for a drink?" They were only a few steps from the Mermaid.

Rachel hid her surprise, both at the sudden appearance of Leah and at her suggestion of a drink. "Sure. In fact, it's my treat. It's the least I can do."

"Tanqueray," said Leah firmly. "Make it a double."

It was still fairly early and the pub was quiet when they pushed their way past the heavy door. They settled themselves in a corner and Rachel went to the bar, ordering a gin and tonic for each of them. She decided not to question Leah's order of a double.

Two drinks later, and Rachel was beginning to feel a warm glow envelop her. Leah too was far more talkative than when they had been at Embers. They had been discussing Rachel's project, and she had confided her promise to stay on the islands to complete it. "It's not necessarily a bad thing, you know," Leah said, her voice slipping on the sibilants. "Stay. Put down some roots. What's the worst that could happen?"

Rachel realized that she didn't have an answer to that anymore.

"Anyway," she said. "You and Jonah—"

"There isn't a me and Jonah," Rachel said quickly. "Strictly in the friend zone."

"Well, you should do something about that; the man's gorgeous."

"I think he's looking for something a bit more serious than I can give him," she admitted.

"What are you afraid of? Everyone needs someone."

"Look who's talking!" said Rachel. "You've cut yourself off completely. Tell me, why did you choose such a life?"

"Listen, Rachel, I've made mistakes in my past, pushed away people who tried to help, tried to help Tabitha too. Perhaps if I'd acted sooner, things would have been different, but at the time I was so caught up in my own dramas . . . getting established as an artist, painting like a demon, ignorant to what was going on right under my nose. I was far from a perfect mother, and then her father . . . well, that's another story again."

"I'm sure you did your best." Rachel guessed that the alcohol was largely responsible for Leah's unexpected confidences.

Leah looked at her sadly. "In the end, that's all we can do."

"But you still haven't answered my question," Rachel persisted.

Leah looked her straight in the eye. "I'm a fraud, Rachel," she said quietly.

"What?"

"A fraud. As an artist. Oh, I had a bit of talent once, but it didn't last. After everything that happened with Tabitha I lost it all. Her, and my work. I couldn't face anyone, none of my friends, certainly not my dealer. I ran away I suppose, first to Scotland and then here. Didn't feel as though I had a right to the life I'd once led, thought I could hide away and everyone would forget about me. That *I* could forget about me."

Rachel went to speak but Leah continued.

"Except it didn't exactly work out like that. I tried to give up painting completely, but I found my way back to it. Somewhere along the way I stopped caring if I was any good. The act of painting was enough. We're not so very different, you and I, you know," Leah continued. "Except that I've the benefit of a few more years' hard-won experience than you. All I'm saying is that shutting yourself away, literally or emotionally, isn't really the best course of action. I believed that by staying away from everyone I couldn't hurt them anymore, nor could they hurt me. I'm no longer sure I was right."

Rachel heard the truth in her words.

"You're young; don't for heaven's sake wait until it's

all too late. Get stuck in this messy life, the joy and the sorrow . . . drink deep . . . speaking of which . . ." She got unsteadily to her feet, squinting at the clock above the bar. "Fancy another?" Her words slurred.

Rachel too noticed the time and peered out of the window, where night had fallen without her realizing. "I don't think you'll be going back to Embers tonight," she said.

Leah shrugged. "S'pose not."

Rachel didn't feel like any more to drink and didn't think it would do Leah any good either. "Why don't we order some food and you can come back and stay at mine?" she suggested. "There's a spare room and I can even rustle up a toothbrush."

Leah smiled widely at her. "Great. I'll get another round in."

Rachel didn't have a chance to refuse.

Chapter Forty-four
Little Embers, Spring 1952

With one arm around her shoulders, Richard guided Esther back to the house and bade her sit in the parlor. She was quiet and clear-eyed, her earlier shivering having ceased, though for years afterward he would be haunted by the look on her face when he had found her. He didn't think anyone could possibly look so pale, paler than winter milk even, blanched of all color.

It didn't appear that anyone else had been woken by Esther's screams and though he hated to leave her, he went to rouse Jean. He knew he could rely on the nurse to keep a cool head and as he explained what had happened she nodded briefly before saying, "We'll need a ladder, and something to cut him down with. Give me a minute and I'll get dressed and come with you. We can put his body in one of the cottages; I don't think bringing him to the house is a good idea." She was matter-of-fact and unemotional, speaking rapidly and quietly. He found himself thankful for her calm presence of mind.

"Absolutely," he agreed. "There's a ladder in the shed and I'll fetch a knife too." It didn't occur to him that he was still in his pajamas and dressing gown, nor to put shoes on his bare feet.

Together they followed the trail of dark footsteps to the orchard.

Jean let out a tiny gasp when she saw Robbie's gently swinging form, but stifled it and held the ladder steady as he climbed.

"Oh God. No." Richard saw that part of the cord Robbie had used to hang himself with was the strap from George's binoculars. He raised his knife and began to saw at the leather. He made short work of it, a quick back and forth and Robbie fell like a lead weight to the ground. There was no kinder way.

"I'll take his arms if you get the feet," Jean instructed after Richard had climbed back down the ladder. He was again grateful for her clear and quick thinking.

Together they made a staggering progress toward the stone cottages on the west side of the island. Richard shouldered the door of the closest one open and they stumbled in. It was a simple dwelling, with two sparsely furnished rooms, but there was an iron-framed single bed in one of them. They hauled Robbie's body up onto the ticking mattress and Jean found a blanket. Richard noticed her cross herself as she laid it over him.

"We will have to notify the police," Richard said as she turned to face him. "It is a good thing the boat is due today. We can get a message to St. Mary's by the evening."

"Yes," agreed Jean firmly. "But I think what we need is a strong cup of tea, first and foremost."

"Right you are. I should get back to Esther too, check on her."

"Why don't you leave that to me. You've both had a terrific shock."

Richard hesitated. Insisting on going to Esther would be to further reveal his feelings for her. "Good idea," he said. "I shall tell the men when they appear, and Mrs. Biggs."

"I expect she'll already be in the kitchen by now."

"Yes, yes . . . I expect she will." Richard suddenly felt himself to be at a loss and dithered about what to do first.

"Strong tea," Jean instructed. "And I think she's got some sugar squirreled away. Tell her to put two spoonfuls in. Heaped."

When Richard reached the kitchen there was no sign of Mrs. Biggs and instead of putting the kettle on the range, he went to the pantry, where he knew there was a bottle of whiskey hidden somewhere on the top shelf. He sloshed a good inch into a mug and sat down at the table, dazed. He steeled himself to tell George. He could well imagine the man's reaction, hoped it would not break either of them. He had to stay strong. He decided to tell them as a group, it would be kinder—to himself as well as the men.

He would also have to inform Robbie's next of kin, his sister, and he had no idea what he might say to her to soften the blow. He felt entirely responsible. She had entrusted him with the welfare of her brother and he had failed her. The mug rattled, jittering against the table as he picked it up. He downed it in one gulp, wincing as the amber liquid flamed down his throat.

Later that morning after Richard had sufficiently recovered his wits, he summoned everyone into the parlor to explain the situation. Reactions ranged from the dumbfounded to the resigned. Wilkie couldn't understand it, asking over and over why no one had noticed, most of all himself. "I thought we were friends," he protested. "He could have confided in me if something was wrong, getting him down, you know."

"Don't blame yourself," Richard said. "Often those people closest to a person still have no idea. Even I was unaware he was having suicidal thoughts. If blame rests anywhere, it should be squarely on my shoulders."

"I have to see him."

George's voice was low and Richard noticed that his right leg was jerking as if it had been electrocuted, though George appeared oblivious to the movement. Richard wanted to place a reassuring hand on the man's knee, but held himself back. He had to try and keep a professional distance, or he would lose control of himself and the situation entirely. He clenched his jaw. "I can't stop you, but I don't think it will help," he replied, trying to sound calm.

"With all due respect, Doc, I've seen more than my fair share of dead bodies."

"Precisely why I don't think it is a good idea," he replied.

"Afraid in this instance, I'll keep my own counsel on that, if it's all the same to you. And if I may, I would like to, to—" He stopped and caught his breath. Richard could see that George was trying not to break down in front of them all. "To prepare his things."

"It's rather unorthodox, but I don't see why not."

"I think that would be a good idea," said Jean.

Esther remained quiet; Richard felt her eyes searching out his across the room. He flashed her what he hoped was a reassuring smile but kept his thoughts focused on George. He was the most at risk of all of them, would need careful observation and the most help.

As the others were leaving the room, Richard signaled to Esther to stay behind. The door closed and they were alone. "Are you sure you are okay?" he asked.

She nodded. "I can't stop seeing his face . . ."

"I know. If it's any consolation, I can't either."

Richard slammed his fist on the table, startling her. "I should have seen it," he said. "I was his *doctor.* I was supposed to be *helping* him. Not this . . . I've been far too caught up with other things and in neglect of my duties."

"It's astonishing what we can hide from others, even those close to us," Esther said, trying to reason with him.

"No!" he cried. "I am responsible for this tragedy. He was under my care. I should have foreseen this."

He took a deep breath.

"I'm sorry you had to find him," he said in a calmer voice. "What were you doing in the orchard at that time of the morning? It looked as though you were on your way to the beach, but that's in the other direction."

"Yes, I know. I . . . well, if you must know I thought I heard someone, someone crying." She sighed. "I thought it was Teddy. My mind still plays tricks on me and even though I told myself it couldn't possibly be, I had to go and look."

"Oh my darling." He placed a hand on her shoulder and she turned toward him. He breathed in her familiar perfume, and something else, something herbal, overlaying it.

"What is that smell?" he asked as he raised her hands to his lips.

"Rosemary. For remembrance. I left a posy outside the back door. Could you tuck it into his pocket? I'll look for Susie too. He'd want her with him." He was touched by her thoughtfulness, and the fact that she had pulled herself together so quickly. She was stronger than he had given her credit for.

Esther drew him into her arms and they clung together, as if survivors of a shipwreck. He felt desire, too long held back, flood through him like a rising tide and he was powerless to resist her lips as she raised her face to his. Esther met him with equal fervor and he looked into her eyes. They held a promise. "Are you sure?" he asked, his breath ragged.

She nodded. "Nothing else matters anymore, nothing except this, this moment."

It was irrational, but it was as if the only way to combat the heavy weight of death was to do something completely opposite, something life-affirming. He let go of the tight control he'd been holding on to for so many weeks. He was oblivious to the fact that someone might walk in on them, no longer cared even if they did. As if in slow motion, he undid the pearl buttons on her blouse and cupped her breasts through the fine lace of her brassiere.

Esther gasped and reached for him again, pulling him toward the chaise. They fell onto it, their bodies pressed against each other, legs and arms entwined, heat rising between them, consuming them. He ran his hands over her skin, lost in the feel of her, the satin of her skin, the softness of her hair, the delicate, familiar scent of her. Esther opened herself to him and they sought each other's lips once more, his gaze locked on hers as he drowned in the depths of her violet eyes. The world around him contracted until all that mattered was them, in a moment that seemed to stretch forever.

Sometimes I think that you are the only thing in this world that makes sense," said Esther as they lay together afterward, entwined, sated.

"I know," Richard said, smoothing her hair from her forehead, placing a kiss on the fine, smooth skin.

"But it can never happen again," she said, resignation in her voice. She was flushed, her face as rosy as the tips of her nipples, her hair a wild tangle. She had never looked more beautiful to him.

"No," he agreed, desolate even as he uttered the words.

"Nothing has changed. I must still leave."

"I understand."

It felt like the beginning of the end.

Chapter Forty-five
St. Mary's, Spring 2018

The accent on the other end of the phone was as thick as custard, and Rachel had trouble understanding it, not least because her head was pounding from the gin and tonics she had downed with Leah the previous night. She'd rung the Lostwithiel library, hoping they might be able to shed some light on the whereabouts of Dr. Creswell. She could only make out about every fifth word and had to ask the woman to repeat herself several times before she got the gist of what she was saying.

"So there was a family with the surname Creswell who lived in the area?" she asked.

"Yarp, 'appen there still is."

"Thank you, thank you so much." Rachel put the phone down, happy to have gotten that far. She would look the name up on the online phone directory for the area. But first, she had to wake her houseguest, who was snoring loudly in the spare room upstairs despite the fact that it was past ten o'clock.

The church bells sounded noon before she dispatched a rather worse-for-wear Leah, who had inveigled a lift back to Little Embers from Tom at the co-op. She promised to call in on her as soon as she was back on the water. "I'd really like that," Leah said, embracing her as she left.

Rachel sat down at the table and was surprised to find that her hands were shaking when she made the call. She'd found the listing she was looking for—there was a Creswell, Dr. R. living in Milltown, North Cornwall. She'd checked it out on an online map, and the village was pretty close to Lostwithiel. It looked like she had the right person.

"Hello," she said when the phone was answered. "I wonder if I might speak to Dr. Richard Creswell."

"Speaking." The man's voice was old, creaky, and he coughed loudly as soon as he had answered. "Sorry about that. How may I help you?"

"My name is Rachel Parker. You don't know me, but I have some information for you," she began.

"If you're one of those wretched salespeople I'm not interested. Go away and bother someone else," he said.

"No, no, it's not that," Rachel said hastily. "Please don't hang up. Did you once know someone called Esther Durrant?"

There was silence on the other end of the line and she thought that he might have hung up on her. "Hello . . . ?"

"What is it? What's happened to her? Has she gone?"

"No, she's still very much alive." Rachel could have sworn she heard a sigh of relief. Either that or it was a crackle of static on the line.

"I'd like to come and talk to you about her if I may?" Rachel held her breath, hoping for a positive response.

"Wednesday, teatime. I'm better in the afternoons."

She jumped at the invitation, such as it was. "Thank you, thank you, Dr. Creswell. You won't regret it, I promise."

There was a harrumph and then more coughing and the line went dead.

Later that afternoon, as cabin fever was starting to set in, Rachel went for a walk. The pain in her wrist and fingers had almost disappeared, as long as she didn't use her hand too much, and she found herself craving some fresh air. The previous day's drizzle had stopped and she looked out of the kitchen window into a bright, clear sky. Luckily, she had a pair of trainers with velcro fastenings, which, although they might not be as suited to the terrain as her new hiking boots, were at least easier to get on and off. Shoelaces were beyond her at the moment. She checked her map and decided that she would attempt a complete circumnavigation of the island.

She hadn't gotten farther than the quay at Hugh Town when she was nearly mown down by a wild-haired woman wearing the same paint-covered fishing smock she'd had on the previous day, carrying a bag of groceries.

Leah again. She hadn't yet made it back to Embers then.

"Hello!" she called out, expecting a warm reply.

"You!" Leah said when she reached her. "I was on my way to see you." She glared at Rachel, her mouth set.

In that instant, Rachel knew right away what must have happened. She did her best to play things down, pretend innocence. "What's up?" she asked. "Did you forget something?"

"What's up? What's bloody up? I'll tell you what's up. Some interfering outspoken little twerp got in touch with my dealer, didn't they? There's only one person who that could have been."

Ouch. Leah was really angry. A small crowd had gathered, hearing her raised voice, but they kept their distance, not wanting to be sucked in to the argument yet keen to hear the particulars nevertheless.

"I can explain . . . ," Rachel began.

Leah held up a hand. "Don't even start. Amber at the post office said Max had been trying to reach me, had called her to leave a message. You know who Max is, don't you?" She glared at Rachel, who nodded dumbly. "What gives you the right to poke your nose into other people's lives? Hey? Who exactly do you think you are? I looked after you, saved your goddamn sorry Australian arse and *this*, this is the thanks I get? You spy on me in my own house, take no heed of my wishes, my strict instructions actually . . . And to think I imagined we might have been friends."

Leah was now standing so close that Rachel felt her breath warm on her face. It had the unmistakable bitter aroma of gin.

"You need to learn to mind your own bloody business, girl."

"I'm sorry, Leah. I thought I was helping."

"Helping? What would you know about helping? You're so sure that you know what you're doing, aren't you? That your way is right? You don't give a shit about anyone or anything else."

"That's not fair," said Rachel quietly. "I *am* sorry for going into your studio when you had asked me not to. It was wrong of me. But when I saw your paintings, I snapped a couple of shots of them without really thinking. Then when I was in London and saw your old gallery . . . well . . ." Her voice trailed off.

"Well what?" Leah asked.

"People should see those paintings, Leah, they're amazing. I was really only trying to help."

"Well it's *my* work and *I* decide what's best for me. Don't *ever* think about interfering again."

"Now then, what's all this?" Jonah had materialized by Rachel's side.

"Ask her, she's the one who's gone and caused all the trouble," said Leah before swirling around and heading back toward the end of the quay.

Rachel had half-expected Leah to be upset when she found out what she'd done, but she was shaken by the anger of her response. And she minded now that she might have encouraged Leah's drinking, as it doubtless made everything worse.

"You okay?" Jonah asked.

Rachel shrugged. "I guess."

"What was all that about?"

"Long story. I've got some apologizing to do when she's calmed down I reckon." Rachel nearly didn't tell

Jonah her news about Dr. Creswell. After the confrontation with Leah, she wondered fleetingly if her other project too would be seen as unwelcome meddling. Perhaps she should cancel her plans, refocus on work, keep her head down. She weighed the possibilities in her mind before deciding that as she had agreed to help Esther, she was obliged to carry on with her plan.

"You, however," she said, "are just the person I need to see."

"I am?"

"Yes. I've found him. Dr. Creswell. He's still alive and he lives in Cornwall."

"No kidding, really?"

"I know. What are the odds? We had a bit of a chat and I asked if I could come and see him about Esther, that she'd asked me to help track him down."

"I see. So when are you going?"

"Next Wednesday. I'll get the train from Penzance I guess, though I'm not sure how close the nearest station is. Would you like to come?" she asked.

"Let me see if I can swap my shifts around. I could drive too. Hiring a car would make the whole trip a lot easier."

"That'd be a big help," she admitted. "But are you sure?" She felt suddenly uncertain of her request, that she might be asking too much of him.

"Why wouldn't I be?" He blew out a breath of frustration. "Perhaps I'm just being nice, Rachel. Can't a person be nice without an agenda anymore? Anyway, I'm not coming just for you—I want to meet the man who wrote those letters."

She didn't answer, ashamed that she'd questioned his motives.

Chapter Forty-six
Cornwall, Spring 2018

The house was a modest one, a cottage tucked away down a lane that led off from the village's main street, but they found it easily enough. It had a white front and dark slate tiles on its steeply sloped roof and twin gable windows that stood out like a pair of watchful eyes. The front garden was a mass of yellow blooms.

"Narcissi," said Jonah. "Just like on the islands."

"They smell divine, don't they," said Rachel. "And they're such a cheerful color. It's hard to be sad when you look at them."

Together they walked up the front path but Rachel hesitated when they reached the door. "Are we doing the right thing?"

"You're having second thoughts? Now? Isn't it a bit late for that?"

"What if it's better to let sleeping dogs lie? You saw what happened with Leah."

"Yes, you still haven't explained about that."

She waved him away. "Later." Still, she hesitated.

"Come on, Rachel, I've never seen you scared of anything, don't disappoint me now."

"I'm not scared. Learning the value of caution per-haps, but not scared," she said.

"Well, I for one haven't come all this way to chicken out." Jonah reached for the bell and gave it a decisive ring.

They waited. And waited.

Rachel was reaching into her pocket for her phone to try and call the doctor, when the door slowly opened.

"Miss Parker?" The man in front of them must have once been tall, but stooped slightly now, his shoulders curved inward. He was thin in the way old people often are, their muscle tone diminished and the skin sitting slack over their bones. But he still sported a thick head of hair and, perhaps surprising for a man in his nine-ties, had bright, inquisitive eyes that swept sharply over the pair, assessing her.

She nodded. "I've brought a friend with me, I hope

that's all right. I can't drive at the moment, you see." She indicated her bandaged wrist.

"You're two more visitors than I usually get in a week," he said. "Come in, come in."

"I'm very pleased to meet you," Rachel said once they were inside. He had ushered them into a room at the front of the house, where a large cat was warming itself in a patch of sunlight on the window seat. The walls were lined from floor to ceiling with books and a pair of old leather Chesterfield sofas faced each other across a coffee table that was also piled with books.

"And I you," he replied, a polite expression on his face. "Now tell me again what this is all about?"

Rachel explained about working on St. Mary's and being shipwrecked on Little Embers. When she mentioned Esther's name, the doctor flinched, as if to hear it still caused him pain. She'd been on the brink of mentioning the letters, but seeing his discomfort, she faltered.

"Rachel found something that she thinks belongs to you," said Jonah, helping her over her hesitation.

"Oh yes?" He looked puzzled.

"Letters," she said. "I apologize, but I read them before I knew exactly what they were. You're the 'R,' aren't you?"

The doctor slumped back in his chair. It was clear he knew exactly which letters she was referring to. "They were merely the foolish imaginings of a much younger man," he said eventually.

Rachel didn't believe him for a second.

"Do you have them?" he asked.

"Er . . ." Rachel hesitated once more. "Actually, I gave them to Esther—Mrs. Durrant. It was her name on the envelopes you see. She told me your name, but that's all I really had to go on to start with. She asked me to help her find you."

He started. "She did?"

Rachel nodded.

"Let me be clear, you're telling me that Esther's read the letters?"

"Yes, I believe she has," said Rachel.

"And that she asked you to look for me."

"She did."

Richard ran a shaky hand through his hair, his eyes glistening. "It feels like it was yesterday. She was the loveliest of women," he said. "Fair took my breath away when I first saw her, I don't mind telling you now. And she had more guts than even I realized. I followed her life—from a distance of course."

"But you never made contact with her again?" Rachel was surprised.

"No. It was best that way . . ." His voice trailed off and he appeared lost in memories.

"Would you like to see her again?" asked Jonah, interrupting.

Surprise dawned on Richard's face. "Oh no. Absolutely not. It's been far too long." Then, a few seconds later, "Does she really want to see me? Where is she? Still in London?"

Rachel nodded, her eyes alight with the possibility of reuniting two lovers after so many years.

"I couldn't possibly manage the trip," he said, a frown on his face. "It's a long way, and then there's Anna."

"Anna?" asked Rachel, puzzled, for she had seen no evidence of a female presence in the house. Was Anna his wife? That could complicate things.

"Anna Freud," he explained. "The tabby lounging in the sun over there."

"Oh, right," said Rachel, breathing a sigh of relief. "I thought you meant your wife."

"No. Never married. Never lucky enough. The cat's named after Sigmund's daughter." He smiled at her.

"Could we leave some food out? We'll have you there and back in a day or two," she suggested.

Richard appeared to consider the suggestion.

"But there's Meals on Wheels," he prevaricated.

"They deliver on a Thursday. Would I be back by then?"

"Why don't we take their number, so we can call just in case we're not?" she suggested, countering his objection.

"Rachel," said Jonah. "How about we let Dr. Creswell have a think about it? There's a fine old church in the village that I saw on the way through that I'd like to check out. Why don't we get some fresh air for a bit?"

She realized what Jonah was doing. Best to give the old man some time to absorb the information they'd just landed him with. "Oh yes. All right then. Would you mind if we called you in the morning?" she asked Richard. "Would that give you enough time to decide what you'd like to do?"

On their way into the village, Rachel had seen a bed and breakfast and she suggested to Jonah that they see if there were any rooms available. As they drove toward it, she got out her phone and called Eve. "I think we're on the way to solving the mystery of why the letters were never sent and reuniting them," she said after hellos had been exchanged. "I'll see you tomorrow. About two? Perfect."

She hung up and looked at Jonah, the satisfied grin of a Cheshire cat on her face.

"I don't understand," he said, flicking a brief look at her before returning his focus to the road.

"Understand what?"

"How you think the doctor will agree to go. Don't you think we should wait until we've spoken to him again?"

"Did you see how he looked when we told him about Esther and the letters? He'll definitely say yes."

Jonah shook his head. "How can you be so cynical about love and commitment, and yet you're like a dog with a bone about this reunion?"

"They've been separated for more than sixty years. She was the love of his life," she said, exasperated.

"I know. Exactly."

Rachel turned to face the window. She, who was normally so rational, who had built her career on the evidence before her, not hunches or feelings, had become involved in something intangible. She didn't have an explanation as to why this had become so important to her, nor why she so fervently believed it would all work out.

"So why don't you believe that's possible for you?" he asked.

She shrugged. "Well, it's never happened, has it? I'm thirty-five. If it was going to happen, it would have done so by now; the odds are against it."

"Says who? There's not a timeline on love, you know."

"Maybe it's not in my destiny—not everyone gets that, do they? And I'm okay with that; there's plenty of other stuff going on for me. I like the way things are, as it happens," she said, a defensive note creeping into her voice. "And there *have* been men in my life if you must know."

"Yes, but being in love and having someone love you back is different. It changes everything. To have someone who sees you for yourself, someone who can read your heart. We all want to be seen, Rachel, to be acknowledged for our true selves. Even Narcissus, who looked into the pool and fell in love with his own reflection."

She looked at him askance. "You can't tell me that you've ever been in love like that. If you had, you'd be married. Kids. The whole shebang."

"Don't be so certain you know everything, Rachel."

"What, then? What don't I know?" She pushed for more from him.

"She left the islands," he said carefully. "Didn't want a bit of them. Getting away was more important to her in the end than me."

"Oh God, Jonah. I'm sorry. I'm being completely

insensitive." She paused, thinking. "Why didn't you go after her?"

"It wasn't that simple. Anyway, it was a long time ago."

They reached the bed and breakfast and their conversation was interrupted. Jonah parked while Rachel went in to inquire about a couple of rooms.

She was signing them in when Jonah arrived, carrying their bags.

The woman handed a set of keys to each of them. "Two rooms. But there's an adjoining door," she said with a wink.

Rachel ignored her, still feeling as if she'd put her foot in it with Jonah.

"Here for the conference, are you?" the woman asked.

"No," said Jonah. "Just a short break."

"Lovely. The food at the pub's not bad, or there's always the Indian. They do a good tikka masala."

"Thanks," he said.

"Just sing out if you need anything."

"We will." His usual good humor seemed to have deserted him.

They walked upstairs and found their rooms. As Jonah reached his, he turned. "I'm tired from the drive. Might have a nap."

Something had definitely changed between them. There was a new coolness in his voice, a distance.

"See you for dinner?" she asked.

"Sure." The answer was curt and before she knew it she was standing on her own in the corridor, his door having shut smartly behind him.

Chapter Forty-seven
Little Embers, Spring 1952

It was several days before the police arrived. Richard had sent a message with the weekly supply boat, but the captain reported that the islands' only police officer had gone to visit relatives on the mainland and they would have to wait until he returned. Wednesday, he reckoned.

By noon of the expected day, the tide was high and the water calm and glassy. It looked like summer, with the sky reflected in the deep blue water, but an unseasonal cold snap chilled the air and Richard shivered in his thick sweater, pulling the sleeves down over his freezing knuckles and jamming his hands in his trouser pockets.

He couldn't confide in Esther, much as he might want to, and he would never dare admit it to Jean. He was her employer, not to mention that there was something in Jean's regard for him that made him wary. He suspected that she would take any confidences as a sign of intimacy and he had no wish to encourage her in that way. He kept his worries to himself, bottling them up in exactly the way he always counseled his patients not to.

Sergeant Taylor, a stocky man with a luxuriant mustache and gimlet eyes, jumped off the boat onto the jetty. He wore the uniform of any British bobby—navy serge trousers and jacket resplendent with silver buttons and a hard domed helmet. A truncheon swung from his belt. He looked smart and businesslike, in contrast to Richard's casual attire, and Richard felt a sense of relief at his arrival. It hadn't been easy for any of them knowing that Robbie's body lay in one of the cottages while their lives carried on. "Dr. Creswell?" he said as he approached.

Richard nodded, extending his hand.

The sergeant's grip was firm and dry. Reassuring. "I understand we've got a body to inspect. The tide will be too low to leave again in a few hours' time so let's dispense with any niceties. If you could show me where it is, I'll get right to it."

Richard led him along the path to the cottages and

indicated the door behind which they'd left Robbie. "I'll need you to accompany me," said the sergeant. "In case I've any questions."

"Of course."

They walked into the small room and Richard pulled back the blanket. "Death by strangulation." He found the only way he could cope with the situation was to maintain a professional distance. "We found him in the morning earlier this week, hanging from one of the apple trees in the orchard. I can show you that later if you like."

"Yes, I shall need to inspect the scene." The police officer leaned forward and gingerly inspected the neck, using one finger to prod the livid mark.

"He used a thin cord, a strap I believe," Richard explained. "It's still attached to the tree. We did all we could to keep anything potentially dangerous away from our patients, but—"

"Did he leave a note? Any sign of his intentions?"

Richard shook his head. "Nurse Bardcombe searched his room, but no, there was nothing."

"I understand this is a facility for the treatment of former servicemen?" he asked.

"It is."

"Then did he give no indication that he was contemplating suicide?"

"None at all. I'll let you have my notes. Of course, we took precautions against this kind of thing, but somehow he managed to get hold of a strap."

The sergeant shook his head. "Poor bugger." He finished his inspection, replaced the blanket, and turned back to Richard. "The orchard, if you please."

When the sergeant returned from the orchard, he asked to interview each of the island's residents separately. "I'll send Mrs. Biggs in with some tea," said Richard as he escorted him to the parlor.

"Aye, I'd be glad of that," said the sergeant, blowing on his hands to warm them up.

"We might as well start with you, Doc. Shouldn't take too long."

"Of course." Richard had no intention of mentioning what he'd seen in the orchard, when he had come across Robbie and George. It wouldn't change anything now.

The sergeant emerged from the parlor an hour later, his movements quick and footsteps certain. He was in a hurry. "Got to catch the tide," he said, looking at his watch.

"I see," replied Richard, relieved that they would soon be away. "Do you require assistance with the body?"

"There's some sailcloth onboard. I'll go and fetch it and meet you at the cottage. We might need one more to help us."

George was the stronger of the remaining men, but Richard immediately dismissed the idea. The man had enough to deal with. "I'll ask Colonel Cooper-Jones to give us a hand."

En route to find Wilkie, Richard stopped at Esther's room. "Do you think you might find George and sit with him?" he asked. "We're moving Robbie's body and I don't want him to be on his own."

"Of course."

He found Wilkie and the two of them met the sergeant at the cottage. They wrapped Robbie's body as gently as they could, securing it with a length of rope, and carried it between them down to the jetty. It was awkward to get it aboard and for a moment Richard worried that they might fumble and drop him into the water, but eventually they managed it.

"I shouldn't need to return," said Sergeant Taylor as the boat prepared to leave. "It all seems pretty straightforward. I'll send a message if there's anything else."

"Right you are," said Richard. "You have the details of the next of kin?"

"Aye. And your letter to her, the sister, isn't it?"

Richard nodded.

"I'll personally see that it gets delivered."

"Much obliged." Richard and Wilkie stood at the edge of the jetty, Wilkie holding a salute until the boat was a dot on the horizon.

While Richard was assisting the police sergeant, Esther went in search of George. She had an idea that he might have gone to the far side of the island, the eastern shore, where waves lashed against steep cliffs and you had to be careful not to lose your footing on the tussocks of grass that fell away to the water below. Every time she went there, she felt her stomach somersault as she looked down onto the whitewash. It was as far away from the main house as it was possible to get and it was where she often found herself on her walks around the island.

She had been correct in her assumption, spotting a lone figure sitting at the edge of the cliff as she drew near. "Halloo!" she called out, giving George plenty of warning of her approach.

He raised his head, but did not greet her. There was a look of complete desolation on his face and his eyes were red-rimmed. It was clear he had been weeping.

"I thought I might find you here," she said gently. "Hope you don't mind. Would you care for some company?"

He didn't reply, staring out to sea as if there were answers somewhere out there beyond the horizon.

Undeterred, she sat down next to him, bringing her knees up and wrapping her arms around her legs. The wind blowing off the ocean was bitter and she could see that he looked nearly blue with cold.

"Desperate business."

She rested her chin on her knees, joining him in his gaze out to sea where the waves lapped at the shore in a never-ceasing motion of water. Esther wanted to scream along with the high-pitched gulls as they hovered above the water, scanning for food.

"The world's gone to hell in a handbasket."

"Oh, George." Esther put an arm around him.

"He was more than just my friend," he blurted out.

"I know."

"I loved him. He made me believe in something good in the world, after all the darkness. But it was impossible. We could never . . . never be. We knew that we would both be leaving the island soon, and we had our old lives to return to, that my wife was expecting me to come home, that I couldn't abandon her, or our son, no matter how I felt. It was the last thing we talked about. We argued, if you must know. I told him that I couldn't continue to see him when we left."

"And you think that somehow you are responsible, because of that?"

"Well, aren't I?"

"Of course not, George. You cannot blame yourself for what he did. It's all so bloody sad and such a waste of his life, but it's not your fault. Do you understand that?"

"This is worse than El Alamein ever was. Even with the drugs."

"Drugs?" Esther was puzzled.

"Bennies. Speed. All of us were hyped up on it, awake for hours on end. That's what I'm here for—got addicted to the bloody stuff, didn't I? Couldn't stop. And it wasn't hard to get hold of, even afterward. My wife was at her wits' end. It was her father who eventually persuaded me to come here. He pays for all this. Which makes me feel even worse."

"Oh, George." She thought of her former reliance on the little red pills she had been prescribed.

He looked at her, his expression stricken. "It feels like everything is coming to an end. Nothing matters anymore. I'm going to miss him so much."

Esther gripped his shoulder as he leaned in to her, his head resting in the curve of her neck. Her own sorrow over Robbie, over leaving Richard, paled in comparison.

Chapter Forty-eight
Cornwall, Spring 2018

By seven o'clock, Rachel was pacing the small entryway of the bed and breakfast. She'd texted Jonah suggesting the time to meet for dinner, but hadn't received a response.

Unable to relax, she had spent the late afternoon tramping through a nearby woodland, finding a narrow footpath that cut between emerald-green fields and curved gently upward toward a long, low hill. As she walked, she had plenty of time to think about what Jonah had said. And to examine her own resistance to love. She reviewed the several boyfriends she'd had over the years. All of them considerably younger than her. She'd told herself that those type of men were easier, more fun, less complicated, that they wanted little from her, an assumption that had been mostly correct.

None of them had been what you might call long term. She realized with sudden clarity that she had become bored with them after only a few months. Had used the excuse of new jobs and new countries to avoid anything deeper, anything that might smack of commitment, might tie her down.

She checked her phone again, still looking for a response that wasn't there, sent another message and continued to pace. After another five minutes and no reply, she decided to go upstairs and see if Jonah was in his room.

He opened the door at her insistent banging. Hair sticking up all over the place. Shirtless. Sleep in the corner of one eye.

She felt a storm of butterflies drum in her belly.

"Dinner?" she said, swallowing. Her mouth felt like the aftermath of a sandstorm.

"Oh yeah. Dinner," he said groggily. "Sure. What time is it?"

"Quarter past."

"Quarter past what?"

"Seven," she said, mild exasperation cutting through the mesmerizing effect of his broad torso, the lean, sculpted planes of which were only centimeters away from her. She took a step back, trying to gain perspective. "Don't tell me you've been asleep all afternoon."

He grinned sheepishly. "Guess I have. Give me five minutes and I'll be right with you."

At dinner, Rachel found herself unaccountably shy. Was it merely the effect of seeing him seminaked, vulnerable? Or was it as a result of their almost-argument in the car that afternoon?

They'd opted for the Indian restaurant, and while she struggled to decide what to order she was aware of him watching her.

"Everything okay?" he asked.

She nodded.

"I hope you're not going to be disappointed, Rachel."

She looked up from the menu with a bright smile that felt forced. "I won't be. However, I can't decide between the dhal and the dhansak."

"Always difficult," he said dryly. "Why don't we get both?"

"Oh, okay, sure." She closed the menu and took a sip of the beer that had been placed in front of her, noticing that Jonah looked as though he was steeling himself to say something.

Sure enough, he was.

"I don't know if this will come as a surprise to you or not, but I like you, Rachel. More than like you actually." He looked at her, then down at the tablecloth, straightening the cutlery, fidgeting. "I've been trying to back off, to get to know you, for you to get to know me . . . to let something happen gradually. But now I'm not sure if I've been wrong about you. Seen what I wanted to see and not what was actually there."

Rachel didn't know what to say. She tried to speak, but no words came.

"At some point you have to make the choice. Leave the shore and strike out for the unknown," he continued. "Otherwise you're only half alive. And believe me, I've seen what half alive looks like." Rachel glanced at him from under her lashes, frightened of what she might encounter if she looked him full in the eye, what might be reflected back at her. He was so earnest, more serious than she'd ever seen him.

"And who wants that, hey?" she said, trying to lighten the atmosphere between them.

"Don't be afraid, Rachel." Anyone else would have chastised her, or given up. Instead, the way he said her name was more a caress, and it sent a shiver through her.

He wouldn't accept anything halfhearted. As she raised her eyes to meet his, she felt something shift.

Intimacy. The word was no longer terrifying. Instead it felt as though it might possibly be quite beautiful.

Just as she was about to tell him that maybe she could, that she did feel something for him, their food arrived and he broke his gaze.

As they ate, he changed the subject and the moment was lost.

"We've got a long day tomorrow, I'll see you in the morning," Jonah said, as they returned to the bed and breakfast after dinner.

"Yes," Rachel agreed, unsure how to gauge his mood. "Good night then. Sleep tight."

He gave her a half smile and opened the door to his room, but then hesitated, stepped backward and turned toward her. Time stood still and she held her breath, not knowing what he was going to say or do.

He obviously thought better of it, as he turned back to the door and disappeared inside before she had the chance to say anything else. She wondered if he was regretting his words in the restaurant, regretting coming on this mad crusade with her. Whether they were both on a fool's errand.

Breakfast the next morning was quiet, saved only by the running interjections from their host, who delivered heaping plates of bacon, sausages, eggs, and tomatoes to their table. Even baked beans.

Rachel looked at him questioningly, pointing her fork to the beans. "Really?" she whispered.

"Uh-huh. That's what you get with the full English." He grinned at her and she grinned back. His good humor had returned and she breathed a quiet sigh of relief.

"North or south?" she asked as she bit into some toast.

"What?"

"Are we driving to London, or back to the islands this morning?"

He gave her a wide grin. "Have a guess."

Chapter Forty-nine
Cornwall, Spring 2018

Richard closed the door gently behind the pleasant but hopelessly naive couple and walked slowly to the kitchen. Filling the kettle, he lifted it onto the stove before turning to the cluttered dresser. It would be here somewhere, he knew.

Riffling through a sea of old papers, bills, yellowing newspaper clippings, several teaspoons—so that was where they'd disappeared to—takeout menus, window-cleaning flyers, and psychology journals, he found what he was looking for, tucked inside a dusty copy of his book on trauma therapy.

The photograph.

He wiped away a mote of dust from the surface with his thumb and held it up. A moment frozen in time. There they were: George, poor, poor Robbie, Jean,

Mrs. Biggs, himself, and Esther. Wilkie, who had given him the print, behind the camera of course.

It could have been yesterday. Events from half a century ago were more immediate to him than those of a few years back nowadays.

All of them—well, apart from Wilkie—so young. He almost couldn't believe they'd once looked like that, especially him. He'd grown used to the sight of an old man with thickening eyebrows, a large nose, and a face marked by deep lines, not this clear-skinned chap with wavy hair, a ready smile, and a naive belief that he could change the world, or at least help put an end to some of its suffering.

His eyes fixed on Esther and his breath caught at her fragile beauty. She faced the camera with a wary look.

He had been unsurprised when he came across an article in one of the Sunday papers a few years back, a profile of her as a female climbing pioneer. Somehow he had known she would go on to achieve great things; he had seen her strength of mind, knew what it had cost her to make the decisions she had. He had briefly considered getting in touch after that; had held on to the article for several months, clipping it carefully, before his cleaner had consigned it to the recycling without asking him.

He had tried so hard to forget her.

The high-pitched whistle of the kettle roused him from his memories and he put the photograph back down on top of the pile. He went to get a mug from the cupboard, noticing that his hands shook even more than usual and that the china rattled as he placed it on the bench top. Taking extra care, he spooned coffee granules from a jar and poured in the boiling water.

He didn't risk carrying the coffee through to the living room, but sat down at the kitchen table instead and stared out of the window, marshaling his thoughts. The cup sat by his elbow, untouched, growing cold.

It wasn't until the cat wandered in from the living room and curled herself around his ankles, purring loudly for her supper, that he got up and went in search of the can opener. "So what do you think, hey, Anna?" he asked. "Should I go and see her?"

When Rachel and Jonah arrived at Richard's cottage the next morning, he was ready and waiting for them, wearing dark trousers, a crisp pale blue shirt that matched the color of the morning sky, a tweed jacket, and a perfect Windsor-knotted tie. He'd combed his white hair into neat furrows that were slicked back from his temples and even trimmed his unruly eyebrows. He was clutching a newspaper-wrapped sheaf of narcissi, picked from his garden, in one hand, and wielded a lacquered wooden cane in the other.

"All set?" Jonah asked.

Richard nodded. "As I'll ever be."

Traffic on the motorway was light and they made good time, stopping for lunch and reaching the outskirts of London in the early afternoon. Rachel chatted to Richard on the way up and he told her about his life as a psychologist and academic, which had helped keep his mind off the purpose of the trip, one that he was still uncertain about the wisdom of undertaking.

"Everything okay?" asked Jonah, after Richard had been silent for some time.

"Oh yes, thank you very much." Richard did his best to sound chipper, but on the inside he was as nervous as a schoolboy on the first day of term. It felt as if sixty-six years had melted away in the time it took a heart to skip a beat and it was as if he had farewelled her only days ago. Now, though, time seemed to have slowed to a slow crawl, even though they were zooming at terrific speed along the motorway. He was anxious to get there. "How much longer have we got to go?"

Jonah peered at the GPS that had been guiding

them. "Not long at all. An hour maybe? Depends on the traffic as we get closer to the city."

Richard's pulse began to quicken, his heart to drum in his chest. He hoped he wasn't about to have a heart attack. One couldn't be too careful, not at his age.

Chapter Fifty
Little Embers, Spring 1952

"I can't go on like this." Esther had to wait until the next day to find Richard alone. She was glad to have escaped the oppressive atmosphere of the house, and they contrived to walk together along the seashore in the late afternoon.

"I know," he said bluntly. His eyes still spoke to her of his feelings. "Neither can I. Jean is watching our every move. Though it pains me greatly, I am thinking of sending everyone home."

Esther started in surprise. "Because of Robbie?"

"Wilkie was due to leave in a few weeks anyway, and George, well, I think it will be better for George if he returns to his wife."

"You're right of course. But what about you? Will you accept more patients?"

"I'm not sure." He looked at her despairingly. "I fear the news of Robbie may spread beyond these shores. People may not be so keen to send their loved ones here in future."

"Oh nonsense, that won't be the case. Your good reputation cannot be shattered by one event."

"Well, I certainly hope not. In the meantime, however, I may go on hiatus. I have my paper to finish . . ."

"And what of Jean?"

"If there are no patients for her to look after . . ." His voice trailed off. "I can cope here on my own with Mrs. Biggs. In fact, she could probably do with a break as well."

"So when will you tell everyone?"

"Wilkie already knows. He'll depart on the next boat with George."

"And me?" Esther asked, holding her breath. Her mind raced. Would she soon see Teddy? It would mean leaving the island, leaving Richard, and she felt ashamed at herself for wondering now how she might bear it.

"I have sent word to John, as we agreed. Selfishly I would wish you to stay a little longer, but we both know it would be best if you too returned to your family posthaste, my darling. Only you can decide what will happen after that."

Esther bit her lip. She knew what he was hinting at, but it was a decision already made.

They were out of sight of the house now, two figures on an empty sweep of sand. He reached for her hand. "I'll write to you," he promised.

She pulled away. "Please don't. I couldn't bear it. I cannot change my situation, Richard, even if I wanted to."

He looked at her, surprised.

"We weren't in love, not really," she said, struggling to keep her voice steady. She couldn't look at him, couldn't bear to see the hurt that was surely written on his face. "We were simply two lonely people who found each other for a while. That's all." She turned back toward the house, stifling a sob.

The mail boat called at the island two days later.

"We've got a couple of passengers for you," Richard shouted to the captain as he made fast to the jetty.

"Oh aye? Reckoned there was a bit of a crowd here this morning."

They had all gathered to wait for the boat and stood surrounded by suitcases, several boxes, and a sack of cabbages and potatoes that the captain would take to the Hugh Town Stores and which would be returned, filled with an order for dry goods—wheat flour, rye, and oats—on the next boat.

The weather was almost warm enough for shirt-sleeves and everywhere she looked, Esther could see swaths of pale yellow flowers, their intoxicating scent borne on the breeze. She had abandoned her winter coat in favor of a cashmere twinset and the feel of the warm sun on her face was a small comfort on such a sad day. Her heart broke once again, for the beauty of the island and for the men who were leaving. Both had become so terribly dear to her.

"Chin up," said Wilkie, catching the look of anguish on her face.

She gave him a wobbly smile. "You too."

"You've got my address," he said. "We'd love to see you in Dorset, once you get settled back home, that is. I know Helen would love to meet you. And you too, Richard. You'll always be welcome."

"Haven't you had enough of my ugly mug, old chap?" Richard's voice was stoic but Esther could see that he too was struggling to keep his feelings in check. She had successfully avoided him since their walk on the beach earlier in the week, but now, standing near him on the jetty, she felt the fresh agony of her words to him. She knew she had been cruel, her words wounding her as much as they doubtless had him. She had uttered them in the hope that he would be able to let her go. That one day he would find love with someone else, someone who was free to be with him, for she never could be.

"Right then, let's get you loaded," said the captain. "Tide waits for no one."

It was the one certainty Esther had learned from her time on the island.

Boxes and bags and sacks were handed across and stowed in the hold, before a flurry of handshakes and hugs from the departing men to those remaining. Goodbyes said, first George then Wilkie hopped aboard.

Esther stood with Richard, Jean, and Mrs. Biggs, feeling suddenly bereft as the boat puttered out into the channel.

Jean had stayed out of her way since the news of everyone's departure had become known and Esther felt sure she must be secretly delighted by the fact that Esther and Richard's relationship would shortly be ended.

According to Richard, Jean was planning a holiday with her aunt in Brighton. "Such a lovely time of year there," she had said to Esther one evening as they all sat at supper. Esther detected a sharp edge to her voice. "You and your husband should try it. I'm sure your little boy would love it; the pier is quite impressive. I believe it even rivals that of Bournemouth." Jean never missed an opportunity to remind Esther of her family responsibilities, but Esther didn't rise to the bait.

"There's a letter here for you," Richard said, his voice terse. He thrust a creamy envelope at her. Esther immediately recognized the handwriting. John.

"Thank you." She barely noticed him take custody of a small brown-paper-wrapped parcel, was too caught up with what her letter might say. Would he come for her? Was she ready? Despite her earlier assertions to Richard, she wavered now. Would everything still remind her of Samuel when she returned? She dreaded falling back into the deep trough she'd been in when she left, didn't think she could bear the return of the dark thoughts. But there would be the living too—especially Teddy. Esther clung to that. She could hardly wait to see him, to hold him close and inhale his sweet little-boy scent, to watch him play in the park, laugh, skip, and sing with him. To kiss him before he went to sleep each night. She didn't think she would ever want to leave his side again.

And what of John? Of him she was far less certain. She had no idea how she was going to live the rest of her life with him, not when she loved another, would always love another. Perhaps there might come a time in the future when she wouldn't mind so terribly much.

She waited until she had reached her room before opening the letter. In it John had enclosed a small photograph of a boy. It took her a few moments before she recognized who it was. Teddy had had a haircut. His toddler curls were no longer, in their place was a much more grown-up style. New clothes too, ones she had not chosen. It had been taken in their small back garden; she recognized the tricycle, which lay on its side in the background. The flowerbeds looked overgrown. He was taller, thinner, as if he had been stretched. Life had gone on apace without her. She scrutinized the photograph, wishing it might reveal more. It was some time before she turned her attention to the letter.

"*My dearest E. I cannot tell you how delighted I am that you are quite yourself again. I was right: Embers was just the place for you to recuperate. Teddy sends kisses—and I thought you would like this photo. We took it a couple of weeks ago, just after his first haircut. He is so proud to be a 'big boy' now, you will hardly recognize him. We have all missed you terribly and are overjoyed to hear that you will soon return home. Unfortunately, I cannot be spared, the reasons for which I will not bore you with, so I have arranged a ticket for you on the sleeper to London on the second of April* and a driver will meet you at the station when you arrive. We cannot wait to see you and have you home with us again. Much love always, John."

The second of April. A little over a week away. The days would go too slowly and yet too fast.

Chapter Fifty-one
London, Spring 2018

Eve brushed her grandmother's long hair, sweeping it back off her face and letting it fall in soft waves around her shoulders. "You look lovely, Grams," she said, handing her a mirror and a pot of Pond's Cold Cream. She'd never known her to use anything else and Grams had certainly never been one for makeup.

"I look so old." Her grandmother uttered a rare complaint, making a face at herself in the mirror.

"Nonsense. You're in better shape than a woman half your age . . . well, at least you were before the accident and you will be again, I have no doubt at all. And you're still beautiful. You always will be." Eve hugged her as tightly as she dared, feeling the knobby bones of her spine beneath the cardigan. She was relieved that her grandmother appeared to have rallied in recent days and that she was now up and about again, moving the few meters from her bedroom to the sitting room with slow but steady determination, refusing the walker that Eve had been advised to acquire. It stood, unused, in the hallway, gathering dust. The GP had visited the day before and given her the go-ahead to venture outside, into the fresh spring air. Their outing that morning, to the café just a few meters away on the corner, had gone well and brought a new touch of pink to her cheeks.

Eve had no idea what she would do once her grandmother no longer needed her. It was too late for her to join David in Africa, and in any case his emails had dried up. She was fairly certain there was little left to salvage of that relationship. She supposed she should have been upset, but strangely it didn't bother her much. What was of more concern, however, was that she had no idea what to do with her life once her nursemaid and transcription skills were no longer required.

They'd made good progress on the autobiography in the last few weeks and Grams had handed over a stack of notes she'd been guarding for Eve to type up. Eve reckoned they'd have a first draft for the publisher by the early summer. However, there was still something her grandmother was keeping from her, she felt sure of it. Perhaps today's visitor would loosen the strings of her grandmother's memory.

"You remember that Rachel is coming again today. You know, the woman who found the letters," she reminded her.

"Yes of course, Eve. I've not lost my memory yet thank you."

As Grams's health improved, her irascible nature had also reasserted itself.

"Perhaps she's found some more things of yours?"

"Possibly. I did leave a suitcase there—I always wondered what happened to a coat I had when I was at Embers. Astrakhan if I remember correctly. It was very expensive at the time."

"What's astrakhan?"

"The fleece of fetal or newborn lambs."

Eve shuddered.

"I know. Sounds barbaric now, doesn't it?" she said with a glint in her eye.

"Just a bit, Grams," Eve snorted.

"Things were different then. In all sorts of ways that you'll probably never understand."

"Maybe she's found Richard?" Eve said, trying to sound nonchalant. She had thought only to plant the idea in her grandmother's head, but she had reckoned without her grams's sharp intelligence.

"Eve," she said, eyeing her in the mirror. "Come on. Out with it. What do you know? What's going on?"

There was no fooling her.

"This is a friend of mine—Jonah," said Rachel when Eve opened the door to them later that day. "Jonah, this is Eve, Esther's granddaughter."

The younger of the two men held out his hand and Eve took it.

"And this, this is Dr. Richard Creswell."

Eve looked closely at the old man in front of her. He had a bright, expectant look in his eyes and clutched a bouquet of bright yellow flowers. Narcissi. Her grandmother's favorites. "Oh my goodness. How lovely to meet you, Dr. Creswell."

"You look like someone I once knew," Richard said. "You have her smile."

"I think I know exactly who you mean," said Eve, her mouth widening further. "Do please come in." She led them into the house and showed the way to the sitting room where Esther was waiting.

"She's just in here," she said, indicating the room along the hallway. "I'll organize some tea. You must be thirsty after your long drive."

"Thank you, my dear. Right you are then."

Eve watched as he steadied himself against the wall for a moment and then grasped the door handle.

"I'd like to hear all about this crazy plan of yours and just how you made it happen," Eve whispered to Rachel as they stood in the hallway, "but first I want to see how Grams reacts. She's been as skittish as a bride on her wedding night ever since she found out he was coming today."

Chapter Fifty-two
Little Embers, Spring 1952

Esther opened the suitcase containing her summer wardrobe. All winter it had remained untouched, but she remembered its contents and there was one item that she wished to retrieve. Shivering slightly, for it was still cool in the mornings, she shimmied into the tight boned bodice, easing the costume up over her legs and waist. She then pulled on her favorite trousers over the top, wrapped a cardigan around herself, and plucked a towel from a hook on the door. Before she left the island, she had a promise to keep.

One afternoon, in the week before he died, she sat down at the beach with Robbie. He was still patiently teaching her to skip flat stones.

"Can you swim, old girl?" he asked.

"Of course," she replied. "My father taught me in the ponds on the Heath."

"Fancy a race?"

She looked at him as if he were mad.

"Not right now," he laughed. "When it warms up, you ninny."

"Well, I'm glad of that. Far too bloody cold right now," she replied with an exaggerated shudder.

"First of April."

"First of April what?"

"That's when I reckon it'll be bearable."

"April Fool's Day you mean?"

"One and the same."

"Well, that's appropriate. You're on." She'd never been able to resist a challenge.

Esther was leaving the island the following day, and Robbie was gone, but she was determined to swim, no matter the temperature. She stood for a moment on the beach, gazing at the vanishing point between sea and sky. The water was calm, barely a wrinkle on its smooth surface. She kicked off her shoes and dug her toes into the sand. She looked at her feet, a pair of half-buried pale fish.

Removing her outer clothes before she could change her mind, she took a deep breath and waded in. The temperature was as frigid as she had feared, but she went deeper until she was up to her waist. Then, before her body went completely numb with the cold, she kicked off the bottom and began to stroke straight out to sea. It had been a long time since she'd been in the water, and to begin with her body felt awkward, uncoordinated, and she flailed about. Until that moment, her experience of swimming had been limited to a few laps of the Kenwood Ladies' Pond, sharing it with families of ducks and waterweed. The open sea was a new challenge. Her strokes were choppy and her breathing labored; Robbie would have had no trouble beating her in a race, of that she was sure. Eventually, however, she found a rhythm and began to move with ease, enjoying the effort of slicing through the briny water. As her arms turned over and over, she lost herself, could have kept on swimming indefinitely. An urge to keep going until she could go no farther danced in her mind. She remembered Robbie, his solid form swinging from the tree and as she did so a dark shape loomed beneath her and she faltered, coming up choking for air and kicking her legs beneath her as she struggled to see what it was. A huge fish? A shark? Were there sharks in these waters? She had no idea.

Esther prayed it was only a dolphin, though it looked far larger than any of the dolphins she'd seen on her walks about the island. Her breath came in sharp gasps now and she turned back to face the shore. She was farther out than she'd intended and she could just make out a small figure, waving frantically, on the beach. Trying to put the unidentifiable darkness beneath her out of her mind, she began swimming as fast as she could back to shore, her strokes sharp and frantic. All thoughts of Robbie were forgotten in her rush to the safety of dry land.

"You look like a mermaid," said Richard as she stood up in the shallow water, her hair streaming. "But you had me worried. I thought you were aiming to swim all the way to the mainland."

Esther shivered and gasped, struggling to get her breath back and feeling the soreness in her shoulders and arms from her panicked sprint. "Don't be ridiculous," she said between breaths. Her earlier terror erased itself as soon as she found land and saw him.

"You put on quite a turn of speed there," he said.

"Might have had something to do with thinking I'd swum over an enormous shark actually," she said.

"If it was . . . it was probably only a seal, or perhaps a basking shark—and you're not exactly likely to be on their menu."

Esther felt only a slight relief that he was still speaking to her, even if his tone was now distant. He handed her a towel and she dried the water from her face, feeling exhilaration, not the cold breeze.

"Oh? How's that?" she asked.

"Well, they feed on plankton."

"That's good then." Esther wrung the water out of her hair. "I was a tiny bit scared," she admitted.

"I don't think there's much that scares you anymore."

The following morning she woke early, her stomach churning at the realization that the day of her departure had arrived. High tide was due at around 10 a.m., so she wouldn't be forced to wait around all day for the boat to arrive, which was some small mercy at least. Now that it would be less than twenty-four hours before she would see Teddy again, she was more confused than ever. Desperate to hold him, she nevertheless wondered how he would be with her after so long away. Perhaps he would have forgotten her, transferred his affections to someone else? Perhaps he no longer needed her. And how would she manage the dull, mundane, day to day of her old life when she was back in London?

She rose and dressed before making her way to the kitchen where the housekeeper was preparing breakfast. Her stomach roiled again at the smell of frying eggs and she poured herself a cup of tea from the large pot on the table. "Nothing for me, thank you, Mrs. Biggs."

"Are you sure, love?"

Esther nodded. "I rather think the crossing might be a rough one and I am not a good sailor at the best of times."

"Probably sensible then," she agreed.

Esther drained her cup and rose to leave. She had no desire to run into Jean before she left.

She remembered again the minute she had felt the imprint of Richard's lips on hers, the way he looked at her when he thought she didn't notice and committed them to memory, sliding them into the box where she intended to keep all the good moments, the ones that would keep her going when she was far away from this place, adrift from him.

"You're up bright and early."

Drat. Jean stood silhouetted in the doorway of the kitchen. Esther was unable to make out her expression, but the tone of her voice was falsely jolly, presumably for Mrs. Biggs's benefit.

"I suppose I am," replied Esther.

"Hardly surprising on such a day. I expect you're far too excited to sleep. I'll wager you can't wait to be home."

"Of course," said Esther carefully. "And I consider

myself most fortunate to have a home to go to." She was determined not to let Jean see her distress, not to let her calm facade slip in front of the woman. "Now if you'll excuse me, I should like to make sure I have everything in order." She made to leave the kitchen.

Jean turned sideways so that Esther could move past her and as she did so, she whispered so that only Esther could hear. "It's for the best, believe me. You'll come to realize that one day." For once she was not sour-faced, her voice softer and more generous than Esther had ever heard it.

When she reached her room she gathered her belongings, including Richard's gift of the walking boots. She had no idea when she might wear them again, but she could not bear to leave them behind. Somehow they symbolized the freedom she'd found since being at Embers. Even though she had effectively been forcibly detained on the island, she had been afforded a liberty that was in stark contrast to the strings that bound her as a wife and mother. But this wasn't real. Real was Hampstead. Teddy. John. The life of a housewife. She hoped it would be enough.

Chapter Fifty-three
Little Embers, Spring 1952

Esther pushed up the sash on the bedroom window and leaned out, straining to see if there was a boat on the horizon. From down below came the sound of strings, the high notes like a soul ascending to heaven, a bird proclaiming the joy of a new day. She smiled sadly to herself. "The Lark Ascending." Again. She stood, lost in the familiar music for several minutes, fixing the moment in her mind. Then, a shout, and she looked out to sea. The shape of a boat plowing through the water, white wake streaming behind it. "Esther!" came the shout again.

When she'd packed her belongings earlier that morning, she had come across the letter that John had written and tucked inside her suitcase. *"I am at my wits' end to know how to help you,"* she read once more. She was more inclined to believe him now, but that didn't change how she felt about Richard. Duty, promises, motherhood: these were the things that mattered, would always matter, she reminded herself.

She gathered her handbag and her gloves.

It was time.

She lifted her suitcase with ease—she had grown strong in her months on the island—and made her way down the stairs to meet him. The second case was to be sent on later, for it contained clothes she didn't immediately need and she did not want the bother of it on her journey home.

Jean was standing in the hallway, Richard next to her. Esther kept her gaze firmly fixed on the front door. Once she walked through it, everything would change.

"Ah, there you are. Here, you shouldn't be carrying that, let me help." She let him take the suitcase from her.

Mrs. Biggs appeared from the kitchen and drew Esther into her ample arms. "We shall miss you," she said, pressing a small bag into Esther's hands. "It'll keep you going on your journey. Travel safe now."

Esther smelled something sweet and yeasty. "I will," she promised as they parted.

Jean gave her a thin smile. "God speed, Mrs. Durrant."

Esther inclined her head ever so slightly.

"Come on then," said Richard. "The boat won't wait for long."

As they all stepped outside, she was enveloped by the fragrant, intoxicating perfume of narcissus, which bloomed toward the horizon in fields of gold. She breathed in deeply, steadying herself. Butterflies—speckled and spotted—fluttered ahead of them, a farewell salutation.

"Ready," she said, fighting to keep her voice from cracking.

The boat puttered away from the jetty and Esther stood at the stern, shielding her eyes against the sun, watching until the figures were mere specks in the distance. She wished there was a way to hold on to the final moments, the last glimpse of him, but they slipped through her fingers like seawater.

She felt in her handbag for a handkerchief and retrieved it to find it had been wrapped around several small papery, brown bulbs that could almost have been onions, though she knew exactly what they were.

As she replaced it, her fingers grazed a small, unfamiliar-shaped box. She brought it out and stared at it. It didn't belong to her, of that she was certain. Carefully, she eased off the lid to find, nestled inside, an oval brooch in silver, decorated with a ring of delicate yellow enamel flowers, their centers dotted with tiny rubies. "Narcissi," she whispered. She turned the brooch over in her hands and saw an engraving. "*Ex tenebris lux,*" she read, running her fingers over the words. From the darkness into the light.

Chapter Fifty-four
London, December 1952

It was a midwinter baby, due at the closing of the year, when the days were shortest and the sun low on the horizon, when the memory of spring was merely a faint, scented breath of another lifetime.

Esther struggled to catch her breath as she walked up the path that led to Kenwood House, her boots crunching through the frost. She had been to the Heath almost every day since her return from Embers, rising at dawn, before John even. It was a habit that she was anxious to hang on to, despite her present condition. It seemed the only way she might remain sane, the effort of walking clearing a blank space in her thoughts, a fresh start every morning. It anchored her, gave a purpose to her days. If it were not for the hours of tramping through the bracken and long grasses that covered the island, she feared her mind would have floated away from her body, thistledown on the wind.

She sat for a while on a bench, legs spread to accommodate the swell of her stomach. Oof. A kick. A footballer in there, or perhaps a ballerina.

Teddy was hoping for a brother. John seemed pleased. She didn't know if he had guessed the truth, gambled that he wouldn't.

She rubbed the great mound of her belly, the skin stretched like a drum, feeling it tighten.

She hadn't wanted to get pregnant again, had meant what she'd said to Richard all those months ago, but by the time she realized, it was too late to do anything about it. It was only the walking that kept the fears at bay. The time was close. Any day now, the midwife had said on her last visit.

She had the baby three days later. A tiny, solemn-faced little girl with her father's eyes, as clear and bright a blue as the waters that encircled Little Embers. Dark winged eyebrows gave her a startled look, as if the world was a delightful surprise. "Hannah," Esther whispered.

Now, she would always have something of him.

Chapter Fifty-five
London, Spring 2018

Esther had taken the memory of Richard up the steep slopes of Mont Blanc and into the Himalayas, when her feet burned with frostbite and she believed her legs could carry her not a step farther. And as she closed her eyes at night she said a silent prayer for him, that he would be safe and happy and, perhaps, occasionally think of her.

And now, here he was. Standing in her sitting room. She had a sudden memory of him on the beach at Embers, the laughter as she fell over in the sand, the mischievous light in his eyes. She hoped he wouldn't care too much that she was no longer a beauty, scarcely resembled the image of the woman he no doubt recalled.

He'd shut the door and it was just the two of them. She didn't move, held her breath.

He looked, despite the gray hair and the lines around his eyes, so much like his younger self that her throat almost closed up with the memories that came rushing back. Her concerns about her own appearance vanished like morning mist as she looked into his dear, kind eyes. "Hello, Richard," she said, doing her best to keep her voice steady.

"Esther."

He said her name so gently, as if he had been keeping it wrapped in layers of tissue for safekeeping and was only now bringing it out again. His voice was the sound of a long ago song, a distant melody that was achingly familiar and all the sweeter for not having been heard for so great a time.

"More beautiful than ever."

She pursed her lips as if to debate the statement, but then smiled and beckoned to him to sit next to her. "Time is not kind to any of us."

"But it allows us still to breathe, to see, to feel. To be alive," he replied.

He sat and took her hand in his and she felt its dry warmth, just as she had on the first day they'd met. She wished hers weren't so aged, the veins standing out like tributaries under the thin skin, knuckles swollen and twisted.

"Sometimes that is more of a curse than a blessing."

"I failed you, dear Esther. I wish you could know how sorry I am." He gripped her hands tightly, as if he feared she might float away if he let go.

"What on earth can you mean?"

"I'm afraid I failed all of you . . . George, Robbie . . ."

"How could you think that? You didn't at all, don't you see?" she looked at him with a fierce expression in her eyes. "I left Embers a very different woman from the one who arrived, and that was all due to you."

Richard smiled weakly. "But poor Robbie . . ."

"You were never to blame. No one was. It was desperately sad, but in the end I don't think anyone could have saved him. Anyway, it is I who should apologize. I was unspeakably cruel. To tell you that you meant so little to me, when in fact you were the world. Please believe me that I only did it to save you heartache."

His eyes softened as he looked at her. "Do you think I didn't know that, my darling?"

She blinked back tears. "Oh."

"I can't quite believe that I'm here," he said. "That you're here in front of me."

"I know, today, of all days."

"I don't understand," he said, looking confused. "What's special about today? Apart from seeing you again, which makes it the most wonderful, the most delightful day in the world of course."

Esther beamed at him. "It's sixty-six years to the day since we last saw each other."

"Surely not?"

"I don't make mistakes about things like that."

He let out a long breath. "Fate?"

She smiled. "Perhaps."

They sat for a moment, each drinking in the sight of the other.

"Have you ever been back?" she asked.

"To the island? No." He shook his head. "It's leased to someone else now in any case."

"Yes, the woman who rescued Rachel. Tell me, Richard, what did you do, afterward I mean?"

"After everyone left?"

She nodded.

He sighed. "Word inevitably got out. Patients stopped coming; no one wanted to send their loved ones somewhere where a man had been allowed to hang himself. I had a little money saved, so I stayed with my father and wrote a number of papers about my treatment theories. Without exactly intending to, I found I'd become an academic, so I took a job at a university. It never quite made up for helping real patients though."

Silence lapsed between them and she felt his hand grip hers more tightly. "I never stopped, you know," she said.

"Stopped what?" he asked.

"Loving you."

"I rather hoped you would have done, for your sake."

Esther shook her head. "The memories of those few short months sustained me for a lifetime."

"As they did me," he said.

"I don't understand; why leave the letters . . . ? Why not keep them with you? Why not send them?"

"You asked me not to write," he said sadly. "And I wanted the memories to stay there, on the island. It would have been intolerable had I taken them with me—I never could have let you go, gotten on with my life. To have some kind of future, I had to leave the past behind. As it was, I never loved another, never wanted to. I got on with things as best I could, kept busy, tried to make a contribution, be of use."

"Oh, Richard."

"I promised John I wouldn't contact you. After you left the island. He never said as much, but I think he guessed there might have been something more between us."

Esther's mouth formed a circle of surprise. "He never said a word to me."

"I read of his passing in the *Times,* and I almost got in touch then, and after that there was the profile on your climbing achievements. But I told myself that too much water had passed under our particular bridge, that it would cause problems for you and your family. I didn't want to disrupt your life, mine either if I'm honest. It was only when Rachel contacted me about the letters and convinced me to see you that I changed my mind."

"Teddy lives in New Zealand now, though he calls every week, and Hannah, well, Hannah died several years ago I'm afraid. Terrible car accident; great—" She faltered, cleared her throat and steadied her voice. "Shame, for she was a damn fine sailor." She fixed him with an unblinking gaze and said quietly, "Eve is her daughter."

"Oh, I am so sorry, my darling . . . may I still call you that?"

She smiled. "I always loved the sound of it when you said it."

"Hannah, you said?" he asked, looking at her with confusion.

"Yes. I named her after your mother."

"I don't understand."

"Don't you?"

The light of comprehension dawned on his face. "Really? How?"

"Don't tell me you don't remember."

She thought she saw him blush.

"Can you ever find it in your heart to forgive me?" she asked. "I could have—no, should have—told you but I was a coward. Weak. I didn't want to hurt John. I fear that making a choice I thought was right meant I had to make so many wrong decisions."

"I had a daughter," he said, sorrow mixed with wonder in his voice. "A daughter. All these years . . ."

"I'm so, so sorry, Richard. I don't know how to make this right. I'm not sure I ever can."

"Do you . . . do you have any photographs?" he asked hesitantly.

Esther pointed to a frame on the mantelpiece. "Fetch that one."

It was a black-and-white picture of a small boy and a younger girl, the girl with the same unruly hair as Richard and an impish look on her face, her eyes lit up with amusement. "There she is, that's her," said Esther. "She was so like you. Always sunny. Tremendous energy. A risk taker. That was probably her downfall, not that I'm one to talk."

He smiled. "And John never suspected?"

"If he did, we never spoke of it. He loved me in his own way, and for that I was always grateful. But I owe you more. More than a mere photograph. I wouldn't blame you if you curse me to hell and back for what I did, what I kept from you. Know that I wished every day that I could tell you."

Richard squeezed her hand. "There's nothing to forgive, Esther. It was an impossible situation, like so many back then."

She had released the tightly bound secret she'd been carrying for so many years. The lump that had been threatening to close her throat since she had read his letters dissolved.

"We all make decisions that are for the best at the time, decisions that we think will do the least amount of damage," he continued. "I have no blame to cast."

"Do you? Do you really understand? I could never have left Teddy, not again."

"I know. I know how much it must have cost you. And I have nothing but admiration."

"You do?" She was surprised.

"You suffered an enormous loss, labored under a

burden of blame that was not yours to carry, but in spite of all that you made a triumph of your life. You have lived with boldness, with courage. I wish we could all say the same about ourselves."

"I never really thought of it like that," she said.

"I'm curious though—why climbing?"

"It was a way of keeping the demons at bay I suppose. The dreads that hit in the small hours. For some reason they didn't come looking for me when I was on a mountain, couldn't reach me. Besides, it was as far from the ocean and islands as I could possibly get."

"I see. Of course. How foolish of me."

"I carried you with me, Richard. Every step."

He was about to reply when the door opened and Eve walked in carrying a vase with the flowers in it. "Dr. Creswell brought these for you, Grams—aren't they gorgeous? Your favorite."

"He has an excellent memory," said Esther, smiling at him once more. Her heart, so long a dried-up, wizened old thing, had bloomed into tender, trembling newness. Life, like the brightness of the flowers, had dazzling color in it again.

"I'll bring the tea in," said Eve before she left the room.

"You say that Eve was Hannah's daughter?" Richard asked.

Esther nodded.

"Oh my goodness," he murmured. "A grand-daughter?"

"Should we tell her?" she asked.

"What do you think they're talking about in there?" Rachel asked.

She and Eve and Jonah were sitting in the kitchen around a square pine table, nursing mugs of tea.

"I'd love to be a fly on the wall," said Eve. "I didn't stay in there for long though—they looked as though they wanted a bit of privacy."

"They've got a lot of catching up to do," said Jonah.

"Have you always lived with your grandmother?" Rachel asked.

Eve explained that she'd been looking after her since Esther's fall. "And I'm helping her write her autobi-ography. Though I'm not really a writer—I've just finished an undergrad degree: physical geography and environmental science. Not that I'm sure how I'll ever use that."

Rachel thought for a moment, an idea forming in her mind. "I might be able to help if you like. I'm a research scientist. That's what I'm doing on St. Mary's. Mapping clam populations. I can put you in touch with a few people. What's your area of specialty?"

Eve's eyes lit up. "You'd do that for me? I've not really thought about a specialty, to be honest. I'm open to almost anything," she said. "Anything that gets me outside would suit me right now. And that would be amazing. Really. Amazing. Thank you."

Eve noticed Jonah looking at his watch. Esther and Dr. Creswell had been together for more than an hour. "Do you have to get back tonight?" she asked.

"Not necessarily, but we'll need to sort out somewhere to stay. Either here or on the way back," said Jonah.

"I'll go and see what they would like to do," Eve suggested. She wanted to see the two of them together once more. They had looked so sweet, sitting with their knees almost touching, hands clasped together as if they were afraid of letting go and losing each other again.

"Eve darling." Esther nodded toward the space on the sofa next to her. "Come and sit down for a minute."

Eve did as she was asked, noticing the serious expression on both of their faces as they looked at her.

"There's something you probably should know."

The feeling Eve had had for a few weeks now, that there was still a missing piece of the puzzle of her grandmother's life, returned.

"It's about Hannah."

"Mum? What about Mum?"

"Your gramps . . . well, your gramps was not her father."

Eve looked at both of them, her eyes darting back and forth. For the first time, she noticed the shape of Dr. Creswell's chin—her mother's had been exactly the same, strong and square, and so was hers. "So that means . . ."

"Yes it does, I'm afraid," said Richard kindly. "Do you mind terribly much? If it's any consolation, I had no idea myself until just now."

"Really? You're sure?" she asked Esther. "But what about Gramps?"

Her grandmother took her hand. "I'm sorry I haven't told you earlier. I thought it would cause more trouble than it would solve. Gramps never knew. At least I think he didn't."

"But why?" Eve asked. "Why didn't you ever tell Dr. Creswell, Grams? Tell Mum? Didn't they deserve to know?" She struggled to make sense of the news.

"Eve darling, times were different then. It would have ruined too many lives. I made the best of things, tried not to hurt anyone more than I already had. It might not have been the right decision, but it was the only one I knew how to make."

Eve took a deep breath and examined Dr. Creswell's face for more similarities. She should be furious, hurt, duped. It took all her courage to look for the best in the situation. "So that means I've gained a grandfather?" she asked finally, smiling at him.

"If you'll have me."

Chapter Fifty-six
St. Mary's, Spring 2018

"I suppose I should be pleased," Rachel said to Janice as they sat in the café one morning a couple of weeks after her return from London. She was filling her in on everything that had happened. "And I am, really. It's a wonderful happy ending. Richard ended up staying with Esther for almost a week and now she has plans to go and visit him in Cornwall, according to Eve. But now I feel a bit flat." She'd replayed her conversation with Jonah at the restaurant over and over in her mind. It was true, she might never experience the kind of love that endured no matter what, the kind of love that she'd seen between Eve's grandmother and Dr. Creswell. It made her feel hollow, as if she'd lost something she never realized she had.

"Well, it was very exciting and I expect you're

floundering a bit now it's all over. How's the wrist, by the way?"

"Doc says I can't even begin to think about using it for another month. I'm going a bit stir-crazy. There are only so many research notes I can read up on, so many hikes I can take. I think I know pretty much every inch of this island now."

Janice nodded sympathetically. "And what about Jonah?"

"We had a bit of a misunderstanding. I think I've missed the boat there."

"Don't be too sure of that, Rachel," said Janice, patting her hand.

Conversation on the long drive back from London had been strained. Jonah had apologized for putting her on the spot. "It wasn't entirely fair. You're entitled to live your life as you want to. I hope we can still be friends?" he said.

She felt an unexpected pang of disappointment. "Sure."

Now, Rachel would have said he was avoiding her. She had hardly seen him since their return, though somewhat frustratingly he'd never been far from her thoughts, even haunting her dreams. Mostly shirtless, with a mocking grin on his face. Always just out of reach. She found herself missing him more than she cared to admit. It was a new feeling for her—she couldn't remember ever really missing someone before, certainly not like this, an almost physical pain, an ache deep inside her.

"Speaking of boats, did you say you could find me one to rent?" she asked.

Janice looked suddenly coy. "As it happens, I do have news of something that might help cheer you up." She looked at her watch and then pointed to Rachel's cup. "Drink up and follow me."

They left the café and walked up Hugh Street, coming to the moorings at Porthcressa Beach. In the sky above the water, kite-surfers hung like seeds blown from a dandelion clock but on the beach there was scarcely a soul around until Rachel noticed a small tinny puttering across the water toward them. She strained her eyes but couldn't make out who it was. Then, as sunlight flashed across the water, she recognized the long auburn hair. Leah.

"Uh-oh," she said to Janice. "She's not my biggest fan actually."

"Just wait and see."

Steeling herself for another dressing-down, Rachel stood at the water's edge. As they helped pull the tinny ashore, she looked at the boat. It was rather familiar. The *Soleil d'Or*? Could it be?

It was. Smartened up, and with a bright new name painted on the side, entwined with a gorgeous yellow narcissus.

"It was washed ashore on the north of the island a couple of weeks ago," said Leah, clambering onto the sand. "Tom at the co-op arranged for someone to come and look over the motor last week. Faulty spark plugs. Simple to fix. And then I thought I should smarten up the old girl for you."

Rachel looked bewildered. So Leah wasn't here to give her another piece of her mind. "Wow. Thanks, that's amazing. Really. That's so incredibly generous of you. I love the artwork."

"Least I could do. Listen, about last time . . . I'm sorry I took it out on you. You didn't mean any harm, I realize that now."

"No, I was wrong. I shouldn't have interfered."

"Well, I'm glad you did. Max tracked me down—can you believe it? He left his swish London gallery and roughed it with me for a couple of days."

Rachel could hardly picture the urbane man in Leah's ramshackle old house.

"Convinced me that I hadn't lost my talent. We're planning an exhibition in the autumn actually. He loves the seascapes."

"That's wonderful," said Janice, who had been looking on with the proud gaze of a godmother.

"It is," said Rachel. "I can't believe it. And thank
you again for the boat; that's going to make everything
so much easier. My supervisor will be delighted."

"Actually, I have a favor to ask." Leah shifted from
foot to foot. "I was wondering if you'd sit for me? I
know you saw the painting I'd started—Max told me.
I think it'll be not too terrible. If I can finish it that is."

"I'd be honored," said Rachel. "I'll be over just as
soon as my wrist is healed."

"Good. This is yours," she said, handing over
the key. Rachel took the opportunity to give Leah a
hug. The older woman briefly resisted, but then relaxed, leaning into her and hugging her back just as
strongly.

"How are you getting back to Little Embers?" Rachel asked.

"Oh, it's all arranged. Tom's giving me a ride home
when he's closed up." She whirled around and strode
off in the direction of town.

"I'd better be off too," said Janice as Leah walked
away. "I'm due at the museum at eleven."

When they'd both gone, Rachel sat on the stone wall
that surrounded the beach and looked across the water.

Now that her boat had been recovered, she began to wonder if Eve might consider coming down to help her with the study. She had a spare room and she reckoned she might be able to re-jig the funding to afford an assistant. It would be fun to have a protégé, not to mention helpful, especially while her wrist was healing.

She was happy to have the boat back and even more pleased that Leah was no longer angry with her, but still she felt an underlying sadness, as if the world was no longer such an exciting place as it once had been. It felt like the end of everything, even the research project no longer seemed as compelling as it once had.

Something her mother once said echoed in her head. "Sometimes love finds you, Rachel, when you're ready. But other times you have to decide. You have to recognize it, to go out and grab it."

She jumped up. The choice was hers to make this time. She knew exactly what she had to do. And who she had to find. This wasn't the end; in fact, it was only just the beginning.

Acknowledgments

When I was about nine or ten and we lived in the Pacific Northwest of the United States, my mother would often take us to visit a ruined, abandoned mental asylum called Steilacoom—it was her idea of an outing. The eeriness of the ruined rooms, the broken furniture, the seemingly random objects left behind, and the air of desolation and menace within those walls have stayed with me.

Some years later, my mother told me of my great-grandmother, who was confined to a mental hospital in England with postnatal depression when my grandfather was a small boy. She said that my grandfather almost never spoke of it, and it was a source of great shame to the family. I only recently discovered that she remained there for the rest of her life. While the reasons for this have been lost in time, it strikes me as utterly tragic.

In addition, when I began to think about this book, I came across stories of belongings—often quite prosaic but that nevertheless had meaning to their owners—left behind in mental asylums, the inhabitants never leaving.

These things gave me the starting point for the novel.

In the course of my research, the Imperial War Museum's oral histories, particularly Ernest Rex Chuter and Eric Norman Foinette's recollections as POWs in Germany in the Second World War, and Percy James Mutimer's recollection of his imprisonment in Changi, were a privilege to listen to. Their accounts of torture and deprivation are bravely and stoically told and their testimonies helped to inspire the characters on Embers Island.

In researching the lives of female mountaineers in the middle of the twentieth century, I came across *The Summit of Her Ambition: The Spirited Life of Marie Byles* by Anne McLeod, and it provided me with such a wonderful example of an adventurous, intelligent woman (she was also the first woman to practice law in New South Wales, the cofounder of the Australian Buddhist Society, an environmentalist, and a staunch advocate for women's rights). I also read of the exploits of three intrepid Englishwomen, Anne Davies, Eve Sims, and Antonia Deacock, who drove sixteen thousand miles from London to India and back, and who trekked for three hundred miles to remote Tibet in 1958. I hoped to instill something of their collective indomitable spirit in the character of Esther Durrant.

I have always been fascinated by islands, their separateness and contained nature, and I knew this story needed to be set somewhere remote, but still in England. I have Michael Morpurgo's *Why the Whales Came* to thank for inspiring me to visit the Scilly Isles and set my story there.

Thanks to my niece Louise for her company on our visit to the Scilly Isles, to Amanda Martin at the Isles of Scilly Museum for her help, and to my early readers Becky, Mercedes, Sanchia, and Rhonda. To my agent, Margaret Connolly, for her wise counsel and continual encouragement, and to my very clever publisher and editors Rebecca Saunders and Alex Craig, and all at Hachette, for their commitment to producing great books and the huge contribution they make to an increasingly vibrant Australian publishing industry.